Staying Out for the Summer

Staying Out for the Summer

Mandy Baggot

An Aria Book

This edition first published in the United Kingdom in 2021 by Aria,
an imprint of Head of Zeus Ltd

9 7 5 3 1 2 4 6 8

A CIP catalogue record for this book is available from the
British Library.

ISBN (PBO): 9781800243095
ISBN (E): 9781800243071

Typeset by Siliconchips Services Ltd UK

Printed and bound in Great Britain by
CPI Group (UK) Ltd, Croydon CRO 4YY

Aria
5–8 Hardwick Street
London EC1R 4RG

www.ariafiction.com

*To our NHS staff and everyone all around
the world in the health and care sectors who are
working tirelessly to save as many lives as possible
during this Coronavirus pandemic. And also to the key
workers keeping essential services and supplies
accessible and putting themselves at risk for us.
THANK YOU all for your amazing service!*

One

Hampshire, UK

Sticky. Slimy. It was impossible to forget the sensation of latex against your skin when you had been covered top-to-toe in it for months. But this didn't feel *quite* the same...

Lucie Burrows made a concerted effort to turn her head on the pillow, in a bed that didn't feel quite as comfortable as it should. Whatever had occurred last night had somehow been worse for her sleep pattern than the utter exhaustion of tending to the patients on Abbington Ward. What *had* happened after she'd finished her shift? She didn't remember landing here... wherever here was. She really should open her eyes but her brain seemed to be saying 'not quite yet'.

Was it even morning? Surely it *had* to be morning. She sniffed. And what *was* that smell? It was a combination of maybe shaving foam meets the perfume counter at Boots. God, the perfume counter at Boots. Even now, months on, it still felt a little bit edgy being able to pick up things other people might have touched. Yes, everyone still carried hand sanitiser and had masks but still... Lucie sighed, shifting position. *Ow, that really hurt*. Despite all her senses suggesting caution, maybe now was the time to open her eyes and find out exactly how bad her hangover *really* was...

'Arrrggghhh!' The scream was high-pitched, hysterical, and not coming from her.

Flicking open her eyelids, hangover pulling into her brain station like it was a high speed to Manchester that wasn't scheduled to stop, Lucie's gaze met her best friend, Gavin Gale. All of him. Naked. Apart from one of the too-short unusable hospital aprons that stopped above his midriff and a pair of disposable gloves. *That* was the rubber she'd been sensing.

'Argh!' Gavin wailed again, gloved hands going to his head, then to the apron – that no amount of tugging was going to elongate – then lastly, *finally* to his penis. 'Luce, what have you done with my clothes?!'

Lucie suddenly remembered she should probably close her eyes. Not that she hadn't seen Gavin in his entirety before. Her friend had a bit of a reputation for flaunting his fruit cluster. At one particular work party, one of Abbington Ward's other nurses, The Other Sharon Osbourne, had actively encouraged using the hydrotherapy pool for skinny dipping and Gavin hadn't thought twice about the consequences. That official warning was still on his record, as far as Lucie knew.

'Gavin,' Lucie began. 'Think about what you just said.' She clawed her way up her double bed – at least it was *her* bed she was in – facing away from Gavin's extremities, that ache in her head thumping back and forth like it was a machine gun in the hands of Chris Hemsworth. '*All* the words.'

She heard Gavin make a sharp inhale. '*Cher* came in and took my clothes?'

The sound of his pleasing exhalation hit the still-scented air as, amid an open packet of paracetamol (Gavin's), an empty packet of Doritos (again, Gavin's) and a wrapper containing a half-eaten Snickers (hers), Lucie found a hair scrunchie on the nightstand. She went to tie back her long dark wavy hair...

Oh. My. God. Where was her hair?!

'Luce!' Gavin screamed. 'Cher took your hair!'

Sheer white-hot fear booted away the now lesser-spotted-still-drunk and Lucie wobbled up and off her mattress, not knowing what the mirror was going to reveal, but feeling utterly terrified about it. How had this happened? What had they done after they left work? She needed to think while she tried to maintain her balance. They had gone to a Mexican to celebrate. Yes! They were celebrating because all the nurses and doctors on duty yesterday had clapped out fifty-seven-year-old Peter from the designated Covid ward. After three weeks and six days of treatment he was finally well enough to go home to his wife and his Pekingese called Trevor. There had been fajitas, sombreros and definitely tequila but... then what?

'Don't panic,' Gavin called.

Was he dressed yet? Lucie gently turned her thankfully pyjama-clad self towards the wall that supported a bookcase of memories – and clutter – plus her full-length mirror. She braced herself. It couldn't be as awful as she was imagining. She leaned a little, then made a bold step right in front of the glass.

Lucie's scream was even louder than Gavin's had been.

'Oh my God! Gavin!' She clamped her hands to the few inches of little more than dark brown stubble, now covering her entire scalp. 'Gavin! What happened?! My hair! I was... I was... always getting called Sandra Oh and now I'm... I'm—'

'Sandra Oh No?' Gavin offered unhelpfully.

'Is your penis covered yet?' Lucie snapped.

This was a disaster! Her hair had always been her best asset. Everyone said so. And now, now her hair was close to non-existent. Almost Gru from *Despicable Me*.

'Shall I use your pants?' Gavin asked. 'Or this undefinable blanket/throw/shawl?'

'Not my pants!' Lucie ordered. She was still turning her head left and then right to see if there was *anything* salvageable about this look. Could she gel it up so it looked even *slightly* longer? And how, *how* had her night gone from beefy burritos to barely-not-bald?

'I'm tying it like a sarong,' Gavin replied. 'One sec.'

Did she have any hats that wouldn't make it look like she was either trying to hide a bad haircut or waiting to knock off someone at a cashpoint? The baseball cap was out. As was the snood that doubled as a face covering when she went to Aldi.

'All done,' Gavin announced. 'You can look now. Well, you know, at my face.'

Lucie turned around. Gavin was still wearing the gloves and apron, but his bottom half was now shielded by an artisan-embroidered Peruvian wrap she'd been planning to give her Aunt Meg for her birthday along with the tights she liked that made you cool if you were too hot and warm if you were too cold.

'Jesus! It looks worse from the front!' Gavin clamped a gloved hand over his mouth. 'Sorry, I didn't mean that. I meant it looks... even more... jaw-dropping from that angle.'

Lucie laughed then, her own hands going over her lips as her body bent double in a happy release. She straightened up the second she began to feel nauseous and her backache kicked in too.

'What?' Gavin asked, hands on his hips.

'Oh, Gavin,' Lucie said through more laughter that was rattling her ribs now.

'What? Tell me, Sinead O'Connor!'

'I think *you* need to look in the mirror.'

Sashaying around her bed, Lucie watched Gavin slowly, perhaps a little hesitantly, swaying towards the mirror in the makeshift sarong like he might be a backpacker in Goa shifting up to a holy shrine.

Trying not to laugh, Lucie realised that Gavin and his love of beard oil was the reason for the high scent of perfume in the room and this other vision in front of her was responsible for the smell of shaving foam.

Standing in front of his reflection, Gavin yelped and took a leap closer, surveying the damage.

'Christ, Luce!' he exclaimed, gloves meeting forehead. 'Someone took my eyebrows!'

Two

'No one noticed, did they? No one, right?'

Lucie couldn't help grinning at Gavin as they both sat on her sofa ready to devour bacon and egg rolls they had purchased from the local café. Ordinarily, still enjoying the novelty of being able to, they would have sat in to have a full hangover curing breakfast. But today, given the hair crisis they were both having, they'd opted for a dash, grab and speedy retreat back to Lucie's flat. Gavin seemed far more self-conscious about the demise of his eyebrows than Lucie was about the loss of her luscious locks. This past year had taught her many things and one of them was definitely what was important and what really wasn't. Her hair would grow back... somewhen. And, at least the crop was the same length all over. A major miracle.

'Gavin,' Lucie said, unwrapping her bap. 'It's really not that bad.'

'I have no eyebrows!' Gavin wailed. 'None!'

'At least we found your clothes,' Lucie countered. 'I'm

not sure why you took them off in the first place or why you ended up in my bed with me but…' She took a bite of the bacon, egg and fluffy Scotch morning roll and rested her back against a cushion as comfort food heaven headed south towards her grateful stomach.

'Name one famous actor without eyebrows. One.'

'Whoopi Goldberg,' Lucie answered, egg running down her chin. She reached for the kitchen roll on the coffee table and mopped up.

'How do you *know* that?!' Gavin complained.

'Your eyebrows will grow back,' Lucie reminded him. 'Probably really quickly. Unlike my hair.' She put her roll down on the plate. 'Why aren't you as concerned about that? Seeing as it was you who obviously made it shorter than… than… one of Cher's Eighties outfits!'

'Oh! The absolute shade!' Gavin said, hands – now gloveless – going to beard.

'Anyway,' Lucie began, shifting on the settee as her shoulders gave a twinge. 'You aren't a famous actor, you're a nurse. Once you've got your hair covered and your face shield on, no one is going to see your eyebrows.'

Still none of the patients saw very much of their features. Albeit slightly more than they had at the height of the Covid-19 pandemic. There were still masks, face shields, gloves and full-length gowns, just thankfully with less of a volume of new admissions. But still they celebrated every single victory against the silent viral assassin. Hence the obvious need to let off steam last night…

'People *will* see if we go on holiday though,' Gavin said, waggling the space that would have housed his eyebrows if his eyebrows were still there.

'Oh, Gav, I thought you'd dropped that plan,' Lucie said, balancing her plate on her knee.

'What gave you that idea?'

'Maybe the fact you asked me about it and I said I didn't want to?'

'You *do* want to though.'

'I said I didn't.'

'But you don't mean that. You can't mean that.'

Did she mean it? Lucie sighed and put her plate on the coffee table, picking up her two-spoon-black coffee. Why was she so opposed to having a break? She, Gavin and the rest of their clinical team had worked their butts off for the past year, surviving on little sleep, little food and only the weeks of clapping from the nation's doorsteps during the peaks of the crisis to spur them on. If anyone deserved a holiday now things had eased a little bit, it was them. But there was her Aunt Meg. Yes, she was still currently independent, but at sixty-five, having suffered a small stroke two years ago, she wasn't quite how she used to be. Not that Meg would be told she ought to slow down. This was a woman who had played bingo three times a week over Zoom last year when she couldn't get out to the social club. But there was also... everything. Yes, the whole wide world was out there, but it was all a little bit different than before. And Lucie was, by nature, always a little hesitant about putting distance between herself and home. There was this little voice inside her head that sometimes suggested breaking a pattern, doing something different, could lead to bad times. And no one wanted any more of those.

'Let me paint you a picture!' Gavin said. He sprung off the sofa, all wild arms and too much enthusiasm for this time on a Sunday morning when she was feeling flatter than a bottle of week-opened lemonade.

'Haven't you done enough of the creative?' Lucie asked, pointing a finger at what was left of her hair.

'Sun so hot it could sear off a tattoo,' Gavin began, waving a hand like he was more illusionist than artist.

'I'm not sure that's selling it to me.' But Lucie *was* enjoying Gavin's floor show. It was amazing he still had the moves if they really had drunk as much as her body was telling her they had.

'OK,' Gavin corrected. 'Sun, deliciously warm... like... being whispered into a nap by Tom Hardy reading a bedtime story.'

That was better. Lucie felt her shoulders twitch in some kind of recognition of that notion being relaxing.

'Sky, the same colour blue as... as... The Other Sharon Osbourne's eyeshadow.'

'You're killing it now, Gavin.' Lucie made to get up. Perhaps a little stroll to the kitchen to top up her coffee would help her feel better. Her back was telling her it needed a change of position anyway.

'Wait! Wait!' Gavin ordered, barricading her path with his body. 'Soft sand running through your toes like you're walking through... talcum powder.'

He really *didn't* have the persuasive techniques and imagery of travel agents.

'No, not talcum powder... better than that... how about...' Gavin pointed a finger like he'd just discovered a new vaccine that could beat *all* the variants. 'Flour. Yes! All that finely milled stuff people had to pay a fortune for just to make white bread during lockdown.'

'Didn't you unfriend people on Facebook if they baked more than once a week?' Lucie said.

'Blocked them if they grew tomatoes.' Gavin pulled a face. 'I was driven to it. Big, fat, foodie show-offs.'

'I'm going to get more coffee,' Lucie said, winding herself around Gavin and the magazine he was now waving like it was a flag and he was in the audience at Eurovision.

'Wait, Luce, come on. Think of… all the wild nights and the cocktails.'

Lucie's stomach actually lurched then. 'Not a great selling point when I have gut rot and would rather drink my own pee than a cocktail right now.' She really wished she hadn't said that. She felt sicker than ever. She didn't even feel like going back to the bacon and egg roll.

'Listen,' Gavin said, touching her arm. 'Luce, please think about it. It would do us good. Both of us. Together.'

Gavin was giving her the big blue eyes and the smile he had whitened as regularly as he could. Her completely lovely best friend who would do anything for her – even cut her hair it seemed. They had been through so much together since they first met as student nurses at Southampton Hospital when they were both twenty. Gavin had been almost close to shy then. How things had changed. And how their friendship had blossomed. But, last year, both running on empty, sore and sweat-drenched, exhausted and deflated for the most part, their friendship had really deepened. In the very worst of times, Lucie had clung to solid, warm, utterly dependable Gavin like he was her personal life raft. She knew that, without him, it was possible she wouldn't have made it through the dark times at the hospital to be here now in

2021 marking recoveries far more than full beds on ICU.

'Please, Luce, please just think about it,' Gavin said again. 'Superhero keyworkers like us deserve this! More than anyone! *You* deserve this! And you know there really isn't anyone else I want to go on holiday with.'

'Hmm, not even Simon from the canteen?'

Lucie watched Gavin flush red from his cheeks to his non-eyebrow-sporting forehead. Her friend had a massive crush on the guy who provided them with coffees at the hospital cafe. But, for some reason, unlike with every other area of his life, where Simon was concerned, Gavin turned back into that self-conscious twenty-year-old who wasn't confident with who he was.

'We agreed not to mention the "S" word,' Gavin said, dropping the magazine to the coffee table where it landed with a splat on Lucie's roll.

'You said you weren't going to mention holidays again,' Lucie said.

'I never said that. When did I say that?'

'OK,' Lucie said, shimmying around Gavin and finally making some headway towards the kitchen. 'Let's make a deal. You say more to Simon than "rich, dark Colombian" next week and I will consider a holiday.'

'Really?' Gavin exclaimed, eyes lighting up like he was front row at a Cher meet-and-greet. 'You'll think about it?'

Lucie nodded and smiled. 'If you speak to Simon about something other than coffee.' It was never going to happen. Gavin had been bashful around the barista for at least eighteen months. But she would still think about it. She hadn't had more than one day off since March 2020. And all that UK sunshine that non-essential workers with gardens had lapped up had been as closed to her as the pubs. Sand between her toes instead of Croc-sweat did have an allure…

'Deal,' Gavin said, lunging to grab Lucie's hand in a shake. 'I would seal it with spit like the old days but, you know, the new normal and everything.'

'More coffee?' Lucie asked, holding her mug aloft.

'Definitely more coffee,' Gavin agreed. 'And a little internet research. Do we think the Balearics, the Canaries or Greece?'

All those places said 'warmth', and the idea of sunshine on her skin and a few weeks of total escape began dancing on her mind. Maybe she could. Perhaps, in fact, she *should*. And her aching spine seemed to agree with her.

Three

Kalamaki Beach, Corfu, Greece

The sun felt *so* good on his skin. As Dr Michalis Andino rested his bare torso against the beach sun lounger he felt his body drop into the material of his towel and deeply rest. This was what he had been missing this past year. Peace. Relaxation. That feeling that everything in the world was going to be OK. He was home and it felt good. Compared to the vibrant and often hectic heart of Thessaloniki, the island of Corfu was a flatline. But in the best of ways. The quiet was exactly what he needed right now. Quiet meant no destruction, no demand, no death. His body bristled then, his thoughts waking up and jumping on a train rather than stilling into a sunshine slumber. He needed to switch his brain off as well as his body. This was what this sabbatical was all about. It was either step away, rejuvenate and take a time-out or… break down.

Slipping his sunglasses upwards to rest on his dark hair, slightly longer than it had been for a while, Michalis surveyed the scene. The golden sand was speckled with loungers and bright blue parasols shading those who required it. Children made holes in the earth, building castles, digging trenches, chasing each other with buckets filled with sea water. The turquoise sea lapped slowly up the beach, swimmers having to wade out a reasonable distance before the sparkling water was deep enough to swim in. He would swim later. Once he had given himself a little peace just lying still, recovering… and not looking at his phone.

'Dr Andino.'

Squinting against the sun, Michalis shielded his eyes and turned his head a little to the left. Had someone called his name? Surely it was his imagination. That was the problem with having lived through the worst time of your career, you were always on high alert. *Dr Andino, this patient is worsening and we do not know why. Dr Andino, we need more Remdisivir.* He wasn't sure exactly how long it was going to take to completely let that heightened awareness go. He settled back on the lounger, discarding his sunglasses on the plastic table to his right that held his bottle of Alfa beer. Then he closed his eyes again.

'Dr Andino.'

There was that voice again. It was female and it sounded vaguely familiar. Was he dreaming? He really didn't want to open his eyes…

'Please, Doctor, it is my eye.'

Michalis jumped then, almost falling from the lounger and into the sand. Feeling someone in close proximity he sat up, opening his eyes and finding himself a lot less than one-and-a-half metres away from Athena Martis from his village. Not only that, but the sixty-something woman was leaning into him, her eyelids prised apart by her fingers, one eyeball bulging like a huge shiny pink marble.

'Mrs Martis,' Michalis began. 'Please do not open your eye that way here.' He tried to lean away from her. 'If the wind blows the sand then the sand will end up—'

'Help me, Doctor,' Athena said, unrelenting in her quest to show him the inner workings of iris, pupil and a white that did look very pink. 'The itch, it is unbearable. I blink. I do not blink. It is all the same. The doctor in Acharavi gave me an ointment, but it makes no difference. Harris says he will not listen to my pain any longer. Nyx tell me you come here so... I come here.'

Nyx. His little sister was going to pay for this. Eighteen years old and still thinking she could play games like they used to. Despite wielding a butcher's cleaver and taking no nonsense from most people, she still seemed to delight in winding him up. It should be comforting that she thought their relationship hadn't changed, but, like it or not, *he* had changed. He had seen things he never wanted to see again and Nyx, fortunately, had been shielded from all that. But being sheltered meant not really having the same level of understanding of the world he had operated in. While she had stayed safe here on the island, he had seen families destroyed, hearts broken, lives lost every single day...

Michalis took a deep breath and focussed on the protruding eye. 'How long has the eye been this colour?'

'Mmm... it was after Easter... but before the end of May... about the time when the fireflies arrived.'

No real accuracy. But likely over a few months as they were now in July. Michalis squinted a little, trying to see if there was anything deeper than what he believed to be a conjunctivitis infection.

'Is it... going to have to come out?' Athena asked, finally letting her eyelid relax a little as Michalis carried out his beachside examination.

'Mrs Martis,' Michalis addressed her. 'Tell me, are you sleeping with the goats again?'

He didn't really need the woman to say anything. The expression on her face said it all.

'After much research,' Athena began, 'Harris discovered that the milk from the goats was much richer when I spent nights with them.'

Michalis was going to have to speak to Harris. He suspected the man's insistence his wife slept in their barn was more about the quality of *his* sleep rather than the quality of the goats' produce.

'You will not sleep with the goats again,' Michalis ordered.

'But...'

'It is the doctor's orders,' Michalis said firmly. 'And I will tell Harris the same.'

'My eye?' Athena asked as Michalis reached for his sunglasses and put them back on.

'I will bring you a solution tonight. Until then,' Michalis said, trying to settle his thoughts, 'do not touch it. Do not poke it. And do not rinse it with ouzo.'

Athena's silence told him she had already tried all of those things.

He closed his eyes and tried to find his way back to the relaxing sea sounds, the gentle in and out of the water and the way the sunlight felt seeping underneath his skin.

'How about *tsipouro*?' Athena broke in.

Michalis whipped his sunglasses off his face and sat up,

annoyed. 'Mrs Martis, you put *tsipouro* anywhere near your eye then I will suggest it is not your eye that gets removed but your brain!'

'Yes, Doctor,' Athena said quickly, her feet shifting fast as she backed away across the sand. 'I will see you tonight. With the solution.'

Michalis shook his head and took a deep breath as the woman finally left. Picking up his bottle of Alfa, he took a hasty swig. Great, even his beer was warm. Relaxing shouldn't be this hard. He inched his broad shoulders upwards, trying to loosen the anxiety. There was nothing to be afraid of here. He had to commit to that feeling and stop searching every shadow. He stood then, leaving his sunbed and raising his arms to the sky. Perhaps the only way to escape any distractions was to throw himself into the sea. Hesitating only for a moment, he sprinted across the sand and splashed into the water.

Four

Cafe Connexions, NHS East Hampshire, UK

'Have a hot chocolate.'

'It's twenty degrees outside!' Gavin responded.

'A cold chocolate then. Uses less energy so a win for the environment.' The Other Sharon Osbourne turned her attention away from Gavin and sent Lucie a wink. Somehow the woman seemed to know this was a crunch beverage buying session that could determine whether they booked a package holiday or not.

Lucie noticed that Gavin had started to sweat in the queue and was pulling the scrub hat he'd insisted on wearing since Monday lower down over his forehead. His eyebrows were four days into new growth and not a lot was happening, despite endless rubbing of moisturising lotion and internet searches for 'cures'. It was a bit like her Aunt Meg impatiently waiting for her chili pepper plants to sprout. Lucie's hair, on the other hand, was already beginning to look a lot better. Well, by that, she meant she had just about got used to catching her reflection and not wondering who the thug was who had broken into her flat in the night. They had also started to piece together some of the rest of that night too. After the Mexican meal they'd gone to a casino. And Sharon had been with them…

'Luce,' Gavin whispered. 'What shall I ask for?'

'A date,' Lucie told him. 'That was the deal.'

'That wasn't the deal,' Gavin shot back. 'The deal was talking to him about something other than coffee.'

'You knew what I meant. And you want me to come on holiday with you, don't you?' Lucie asked, toying with the lanyard around her neck.

'You going on holiday?' Sharon asked. 'Whereabouts?'

'We don't know yet,' Gavin answered.

'I've always fancied Costa Rica,' Sharon breathed.

'I thought you'd always fancied Jason Momoa,' Gavin said.

'Pot calling,' Sharon replied with a smile.

'You'd better get your game face on,' Lucie told Gavin as the person in front moved up a place in the queue. 'It's nearly your turn to order.'

'Not "rich, dark Colombian". Not "rich, dark Colombian",' Gavin chanted like it was a mantra for life.

The Other Sharon Osbourne turned towards Lucie then. Was it Lucie's imagination or was her trademark blue eyeshadow even more vivid today? She tried not to get distracted by it.

'I've heard very good things about Greece,' Sharon said, touching her nose with her finger. 'Handled the global pandemic efficiently and effectively. Has all the beautiful sea scenes, a cuisine Rick Stein gets excited about and have you *seen* their prime minister?'

'Does he knock Boris off the beauty pageant podium?' Lucie asked.

'Watch him on YouTube is all I'm saying.' Sharon let out a lusty sigh. 'I have no idea what he's talking about. It's all Greek to me. But those eyes…'

'Hey, Gavin.'

It was Simon's voice. Lucie focussed everything on what was happening ahead of her. It was Gavin's turn to be served and Simon had greeted him with a warm smile like always.

'Hi, Simon. Could I have…' Gavin began, all pink cheeks and the scrub hat almost getting caught up in his eyelashes.

'Let me guess?' Simon started. 'A rich, dar—'

'No,' Lucie butted in. She didn't know why she had broken in, except she knew if Simon completed Gavin's sentence for him then Gavin would bottle it.

'No?' Simon asked, looking close to astounded.

'N…o,' Gavin managed to mumble.

Lucie gave him an elbow as his cheeks turned quickly from a light pink shade she'd once tried as nail varnish to the menopausal-hot-flush-red The Other Sharon Osbourne had turned last winter.

'I've heard,' Sharon began, 'that Gavin fancies something rich, dark and from Hampshire.'

Now Gavin was turning as purple as an aubergine, which was kind of ironic… But Lucie felt for him. Trust Sharon to put her size eights in it.

'Really?' Simon replied, his expression giving away absolutely nothing.

'No,' Gavin interrupted. 'No… I… very much… still want my coffee from South America.'

'Oh,' Sharon exclaimed. 'We were talking about coffee, were we?'

'Gavin,' Lucie said softly. 'Tell Simon what you want.'

'What you really *really* want,' Sharon added, all Spice Girl.

'I'll,' Gavin began, fingers scratching nervously at his scrub hat, 'have... a sausage... roll.'

'O-K,' Simon replied. 'To eat in or to go?'

'I expect the answer's any way up, darlin',' Sharon responded with a cackle.

Gavin looked so hot now that Lucie was worried he might actually faint. It was time to come to her best friend's rescue.

'Two rich, dark Colombians as well,' Lucie ordered. 'Gav, why don't you go and find us a seat? I'll bring everything over.'

'Yeah,' Sharon said. 'Go and sit down before you fall down. I'll have a hot chocolate, Simon, and don't be stingy on the cream.'

'Is Gavin OK?' Simon asked, his dark eyes following the unsure steps of the nurse as he retreated from the queue and headed towards the tables.

'He's OK,' Sharon said. 'If you *can* be OK when you've got drunk enough to have your eyebrows shaved off.'

'He shaved off his eyebrows?' Simon remarked. Lucie couldn't tell if he was appalled or impressed. And no one actually remembered anything about the shaving...

'We don't talk about that, Sharon,' Lucie reminded.

'Like we don't talk about your hair either?'

'Sharon, why don't you take the weight off your feet too and I'll bring your hot chocolate over,' Lucie said, desperate to get rid of the woman whose jaw was currently seeing more action than a hairdressing salon after lifted restrictions.

'And pay for it?' Sharon asked, grinning because she already knew she was on to a winner.

'Yes, I'll pay for it.' Lucie smiled at Simon while she waited for Sharon to depart.

'So,' Simon said to Lucie. 'One hot chocolate with too much cream. Two rich, dark Colombians. And a sausage roll.'

Lucie held her breath. Should she? Would Gavin thank her or maybe shave off something else that belonged to her? It didn't bear thinking about. Or was it worth the risk? Perhaps sometimes you had to take one…

'And a phone number,' Lucie blurted out. '*Your* phone number that is.' She smiled and silently prayed.

'Oh, wow,' Simon began, his cheeks reddening now. 'I don't know what to say.'

'Say it with digits,' Lucie pleaded. 'Please!'

'Well, I…'

'Come on,' Lucie carried on. 'You must know Gavin's been trying to attract your attention since way before anyone knew who Chris Whitty was. And—'

'Oh,' Simon said. 'I thought you meant *you* wanted my phone number.'

'What? No. God, no,' Lucie said quickly. 'Sorry… that came out far harsher than I meant it to. And you're lovely. Really lovely. But you're—'

'I'm not gay,' Simon butted in.

Lucie pulled a face like someone had just told her Graham Norton was straight. '*Not* gay?'

'Not gay,' Simon repeated. 'Sorry.'

'Oh.' Lucie didn't know what to say. How had they all got it so wrong? Her profile-building hadn't been from looks or mannerisms alone. Although Gavin had insisted Simon always wore 'queer jeans'. She had, over the months, asked him all sorts of leading questions about his weekend pursuits and musical tastes. Granted, he had never admitted to being all over Sam Smith, Panic at the Disco! and Cher like Gavin was, but she'd discovered Simon spent a disproportionate amount of time at the gym, had deep opinions about fashion and seemed to know exactly who Carson Kressley was. And surely Gavin had to have a gaydar that worked, right?

'*Not* gay?' Lucie asked again. 'Are you sure?'

Simon seemed to wince then, looking increasingly uncomfortable as the conversation continued. 'I think I'd know.'

Lucie nodded. 'Yes, yes, I guess you would. Of course you would.'

It took Simon seconds to rustle up their orders, all done in complete silence with neither of them knowing where to look. Lucie was glad to leave the counter even when she knew she was swapping it for the eager anticipation in Gavin's eyes and despite knowing she was going to have to break devastating news.

'Well?' Gavin asked immediately, before Lucie had even had a chance to sit down.

'Well,' Lucie said. 'Here's your sausage roll and your coffee. And, Sharon, one hot chocolate with more cream than an Elmlea factory.'

'Ta,' Sharon answered, grabbing the mug.

'Is that it?' Gavin wanted to know. 'Because you were talking for forever and Simon went red.'

'Well, I have good news for you,' Lucie said. 'That's all you need to know.' She plumped down onto a seat and smiled at her best friend. 'We're going on holiday. And you can even choose the location.'

Lucie watched Gavin's whole face light up in excitement. She was an excellent best friend. And Gavin was right, they did deserve a time-out after all they had been through. She just needed to trust that breaking her routines for once couldn't really kick off a tsunami.

'Really?!' Gavin exclaimed. 'You really mean it?!'

'I really mean it,' Lucie told him, nodding. 'I'm in.'

The bad news about Simon was going to be much better delivered with a cooling cocktail in her hand while Gavin coated himself in coconut oil under a tattoo-searing hot sun.

Five

'In how many pieces would you like me to cut the rabbit?'

'I do not know. How many pieces do you usually cut a rabbit into?'

Michalis looked up from where he was stacking his father's jars of homemade spiced sauce in the window display of the family butcher's shop and surveyed his sister, Nyx, and the customer he did not recognise from the village. The man did not look like a tourist, here only briefly for a holiday. He had the look of a Greek. He was perhaps mid-sixties, wearing dark trousers, a short-sleeved white shirt, open at the neck, glasses on his face, and his dark hair was slightly greying at the temples. Andino's was known as the best butcher's in the north-east of Corfu, perhaps while Michalis had been away their fame had spread further down the island.

'What are you making with it?' Nyx demanded to know, her cleaver raised high in the air and seemingly staying there for the time being.

'Dinner,' the customer answered, his confusion seeming to gain momentum as this conversation continued.

'I know that! I am not an idiot!' Nyx growled, and then swung the cleaver down onto the chopping block with a hideous thud.

'Nyx,' Michalis said, making his way around the counter to stand next to her.

'What?' Nyx asked, pulling a pop-eyed face as she turned to face him. She looked six years old when she did that. You could just see the edge of the two doughnut rings of plaits she pinned to her head and covered with her white cap. Her apron was splattered with so much blood she might be confused for someone in the middle of a murder scene or an operating theatre. He recalled a time when she had looked similar, coated in strawberry juice when he had helped her make a strawberry yoghurt cake. Little Nyx standing on a chair to enable her to mix the ingredients together, somehow covering herself more than the inside of the baking tray.

'Please excuse my sister,' Michalis addressed the customer. 'She suffers from a rare condition where she is overcome with rage for no particular reason.'

'Really?' the man asked, shuffling backwards a little in the small shop.

'Yes,' Michalis said. 'It is known as… so-angry-itis.'

'Micha!' Nyx yelled. 'Do not make excuses for me or I will cut you into more pieces than the rabbit!'

Mee-sha. She had called him that as soon as she could speak. 'Michalis' had been too complicated for an eighteen-month-old and even as she grew, the nickname stuck.

Michalis leaned over the counter and whispered to the man. 'She does not mean it.'

The man swallowed then, dropping his eyes to the piece of paper in his hand that looked like a shopping list. 'I am not sure if...'

'Please,' Michalis said calmly. 'What dish are you making with the rabbit?'

'That is what *I* asked!' Nyx exclaimed, thumping the rabbit down on the block.

'*Stifado*,' he replied, sounding harried.

'At last!' Nyx declared and began thwacking the rabbit with the cleaver, dicing it expertly into bits.

Michalis tried to draw the customer's attention away from his sister's dissection of the animal and, instead, to him. 'Cook the rabbit for as long as possible. All day if you are able. My sister will prepare the animal, so you have the very least to do. Bite-sized chunks are best, but be sure to include some of the belly and the kidneys when you prepare. These can be the most succulent of surprises.'

'OK,' the man said, visibly brightening.

'You are making this for a special occasion?' Michalis asked, smiling.

The man nodded then. 'Yes... it is an anniversary.'

'Well, congratulations! How many years?'

'Too many,' he responded with a sigh.

'Well, you cook your wife rabbit like my brother tells you,' Nyx called. 'And she will love you forever.' She sniffed, then pointed the cleaver at him. 'That is a warning.'

The door of the butcher's shop opened then, the brass bell sounding as Melina Hatzi, the village president, swirled in like a tornado. With her lacquered black hair, pinstriped skirt and matching jacket, Michalis almost didn't recognise her. This was the woman who had always been in charge of village life, yet even though she had held this position for as long as he had been alive, her business was her allotment, her chickens and making sure everyone attended church. None of those things would usually involve a smart suit.

'Michalis! How are you? Come here! How long do you stay? Are you married?'

Before Michalis could offer any greeting whatsoever, he had been bundled into a hug that constricted his rib cage to the point of actual pain. He extricated himself as soon as he could and smiled at Melina.

'I am very well,' he answered. 'And no.'

He had no answer to the question of how long he was staying. As long as it took to feel better was his only estimate, and he was keeping that to himself. He had been as vague as he could get away with with friends, colleagues and his landlord in Thessaloniki. He didn't want the attention, even if the enquiries as to how he was were all well-meaning.

Melina gave a whistle through the gap in her front teeth and shook her head. 'You need to have children soon. There are a few candidates in Sortilas who have perfect health scores. Ideal to breed with a *doctor*.'

Perfect health scores. Michalis simply smiled while the customer waiting for his rabbit looked like he wished he had done his shopping in nearby Acharavi.

'The window for breeding is getting longer, Mrs Hatzi. People have young into their fifties and sixties now,' Nyx offered, bringing her cleaver down onto the rabbit's leg and separating it cleanly. 'I read that one woman in China had a baby at sixty-seven years old.'

'Not in my village,' Melina said forcefully. 'At that age,

the only young that people should be taking care of is their grandchildren.'

'Or their kids,' Nyx suggested.

'That is what I said,' Melina replied.

'I meant their baby goats,' Nyx said, frowning.

'Can I help you?' Michalis asked. 'You would like some meat? Or some of my father's special sauces?'

'No,' Melina answered. 'I would like to leave these leaflets. And a poster for the window.'

There seemed to be no asking if it was acceptable to have the poster displayed, just the order. Michalis took the papers the president was offering.

'What is this?' Michalis asked.

'It is what it says.'

Michalis turned his attention back to the poster in his hand. 'Day of the Not Dead,' he read aloud. Without even looking up he saw the customer's shoulders flinch a little.

'Is it not the best idea?' Melina asked, seemingly not expecting any contradiction.

'Do we get to dress up like zombies?' Nyx asked. Michalis watched his sister roll her eyes into the back of her head, arms stretched out like she was acting, steps faltering and off balance, knife still in her hand.

'The rabbit?' the customer asked, pointing a finger to the glass behind which his purchase was on its way to being isolated in sections.

'OK! OK!' Nyx said, frustrated. 'Do not aggravate my so-angry-itis.'

'It is a new festival,' Melina announced. 'If anyone from your family had attended the last village meeting you would know everything about it.'

The village meetings. Michalis recalled those in graphic detail. They lasted for hours and discussed matters such as a rota system for communal parking spaces and the colour they were all going to repaint their houses. These meetings were meant to be attended even more regularly than church services if you wanted to remain in favour with the president. Although, it was unusual for their father not to be involved. His dad wasn't quite himself at the moment and apart from Michalis recharging and re-evaluating while he was back on Corfu, he wanted to get to the bottom of what that was all about. Nyx seemed clueless there was even something amiss about their father. But Michalis saw it and, since he had been back, he had felt it too. Dimitri was distant, distracted, there but somehow, also, not.

'This year we will begin the biggest celebrations of our health status,' Melina announced. 'You have seen the golden plaque on the church?'

Michalis nodded. 'I have seen it.' There was no chance of missing it. It stood out like a clown at a funeral. The beautiful muted yellow paint of the old church building – all crumbling arches and a historic bell tower – and then this sign and a bright golden effigy of a tortoise.

'We are the *only* village to have received world gold status from the Worldwide Good Health Federation. This year, with special measures, we should be able to receive a record number of tourists wanting some of our vigour and vitality!'

'And virility!' Nyx added, making a fist and punching the air.

Melina studied Nyx suddenly, her gaze intensifying until his sister seemed to grow self-conscious under the scrutiny and she turned back towards the battered rabbit.

'You are eighteen now,' Melina said to Nyx. 'You will soon need to look for a husband. I can—'

The end of Melina's sentence was deftly cut off by Nyx delivering another blow to the animal carcass.

'Should I come back for the rabbit?' the customer questioned softly.

'Be patient!' Nyx ordered him. 'If you cannot wait a few moments for the animal to be ready, how are you going to wait all day for the *stifado* to be perfect?'

'I will put up the poster,' Michalis told Melina.

'And the leaflets. Left on the counter. And to be given to everyone who comes in. Not just those who make a purchase.'

It was craziness to even think of objecting. 'Of course,' Michalis answered.

Melina nodded. 'Very good.'

'Was there anything else?' Michalis asked.

Melina seemed to muse for a moment and then she held a finger in the air. '*You* will be the star of the festival! I do not know why I did not think of it before.'

'What?' Michalis gasped. He could think of nothing he wanted less... except perhaps Coronavirus.

'You are the hero of the village! Our doctor!' Melina continued. 'Early in 2020 you helped us be prepared for what was to come. When the world was under attack and no one knew what to do, you showed calm and you made decisions for the good of our community. Sortilas will never forget that.'

'Mrs Hatzi,' Michalis began. 'Really, I do not think that—'

'We could make balloons with Micha's face on them,' Nyx suggested, drawing a balloon shape in the air with one of her bloodied fingers. 'And he should be carried. On a throne. From here, to the village square, where there will be another throne. I can make a large staff out of the rib cage of cows.'

Michalis looked at Melina and said a silent prayer that this was going only one way. But then the woman smiled at Nyx and Michalis's heart dropped, until…

'You are crazy!' Melina stated. 'There will be no balloons or sticks made of cows! But maybe the throne. I will talk to my festival committee.'

'Micha should be *on* the festival committee,' Nyx offered.

Now Michalis wanted to lock his sister in the cold store for a few hours until her doughnut hair turned to ice. He had to get himself out of this, and fast.

'I am very busy,' he said. 'I will not have time.'

'Busy?!' Nyx countered. 'You are on holiday!'

'I am… working here with you and I am… considering opening a… practice in the village.' What was he saying? This wasn't what he wanted! The very last thing on his mind was opening a surgery! This was a sabbatical, not a busman's holiday!

'That is wonderful,' Melina said, beaming. 'Some of the villagers are struggling with the new doctor in Acharavi. A fever. He prescribe antibiotics. A stomach-ache. Antibiotics. Pregnant…'

'Condoms!' Nyx shouted.

It was a tumbleweed moment that Michalis should have used to extricate himself from the idea that he was going to start seeing patients in the village.

'Have you found a premises?' Melina asked him.

'No. I...' Had only come up with the whole idea two seconds ago and was deeply regretting the oversharing.

'I will find you somewhere. Leave it to me.'

And with that parting statement made, Melina swept from the shop as quickly as she had entered and was gone.

'Is my rabbit...' the customer began.

'Take it!' Nyx screamed, deftly wrapping limbs, body and head with plastic, then paper, then thrusting it all in a carrier bag and literally chucking it at the man.

'And... a leaflet,' Michalis said, offering one of the advertisements to him.

The man left the money for the animal on the countertop, snatched a leaflet and departed.

'What a day!' Nyx exclaimed, wiping her face with the sleeve of her white coat.

Michalis had no energy left to agree or disagree.

Six

Aunt Meg's house, Southampton

A week later

It was early evening and Lucie parked her little blue Fiat outside the substantial semi-detached home on the outskirts of the city. The house was way too big for a woman on her own, but Lucie knew that downsizing wasn't yet on her Aunt Meg's agenda. There were a lot of memories tied up in each and every room of this former family home. Looking to the front garden, flowering bushes in full bloom, burgeoning hanging baskets displaying the reds and pinks of fuchsias and geraniums, Lucie saw Meg in her usual summer sitting position. Folding chair set up by the front door – a little bit on the small lawn, a little bit on the path – adjusted to get the prime view of all the goings-on of the street. Lucie waved a hand and Meg deliberately turned her head away like she hadn't seen her arrival and wasn't really watching what her neighbours got up to on a minute-by-minute basis.

Lucie got out of the car, locked up and headed up the path of her aunt's home. 'Hey!'

Meg let out a tut of annoyance. 'I wish you wouldn't use that word.' She shook her head. 'It sounds like you're asking for something to feed your horse with.'

Lucie grinned. She loved her Aunt Meg with every fibre of her being. Yes, she might have an overprotective nature, but the advice was mostly given with the best of intentions. And this large house Meg was sitting outside of, its bricks creaking with nostalgia, had once been *her* home too. Ten years ago now, Lucie, Meg and Lucie's grandparents, David and Sheila, had packed into the three bedrooms and the rest of the home had been filled with books and music (her), baking and cross-stitch (Meg) and porcelain-faced dolls and marrows (her nan and grandad). Lucie had never really known what her mum had filled the house with. She'd only been two years old when Rita passed away, aged just eighteen.

It was Meg who had always been there – back in the family home after her marriage failed – being both aunt and mother to a little Lucie. And now that her grandparents had both passed, Meg was the only one left.

'Good evening,' Lucie began again, sounding all her letters with sarcastic intent as she bent to settle on the grass. 'How wonderful to see you.'

'Lucie!' Meg exclaimed. 'Don't sit on the floor. Get a chair. You know where they are.'

'I'm good.'

'Ugh. Now you're using an Americanism.' Meg rolled her eyes and pulled the super-large straw sun hat she was wearing over her brow. 'Next you'll be saying "my bad".

There's no such thing as a "bad". You do know that, don't you?'

Lucie sat unmoved on the grass, legs crossed in front of her, somehow feeling the same way she had at sixteen when she'd wanted Meg's opinion on asking her crush, Jason, to the leavers' dance at school. Jason was still around. His plumbing business often advertised on local radio and she'd seen him a few months ago in the newsagent's. These days though he looked a lot more high-pressure ball valve than he did Zac Efron…

'Well?' Meg said, glasses slipping down her nose, eyes beneath direct.

'Well what?' Lucie asked.

'What are you doing here?' Meg asked. 'It's not a usual day for a visit. Is something wrong?'

'No,' Lucie said quickly. 'Nothing's wrong.'

'Then you should be out having cautious fun with people your own age.'

Lucie laughed then. 'All the people my age I know are married with children. Except Gavin and Gavin's busy trying to grow his eyebrows back tonight.'

'Well,' Meg said with a sniff. 'Perhaps you should be busy trying to grow your lovely hair back so someone will want to marry you. It looks worse now than the photo you sent me.'

Lucie laughed. She knew Meg didn't really mean that. About marriage, not her hair. Throughout Lucie's lifetime, Meg had always been the most uncompromising person she knew. She used to say, after her divorce, that it was out with men and in with self-care. One time, when Meg had stumbled across a few too many memes, she had actually said 'fries before guys'. Lucie smoothed her hand across the crop that was actually getting a tiny bit longer by the day. She was getting used to having short hair. It was quite liberating having nothing to hide behind. Perhaps a whole new her could start with this new haircut. And a holiday...

'Well, I have actually come to tell you something,' Lucie admitted, plucking a piece of grass from the ground and twirling it around between finger and thumb.

'Oh?' Meg said. Straight away, her aunt's hand went to the locket around her neck that Lucie knew held photos of her, Rita, Sheila and David. 'Should I be worried?'

Meg always worried, even more so now she was older. If it was icy in the winter Meg would text Lucie and tell her to drive with extreme caution and message as soon as she arrived safely at the hospital. If it was a heatwave there would be a discussion about drinking plenty of water and staying in the shade. And when it came to meeting new people, Meg would feel happier if Lucie knew their surname as well as their first name so she could settle herself with finding them on Facebook and be content that, from the information available, they weren't running a people-smuggling ring...

'No,' Lucie said quickly. 'Of course not. Anyway, when have you ever *really* had to worry about me?'

'Well, where do I start?' Meg asked, sighing. 'There was one time when you were six. You got four Maltesers stuck up your nose and we had to take you to the hospital to be "flushed". Then, when you were eighteen, you walked into a field containing a prize bull and had to be rescued by me, the farmer and half a turnip. And then there was—'

'OK, OK, stop,' Lucie begged, inwardly cringing. Perhaps

the hair mishap with Gavin wasn't so bad when put in the context of her youthful misadventures. 'I should have clarified. You haven't had to worry about me since I became a nurse.'

Meg seemed to muse on that statement a little, fingers going from the locket to the few strands of hair that framed her face and were always left purposefully out of her bun. 'Yes,' Meg finally answered. 'I suppose you're right. Although, after this past year, I have worried about you being safe doing what you do.'

Lucie swallowed and her back gave a twinge as she remembered all those weeks and weeks of not being able to see Meg at all. They had had to rely on FaceTime, then doorstep conversations from two metres away, until finally they'd been able to share a few glasses of gin and tonic a little closer – with wipes. Until it had all be taken away again, tiers had been set up and they'd counted down to Christmas. And then Christmas had been all but cancelled, plans had to change and Lucie had had to pay ridiculous amounts of cash she didn't have to get her hands on anything that contained turkey... while working double shifts as Covid case numbers rose again.

'Well,' Lucie said, biting back the unpleasant memories. 'You can stop worrying. Because... I'm taking some time off.' She drew in a breath as if the air would somehow validate the decision she had made. Why did agreeing to a holiday feel so momentous? Because it *was* momentous. This past year she'd had a fully formed rigid routine that barely changed unless Boris Johnson said so. People relied on her. In the back of her mind she was still worried that if she went away, something would get missed, or someone would be lost and that her not being there would somehow cause an avalanche of unfortunate events. Her sensible side knew she wasn't a modern day Nostradamus, but she did believe in cause and effect and she didn't want to be the catalyst.

'Time off?' Meg asked.

'A holiday,' Lucie elaborated. 'Greece.'

Meg's eyes lit up then. 'Greece,' she purred, like she'd suddenly been hit with a shot of nostalgia, plus all the golden sand and sunset nights.

'Yes... have you been?' Lucie asked.

Meg gave a slow nod, her eyes looking towards the begonias swaying gently in the sunshine. 'I have.'

There was a distant look in her aunt's eyes Lucie hadn't ever seen before, but it didn't appear that Meg was going to elaborate unless she was directly pushed.

'Well,' Lucie said. 'I don't remember you telling me about it. What's it like?'

Her aunt had told her many stories over the years of her adventures. Before marriage, it had been grabbing rucksack, passport and simply taking off. Then during marriage it was slotting in two weeks' holiday from her office job and visiting caravan sites in the UK in her and ex-husband John's campervan. After that she had hung up her wanderlust in the back of the cupboard with glitzy shoes she kept but never wore anymore. But Meg had never mentioned Greece, Lucie was sure of it.

'It was...' Meg stopped talking and gave a visible shiver. 'A long time ago.'

Lucie smiled, edging closer to her aunt's chair. 'Was there a man?'

'Don't be silly,' Meg protested, waving a hand as if she was swatting a fly. Her expression told a different story, though.

'There was a man, wasn't there?' Lucie said again. 'What was his name?'

Meg sniffed. 'You do know that all the best stories don't have to begin and end with a man, don't you? Haven't I taught you that much?'

'Of course,' Lucie said firmly. 'You bought me a T-shirt that said almost exactly that when I was twelve.'

Meg nodded, as if wholly satisfied. And then she answered the question:

'His name was Petros.'

Lucie put a hand to her chest in mock shock. 'Aunt Meg! There *was* a man!'

A small smile started to spread across her aunt's lips while Meg attempted to tighten her mouth as if she didn't want to let her expression give her away. 'As I said, it was a long time ago.'

'But you still remember it,' Lucie said, edging closer still. 'Still remember *Petros* after all this time.'

Meg shook her head, but she was smiling even wider now and seemed unable to do anything to stop it. 'Don't be silly. It was just a crush. I was eighteen. I didn't know what I was going to do with my life. I was—'

'Wild?' Lucie suggested with a wink.

'Lucie, you know I was never the wild Burrows sister.' Meg's voice almost sounded a warning and Lucie swallowed, remembering every cautionary word Meg had delivered to her as soon as she had hit secondary school. Given what had happened to her mother she understood why. Meg and her grandparents had been desperately determined not to let history repeat itself. And if providing advisories at every opportunity helped them as well as her, then it couldn't ever be a bad thing. Could it? Except there were times, still, when the re-enactment her nan had done with three of her creepy dolls to underpin the importance of stranger danger precautions came to her in her nightmares…

'I'm sorry,' Meg said quickly then. 'I didn't mean…'

'It's OK,' Lucie insisted, putting a hand on Meg's knee and squeezing gently. 'I know what you meant.'

'I was silly to get all starry-eyed at the mention of a European country,' Meg continued. 'I suppose it reminded me of endless sunshine days and that feeling of complete calm and tranquillity. It really is like another world. Well, it was, all those years ago. It might have changed.'

'I hope not,' Lucie said, letting go of a sigh. 'That's exactly what I'm looking for.' She leaned her head against her aunt's knee, resting it there and instinctively knowing Meg was going to caress what was left of her hair. She smiled to herself as she felt her aunt's hand on her scalp, fingers gently massaging like she had when Lucie was much younger and sporting pigtails.

'Where exactly are you going?' Meg asked. 'And when? Does your hair have *any* time to grow?'

'One of the islands,' Lucie breathed. 'That's the only detail Gavin's giving up. I've left everything up to him. It's a long story but he needed a nice focus and—'

'Oh, Lucie,' Meg said. 'You've left organising a much-needed break to a man who would happily spend two weeks covered in glitter and doing TikTok routines.'

Lucie laughed. 'What do you know about TikTok?'

'Occasionally we do them at physiotherapy when there's a group of us,' Meg said. 'My favourite is The Renegade.'

Lucie looked up then, to check if her aunt was serious or not. It appeared from the twinkle in her eye that she was... 'Wow.'

'You must want *some* input into where you're going though, surely.'

And Meg would be itching for a full itinerary. Lucie had had to give her all the details of one training day in Portsmouth because she had read Cosham crime rates were on the rise. 'Well,' Lucie started. 'I didn't know that I really wanted to go anywhere to begin with but...'

'But?' Meg asked, stroking Lucie's head again.

'But now I think... maybe I *need* to get away,' she admitted. 'I mean, I've barely ever left Southampton.'

'We've had some lovely excursions to the Isle of Wight,' Meg countered.

They had. By hydrofoil, ferry and once on the hovercraft from Southsea. But no matter how nice fish and chips and a train ride up the pier was, a few miles across the Solent wasn't really abroad. And Lucie's heart, when she turned off the worry button, told her she wanted more. Even just for a couple of weeks. She wanted to be something different to Lucie Burrows, Staff Nurse. She wanted to try to redefine herself and, most of all, she wanted to be more than the tragic girl whose mum chose partying over motherhood.

'We have,' Lucie answered. 'I just need to see what else is out there. A little further away. Just for a bit.'

She felt Meg's hand brush her hair a touch more tenderly. 'You do work so hard, Lucie-Lou.'

Lucie nodded and closed her eyes, letting the evening

sunshine warm her cheeks and wind its way through her body. Work had always been her focus. And she knew having that career stability pleased Meg. Her aunt had often told her that Rita's lack of a plan had most probably contributed towards her undoing as much as anything else.

'Well,' Meg began. 'I want you to have the most fabulous time. But please, let me know when you get there and let me know what island it is and the name of your hotel and I'll check I still have Gavin's mobile number. And you'll need insect repellent and factor thirty sun cream and… I'll probably still worry when I have all of that.'

'I will let you know where I am,' Lucie said. 'Of course I will.' She turned her head, looking up into her aunt's face like she had so many times from this exact position over the years.

'And I want to see all the photos of the fabulous mountain backdrops, the turquoise water and the—'

'Men called Petros?' Lucie jumped in. 'What island was he from?'

'Ah,' Meg said, putting a finger to her nose. 'There will be plenty of time for talking about Petros on another occasion. When do you leave for this Greek odyssey?'

'Tomorrow,' Lucie announced, bracing herself for what she knew was coming.

'Well, what are you doing here?! Haven't you got packing to do? You need to be organised. You'll need to print off boarding passes and photocopy your passport in case it gets lost.' Meg shooed her off her leg, wriggling her knees until Lucie had no choice but to stand up.

'I do have a million things to do, and Gavin's coming over to stay because we have to head for the airport at two a.m. or some other equally mad time. And even though we swore no alcohol, he's already messaged me a photo of a bottle of retsina with the caption "so we're acclimatised".'

Lucie took a breath before it ran out.

'Then go, my Lucie-Lou, go and get ready for your Greek adventure,' Meg urged. 'And don't forget aftersun… and travel sickness bands.'

'I don't get travel sick.'

'No, but someone else on the plane might and it's always good to be prepared.' She smiled. 'You will be careful though, Lucie, won't you?'

She nodded. 'I promise.'

It was real! She was going away tomorrow! To *Greece*. And Greece was going to be Greek-tastic!

Seven

Ioannis Kapodistrias Airport, Corfu

The Greek island location had been revealed. Corfu. Or, as Gavin had kept saying, Kerkyra. That was Corfu's Greek name and Gavin said it sounded more mysterious and sexy. Kerkyra had a surprisingly smart and obviously recently-updated airport terminal. Everything was grey, with a touch of muted turquoise on the signage, and the toilets were modern and clean. Meg had sent her a text about Greek toilets late last night, after Gavin had drunk most of the retsina and started up a rendition of 'Super Trouper' like he was a member of an ABBA tribute act. Meg had told Lucie: 'Hover at all costs, as a lot of the toilets I remember were no more than holes in the ground'. Apparently the ones that weren't holes in the ground never had any seats. Meg had also suggested adding nappy sacks to her luggage. The following note about having to put your soiled toilet paper in a bin rather than down the loo had actually been true.

'Feel that heat!' Gavin exclaimed, tilting his face to the sky. 'I reckon it's enough to singe off your eyebrows.'

He faced Lucie. 'Lucky I still don't have any.'

Lucie smiled and drew in a breath of the sweet humid air as she let herself take in the buzz that surrounded Corfu's airport. There were travel representatives sweating a little in their uniforms, clipboards at the ready to check passenger names, cleaners with their trolleys and mops, endless amounts of Greek men with mobile phones clamped to their ears, coaches with engines idling adding to the heat of the atmosphere and a row of dark blue Mercedes taxis, yellow signs on their roofs. It wasn't anything like standing outside the hospital in Southampton not knowing what they were going to be faced with when they went through the front doors. This was uncharted territory, yes, but the anticipation was giving her all the good tingles.

'Right!' Gavin announced, dipping fingers into his neon orange flight bag. 'Let me check the name we're looking for here for our transfer.'

'Aren't we looking for *our* names?' Lucie queried, shielding her eyes from the sun and wondering which compartment of her trolley case she had put her sunglasses in. It was hot and she also needed to remember that she didn't have copious amounts of hair on her head to barricade her scalp from the UV rays. She looked to Gavin. 'That's what they do, isn't it? Write *our* names on a board, spelt wrong if you believe the films, and—'

'And then we get kidnapped by guerrilla drag queens. And then after a tough few weeks of wig envy and a lack of tea, we get rescued by Gerard Butler.' Gavin giggled and then snorted. It had to be the Aperol Spritz. Gavin didn't seem to have any nervous hesitation about leaving work for a few weeks like she did.

'Gav, do you have paperwork or just… stuff that might one day make a good screenplay?'

'I have paperwork!'

He was making a real meal out of finding anything in the neon bag though. For someone whose trolley case was on the larger size of easyJet dimensions, he'd definitely made the most of all the available space. Was that golf balls he had in a zip-lock bag? Since when had Gavin been into golf? She watched as Gavin returned the packet to his bag and finally pulled out a cardboard folder.

'Here we are! *Sortilas* is what we're looking for.'

Lucie wasn't sure if 'sortilas' was the name of a Greek food, a Greek man or the Greek word for 'luxury transfer'. Right now, any one of those would have done.

'There should be a man, or a woman, greeting us with a sign saying "Sortilas",' Gavin said.

Perhaps 'sortilas' was the Greek word for welcome. Lucie pulled her trolley case a little closer to her and squeaked as she ran over her own bare toes. They might be freshly coated in an Avon shade called Pink Obsession, which The Other Sharon Osbourne had palmed onto her because apparently the hue clashed with Sharon's spider veins, but they were only just getting over the near-frostbite from very early morning temperatures waiting for a transfer bus at Luton Airport. She should have asked Meg a few Greek words to get her started. Lucie imagined even a young Meg would have been highly organised in her adventuring.

'There!' Gavin announced, pointing across the road and a yellow zebra crossing to who-knew-what. 'Sortilas.'

'Gavin,' Lucie began as her friend started to tear off, striding forward as if he was the founding father of power-walking. 'Is Sortilas the name of our hotel?' That's what it had to be, didn't it?

'Hotel?'

Why had Gavin said the word 'hotel' like it wasn't a full member of the English language and could not ever be used as such in Scrabble? Lucie was beginning to worry that the faith she had in Gavin choosing somewhere relaxing and away-from-it-all might have been ill-placed. As much as Lucie wanted chill time, she had absolutely thought that would involve a hotel, be it an apartment to cater for themselves or an all-inclusive free-for-all. Granted she hadn't paid out all-inclusive prices but...

'Yes,' Lucie said, still trying to catch up to him. 'You know, the place we're staying.'

Gavin laughed then, one hand going from the strap of his bag to his mouth, eyes alive with surprise. 'I keep forgetting I've kept the whole trip under wraps!' He giggled. 'Let's keep that going.' He grinned at her. 'There's no hotel, by the way.'

Lucie's stomach plummeted like the plane had during a bump of turbulence on their final descent. There was no hotel. Oh, God. The only thing coming to mind now was the memory that Gavin had once taken part in a weekend in deepest, darkest North Wales where he'd had to make a shelter out of sticks, leaves and crisp packets made into triangles for waterproofing. No, it couldn't be anything like that. Gavin had cried for a week after that experience and said he was never going to pursue a relationship with anyone whose Grindr profile said they liked communing with nature. Gavin had translated that as 'might indulge in al fresco relations' when really it had meant 'possibly Ant Middleton's twin brother'.

'Don't look so worried, Luce,' Gavin said, putting an arm around her shoulders. 'When have I ever let you down?' He continued his trajectory with Lucie now on the same squashed-to-his-side course.

'You shaved off my hair,' she answered without hesitation.

'We don't know *I* did that.'

'Gavin, I can't even do my eyeliner straight. There's no way I cut my own hair.'

'When have I ever let you down *apart* from that?' He sniffed. 'If I *did* do that. Sharon's being very sketchy about her whereabouts after the casino.'

'Well… you dropped hot glue on the upholstery of my car trying to fix your leather trousers on the way to Sharon's probably-not-fiftieth-birthday.'

'*That* was not my fault!' Gavin exclaimed. 'That was your driving!'

'The main thing people do in a car is drive! I'm pretty sure gluing clothes together isn't in the Highway Code's list of common practices.'

'Listen,' Gavin said, smiling. 'Everything in the UK is way way behind us now. Miles and miles back there over seas and clouds.' He waved a hand at the pure blue sky. 'All that matters for the next few weeks is you, me and total relaxation.'

The word 'relaxation' from Gavin's lips actually made her whole spirit thrum in that moment. Her whole self – so much more than her dodgy back – was crying out for it. She needed to completely ease off the gas, take her foot off the pedal and let her soul do the driving…

'*Yassas! Yassas!* You are the Gaveen and Loosely?'

There was a man in front of them now, a paper sign in his hand bearing the word 'Sortilas'. He had thick black hair and a cigarette hanging from his lips. The suit he was wearing was a little too small for him and the belt he really didn't need was set to the last notch.

'I'm Gavin,' Gavin announced. 'Gav-in... and this is Lu-cie.'

'I am Miltos. Mil-tos. The driver for the van to Sortilas.' He grabbed Gavin's suitcase with one hand and Lucie's with the other before either of them had time to blink, let alone respond.

'Did he say "van"?' Lucie asked Gavin as they hurried after Miltos, past the line of luxurious taxis.

'I'm sure he meant "minibus",' Gavin replied, with little conviction. 'Minibus, van, they're probably one and the same in the Greek language.'

Lucie's heart brightened as she set her eyes on a small, sleek, silver coach ahead. It was all polished chrome and blacked out windows, as if ready to transport Lady Gaga and a full entourage. This was more like it!

Except Miltos wasn't stopping at the mini-coach. *Stop! Stop at the coach!* Lucie held her breath as Miltos halted not at the door of the bus she had convinced herself would contain air-conditioning to simulate Iceland – which was exactly what she needed right now – but instead at the rusty framework of a van. A van plastered with effigies of every fruit you could imagine. Miltos now had his hand on the wing-mirror that was wobbling in the humidity so much it could barely be attached to the vehicle. Then he opened a sliding door, popping in their cases and then holding out his hand.

'Loosely,' he greeted with a smile.

Lucie now wanted to cry. The interior of the van was dark. Were there even seats in there? There had surely been a mistake. She stayed still, waiting for Gavin to point out the obvious error in their transfer.

'Please, Loosely,' Miltos spoke again, taking the cigarette from his lips, dropping it onto the ground and crushing it beneath his shoe. 'Let me help you with the step.'

'Gavin,' Lucie said, her throat tightening. She didn't know what else to say. She hoped saying his name would be enough to spur action.

'This is…' Gavin began, drawing up to Lucie's shoulder, 'so not like anything in Southampton, right?' His voice lowered to a whisper then. 'Think of it as a grade up from the shittiest Uber you've ever been in. The info said it was a thirty-minute drive at most.' He smiled at Lucie. 'Dark means it will be cool inside there.'

'All I can smell is…' Lucie stopped talking and really breathed. What *was* that scent?

'Cherries,' Miltos offered. 'I have sold many cherries this morning, but there are a few containers left. Do not worry. Plenty of space.' He put his hand out again and Lucie felt Gavin nudge her forward.

'I promise you're going to love it when we get there,' Gavin whispered.

'Well, I think you need to tell me where "there" is now,' Lucie grumbled, stepping up into the fruit van with Miltos's assistance and thumping down onto a seat that appeared to be next to an over-spilling tray of nectarines.

Gavin hopped in alongside her, orange bag catching on a set of weighing scales as his bottom found slightly torn pleather. 'You said you wanted a surprise.'

'*You* said I wanted a surprise,' Lucie answered, gathering herself together in as minimal space as possible. She was afraid that any movement might involve the juice of fruits she suspected would stain the white trousers she had bought on impulse when a holiday clothing ad had been fed to her on Facebook.

'We go to Sortilas!' Miltos reminded them, sliding the door closed then hopping up into the cab at the front. 'Your health holiday begins right here. With the fruit!'

Health holiday. Had he said 'health holiday'? She didn't want a health holiday. She wanted cocktails and not having to watch her weight. As much as Gavin worked out at the hospital gym, he wasn't really one for nuts or seeds, and the only pulses he was fond of usually involved a heavy dance track at nightclub The Edge. And she really wanted something different to measured and cautious, or her mind was going to be trying to tell her she shouldn't have even left her safety net in the UK…

'Gavin,' Lucie said. 'Please tell me this isn't some sort of… fat camp.' For some reason she was conjuring up images of celebrities having their girth measured and progress tracked as they went from slob to slim in a series of challenges that involved coloured tracksuits.

'What is "fat camp"?' Miltos asked as he started the engine and the van began to whine and groan like Lucie might soon if she didn't get something alcoholic in her system. Maybe that was why Gavin had been Mr Italian Aperitif on the plane! Because he knew that was the last of his alcohol!

Gavin placed a hand on Lucie's knee and squeezed. 'Mr Miltos, please reassure Loosely that Sortilas is going to have plenty of food and plenty of wine before she faints.'

Lucie pulled a face at Gavin's use of her name.

'Oh, Loosely,' Miltos answered, looking at her in the rear-view mirror. 'In Sortilas no one goes hungry. Not even the fat camp ones.'

Eight

Sortilas Village Square, Sortilas

'Let me shoot one of them. Just one. I will aim for their arseholes.'

From their seated position on one of the dark green painted iron benches in the village square, Michalis watched the gathering over his extra-strong frappe as Nyx made guns with her fingers and made the sound effect of pistols shooting towards the tourists who were arriving, led by Melina. The village president was carrying a big chunky wooden staff that had a large *mati* – evil eye symbol – on its top. The Greek legend was that items bearing this symbol were talismans, meant to ward off any unpleasantness.

'Why do you want to shoot the tourists?' Michalis asked.

'They are stupid,' Nyx answered, now pretending she was looking down the sight of a sniper rifle and lining her vision up with a man wearing a very bright palm-tree-patterned shirt. Michalis couldn't pretend *that* wasn't a crime against fashion but still, tourism was as vital to Corfu as having air to breathe.

'Nyx,' Michalis said. 'They come here and give money to the tavernas and the bars.'

'They come here and think it is paradise,' Nyx told him. 'Sooo dumb.'

He had come back here and thought it was paradise too. And it was, compared to what he had been living with in Thessaloniki. Arriving back on this quiet, beautiful island, he had immediately felt a change in pace. But, exactly like he had at Nyx's age, his sister wanted to escape the confines of village life and familiarity to visit new places and have different experiences. He could tell her that life outside of Corfu might seem naturally appealing. He had thought a vibrant city existence was for him, once upon a time. He had longed to be a doctor who worked miracles, made big changes and discovered cures. And then, when he wasn't being a hero, he would have time to go out, enjoy the buzz of a new scene, meet many people from all over the world, live the largest of lives, fall in love... Yet now, after doing all of that, after everything that had come to pass over the last eighteen months, he felt it would be important to remind his younger sister that happiness came in many forms and she should not take for granted the slow pace of life and peace here. Because one day, just like him, she might want to cling to it. Though, having said that, and looking at Nyx now, his sister aiming a pretend bow and arrow at the group mainly dressed in shorts and T-shirts, he knew it was doubtful she would listen. She was filled to the brim with that confidence of youth, that feeling that she was ungoverned by anything or anyone, invincible.

'Well... they will spend money at your shop,' Michalis stated, sucking at his drink again.

'*Papa's* shop,' Nyx said with a grunt. 'Not mine. And, really, how many holidaymakers want to spend their time in the sun cooking lamb testicles?' Nyx widened her eyes then, showing slight macabre excitement. 'I have started selling them marinated in a lemon and garlic sauce by the way. They are very popular.'

'Not all tourists want to eat out,' Michalis reminded her. 'The ones staying here in Sortilas, those who do not want to venture far, will need ingredients to cook. We are the only shop in the village that sells meat.'

Nyx pulled another face. 'They always ask me for "burgers" and "English sausages". If they want "burgers" and "English sausages" why have they come to Greece? Why do they not take their holidays in… sausage-shire.'

'Nyx,' Michalis said. 'You are becoming more and more intolerant.'

'I am?' she asked, this time her expression spelling out 'astounded'. 'How was I not getting this right before?'

'Do you not need all the business you can get?'

Nyx sighed and slurped at her frappe. 'That is what Papa says. But, you know, sometimes there are more important things in life than being nice to dumb people for their money.'

Michalis focussed closer on the activity in the square and the village president. Melina seemed to be leading the group of newcomers towards a wooden trestle and behind the table stood two people dressed in what looked like hospital gowns, gloves and masks. 'Nyx, what is going on over there?'

'Oh, Micha!' Nyx exclaimed almost excitedly. 'I forgot to tell you about the new procedures here. This is *great* to watch! It has been going on ever since the golden tortoise and plaque arrived on the side of the church.' She giggled. 'It is health screening.'

'What?' Michalis asked, adjusting his sunglasses.

'Yes! Melina has decided that, with Sortilas getting the award for longevity and excellent health, the village must do everything they can to ensure this is not undermined. So, screening and tests.'

Michalis was up on his feet. 'This is madness. She can't do that. And who are the people dressed in PPE?'

'Ah, well, one of them is Stavros and—'

'Stavros? Who hires mountain bikes?'

'Melina said he was used to wearing gloves and using fluids to lubricate the bikes, so he was a perfect candidate to take swabs of oily snot and mouth juices.'

Michalis shook his head and wondered what to do. This was complete craziness. There were still enough tests and isolation measures without this. These were people looking for a break from their lives, people, like him, who were desperate for a relaxing escape. You did not start that off by shoving a six-inch cotton bud down someone's throat if it was no longer an absolute necessity.

'The other one, it is Athena,' Nyx said. 'She has provided the goat piss.'

'Goat piss!' Michalis exclaimed.

'That is my very *favourite* part!' Nyx told him. 'I think we should move benches. Get closer.'

'*I* am getting closer,' Michalis stated brutally. 'I am shutting this down.'

Nine

'Gavin,' Lucie said, her voice wobbling. 'Why are there people in PPE here? You promised me this was not a health holiday.' And the figures clad from head to toe in protection were causing flashbacks to some of those harrowing nights she was desperate to get some distance from.

Despite the latex apparitions ahead of them, they were standing in the most picturesque village square that really did look like the quintessential depiction of Greece from bygone times. Wrought iron benches housed elderly men passing the time of day and snoozing cats stretched out, bellies up, or curled into a tight bundle protecting paws from the sun. They had been dropped off a mere few hundred metres away before being roughly greeted by a woman with a big stick, then urged to join another group of people who seemed to have got down from a very luxurious coach...

In a stark comparison, Miltos had given them less than twenty seconds to unfurl themselves from the confines of the fruit van, stretch their legs, check their clothes for cherry juice and marvel at the glorious view down over the mountainous terrain towards a glistening sea. And now they were here. Faced with figures who looked a lot like she and Gavin had last year. And the intense Greek heat had to be a number of degrees hotter than Abbington Ward. She felt for them.

'It's not a "health holiday" as such,' Gavin began.

'What's that supposed to mean?' Lucie snapped back. 'Because, right now, I'm still wondering how you managed to book a fruit van to drive us from the airport. *And* marvelling how we got here without being crushed against a couple of pounds of nectarines, given the hairpin nature of the roads!'

'I think someone needs a drink,' Gavin replied.

'Yes,' Lucie agreed. '*Someone does* need a drink. Because *I* didn't mainline all the airline Aperol!'

'Maybe a little siesta when we get to where we're staying? They do that in Greece, you know. An afternoon sleep to prepare for the evening.' Gavin sighed. 'That's a ritual I could fully embrace and bring back to England. Along with some tapenade. It's so expensive in Tesco.'

'Where *are* we staying?' Lucie continued to rant. 'Because I can't see any hotels here, Gavin. Just a… mini-market, a sort-of restaurant and a…' She wrinkled her nose, still without sunglasses, and tried to see exactly what the other shop with a large glass frontage was. 'Are those pig trotters hanging with that bunting?'

'The Greeks make all sorts of interesting dishes. Didn't you look at the in-flight magazine? There was a whole page on frying an octopus's ink sack.' Gavin shivered. 'I had to jiggle a little bit and adjust my seat back after reading that.'

'Gavin, please,' Lucie begged. 'What *is* this place? Because it doesn't seem like anything out of a TUI brochure.'

Gavin slipped an arm around her shoulders and drew her closer to him as they moved along a little in the queue of approximately thirty people. 'Well, a friend of a friend recommended it to me. She said this place, this lovely *village*, was known for being one of the safest, healthiest places in Europe. There are actually people living here who are over a hundred years old. And they're still active! All, you know, gadding about like the late great Captain Sir Tom Moore did.'

'So, it *is* a health holiday!' She didn't want to live to one hundred if it meant eating the sack of an octopus or pigs' trotters. She just wanted a nice cool glass of wine and this fluffy pita bread everyone said the Greeks did better than anyone else. Was that too much to ask? Particularly as the sensible voice in her head, that sounded very much like a version of Meg, was still whispering that she needed to hover her foot over life's brake pedal instead of caressing the accelerator.

'Hear me out,' Gavin begged. 'I did my research. We have all the calm and tranquillity here in Sortilas. And then we have the lively villages of Sidari and Roda within easy reach for when we want to live it up with cocktails, karaoke and... a Cher tribute act.'

Lucie closed her eyes. She was really hoping Gavin hadn't booked their trip based entirely on the fact there was a Cher tribute act nearby. But right at this moment, watching people sipping at a strange cloudy gold-coloured solution in a small plastic beaker, all the renditions of 'If I Could Turn Back Time' seemed preferable to this current charade.

'Wait until you see the house we're staying in,' Gavin said, nudging her rib cage with a teasing elbow. 'You're going to love it. It's literal history.'

No canvas. That was a plus. 'House' meant bricks and mortar, didn't it? Lucie breathed a humid breath of relief. She had been imagining communal showers and hunting local wildlife for dinner...

'*Kalispera!* Welcome to Sortilas!'

It was the woman with the stick proffering a tray of the funny plastic cups their way. Gavin plucked one straight up and raised it in the air in a gesture of 'cheers'.

'Please,' the woman said to Lucie. 'A drink for you.'

'No, thank you,' Lucie answered. 'I'm not really thirsty.'

'What?!' Gavin remarked, his tiny cup as yet undrunk. 'It's sweltering out here.' He lowered his voice a notch. 'And it's probably rude not to accept a welcome drink.'

'Can't you smell it?' Lucie whispered. She was trying to keep a smile on her face for the woman's benefit, but she also wanted to communicate her concern about the contents of the cups.

'Smell what?' Gavin asked, putting the little beaker nearer to his face.

'Gavin, you're a nurse! The drinks smell like wee,' Lucie whispered, hiding her lips from the woman with the flat of her hand. 'Wee that's harbouring a week-old urine infection.'

Gavin gave a good long sniff, dipping his nose into the cup. And then his eyes rolled into the back of his head like he was about to be overcome by fumes.

'Please,' the woman said, taking a cup off the tray and holding it out to Lucie. 'It is tradition.'

'What is it?' Gavin asked her, holding the cup by his fingertips now.

'It is traditional,' the woman replied. 'You drink, you have good holiday in the village.'

'And, if we don't drink?' Lucie asked, still not accepting the cup.

'It can't be wee,' Gavin whispered. 'Can it?' He took another sniff and his expression seemed to give off the impression he was settling himself with the idea that it might be something that *hadn't* come out of someone's urethra.

'Local delicacy,' the woman said, nodding rather excessively and trying to press the cup in between Lucie's fingers.

'How bad can it be?' Gavin asked Lucie, already looking like he was bracing himself. 'It will be something like *raki*. Remember that *raki* night we had with Sharon?'

'I do,' Lucie answered. 'The taste was so bad we were both voluntarily licking her "lucky" cactus plant to take away the taste.'

Lucie watched Gavin take an almighty breath and then he put the rim of the cup to his lips and tipped it down his throat in one slick action. He let out an accomplished gasp and put the beaker back on the tray. 'Done.'

'*Na stamatísei!* Stop!'

Lucie turned her head at the deep command and saw a man striding towards their group. Dark hair, short but not too short, sunglasses covering a good portion of his olive-skinned face and dressed in a plain white T-shirt and faded denim jeans. In his hands was a takeout cup of something brown with ice cubes. Quickly the man put his drink down on the long table and snatched the cup of might-be-wee out of the space between Lucie and the woman trying to press it on her.

He looked somewhere between angry and agitated, as if he hadn't quite decided which way to go. Lucie could smell a hint of aftershave that wasn't at all unpleasant and was, in fact, a whole lot better than the aroma of the 'welcome' drink. Next to her she could feel Gavin rippling with interest as the new arrival began to speak quickly in what she assumed was Greek. She couldn't understand a word, but she *could* understand that this man was unhappy with this lining up and drinking procedure. She was quite impressed with the fact he was wearing jeans when she was currently melting like a cheap candle in her thin white cotton trousers.

'Excuse me,' Gavin said with a bit of a throat clear. 'What's going on?'

'Nothing is going on,' the woman said quickly. 'We are welcoming you to Sortilas in our customary way.'

The man pulled off his sunglasses then and looked directly at Lucie. 'My apologies. You did not take a drink, right?'

'No,' Lucie answered. He had the most deliciously dark eyes. She should definitely say more than one word if she wanted to keep him looking at her.

'*I* did!' Gavin exclaimed. 'I drank one of those traditional drinks. What was it? Should I gag?'

Gavin already had his tongue out in the air making a noise like he might be a three-year-old with a handful of Lego stuck in his throat.

'Mrs Hatzi!' the man exclaimed. 'You cannot make tourists drink goat urine.'

Gavin bent double then, starting to make a horrendous retching sound. Lucie put a hand on his back and patted in a half-hearted attempt at consolation. There was time for 'I told you so' later.

'It is a natural deterrent!' the woman called Mrs Hatzi insisted. 'We have done much research. The urine of the goats has many benefits. Including aiding with respiratory disorders.'

The man was shaking his head now and seemed to be chewing on his bottom lip. It was a nice bottom lip, pink and plump, bare when compared to the layer of beard on the rest of his face. Lucie had almost blanked out the fact that next to her Gavin was still trying to draw out the goat piss from his stomach.

'This is craziness. And dangerous,' the man warned. 'These people are here for Greek hospitality, not being force-fed the by-products of our animals. I cannot let you continue with this.'

'Lucie! Help me get this stuff out of me! Argh! Ugh! Where's the nearest cactus?'

'You don't need a cactus,' Lucie told him. 'It's only a bit of wee.' If anything it might dilute the Aperol high Gavin had been floating on since they landed.

'Here. Give him this.'

The man was holding out his plastic cup from the table, now devoid of its lid and straw.

'What animal did *this* come from?' Lucie asked him, half-serious, half not. It *was* brown after all…

'Cow,' the man answered without flinching a muscle.

It took Lucie a second to realise exactly what he meant and she smiled. 'Milk?'

'And coffee,' he said, returning the smile. 'Frappe.'

'Give it to me!' Gavin hollered, reaching out a hand and snatching it away from Lucie.

She went to say something else to the rather hot guy but saw he had turned his attention back to the woman.

'Mrs Hatzi, no more of this,' he warned. 'You know where the people stay. And, if there are any problems, *I* am in the village. No more goat urine.'

Lucie watched him put his sunglasses back on before turning around and heading across the square. He stopped at a bench next to a really pretty young woman with amazing buns in her hair. Together they looked like a poster couple for Brand Perfect Marriage. Just her luck. Not that she was really *seriously* looking. This break was about relaxation, putting the ugly past behind her and trying to get back to somewhere near normal. That stability had to come first before anything else. It would be a tip-toe into the adventure arena if anything, not a full-on face-plant.

'Can we go now?' Gavin groaned. 'I think I need to lie down.'

'One moment,' the woman said. 'First we check temperatures.'

Lucie shook her head, trying to pull Gavin into an upright position. 'Let's hope they're not using any part of a goat for that.'

Ten

Villa Psomi, Sortilas

The view was phenomenal. There was no other word for it. Lucie was standing – case at her feet – under a wooden pergola, its roof strung with lush vines that were bursting with grapes. There were so many bunches of muted green and vibrant purple fruits tumbling and twisting down from the canopy, all providing welcome shade. But all she could really do was gaze, and gaze some more, at the panoramic view of the sea. It was below their position here on the side of the mountain but looked close enough to reach out and touch... or perhaps dive into. Lucie could almost feel the coolness of the water on her shoulders, gently flowing over the skin and removing all that built-up tension she tended to carry at the back of her neck. This was what she needed but hadn't quite *accepted* she needed. This sense of complete tranquillity. How fortunate was she to be on holiday in a new country? How lucky was she to be here at all? Her thoughts turned to all those families she had witnessed – sometimes only over FaceTime – in the midst of grief when they had lost a loved one to Coronavirus. Sometimes it had been so quick, the change between someone needing a little help with their breathing to being admitted to intensive care. Other times it had been a long, drawn out debilitation until the end. Nothing changed the goodbye though. Be it by the bedside or over Zoom, everyone had been given the chance to say a final farewell. Lucie swallowed as her thoughts drifted back over the years, halting inside the confused mind of her two-year-old self, being told Mummy had had to go away. That last goodbye was something she'd never been able to have…

'Argh! Get it off me! Get it off me!'

Lucie's thoughts were interrupted by Gavin running onto the terrace, all flapping arms and hysteria, straight away shattering the stillness.

'What's the matter?' Lucie asked.

'It's a praying mantis! It's huge! It's going to get in my throat! Don't let it get in my throat!' Gavin clapped a hand over his mouth, turning the panic internal at least.

'Where is it?' Lucie asked. She didn't have an aversion to critters. She'd spent a large portion of her childhood making homes for worms while Meg dug earth for mini-allotments in planters in their back garden. She hadn't taken much in about the growing of vegetables, but she did know the difference between a red admiral and a cabbage white in the butterfly world. Meg had also made sure she knew the difference between sweets and slug pellets.

'Left breast! Left breast!' Gavin was practically hyperventilating now. His hand was still close to his mouth and now he had closed his eyes. He was still pumping his legs up and down though, like he was taking part in *PE with Joe.*

Lucie couldn't see a thing on his T-shirt except a hint of perspiration – or perhaps it was a dribble of goat wee from the welcoming committee.

Gavin opened one eye. 'It's not there. Where's it gone? Where's it gone?'

'It probably couldn't stand the noise,' Lucie told him with a smile.

Gavin took a nervous breath and spread his fingers over his T-shirt, brushing down tentatively but thoroughly. 'The nature element of the house was the only drawback, I have to admit.'

'But look at the view,' Lucie said, sighing with contentment as she linked her arm with Gavin's and turned him ever so slightly towards the fantastic outlook.

'I knew you'd like the view. It's gorgeous, isn't it?'

'Completely gorgeous.' She took a breath. 'I think it's the most gorgeous view I've ever seen.'

'Well,' Gavin said, giving her a squeeze. 'Wait until you see the *inside* of the house. I think we're going to have to draw straws for the "oven" bedroom.'

'Oven bedroom?' Lucie queried. She wasn't sure she liked the sound of that. It sounded stifling rather than optimised for sleep.

'I love that you haven't seen any of the photos. The absolute power!' Gavin said, grinning. He put an arm around her shoulders. 'Come on. Come and meet Villa Bread.'

'What?' That didn't sound like any kind of relaxing holiday retreat. 'Villa Bread?'

'Villa Psomi. *Psomi* means "bread" in Greek. It's called that because part of it used to be a bakery. Getting the whole oven bedroom thing now?'

This place had history, roots, a story. She shouldn't have assumed Gavin wasn't capable of booking more than a studio apartment with a view of a pool and its resident flamingo floaty. Yes, the centre of the village might have had the maddest people wanting to probe and assess, but they were all a short walk away. This place was isolated in the very best of ways.

'Ta da!' Gavin said, throwing his arms out and waving excitedly like the best game show presenter revealing a grand prize.

Lucie gulped. The house, exactly like the view, was something special too. It was every kind of strong and traditional, yet there was a deep warmth coming from the stone and cement, rendered in that perfect rustic way travelogues rave about. There were glass blocks in the shape of a cross on one wall, other windows half-covered with wooden shutters brightly painted white. A grey stone paved area led to the large front door and across this courtyard was another separate building. More living accommodation? Lucie was starting to worry that Gavin had invited other people... or was this going to be communal space? Or perhaps it was a guest house to share?

'You love it, right? Tell me you love it!' Gavin said, taking her case from her.

'Are there other people staying here?' Lucie asked. She tried to keep the disappointment out of her tone, because they *were* on a budget. It was a little bit optimistic to think the few hundred pounds she had parted with for this trip was going to buy them a huge mansion house with panoramic sea views all to themselves.

Gavin looked over his shoulder suddenly. 'Shit, there's no one else here, is there? Don't tell me I arsed up the dates!'

'No,' Lucie said. 'I can't *see* anyone. But, you know, this house, it's so big. Have we got a room each and use of a kitchen or...'

'Oh, Luce,' Gavin said, all smiles again. 'It's all ours. The whole thing. And there's three bedrooms in the main house, plus this building here is a separate studio.' He pointed to the stone structure opposite, which *did* look like a whole small house on its own. 'Plenty of space to spread out and enjoy. Plus there's a pool, tucked down over there.' He pointed over the tumbling greenery and Lucie caught sight of a couple of white parasols rippling in the breeze, the glimmer of turquoise water...

Now she wanted to happy-cry. This was *perfect*. This was so much more than the tiny balcony and twin beds in one room she had been envisaging. Not that sharing with Gavin wouldn't have been OK, provided she kept him well away from shaving equipment. But to be in this serene location, in an entire, vast property, Lucie suddenly felt like she'd won life's lottery. Nothing but gratitude flowed through her veins.

'You're not going to cry on me, are you?' Gavin asked her, dropping his head a little into her space like he had on so many occasions when Lucie had almost lost it during a long, hard night shift at the hospital. Times when she had almost wanted to give up...

'No,' she said firmly, determined that her chin was not going to give out a tell-tale wobble. 'Show me this oven bedroom I'm going to be sleeping in.'

'Ah!' Gavin exclaimed. 'I think I said we would draw straws, girlfriend!'

Lucie smiled and put her hand on her case. Somehow, through the madness of the ride in the fruit van and the ingestion of the wee of goats, she was finally relaxing into the idea of this Greek getaway.

Eleven

The Andino apartment, Sortilas

'What do you think?'

Nyx's mouth was slick with oil, her eyes bright and enthused like they always were unless she was channelling angry and annoyed. Michalis nodded his head while his taste buds worked themselves into a frenzy with every motion of his mouth. They were sitting together, with their father, Dimitri, at the family dining table, wedged onto the balcony above the butcher's shop, under a canopy of faded and weary bamboo sticks that had been providing shade as long as Michalis had been alive. It was looking all the more dilapidated now though, and there were none of the pots filled with bright geraniums and bougainvillea or planters housing fresh thyme, rosemary and dill that his mother used to tend. From the moment she passed, seventeen years ago, the family home became slightly less cared for and cherished. Perhaps a little like them as people too.

'Papa? What do you think?' Nyx asked, louder, as if they were all deaf.

Dimitri looked up from his plate, some of the food hanging from his fork. Michalis had noticed that not much sustenance had met his father's mouth yet.

'It is like nothing I have tasted before,' Dimitri answered.

Michalis's eyes went to the sheep's head that had been carefully presented on a silver platter and placed in the centre of their table. Nyx had even widened the mouth of the animal into some kind of manic grin. Although they always had lamb for Easter and ate most parts of it, Michalis wasn't quite sure what parts were in the ball-shaped pieces his sister had served up from the skull onto each of their plates. But the food was actually surprisingly good.

'So, I was looking at recipes on the internet and did you know that we Andinos are uninventive when it comes to lamb?' Nyx reached forward and dug her fork into the skull, pulling out another crispy ball. 'We put it on a spit, the same every time. So, today, I cooked the head for all of the day. Then I took out the brain, the cheek, the eyeballs and the tongue and I cut them into fine, tiny little pieces. Next, I added feta, mustard, peppers and gently massaged it all together to form perfect egg shapes, before I deep-fried them in olive oil.' She laughed. 'Then I serve them in the skull. Like balls for brains! Ha!'

Michalis watched his father drop his fork to his plate and instead pick up his glass of ouzo and ice.

'Are you feeling OK, Papa?' Michalis asked him.

Dimitri gave a shrug of non-commitment. 'I would prefer fish.'

Nyx gave a gasp like their father might have asked to

invite the devil for dinner to meet with the priest. 'Fish! I... cannot even speak! You are a *butcher*!'

Michalis was a little surprised himself. Despite living on Corfu where seafood was plentiful and excellent, Dimitri had always been more of a meat lover. It stood to reason, it was his occupation and his father's occupation before him and his grandfather's and so on. It would have been Michalis's occupation too if he hadn't made a stand when he left school with good grades. Being a doctor had been on his mind from the moment he had time to really acknowledge his mother's passing and Dimitri was smart enough to realise that trying to make him stay in the family business was only going to make Michalis more determined to fly the nest. Studying for a job in the medical profession was about so much more than being the first in his family to go to university, it was about understanding what had happened to his mum and trying to prevent something like that happening to another family.

'Fish is good for you, I read about it,' Dimitri answered.

'Fish is thin,' Nyx countered. 'All fish are thin. Even the fat ones.' She put another whole ball in her mouth and chowed down.

'Fish *is* good for you,' Michalis offered to them both. 'But a varied diet is best.' He looked at his father's full glass of cloudy liquid. 'Perhaps... a little less ouzo?'

Dimitri took a hearty swig of his drink and smacked his lips in something like obstinance. 'I read that a little alcohol every day has many health benefits.'

'All this reading,' Nyx remarked, shaking her head. 'Nothing good can come from it.'

'You are worried for your health?' Michalis asked

him. Perhaps there was something physically wrong with their father and he was keeping it from everyone. He had said very little since Michalis had arrived back. His father wasn't the greatest of talkers at the best of times, but he hadn't engaged at all. In fact, the only stories of village life – births (not many), deaths (even fewer) and marriages (somewhere in between) – had come from his sister.

'Melina tells me you are setting up a surgery in the village,' Dimitri said, changing the conversation.

Michalis shook his head, sighing. 'Melina is making visitors drink goat urine before they go to their accommodation, did you know that?'

'I knew of it,' Dimitri admitted with a shrug. 'What can anyone do? She is the president.'

'She has got even more crazy since the golden tortoise arrived. When she is not giving orders to people, she is polishing it. Around and around. Up and down. Side to side.' Nyx made a mime of someone cleaning in all the motions. 'I think she expects Kyriakos Mitsotakis to visit and present her with something even bigger.' She grinned at her own euphemism. 'Another ball?' She picked up the platter and offered the skull across the table.

'I have enough,' Michalis answered his sister. He was five balls down and unable to breathe without leaning back in the chair. And if he leaned back too far he would be in danger of falling from the balcony to the street below. The railings had been shaky for years. When Nyx had turned six and was old enough to climb olive trees and skilled enough to dissect a pig, no one considered it a hazard any longer. But perhaps he could fix it himself while he was here. His father wasn't getting any younger…

'Papa?' Nyx asked.

'Not for me,' Dimitri said, putting down his fork. He took another slurp of ouzo. 'So, where is this surgery to be? And why does the president know about your plans before your own father?'

Michalis let out a sigh, but his father showing interest in his plans was an improvement on his general demeanour. 'This was not my intention.'

'But you are going to do it?!' Nyx exclaimed.

He wasn't going to do it. Was he? The truth was he didn't know what he was going to do. He hadn't thought of anything much past the ripping off of his scrubs and the pain in his own heart as he lost yet another patient. He'd tried to talk about it with his friend, Nikos, once. After three bottles of Alfa and a shot called Kamikaze at a bar not far from the hospital, he had tried to explain a little of how he felt. But the words had stuck in his throat as Nikos claimed everything could be rinsed away with alcohol and the freedom of the dancefloor. It was then that Michalis knew not everyone felt the same. At times, Michalis had felt like he was cycling up the steepest of mountains. The summit was there, just out of reach, behind the clouds, until you rounded the very next corner and it completely disappeared. Did you stop pedalling and turn back because there was no guarantee the end would ever be there to reach? Or did you carry on regardless because not giving up had to make some kind of difference? He still didn't have the answer to that question.

'You are too good for this village with their earaches and their piles,' Dimitri scoffed.

'And,' Nyx began, 'there are certain creams it would be embarrassing to ask your brother for.'

'Although the large amount of medicines Miltos goes through would pay a deposit on a house for you,' Dimitri stated.

'It was something I said to get myself out of a situation,' Michalis continued. How many times had he done that before?

'He is to be paraded through the streets,' Nyx told their father, bouncing a little on her chair. 'For the new festival. The Day of the Not Dead.'

'I have seen the posters. They make you look like Superman.'

'There are more posters?!' Nyx said. 'With Micha's face on them?'

'This is insanity,' Michalis said, shaking his head. 'From where has Melina got a photograph of me?'

'It is not a photograph,' Dimitri told him. 'It is an artist's impression.'

'Someone has drawn him!' Nyx laughed out loud, banging the butt of her fork on the table and making everything shake. 'Please tell me it is a cartoon!'

'This village!' Michalis exclaimed in irritation.

'Despite what you say,' Dimitri said, 'the village is changing. It is not how it once was.'

His father's tone was reflective. It was almost as if this conversation was no longer about pills for haemorrhoids or the *panegyris*, but something deeper. Michalis's gaze went to a small wooden basket on the shelves of the balcony wall. Its weaving was coming apart at the joins and there was evidence on the outside that swallows had been nesting in it. He had made that basket when he was eight with his mother. It was one of the last things they had done together…

'I agree it is changing,' Nyx said. 'You are wanting to eat fish instead of meat!'

'The village is old,' Dimitri continued.

'Mrs Kanaris is turning ninety-five on Christmas Day.'

'The village is dying,' Dimitri said again.

Michalis wasn't sure he liked the way this conversation was going. Perhaps he could get his father to consent to a small series of tests to put Michalis's own mind at rest. Blood pressure, blood sugar, perhaps a small body MOT to test the function of his liver and kidneys…

'The village is not dying,' Nyx scoffed. 'That is one of the problems. *No one* is dying!'

'But they will,' Dimitri said. 'And when they do, they will all go at once.'

'Mrs Kanaris will be the last,' Nyx mused. 'Anyone who can eat *baklava* without their teeth has the will of a warrior.'

'There are no new people coming into the village. There were only two births last year. Two!' Dimitri stated, sipping at his drink.

'Maria is pregnant,' Nyx reminded. 'Twins. She is due very soon. She is dying to eat offal again, did you know?'

'And after that?' Dimitri asked. 'There are very few young people to reproduce but… you two.'

'Oh my God!' Nyx exclaimed. 'Why does everybody want me to marry and breed?!' She dropped her fork and folded her arms across her chest. 'I am not a horse.'

'You are thinking about grandchildren?' Michalis asked.

Perhaps his father was simply wallowing in the natural life process of getting older and hitting all the expected milestones.

'I am thinking that, by now, I thought I would be teaching someone else the trade of butchery,' Dimitri said.

'Well,' Nyx said, leaning forward and unwrapping her arms from around herself, 'you could put the machetes in the fists of Maria's twins when they get to five. Better butchers than policemen like their father, am I right?' She grinned. 'I am right, right?'

'I am talking about family,' Dimitri said, seeming to get a little frustrated. 'Your mother, she always assumed there would be grandchildren.'

'But she is not here.'

Michalis didn't really know why he had felt the need to say that sentence aloud, but he had. They never talked directly about his mother, Lola, now. At first Michalis was desperate to keep the memory of her alive – more so for Nyx who barely remembered the woman who had raised her for only a year – but whenever this happened his father would leave the room and change the conversation until even speaking her name felt too challenging and intrusive somehow.

No one was saying anything in response now either, and Michalis's words were hanging in the air above the sheep's skull, perhaps longing to be deep-fried.

It was Dimitri who finally broke the silence.

'Forget I said anything,' Dimitri said, getting up from his seat. 'Your lives are full. You do not need the advice of an old man from an even older village.'

'Papa,' Michalis said, rising from his own seat to try

and stop his father from leaving the dinner table.

'Sit,' Dimitri ordered. 'Finish your sister's balls.'

Michalis sensed there was going to be no further discussion and he held his position, hovering over his chair until Dimitri left the balcony.

'That went well,' Nyx said, letting out a deep exhale. 'I make balls and he starts to talk about reproduction. I will never make these again.'

'How is he when he is at work?' Michalis asked, retaking his seat.

'Silent,' Nyx answered. 'Unless he is whispering into his phone on his breaks.'

'Whispering into his phone?' Michalis didn't even know his father *had* a mobile phone.

'Mmm. It was a purchase he made a few months ago. He says it allows me not to worry so much when he goes out at night on his moped.'

'Where does he go at night on his moped?' Now Michalis felt completely out of the loop.

'I do not know! I am not his prison governor! I am too busy at night going out on my own moped!'

Was Michalis the only one in this family who did not have a two-wheeled vehicle?

'I want to give him a medical,' Michalis said, decided.

'He will not agree to that. You know how he hates to go to the doctor.'

'He will not be going to *any* doctor. He will be coming to me. His son.'

'I think that will make the idea even less appealing,' Nyx said, leaning back in her chair.

'You think he does not trust me?'

'I think he does not trust the whole world after Mama died,' Nyx said. 'And you do not visit very much. Too busy with your new friends and your fancy career in Thessaloniki.'

Michalis sighed. His sister had no idea about the difficult parts of his life on the mainland, with good reason. He only shared with her the loud, crazy bars he knew she would love, the heartwarming success stories of his work, the beach parties he'd attended at the start of his career – when he'd actually had days off. But it hadn't been like that for some time now.

'And apart from the night riding and the mobile phone,' Nyx started, 'Papa still feels the same about everything. Life has dealt him shit and he is simply getting older.'

Michalis didn't know how to respond. He had been so focussed on what was going on in his own life he had taken his eye off the ball when it came to things in Sortilas. Nyx had done her main growing up with only Dimitri. Their father had spent a large portion of his life as a widower solely responsible for a young daughter. That can't have been easy for either of them. Perhaps sending home money and visiting sporadically hadn't been enough. Maybe he had ended up putting his patients before his own kin.

'So,' Nyx began. 'Are you going to open your surgery or not?'

Michalis sighed, plucking another lamb ball from the skull and holding it between his thumb and forefinger. 'Yes,' he answered finally. 'If only to get Papa to take some tests.'

Nyx grinned. 'Perfect. And, if he does not comply, I can help you collect samples in inventive ways.'

Michalis was certain he did not want to hear any more about that.

Twelve

Villa Psomi, Sortilas

'Gavin's room has an oven in it,' Lucie spilled into her phone. She was standing on the terrace that led out from the upper sitting room, gazing at the glorious span of cerulean sea set out before her. Her now sun-cream-coated shoulders were soaking up the hot early evening sunshine as she chatted to Meg back in England. 'It used to be a bakery apparently and you could actually crawl into the oven and sleep there, you know, if you wanted to.' Lucie smiled to herself. 'Gavin said there are groups who pay a lot of money to stay somewhere with confined spaces.'

'How ridiculous,' Meg replied. 'Don't they know they will end up confined in a coffin soon enough?' She tutted. 'Now, tell me more about the view and the village. I just can't believe you're in Corfu, Lucie-Lou.'

When Lucie had told Meg she was in Corfu, her aunt had made a noise that sounded like a cross between the mew of a cat and a purr of the engine of a well-looked-after classic car. It turned out that Corfu was the island where

Meg had met Petros. But that was still all the detail Meg was currently divulging.

'Neither can I,' Lucie admitted. 'And I can't believe how beautiful it is.' She let the sigh of contentment leave her and felt her soul soar as it gently pulsed in reaction to the magnificent vista.

'Tell me what it looks like,' Meg begged.

Lucie wasn't sure she had heard Meg so enthusiastic about anything before. Not even the Isle of Wight. 'Well,' Lucie started. 'The sea is the colour of... the mix of blues in your favourite blouse. It's pale and then it's deep and then it's turquoise and, from where I'm standing right now, it's so wide and peacefully still.'

Meg sighed, satisfied. 'What about the mountains? Can you see the mountains?'

'I can see Albania,' Lucie said, nodding as she took in the dramatic backdrop where the sea stopped. 'It's like nothing I've ever imagined. Here I am, in Greece, and I'm looking at another country across the water.'

'I can't believe you're in the north of Corfu too.'

'What was the name of the place you stayed?'

'Perithia,' Meg said. 'A tiny little apartment I didn't spend any time in because it was so small. It had a lovely view of an olive grove, but the mosquitos were quite fierce in the evenings. The little village was lovely though. There were two tavernas, both equally delightful and...'

'What's the matter?' Lucie asked as Meg suddenly stopped talking.

'I'm here reminiscing about times long gone by and you're the one who's having your first summer in Greece. This is your story, Lucie-Lou. Tell me more.'

Suddenly Lucie didn't want to tell Meg more. Something inside was nudging her to instead ask a question, as tiny snippets of maybe-memories prickled her subconscious. She was thinking about her mum again in this moment. Had she had any dreams to travel? How would Rita have felt in front of this view? Would her mum have breathed it into her soul like Lucie was, or would she have been more interested in finding the partying and late nights like everyone seemed to recall. Lucie shook her head.

'Lucie, is everything OK?' Meg's voice asked down the phone connection.

'Yes,' Lucie said quickly. Now wasn't the time. 'We… we have a huge garden. Half an acre all to ourselves, with olive trees, and there's herbs and beautiful pots of flowers and there are ruins next door that are all crumbling and atmospheric. Gavin's already a bit worried about ghosts.'

Meg laughed. 'He should be more worried about snakes if you have half an acre of grass.'

'Really?' Lucie swallowed. She might not be afraid of insects but she wasn't quite sure how she felt about snakes…

'There are many snakes on Corfu,' Meg informed her. 'But the majority are harmless and very beautiful. Just be noisy when you walk. Stamp your feet and chat. I cannot think that Gavin will have a problem with that.'

'There are four bedrooms. Three in the main house and one in the cutest little studio outside. It even has its own terrace with more incredible views.' Lucie took a breath. 'Honestly, Meg, so far it's the most amazing place I've ever been.'

'You sound more relaxed than I've heard you in a very long time. After only a few short hours on Greek soil.'

'And after riding in a fruit van and watching Gavin drink goat wee.'

'What?' Meg exclaimed with a chortle.

'That's a whole other story.'

'What do you have planned for tonight?' Meg asked. 'Are you cooking in? Eating out? Honestly, I can almost taste the tender chicken *souvlaki*.'

'Gavin said we need to celebrate our first night so absolutely no cooking. He's going to arrange a taxi to take us somewhere. I don't know where. What's chicken soo-vaki?'

'*Souvlaki*,' Meg repeated. 'Tender chunks of chicken on a skewer, usually served with chips and salad. Delicious.'

'That sounds really nice.' Lucie's stomach gave a rumble of appreciation at the idea of the dish. 'But, we will eat in too. We both agreed we have to do this as cheaply as possible. So tomorrow we will find a shop and get some supplies.'

'Fresh salads,' Meg said. 'Those ripe, plump tomatoes, and cucumber and red onion... then add in that salty, creamy and crumbly feta cheese. You definitely don't have to have Gordon Ramsay cooking for you to experience five-star tastes in Greece.'

'I can't wait,' Lucie answered.

'Oh, Lucie-Lou, have an amazing time. And keep ringing me. I want to hear all about it.' There was a pause and then: 'And, be careful won't you? I mean, as much as I adored Corfu, it's a foreign country to you and—'

'Meg, you have to stop worrying about me so much,' Lucie interrupted. 'I always do the right thing.' She watched a cream-and-black striped butterfly take flight from the tendril of a plant and for a second she contemplated its utter freedom, happily gliding from one flower to the next, no set routine or plan, no aunt suggesting the best route…

'Lucie! That mantis is back! Help me!' It was Gavin, loudly and from inside the house.

'What's that dreadful shouting?' Meg asked.

'Gavin communing with nature,' Lucie said with a laugh. 'I'll call you tomorrow and describe the chicken on a skewer in minute detail.'

'I might have to make one myself,' Meg replied with a heady sigh. '*Yassas*.'

'What does that mean?'

'It means "goodbye". *And* "hello". In Greek.'

'*Yassas*,' Lucie said, loving the feel of the foreign word on her tongue.

'Goodbye, my darling. Speak soon.'

'Bye.' She ended the call and shivered as she looked again at the beautiful sea view.

'Lucie! Pur-lease!' Another wail from Gavin ensued.

'Coming!'

Thirteen

Vouni

'And we have arrived! Come, Loosely, Gaveen. Come to experience the real Corfiot cuisine.'

Lucie couldn't quite believe she was packed into the very same fruit van *again*. This was the 'taxi' that Gavin had booked to take them out for dinner. Miltos's van was now jam-packed with large green striped watermelons that had felt like bowling balls to her kidneys when they had veered around more tight corners.

'His price was very reasonable,' Gavin whispered. 'Dinner with drinks and a taxi both ways for only thirty euro. You did say you wanted to do things cheaply.'

'I didn't think doing things cheaply would involve getting intimate with a watermelon.'

'Hark at you, Baby Houseman!'

'Gavin, seriously, if I have to ride in this fruit van once more I'll... cut up your Cher tour T-shirt before you even get a chance to wear it here.'

'Well, we obviously have to get the fruit van back to Villa Bread but after that...'

Lucie yelped as a watermelon shook with the vibration of Miltos pulling open the sliding door and rolled into her lap.

'Come, Loosely! Leave the watermelons behind and get ready to taste *sofrito*.'

'*Sofrito*?' Lucie queried. 'What's that?' She had her heart set on the *souvlaki* Meg had talked about.

'Very nice Corfu meal with veal and garlic. My grandmother make. Come.'

Before Lucie could say anything else, Miltos had grabbed her hand and pulled her down from the van. She was regretting the wedged sandals now. Here in this hamlet there were weeds thriving between the gaps of the concrete ground and chickens roaming free, eyeing the newcomers like Lucie and Gavin might be next on the menu. One of the chickens let out a squawk and Gavin squealed as Miltos began striding towards a ramshackle house just ahead that seemed to be made up of stone, corrugated iron and washing lines...

'Gavin,' Lucie said, trying to wiggle her toes and remove the dust motes that had settled inside her shoes already. 'This isn't a restaurant, is it?'

Gavin was brushing down his Armani T-shirt and being as unresponsive as their Annie resus dummies during nurse training.

'Gavin!' Lucie said again. 'Miltos meant this place makes this *sofrito* like his grandmother *used* to make, right? Not that his grandmother is actually making it now... for us.'

'I don't actually know,' Gavin admitted tentatively. 'But,

focus on value for money. I'm starving. This dinner sounds authentic. It was *cheap* and we can both have a drink because we have a ride back to the house.'

First thing tomorrow Lucie was going to see about hiring a car from somewhere. So she might be a little apprehensive about driving on the other side of the road and there was the fact that *every* side of the road here in Corfu seemed like it contained more peril than a well-written road trip thriller. But, on the plus side, there would be no more fruit and she and Gavin could explore the island a little more. Find places that weren't going to make them drink the urine of a local farm animal.

'They better have wine,' Lucie told Gavin. 'And lots of it.'

Gavin linked arms with her and grinned. 'This is great, isn't it? Completely rustic... real Greece.'

'And here I was thinking you wanted karaoke and bingo.'

'There's going to be plenty of time for that too,' Gavin assured. 'Come on... oh, but mind that chicken, step there.'

The cockerel in Lucie's path gave out a growl like it might suddenly morph into a slavering beast of a dog instead of a ruffled and bedraggled Foghorn Leghorn.

'Excuse me,' Lucie said, bowing a little to it then quickly scooting past.

'*Kalos irthate! Kalos irthate!*'

Lucie and Gavin had walked through an entrance porch that contained piles of wood, fishing rods, wellington boots and a collection of hats for all occasions. And now, here they were, in a large farmhouse style kitchen – thick flagstones on the floor – where pots and pans hung from ropes attached to the ceiling. A tiny silver-haired Greek woman was at its centre, giving off the kind of excitement you'd expect for the entrance of holy prophets. She was wearing an ankle-skimming grey dress with a full-length flowered apron over the top of it. Her hair was long and tied back from her face into a bun at her nape. There were slippers on her feet.

'"*Kalos irthate*" means "welcome",' Miltos translated.

'That's nice,' Gavin said, quickly ducking as a frying pan blew in the hot breeze. 'Isn't it, Lucie?'

'Yes,' Lucie bleated. How old was this little lady? She couldn't *really* be Miltos's grandmother, could she?

The woman said something else and Miltos smiled and nodded before speaking to them again.

'My grandmother says you must treat her home as your own. That is what we do here in Greece. We are all about the *philoxenia*. Kindness to strangers.'

'Ooo,' Gavin began, turning a one-eighty spin as two fish slices banged together like a wind chime and threatened to slice off his ear. 'I read about that on the plane. It's a beautiful thing.'

Lucie was still staring open-mouthed at the small woman, who was now powering around the kitchen, lifting lids from steaming pots and plucking utensils from the hooks of the suspended strings. Miltos had to be in his fifties, didn't he? Even a rough calculation would put his grandmother at... over one hundred?

'What is your mother's name?' Gavin asked Miltos.

'*Yiayia*,' Miltos answered with a grin. 'Grandmother.'

Gavin laughed. 'No, I think this is getting lost in translation somehow.'

'*Ochi*,' Miltos said with a shake of his head. 'My mother's mother, she is my grandmother. *Eki*. There.' He pointed to the woman pulling a crockpot out of the oven. 'And her name is Mary.' Miltos turned around and pointed. 'And this is my grandmother's sister, Ariana.'

Gavin squeaked and jumped, hitting his head on the side of a cast iron wok. Lucie's gaze went to an armchair in the far corner of the kitchen at which another woman no one had noticed was sitting. She looked identical to Mary, from the clothes, to the hair styling, to the age.

'*Yassas*,' the woman said, waggling her fingers and smiling at them.

'Twins,' Miltos stated. 'One-hundred-and-one this last birthday.'

'What?! Seriously?' Gavin exclaimed, holding a hand to his bumped head.

'Seriously, Gaveen,' Miltos told him, nodding. 'They are the oldest living people in Vouni. But not the oldest in the area. The very oldest people are in Sortilas.' He smiled. 'That is why everybody want to come there.' He inhaled deeply, straightening his back, the bottom button of his shirt popping undone. 'Is it the air we breathe? Is it the soil in which we plant our seeds? Is it that we are blessed by the gods? No one really knows, but you cannot deny the facts. We are strong and healthy and living for a long time.'

'And looking very well on it,' Gavin replied. He got closer to Lucie and dropped a whisper into her ear. 'She hasn't exactly got the looks of the Ariana we know and love, but if I look like that when I'm a hundred-and-one I'd take it.'

Yes, Lucie would take it too, because after the year they'd had, she knew all too well that not everyone made it into any kind of old age.

'The food does smell delicious,' she said, still watching Mary diving around her kitchen space like she was sprightlier than any of her chickens scratching around outside.

'It *is* delicious,' Miltos assured. He dropped another quick few lines of Greek into the air and Mary gave a rapid response that Miltos laughed at.

'What did she say?' Lucie asked. 'Would she like us to do anything to help?' It felt right to offer, seeing as they had been told to treat the house as their own home. But, then again, women could be funny about their kitchen space. Meg wasn't a fan of Lucie dipping in to help with serving up, even when she was red-faced and in danger of burning Yorkshire puddings. Lucie knew it was because she had burned her little finger on a hot pan when she was seven and even now, in her twenties, Meg didn't trust her not to blunder around and scald herself.

'No,' Miltos said. 'My grandmother said it is perhaps her home-cooked *sofrito* that is the key to long life here.'

'Put me down for a double helping in that case,' Gavin said, grinning.

Fourteen

Sitting back in her chair, Lucie put her hands on her belly and held it. She was so full. She couldn't remember being this full ever in her life. First there had been homemade bread – fluffy, soft, huge – and then there had been the *sofrito*. Well, it really had lived up to the deliciousness rating that had been promised. Lucie had never tried veal before, but she would definitely be eating it again. It was rich in flavour, tender in texture and had been served gently resting in the sauce it had been cooked in. Garlic was the overriding taste, but it had been succulent and perfection to the palate. The meat had been accompanied by the freshest courgettes and carrots, a little plain rice, and roasted potatoes that were a world away from frozen Aunt Bessie's.

And the eating area was rustic perfection too. There was a large patio area outside, underneath a wooden and pipework pergola, where a thick hunk of a table sat in pride of place. It looked like someone had chain-sawed down an ancient oak, split it in the middle, and hand-sanded off the rough edges. It was covered in a pristine white tablecloth

Lucie had been terrified to drop food on. Around it were six chairs, one for each of them plus one seat for four cats – one black, one black-and-white, and two a mottled grey-and-ginger colouring – who were ridiculously well behaved and ate in turns from a platter Ariana had put in front of them. Their view was green trees cascading over the side of the drop and ending at the blue of the sea.

'I think my stomach is doing my lungs out of room,' Gavin said.

'You are too full for dessert?' Miltos asked, looking like he might be angry if the answer was yes.

'I… no,' Gavin said quickly. 'I mean, no one is ever too full for dessert, right, Luce?'

Why was she nodding her head when there was no way she was going to be able to fit another thing in her stomach? She was praying it was only ice cream because everyone knew ice cream took up no room at all.

Mary and Ariana got to their feet and disappeared inside the house again. Neither of them spoke any English, but Miltos had played the role of translator. It had made Lucie feel a little bit lacking when it came to languages. Perhaps, with Meg's help over the phone, she could at least learn a little of the local lingo while she was here.

'You like the *sofrito*, *ne?*'

'Miltos, it was amazing,' Gavin said. 'Please tell your grandmother and your great-aunt that when they come back.'

'Ariana has made *kataifi*,' Miltos informed them, sipping from his water glass.

Was that the Greek word for ice cream? If not then Lucie's stomach was in real trouble…

'What is that?' Gavin asked, cupping his hands around his wine glass.

'Almond and walnut pastry in syrup,' Miltos said, chuckling. 'It looks like the hair of Donald Trump.'

Lucie's stomach braced itself at the word 'pastry'. There was just no way... Perhaps she could sneak some over to the cats.

The sisters arrived back outside, holding an edge each of the most enormous silver tray Lucie had ever seen. On it were piles and piles of rolled up oblongs that looked like Shredded Wheat, all swimming in syrup. There had to be a hundred of them and Lucie wondered who else was going to be joining them for pudding...

'Wow!' Gavin exclaimed, picking up the copper wine jug and refilling his glass. 'Fantastic!'

'*Fandastika*,' Miltos translated, jumping to help his grandmother and great-aunt get the platter over to the table.

Once it was in front of them and Lucie could smell the sweet scent of the syrup, her stomach reacted in quite a different way. Perhaps a few teeny little bites might be possible...

Miltos picked up large wooden salad servers and began plating up for them. How many was he putting out? Five? Six?

'These look so delicate,' Gavin said, nodding and trying to engage with the two ladies. 'Beautiful.'

Mary said something in Greek and Miltos laughed out loud. 'My grandmother says you are very handsome and she wishes she were twenty years younger.'

'Only twenty?' Gavin whispered to Lucie. 'How old does

she think I am? Maybe my eyebrows being gone has aged me!'

Ariana asked a question then as Lucie accepted a plate from Miltos. A serving was put down in front of the cats.

'Ariana wants to know when you two are going to get married.'

The *kataifi* Gavin had just put into his mouth came shooting out and Lucie watched her friend deftly hide the mouth missile under a serviette.

'We're just friends,' Lucie said with a smile.

'Oh, Loosely,' Miltos said softly. 'That is the way it always begins.'

The sisters were giggling to each other and whispering now. The cats even seemed to be paying attention.

'My aunt longs to make a wedding dress,' Miltos said, translating the excited babble. 'In our villages there are not many weddings any longer.'

'Oh,' Lucie said, not really knowing how to reply. 'Well, as I said, Gavin and I are just friends. We work together.'

'What do you do?' Miltos asked. He spoke in Greek to Mary and Ariana, presumably translating.

'We're nurses,' Lucie said.

'You are a nurse, Loosely?' Miltos asked.

'Yes. And Gavin's a nurse too.'

Gavin was saying nothing but was now picking up the roll of *kataifi* that had previously been in his mouth and jamming it back in there again.

'You mean Gaveen is a doctor?'

'No,' Lucie said. 'A nurse.'

'Nurses are women.'

'Not anymore,' Lucie countered.

'Well,' Miltos said. 'We will tell my grandmother and my aunt he is a doctor, because they will not understand.'

He gave this message over in Greek and Mary and Ariana clapped their hands together and chattered away excitedly.

'What are they saying?' Lucie asked.

'They are saying that Gaveen must meet the doctor in Sortilas. He has come back from Thessaloniki. The rumour is he will be starting a practice in the village any day now. Even more to celebrate at our new Day of the Not Dead festival.'

'Well,' Gavin began, bits of pastry all over his teeth. 'That doesn't sound creepy at all.'

'What is creepy?' Miltos asked, slamming his palms onto the table and looking a little cross. 'You think it is wrong to celebrate our health and well-being?'

'No,' Lucie said quickly. 'Of course not. Gavin didn't mean that. And I think if ever there was a reason to celebrate, then health and well-being is completely the best thing to have a festival for.' But she hadn't noticed any posters advertising it. Perhaps they were all in Greek and her mind hadn't acknowledged them.

'And wine,' Miltos added, calming slightly. 'And olives. And saints. And, of course, sardines.'

'You have a lot of festivals,' Gavin said. 'I mean, of course, why wouldn't you, when there's so much to celebrate?'

'What can I say?' Miltos replied with a shrug. 'We are Greece.'

Mary said something to Miltos, but her eyes were fixed on Lucie.

'My grandmother says she would like to make you

a wedding dress,' Miltos stated. 'She is going to get her measuring equipment.'

With that said, Mary was up from the table and disappearing into the house with all the enthusiasm of a mother to the bride. Except there was no bride here. And there wasn't likely to be one, seeing as Lucie didn't have a significant other. She hadn't actually ever had anyone significant enough to call a significant other. She'd only taken one guy to meet Meg – Gabriel. And Meg had given him quite the inquisition over a stilted meal of bolognese, which Meg had added anchovies to, even though Lucie had forewarned her that Gabriel wasn't a fish fan. Asking someone if they had a ten-year plan and their opinion on over-the-counter medication was too much for a fourth date and Lucie had told Meg exactly that when Gabriel decided he wasn't ready for a fifth date commitment. It was one of those times when Meg's care had turned claustrophobic. For the most part Lucie let those situations slide, but on some occasions she tried to explain to Meg that it wasn't fair for her to attempt to control everything, despite the good intentions behind it. But Meg never reacted very well to criticism and after a week or so of radio silence, it was usually Lucie who had to settle things between them with a box of cakes from the baker's.

Lucie shook her head to try to clear her thoughts, taking a swig of her drink. This wine was very nice but was obviously even more potent when you'd only just got to Greece and were a little jaded from the travelling. And she had come here to forget! Ha!

'Honestly,' she breathed. 'I really think your grandmother would be wasting her time making a wedding dress for me.

It might be twenty years before I get to wear it.' *If at all*, her brain said. Marriage hadn't worked for Meg. Her mum had never got old enough to be asked. Why would it work for her? And wasn't it an outdated concept anyway? People changed and grew and, in her experience, they moved apart from each other's original remit. The Other Sharon Osbourne was on her third husband...

'You think my grandmother has time to waste?' Miltos said, scowling. 'She is one-hundred-and-one. She wastes nothing. She does not know how many more mornings she will wake up.'

Lucie swallowed. She didn't want to be rude to their hosts but... being measured for a wedding dress. On her first night in Corfu...

Mary was back now, a huge circle of rope around her shoulder like she might be about to attach it to a boat and haul it into shore. This was the strangest dinner Lucie had ever attended. And was she really going to play mannequin and have her sizes taken to fill the wishes of a one-hundred-and-one-year-old woman she barely knew?

'Come on, Luce,' Gavin said, encouraging her out of her chair, a bit handsy after all the Greek wine. He lowered his voice a little then. 'Before we have to tell them that I actually like boys.' He sighed. 'If Miltos couldn't understand I was a nurse, he's not going to be woke enough to understand I prefer an aubergine.'

Mary was beckoning Lucie forward, Ariana was also on her feet now too, the rope being unravelled much to the delight of the cats. Lucie sighed. What harm would it do to be measured? It would make these two sisters happy and they had just provided them with the most exquisite meal in a gorgeous setting. She splayed out her arms and got ready.

'Lovely jubbly!' Miltos said, clapping his hands together. Then he turned to Gavin and his forehead creased into seriousness. 'Now, Gaveen, tell me, what do you do with your eyebrows?'

Fifteen

Andino Butcher's, Sortilas

Michalis held the machete in his hand and looked at the large cut of meat on the chopping block in front of him. It was five a.m. and he hadn't been able to stay asleep. It was hot. His family home had no air conditioning and there were only a few windows of the house fitted with mosquito nets. Still, no modernisations had been made in all the time he had been alive. Again, he did not know if this was because his father was lazy, tired or still just wanting to keep everything exactly as it had been before his mother had died. He'd also had another nightmare. He'd been in a hospital cubicle, the curtains drawn, the body of a patient in the bed beside him. But when he had gone to leave, the curtains would not open no matter what he did. He had woken up sweating, scared, pins and needles in his fingers like he had been clawing in reality.

Suddenly, he jumped. Had that been a noise outside? He held his breath, his heart pumping hard, the sound echoing through his ears. He looked to the door of the shop and out into the darkness. Was someone there? Creeping out from behind the counter, the knife still in his hand, trainers moving silently across the stone floor, he moved to the door, eyes staring into the blackness, searching the shadowy village square for sign of movement. He was holding his breath now, trying to stop adrenaline from flooding his body. And then there was a yowl that momentarily had him panicked, until he saw two cats springing out from behind the bins. Relief was instantaneous and he held onto that feeling until his heart got in line too. Returning to his position behind the counter, he drew up the knife still in his hand and slammed it down onto the meat with force. The slab of meat cleaved in two and the blade stuck into the wood. He wiggled the blade out. It was super-sharp. You wouldn't want to get your hand caught beneath it. Particularly if one of your specialties was delicate surgery...

'What are you doing?!'

Heart pulsing again, Michalis almost dropped the knife at the sound of his sister's hissing and the machete fell onto the chopping block, missing his left hand by millimetres.

'Nyx!' he exclaimed, turning to face her. 'How many times do I have to tell you not to sneak up on people?'

'You told me around twice... when I was ten.' She scowled, her blonde hair wild and untamed, shorts and a vest covering her slender frame. 'You told me that more often than telling me if I did not eat vegetables I would not grow... and here I am.'

She had always looked tiny to him, always his little sister. But he knew how strong she was on the inside. How strong she had to be growing up without a mother...

'And, again, what are you doing?' Nyx wanted to know. 'You are not a butcher.'

'Ah,' Michalis said. 'I am not a butcher every day like you, but I am the son of a butcher and I have been taught the art from a young age, just like you.'

'So,' Nyx said, still scowling and seeming to widen her body and edge him out from behind what was usually her spot in charge of the establishment. 'You think you will come here and start up again? Just like that?'

'No, well... OK, I could not sleep,' Michalis admitted.

'So you thought you would take over my job?'

'No,' Michalis said. It was really more a case of putting himself in his father's shoes, trying to reconnect with Dimitri's everyday life and figure out exactly what was going on with him. All the talk about the village dying and the need for grandchildren had to stem from somewhere. And Michalis really hoped that it wasn't Dimitri's health.

'Good,' Nyx replied. 'Because you are doing everything wrong.' She went towards the sink and began vigorously scrubbing at her hands. 'You did wash your hands, I hope? Because being a butcher is exactly like preparing for surgery.'

'I scrubbed up to my elbows,' Michalis confirmed.

'Right,' Nyx said, coming back over to the block. 'So now you have literally butchered this calf, what are you going to do with it?'

'I...' Michalis hadn't thought that far ahead. His dissection of an animal was rusty. He had only thought about trying to get into his father's head, not into the internal cavities of the baby cow. Perhaps it had been both selfish and stupid.

'Chuck,' Nyx said, taking hold of the animal's shoulder. 'For burgers, flat-iron steaks, ribs, medallions and meat for stews.' She thumped a fist onto the breast of the animal. 'This?'

'Brisket,' Michalis answered.

'This?' Nyx said, poking fingers into the calf.

'Ribs.'

'This?'

'Loin.'

'Which one?'

'The sirloin.'

Nyx grinned. 'You *do* remember!'

The door to the butcher's shop suddenly opened and Nyx grabbed the machete before he could, raising it like she might throw it toward the person coming in.

The bell tinkled and Michalis took hold of Nyx's weapon-wielding arm and drew it back. The figure creeping in was…

'Papa!' Nyx shouted with an annoyed sigh. 'What are you doing?!'

Dimitri jumped. The shock on his face said that he expected to be alone when he opened the door. Michalis watched Dimitri put a hand to his chest and take a deep breath. He noted that his dad was dressed in the same clothes he was wearing last night…

'What are *you* doing?' Dimitri bit back. 'It is not even six a.m.' He sniffed, prowling forward. 'And why is there a calf out here with its middle savaged?' He stared at the animal from the customers' side of the counter and then raised his eyes to the pair of them like he couldn't work out which of them was to blame.

'Do not look at me!' Nyx exclaimed in horror. 'As if I would carve the calf in two like that! This is all on your son, the doctor.'

Dimitri stared directly at Michalis then and Michalis was transported back to being five years old and getting caught with a spoon in the syrup destined to trickle over *loukoumades* (doughnut balls).

'I was... paying some interest in the family business. Seeing if I might remember what to do.'

Dimitri snorted. 'And it is clear that you do not.' He stepped away from the counter, heading around it and towards the back of the shop that led to the stairs to their apartment.

'Wait, Papa,' Nyx said, budging past Michalis at speed. 'We could show Micha how to do this correctly. Together.'

Dimitri waved a hand. 'I taught you everything I know. You can show him if he is really interested.'

'Papa, why are you up so early?' Nyx asked, folding her arms across her chest. 'Are you unable to sleep?'

'Why are you so concerned with what I am doing?'

'Because we care about you,' Michalis jumped in. 'You are behaving a little out of character.'

'And what would you know of my character?' Dimitri snapped a reply, turning in the doorway and facing them again, Nyx a barrier between them. 'You have all the time been in Thessaloniki.'

Michalis shook his head. There was definitely something going on with his father and he wasn't going to let this go on any longer. 'I have decided. I *will* start up a small surgery in the village. I will open for a few hours on certain days, for the time I am in Sortilas.'

'Really?' Dimitri asked, tutting. 'Did I not say that you were too good for this village?'

'I think the village needs someone looking after their

health again,' Michalis said matter-of-factly. 'I think, the villagers have forgotten everything I told them back before Coronavirus got out of control.'

'Cigarettes are back,' Nyx admitted with a nod. 'Although Mrs Kanaris never really gave up. She would puff away when your back was turned.'

'Where is your premises?' Dimitri asked. 'And your things? Do you even have a stethoscope?'

'I will speak to Melina today,' Michalis said with determination. 'If she has made my face into Superman on posters then she owes me. And, Papa, I would like you to be one of my first patients.'

'Me?' Dimitri asked, body language giving off his desperation to get out of this conversation.

'You have started eating fish,' Nyx stated as if that explained everything.

'Well, *you* keep colouring your hair,' Dimitri countered. 'Are we to attend psychiatry appointments together?'

'What is wrong with my hair?' Nyx gasped. 'Is it the fact I have some?'

'You are not too old for the wooden spoon!'

'You forget I have the machetes now!'

'Stop!' Michalis ordered. 'Stop. Both of you.'

He watched his father and his sister both move their lips into identical firm lines, eyes fixed on each other, tempers simmering.

'Is this how it has been all of the time while I have been away?' Michalis asked.

Neither Nyx nor Dimitri said a word.

'Perhaps I *should* make appointments for you both,' Michalis suggested firmly.

'There is nothing wrong with me!' Nyx and Dimitri said in perfect unison.

'I think the doctor in the family will be the judge of that,' Michalis stated. He let that statement settle for a beat before continuing. 'I will let you know when my stethoscope is ready.'

'Pfft!' Dimitri exhaled before marching off towards the stairs.

Nyx glared at Michalis as she stalked back behind the counter and grabbed a sharp blade, pointing it at him. 'Do not even think about examining me. Or I will separate you a lot worse than you have separated this calf!'

Michalis shook his head. His family and other – dead – animals...

Sixteen

Villa Psomi, Sortilas

Lucie threw open the shutters in her bedroom. There were three sets. Two on the main wall opposite the bed and another set to the left, all with ludicrous views of the sea. The sun was already up, but there was slightly fresher air coming into the room now and the scent of salt water, heat and olive groves. How lucky was she right now? She leaned against the windowsill, looking out and breathing in, making a gentle stretching suggestion to her spine. And relax...

'Lucie!'

She shivered. It wasn't a beckoning that might accompany an invitation to swim or a call that breakfast was ready. This was a warning cry coming from downstairs, from Gavin's oven bedroom.

Not wasting any time shouting back, she pulled a pair of denim cut-offs over her legs and padded over the aged floorboards towards the stairs that led the way down to the kitchen and then on to Gavin's room.

'Don't make any sudden moves!' Gavin announced once she got there.

Her best friend was underneath the sheet, its length pulled up to his chin, a terrified expression on his face. If this was no more than another insect, she was going to be cross her attempt at channelling mindfulness had been disturbed.

'What's the matter?' Lucie asked him.

'There!' Gavin said, pointing to the bottom of the double bed.

'Where?'

'It's camouflaged,' Gavin whispered. 'It's brown and… oriental… *exactly* like this cover sheet.'

Lucie's first thought was Gavin had drunk *way* too much of the wine in Vouni while she was being measured for a wedding that was never going to happen and that he was hallucinating. But then, on closer inspection, she saw it…

'Aww, it's a cute tortoise!' Lucie stepped towards the bottom end of Gavin's bed and had a better look at the animal. It was cute. Its turd-like head stretching out from its shell as it debated where to put feet down next.

'I know it's a tortoise! I'm not that stupid! But, you know, pet management wasn't in any of the details I got from the travel company and… where's its hutch?'

'Well,' Lucie said, putting a finger out towards the animal and watching it seem to debate how to react. 'We haven't fully explored the whole house yet, have we?' And that was the strangest thing to say when somehow she had found the time to have her wrists, waist and ankles measured. Who knew what this wedding outfit was going to resemble…

There was a knock on the door and Gavin yelped, drawing his legs up to his chest under the sheet and sending the tortoise closer to him like it was now on a linen conveyer belt.

'You haven't booked another fruit van taxi, have you?' Lucie asked him. If she ever saw another *nektarini* it would be too soon.

'Not that I remember,' Gavin stated. 'But things did get a bit hazy between all those dessert rolls and you standing on a chair like Meryl Streep.'

Another louder knock ensued and Lucie padded to the doorway of the oven bedroom.

'Wait! Luce! Don't leave me with the tortoise!'

Crossing the pink-and-cream striped marble floor of the kitchen, Lucie pulled open the heavy wood door and in flooded sunshine and heat, followed by a woman in a pinstriped skirt suit who looked a little bit familiar.

'*Kalimera*,' the woman said, striding into the space without invitation.

'Er, hello,' Lucie replied. *Now* she recognised her. It was the woman from their welcome gathering in the square yesterday. The one trying to get everybody to drink goat 'nectar' and holding a big stick.

'The studio building is no longer available,' she stated, pointing across the courtyard at the lovely little annexe opposite. That was one corner of the property Lucie had yet to explore. But it gave off all the artist/writer studio vibes with sea views from its window and a cute terrace outside of it.

'What?' Lucie asked. 'I don't understand.'

'You are two, *ne*?' the woman continued. 'No more.'

'Yes, it's only me and Gavin but…'

'Good,' the woman said. 'Then you do not need.' She

turned like she was about to leave again. That couldn't be how things worked in Greece. Surely you didn't walk into someone's holiday home, tell them something they weren't going to like and then leave again without discussion. And where was her authority? Did she *own* this house? She didn't really look like a representative of a travel company...

'Wait,' Lucie said. 'I mean... I really don't think you can do that.'

The woman turned around again, eyeing Lucie like she might have insulted the entire Greek nation by questioning her authority. 'I *can* do that.'

'But,' Lucie began. 'We've... paid and...' She stopped talking as the woman's eyes turned all Vanya from *The Umbrella Academy*. Was she about to be bewitched?

'*Signomi*. I have not formally introduced myself,' the woman said, taking steps back into the kitchen space. 'I... am the president of Sortilas and I need to take ownership of this studio for the health and safety of the village.' She stuck her hand out then. 'Melina Hatzi.'

'Lucie Burrows,' she replied, taking the woman's hand and giving it a firm shake.

No sooner had their palms disconnected, Melina was unzipping and dipping her fingers into the leather bumbag around her middle and, producing antibacterial gel, she expertly squirted, rubbed and massaged in one quick motion.

'I need a small space for the doctor,' Melina informed matter-of-factly. 'I had hoped that there would be some room at the back of the mini-market, but this is now filled with food for apocalypse purposes.'

'Apocalypse purposes?' Lucie queried. Surely after the

shitshow of 2020 the world wasn't due any more disasters.

Melina shook her head. 'It is Ajax's way. One year it is time travel. The next it is aliens. This year, the end of the world.' She tutted. 'The only good thing about that is if he thinks the world will end he cannot plan a theme for next year.'

Now Lucie was really thinking all the people in this village were mad.

'The goat shed is not hygienic enough, so we need the studio,' Melina stated.

'Well… I… it isn't really up to me.' She swallowed, wishing that Gavin would get over his ridiculous panic about a tortoise and come and help her out. 'It's up to…'

'Me,' Melina stated firmly. 'I have a key already. The doctor will move in later.'

'Move in?!' Lucie shrieked as Melina stepped back out of the house and onto the cobbled courtyard. No amount of beautiful dappled sunshine was going to boost her mood now.

'*Yassas!*' Melina called, waving a hand as she walked away.

'Lucie!' Gavin screamed. 'The tortoise is growling at me!'

She needed Gavin to start manning up, and quickly! Corfu had been *his* destination of choice. If he was this shit-scared of creatures, perhaps he would have been better looking at a caravan break in the Isle of Sheppey instead of an isle belonging to Greece.

'Gavin! Get out of bed and get out here! Someone's moving into the studio unless you help me stop them!' She rushed out of the front door in a bid to halt this woman who seemed to be in charge of just about everything. 'Excuse me! Excuse me! Wait a second.' The woman was already disappearing into the distance…

'Take it from me! Take it!'

Suddenly Gavin was next to her, the bed cover tied around him like a sarong, exactly like that morning after the night before the eyebrow/hair incident. He had the tortoise held precariously between thumb and forefinger like it might be soiled hospital sheets or something odd from The Other Sharon Osbourne's lunchbox…

Lucie took the tortoise out of Gavin's grasp and put it down under the shade of the herb garden. There was definitely rosemary and thyme in there, and she made a note to remember to use the fresh, fragrant leaves in anything they cooked later.

'You can't put it down here if it's a pet!' Gavin screeched, reluctantly picking the animal back up and folding the front of his sarong to create a hammock of material for it to sit in.

'That strange woman from the square,' Lucie began. 'The one with the welcome wee-wee. She's apparently the president of the village and a doctor is coming to commandeer the studio. *This* studio.' She pointed at the adorable little building she had imagined having one or two nights sleeping in herself…

'A *doctor*,' Gavin breathed. 'Well, if he looks anything like Dr Kashuda from our hospital I'll be quite happy to make him welcome.'

'Gavin,' Lucie said. 'We don't know it's a man and it doesn't matter what they look like. They're coming here. To *our* studio. To the place where you said we had all the space!'

'But we don't *need* all the space, do we?'

Lucie sighed. No, perhaps they didn't need all the space, but having been handed a gorgeous ancient house with walls of thick rock and olive trees meandering down to the water, she didn't really want it snatched away again. It felt exciting to be the lady of this Greek manor for a little while. It was less exciting when someone else seemed to be calling the shots over her holiday accommodation.

'I'm going for a walk,' Lucie suddenly announced. She needed to breathe. To find out about a hire car. To get something, *anything* for breakfast.

'OK,' Gavin said, stepping back into the house, hammock sarong swaying in the breeze. 'I'll shut the door so the grasshoppers don't get in.'

Seventeen

Andino Butcher's, Sortilas

Nyx had an appointment in Acharavi, his father was still in bed, so Michalis was in charge of the butcher's. He wasn't sure how he felt about managing something he had clearly forgotten almost everything about, if his dismantling of the calf was anything to go by. He also suspected that Nyx's appointment was simply sitting in Ilo Ilo for coffee…

The bell over the door of the shop tinkled and a woman stepped inside. Slightly wavy dark hair cropped short, wearing denim cut-offs and a light pink T-shirt. He recognised her immediately as the woman whose partner had drunk the goat urine yesterday.

'*Kalimera*,' Michalis greeted, hoping she didn't want anything that wouldn't be acceptable rustically carved.

'Oh, hello,' she answered. 'I… you… were at the square yesterday. You sacrificed your coffee for Gavin, so he wasn't sick.'

Michalis nodded. 'I did. And once again, I apologise

for the village craziness. What must you think of us?'

'I think,' she began, stepping a little closer to the counter and surveying the meat goods on display. 'That I have no idea what half of these things in here are.' She pointed at the rolls of *kokoretsi*.

'You most likely do not *want* to know what that is,' he answered.

'Well now I'm intrigued,' she said, lifting her eyes to his. 'I'm looking for something to cook tonight.'

'This,' Michalis began, 'is the intestines of a lamb.'

'Ugh! God, no. No, I don't want that.'

Michalis laughed at her shock. 'I told you we were a little bit crazy here.'

'Trust me, after you've gone to dinner in a fruit van, been literally force-fed something called *sofrito* and had your measurements taken for a wedding dress, you know all about crazy.'

Michalis nodded. 'It sounds to me like you have been to Vouni and met with Mary and Ariana.'

'Oh my God,' the woman exclaimed. 'How did you know that?'

Michalis laughed again, enjoying her surprise a little. 'Everyone knows everyone around here. Plus, Mary is a little obsessed with weddings. My sister has three wedding dresses made by Mary. She was measured for her first one when she was thirteen.'

'Is she married now?'

'No,' Michalis replied with a smile. 'But she is well prepared.'

'I don't need a wedding dress,' the woman stated. 'But it seemed rude to decline and—'

'Ah, there would be no saying no, I understand,' Michalis admitted. 'You would have to have eaten all the *kataifi* before they let you leave.'

She laughed. 'You really do understand. And, believe me, if I had eaten that, I would never have fitted into *any* dress ever again.'

He couldn't stop his eyes from dropping to appraise her body then. She was petite but looked strong. Not someone who could easily be blown over in a storm, his mother might have said. There was energy about her, a liveliness and perhaps a little mystery. But, she was here with her partner and he was definitely not looking for romance. He was still recovering from the last one, a relationship that had ended so badly – and then turned even more tragic. He was still hoping his mobile didn't ring. Still a little more cautious when night fell. He took a breath.

'Do you have chicken *souvlaki*?' she asked him.

'*Ne,*' he replied with a nod. 'Would you like just the meat? Or would you like me to prepare it with pepper and onion?'

'Oh, well, I don't know. What would you recommend? I'm a bit of a Greek cuisine novice, but my aunt said that chicken *souvlaki* was one of her favourites so...'

'Your aunt is here with you?' Michalis asked, taking skewers of meat from the display and setting them on the board.

'No,' she answered. 'No, she came to this island many years ago and she's a little excited that I'm here now. Excited and pretty much texting me every second minute to make sure I wear a hat.' She put a hand to her short hair.

'Please,' Michalis said, raising his eyes out of his

arrangement of the chicken. 'Do not tell your aunt that the village president is trying to get tourists to drink the secretions of local animals.'

'Ah, well,' she began. 'I can't make any promises about that. But, if you make me the *souvlakis* with the onion and peppers and they're really as delicious as my aunt says they are then I promise to talk more about the chicken than the goat.'

'*Souvlakia*,' Michalis said.

'What?'

'More than one *souvlaki*, we say *souvlakia*.'

'Oh, OK. Well, can I have four *souvlakia*, please? Gavin's a pig when it comes to all foods. How do you say "four" in Greek?'

'*Tesera*,' Michalis told her. He washed his hands before changing from handling meat to salad. '*Pos sas lene?*'

'Oh… was that "will four be enough"?'

Michalis smiled then, deftly cutting thick chunks of yellow and green pepper then moving on to red onion. 'No, I asked you what is your name.'

She seemed to turn a little bashful then, her gaze falling to his hands as they moved salad onto skewers, alternating with fat pieces of chicken breast.

'Lucie,' she answered.

'I am Michalis,' he replied.

'It's nice to meet you.'

'*Ki ego*. You too.'

The bell above the door chimed again and Michalis looked up. It was the customer who had bought the rabbit for *stifado* just the other day.

'*Kalimera*,' the man greeted quietly, standing beside

Lucie at the counter and seeming slightly ill at ease.

Michalis spoke in Greek. 'Can I help you?'

'The woman is not here?' the man whispered.

'The woman?'

'Has her hair in two doughnuts and shouts a lot.'

'Ah, my sister,' Michalis said, nodding. 'No, she is not here right now. Do you need me to give her a message?'

The man shook his head vigorously then. 'No. Not at all. She terrifies me.'

'O-K.'

'I would like some steak mince.'

'No problem. I will just finish the *souvlakia* for this customer.'

The skewers of meat, peppers and onion were almost done and Michalis felt disappointed for the end of the interaction. Stupidly so. He was not in the right headspace for making any kind of new connection. He looked up at Lucie. 'You are staying here long?'

'A few weeks,' Lucie replied.

Michalis watched her eyes going to a new large poster he hadn't even noticed was stuck to the inside of the shop window. Oh God! What was that doing there? Nyx must have put it up in between them talking about the oddness of their father, him having a shower and her disappearing to Acharavi. He wanted to leapfrog the counter and tear it down before Lucie could see. But then the already traumatised customer might be terrified of *him* as well as Nyx.

'Is that you?' Lucie remarked, stepping towards the window and surveying the billboard. *Too late.*

He looked like a gladiator with the bulk of Ironman.

Who *had* drawn this cartoonish figure with bulging veins and rippling biceps? It was true he liked to keep himself in shape, but this depiction had pitched him at professional bodybuilder...

'It's you, isn't it?' Lucie said, standing right in front of the poster now. It was obviously double sided. His blown-up body visible from inside the shop as well as from the street.

'I did not pose for this,' Michalis told her. He felt himself blush. What else could he say? Damn Melina and her new festival...

'The Day of the Not Dead,' Lucie read. 'Miltos told me about this last night.'

The man in the shop shook his head then spoke in English. 'Always about health here now.'

'It sounds like fun,' Lucie said. 'Dancing and music.'

'Overpriced *loukoumades* and gypsies selling roses,' the man informed.

'Your *souvlakia* is ready,' Michalis said, carefully wrapping the portions in paper and fastening it all together with a rubber band.

'Thank you,' Lucie said. 'How much is it?' She came back to the counter and drew out a purse from her bag.

'Half price,' Michalis found himself saying. 'If you come back and tell me what you thought of them. Three euro.'

'Well, thank you. That sounds very fair. I will.' She placed the money on the countertop and picked up the parcel.

'*Yassas*,' Michalis said as she made her way to the door again. 'Goodbye.'

'*Yassas*,' Lucie answered.

The bell rang as she departed and the customer gave a cough. 'Do I get my mince for half the price if I come back and tell you what I thought of it?'

Eighteen

Woody's, Acharavi

Despite having successfully purchased that evening's meal of *souvlakia*, when Lucie got back to the house Gavin was craving more than the simple bread and ham she had picked up for breakfast from Ajax's apocalypse-ready mini-market. Gavin *had* dressed though. Then he had squealed at two large yellow-and-black butterflies and ran around the courtyard as if they were both hunting him down as prey. After that he had demanded sausage and bacon and was on his mobile to Miltos for a lift to one of the nearby towns that catered for hungry Brits in need of something that tasted like home. Despite Lucie's protests about being knee-deep in apricots again, here they now were, courtesy of another ride in the fruit van, Gavin devouring the big breakfast that did look spectacular. She had ordered what she thought would be the healthy option – a continental – but it was as huge as Gavin's meal and came with cake… She had thought of sending a photo to Meg, but then decided that cake for breakfast might have tipped her aunt into a message rant about cholesterol.

'It's time to really unwind now,' Gavin mused through a mouthful of sausage.

'It's time we got our own transport,' Lucie told him. She looked out over the white stone beach little more than a few paces away and watched the froth of the waves spraying foam all over the shoreline. The sound was really quite soothing.

'I know,' Gavin agreed, slurping at his coffee. 'I spoke to Miltos while you were moaning on about cherries in your lap.'

Of course Gavin had leapt into the *front* of the fruit van for their drive down the mountain while she had been consigned to the produce section...

'What did you say?' Lucie asked, dipping her spoon into her Greek yoghurt and fresh fruit.

'I asked him if he knew where we could hire some transport at a good price.'

Lucie shook her head. 'Oh God.'

'What?'

'I hope you made it clear that transport didn't mean "fruit van" or "donkey".'

'He's going to pop in later this afternoon – after his siesta – and let us know the options.'

'Or we could just visit one of those little places with actual real cars outside called "rental companies" and get something that hasn't been organised by someone whose relatives want to dress me up like a bridal collection.'

'What's the matter, Luce?' Gavin asked, putting down his knife and fork. 'You seem tense.'

She wasn't tense. Was she? She was enjoying being here. It was lovely. But something inside was telling her she needed it to be perfect. She wanted to gather up *all* the Greece in the short time they had, experience the whole shebang and not miss a thing. Somehow this felt like a monumental journey rather than a cheap few weeks' break, and she didn't exactly know why that was the case. Perhaps it was the fact there had been no real respite from the horrors at the hospital for a year, or maybe it was more deep-rooted than that. Maybe it was about uncovering another part of herself she hadn't been fully introduced to yet…

'Well,' she started. 'We also have the matter of someone moving into our studio. What are you going to do about that?'

'The doctor,' Gavin breathed. He'd said 'doctor' like he'd meant 'potential sex slave'.

'It's our place, Gavin. For *our* holiday. I don't know if I'm very happy about bumping into someone I don't know. I mean, the studio doesn't have a separate toilet. They'll need the toilet. In our house.'

'Well,' Gavin began. 'Shall we reserve judgement for a bit?'

'What do you mean? We need to stop them coming. If they come then the decision is made. But if we want to not have them there then we need to say something or do something.'

'Well… shall we see if it's a man and, if it is, see what he looks like first?'

Lucie's mouth dropped open. 'Gavin!'

'What?'

'You can't say that!'

'Why not?' He sighed. 'I mean, Simon's not taken the bait yet, so I need to be getting on top of someone else. And I do love a doctor.'

And she still hadn't had the courage to tell Gavin that the only way he would ever be getting on top of Simon would be if he was intubating him. 'You work at a hospital,' Lucie reminded him. 'There are wards full of doctors you could pick from.'

'So, I'm not allowed a *Greek* doctor?'

'No... well... I...'

'Put the fruit down and have a sausage,' Gavin said, winking as he speared one on his fork and offered it over to her. 'That's my prescription. And my diagnosis is that the health is making you grumpy.'

Lucie shook her head and folded her arms across her chest. She didn't want to be grumpy. She wanted to strip off her vest and shorts and run into that rumbling sea, letting the waves crash all over her skin and cover her in salt... And why couldn't she? What was stopping her from doing just that? She had her bikini on. They were steps away from the beach. A quick dip and then back to finish breakfast. No regrets. No second-guessing. She stood up.

'What are you doing?' Gavin wanted to know.

'I'm going for a swim.' She wrenched her vest over her head and dropped it to her chair.

'Now?!'

'Yes now.'

'No one else is in the water right now.'

'So?' And he was wrong anyway. She had spotted a man in a full rubber diving outfit submerging himself only moments earlier. A small fluorescent flag marked the spot.

'Don't leave me on my own,' Gavin said like a four-year-old. 'There might be wasps and I'm enjoying this breakfast.'

'And I am your best friend,' Lucie said. 'Not your carer.'

'I promise if Miltos arrives with a donkey we can head to the very first hire car company.'

'I'm going swimming, Gavin. I won't be long.'

She took off her shorts, left them on the chair too and padded across the road to the shoreline of stones. The warmth in the air made the fine hairs on her arms react and she found the rest of her bubbling at the thought of getting into the water. Was this how a young Meg had felt in Corfu all those years ago? Was this maybe how her mum might have felt if she had lived to have the opportunity?

That cloaked feeling you got that people described as 'someone walking over your grave' crept over Lucie's bare shoulders and she felt herself shiver. She was thinking about her mum much more here in Greece. Why? Was it this change of pace, this time to think, that was unlocking feelings she'd buried? Or was it because now, away from the pandemonium of the hospital, she was slightly distanced from what she had witnessed, could now truly acknowledge loss with a new, shuddering perspective. She took a deep breath and focussed again on the beauty of the water and the hypnotic sound of the waves. Leaving all her thoughts behind she stepped into the sea and got ready to dive deep.

Nineteen

Villa Psomi, Sortilas

Michalis didn't feel entirely comfortable about this, but if it was what it took to get his father's health looked into then it would be worth it. He had forgotten how beautifully rustic this house was. Years ago, when his mother was alive, before Nyx was born, he had run around this courtyard with other children from the village. Wispy branches of olive trees in their hands, swishing and swiping away the mosquitos, pretending they were great warriors as they sprinted over crumbling bricks and tumbled into the garden loudly, letting the snakes know they were there. It was a place for solace now – no war cry of playing children – the only thing unchanged was the age-old olive trees and the panoramic sea view.

Melina wrenched open the heavy wooden door of the studio building opposite the main house, shunting and pulling with a combination of strength and desperate willpower. Wood splintered as the slightly warped bottom of the door met with the cobbles of the terrace, straining at the intrusion.

'Let me help you,' Michalis said, worried that the president was going to be his very first patient if she kept this exertion up.

'It is not used as much as it should be,' Melina said, wiping a hand over her perspiring forehead. 'When things are not used they rot. I try to tell this to the community when I talk about breeding.'

And from what Michalis had learned since he had been back on the island, Melina was not talking about livestock... 'Who owns this now?'

'The village,' Melina answered. 'Remember the American couple who walked all the time? Up the mountain. Down the mountain. Around the garden. To the beach. Always always walking.'

Michalis did remember them from his youth. They were kind and they were different and Michalis had been intrigued by their accents. 'They have sold the house?' he asked.

'They went back to America and... they died.'

'Both of them?' Michalis exclaimed.

'I cannot remember which one was first.' Melina shook her head. 'But the house was left to the village and the village has been renting this out for holidaymakers for the past few years.' She sniffed. 'While you were away fighting disease and devastation.'

His father hadn't told him anything about this either. Michalis was starting to wonder what else Dimitri had held back. It wasn't as if Michalis had completely abandoned the village. He had made visits when he could. To begin with, at university, Thessaloniki had been new and exciting. He had wanted to spend time with his friends, drinking in the atmosphere of the city, drinking in the beer and meeting like-minded others who had grown up in many different places. Then, once he was qualified, it had been all about making an impression. Being on call for whatever was needed, getting known as reliable and trustworthy as well as knowledgeable and skilled. That ongoing commitment had earned him the job he had wanted from the very beginning within just five years. He had done good works, was still doing everything he could. He shouldn't feel guilty about it. But somehow being back here and seeing his father and his sister existing like they always had, it felt a little like he had abandoned them.

'The profit,' Melina continued. 'It goes to village projects like... Andreas Kousaris's son Spiros's dream to build a lift that will transport villagers down the mountain from Sortilas to Acharavi via cable car.'

Michalis blinked, not entirely sure he had heard correctly. Everyone had cars these days. Why did they need a cable connection? And what an eyesore that would be!

'And, of course, the Day of the Not Dead festival,' Melina concluded. 'So, I am commandeering the studio for health purposes and there will be a wage for the doctor. Your surgery. *Ela!*'

Melina beckoned him into the space, leading the way, and Michalis followed, stepping over the tiny form of a light-coloured gecko making its escape over the threshold. The room wasn't exactly spacious, but it was enough. There was even a desk under one window and that incredible view of the sea. The floor was tiled and there was a small sink for handwashing and a bookshelf he could store supplies on. He'd brought a small amount of equipment with him from Thessaloniki, not knowing what he might need, not knowing when he was going to return. He needed to make a decision about his apartment there soon. His friend Chico, a fellow doctor, had always admired its view over the park when he'd stayed over. It could be an easy transition if the landlord was agreeable…

Michalis put his hand on the chair with wheels and it listed a little to the left. That would need some adjustment.

'Your first patient will be here at six,' Melina stated.

'What?' he asked, turning to face her again.

'If I have to hear another word about Athena's eye condition I will need a doctor for myself.'

Michalis shook his head. 'I have told her what to do for her eye. I gave her a solution over a week ago.'

'Well,' Melina began. 'She has one more chance to listen correctly this time. No follow-up appointments. I have a list that will keep you going for a few weeks.'

A list already? Maybe this wasn't such a good idea. He needed to assert his authority on this, and fast.

'I will set my own hours,' Michalis told her, turning the chair upside down and toying with the wheel.

'Five days a week.'

'Three,' Michalis countered. 'One day the morning. One the afternoon. One evening.'

Melina seemed to muse on this point, head gently swaying to the left and then the right until… 'OK. But what about emergencies?'

'No emergencies,' Michalis said quickly. 'That is what the healthcare establishments in Roda and Acharavi are for.' He sniffed. 'Besides, I know what Sortilas is like. The emergency would be the cat with only three legs has got stuck up the tree again.'

'But,' Melina began. 'If there was a *real* emergency...'

Michalis sighed. He was a doctor. It was his duty to preserve life. Help in any way he could. It therefore seemed being taken advantage of was also going to be forever in his remit.

'We will see how it goes,' Michalis finally agreed.

Melina slapped a hand on his shoulder, smiling. 'This is a very good thing you do for the village. A very good thing.'

He nodded, hope in his heart. But, in all honesty, he wasn't quite sure this *was* the right move to make. His confidence had taken the biggest battering on the mainland. General practice here might seem much slower-paced and less intense than the hospital, but what if he made a misdiagnosis and put someone in jeopardy? He swallowed. That was the very last thing he wanted to do.

'Now,' Melina said, clapping her hands together and turning a full three-sixty in the centre of the space. 'Where will be the best place to set up your skeleton?'

Michalis shook his head. 'I do not have a skeleton.'

'But,' Melina began, looking exasperated. 'Every doctor has a skeleton. What about a white coat? The village will be expecting a white coat...'

Twenty

'I've written a list,' Gavin announced.

It was late afternoon and after the swimming, the breakfast and a good explore of Acharavi – the nearest town to Sortilas with supermarkets, tourist shops and about a gazillion restaurants Lucie was now aching to try – they had returned to the house to make the most of the sunshine weather and the luxurious sun loungers around their pool area. And, up until this slightly rude awakening, Lucie had been enjoying the complete switching off. Her back pain was waning a little and the only sounds to interrupt the utter peace were the cicadas, the whisper of a breeze and a sporadic chainsaw echoing up the mountain. Everything she had been caught up in in England over the past year was far, far away. Work was completely out of reach. The Other Sharon Osbourne's constant invitations to virtual make-up parties were muted. This was her chance to press the reboot button, maybe even completely re-invent herself. She could be whoever she wanted to be. No one here, apart from Gavin, knew her past.

It was like a clean blank slate, ready for the chalking…

Lucie opened her eyes and looked at her friend. 'Is it your favourite drag queens?'

'No!' Gavin exclaimed. 'I did that up to Season 12 of *Drag Race* already. Mmm, Gigi Goode.'

Lucie shook her head, smiling. 'If it's a list of favourite fruits, I'd like to remove apricots if they made the cut.'

Gavin huffed a sigh and plumped down on the edge of Lucie's lounger. He was wearing very small neon pink trunks that scarily didn't look too far away from the shade of his thighs. She hoped he had put enough sun cream on. She silently cursed herself. Now she was sounding like Meg and, as solidly wholesome as her aunt was, Lucie wasn't up for becoming a carbon copy.

'I never knew you had such an aversion to fruit!' Gavin said, pen and paper in hand.

'Eating it, no. Riding around like I'm in a relationship with it, yes.'

'Well, it's not fruit. It's a suggested list of experiences we could try while we're here in Corfu. Number one,' Gavin began. 'A banana boat.'

'Gavin! You said it wasn't fruit!' She knew what it was really. It was a huge floaty shaped liked a banana, attached to the back of a speedboat. And that speedboat's whole purpose was to drive as fast as it could and try to fling you into oblivion… or further.

'Very funny. Number two. Wine tasting.'

'I thought we started that last night.'

'I mean properly. Not slugging them back to get that Pinot high.'

'You've never complained before,' Lucie reminded him.

In fact, knocking them back as quickly as he could was usually Gavin's pre-going-out warm-up routine. That and a short salsa to something by Lauv... 'And I'm not sure that wine we had last night was even a long-lost relation to anything Pinot.'

'Well, perhaps if we concentrate on enjoying and understanding the undertones and the top notes we might not end up shaving each other's body hair off.'

He had a point on that one. She was still trying to dredge up memories of that night and there was the vaguest recollection that Sharon had, at some point, been in her flat. 'What's number three?'

'Karaoke.'

'Oh, Gavin, really? We can do karaoke anywhere!'

'We couldn't last year! Singing was outlawed and I'm never happy to get to the end of a year not having publicly sung "Bohemian Rhapsody" at least twice.'

Lucie smiled, shaking her head. 'Number four?'

'Donkeys,' Gavin said. 'There's a sanctuary on Corfu.'

'And you do love a nice soft ass.'

'It has been said.'

Lucie went to form the words 'number five' when suddenly her gaze went across the pool and met the form of an old woman. She was dressed all in black, casually leaning back on a sun lounger like a demonic apparition. 'Gavin! Who... is that? And, please, tell me you can see her.'

'Jesus!' Gavin exclaimed, hand planting onto his chest. 'It's like something out of *The Woman in Black*. Literally.'

'Well, *who* is she?' Lucie asked. She felt the need to pull her swimming towel out from underneath her and cover her bikini top with it.

'I don't know,' Gavin answered. 'But I really hope it isn't the doctor.'

'Oh God!' Lucie exclaimed, looking up the stone steps that led the way down to the terrace and pool area. 'There are more of them outside the house. Gavin, what's going on?!'

Michalis was wearing a white coat. He couldn't remember the last time he had worn a white coat. Back in Thessaloniki it had been disposable PPE, not cotton. And this was too small, something his father had worn for butchery circa 1980. But he also knew Melina was right about the village looking for something they defined as old-fashioned authority. The outfit of a doctor. The stethoscope hanging around his neck. To them, the almost fancy dress was the mark of a professional, not the certificates and qualifications for the years of work he had put in to achieve the status. It said everything. But, he supposed, in some ways his own feelings were similar. Medicine to him had always been more about the people than the paper.

He breathed in the fragrance of herbs in the stone-wrapped beds next to the *klimataria* covered by grapevines, their fruit plump and ripened. And, just like that, the memories of his mother's home-cooking were demanding his attention. Steaming pots of Greek specialities, something new she had seen made by a chef on television, the freshest ingredients, the healthiest cuts of meat. She had always *always* done the right thing in her life. It had been a simple life, being a wife, a mother, running a home, but she had revelled in it. And where had it got her in the end? He put fingertips to rosemary, running the fronds over his skin until he knew the smell had impregnated. Putting a finger to his nose, he closed his eyes and inhaled. So soft, so light, but it had the strongest of reminders of what their family had lost. Its core. Its quiet yet strong and fearless queen bee. Even after all these years, they still hadn't quite worked out what they were without her.

Then, just like that, the peace was broken. Conversation. Chatter. As he walked on and rounded the corner, Michalis stopped still. There were people. A line queuing up on the courtyard of Villa Psomi. They were snaking around the stone building, some sitting on the low wall, others tucked into shady nooks. It was too many people to be the guests staying at the property. He swallowed. Melina had said a list but... were they *all* waiting for him? It was only half past five and he was expecting Nyx to bring their father here before six...

Then, as they seemed to notice his presence, the volume of their conversation rose.

'*Yatros!*'

'Michalis!'

'Dr Andino.'

What had he started? He felt like a startled pine marten not expecting traffic. He could feel his hands begin to shake and he grabbed one with the other, trying to stop his emotions from snowballing. *This was not like what had happened at the hospital. This was not going to be the same at all.* He took a deep breath... and then he turned his back on them all. Everything felt like it was suddenly shrinking in on him. Exactly like it had that very last day before he got on a plane.

'Hello? Are you the doctor?'

Michalis squeezed his eyes tight shut. Why couldn't he just take a break? He wasn't meant to be practising medicine at all. Why had he set this up? He clearly wasn't ready. He didn't want to think. He didn't want to feel. But most of all he wanted to forget...

'Hello? Can you hear me?'

He needed to focus. Retrain his brain to find something else. Anything else other than this overwhelming urge to run away or hide. *The rosemary*. Simpler times. Happy times. His mother's proud smile when he learned to ride a bike...

'Excuse me! I'm talking to you and... oh!'

Michalis forced himself to turn round then and he was greeted not by one of his would-be patients but by the woman from the butcher's this morning. Lucie. Wearing nothing but a towel from what he could see. And he couldn't seem to divert his eyes...

'Sorry,' she said. 'I... thought you were someone else.' She pulled her towel a little tighter around her body. 'I think all these people are waiting to see a doctor who's meant to be coming here. Do you know the doctor in the village? Are you waiting to see him too?'

'I... am the doctor,' Michalis said. He sounded awkward, unsure of himself. He definitely couldn't see patients like that. He thought about the buffed image of himself on those festival posters. He wasn't that man. He was as far from that superhero image as could be. He shook himself. 'Sorry.'

'*You're* the doctor?' Lucie asked, tipping her head to one side. Droplets of water were sliding down her cheek from her short crop of wet hair now. 'But... you're the butcher.'

He nodded. 'In Corfu, people wear many hats. In the village of Perithia, the postman is also the mayor.'

'I... don't know what to say to that.'

He felt himself slowly begin to recover. This *was* different. There would be warts and infected insect bites, not life-saving surgery or tiny underdeveloped babies. He *could* do this. He *had* to. To prove that his life could still be about helping those in need. That his course and purpose was true.

'And this is where you are staying,' Michalis remarked, indicating the old stone house. 'I am so sorry for my intrusion. If you are unhappy, I will do my best to arrange another place for my surgery as soon as possible.'

'Ah, let's not be too hasty there!'

It was Lucie's partner. The man who had rinsed away the goat urine with Michalis's coffee. Was it... Gary? Whatever he was called, the man was smiling at him, his eyes appraising the white coat like it was high fashion from a Paris runway. The man was wearing bright pink underwear. Very small underwear.

'I'm sure we can make this work,' the man stated. 'But the woman on the sun lounger has to go. She's started knitting and I'm worried it might be a jumper to cover me up.' The man moved a little closer to him. 'And I want an *all over* tan while I'm here in Corfu.' He waggled his forehead. He didn't seem to have eyebrows.

'Again,' Michalis began. 'I apologise. I intend only to be here for three days a week. One morning surgery, one afternoon and one evening. But if that is not OK for you I can rethink.'

Lucie was still looking at him like she thought he might

pull a side of beef out from under his white coat. He put his hands into his pockets.

'Well,' the man began. 'If you need any assistance, then Nurse Burrows or Nurse Gale are on hand right across the courtyard.' He grinned. 'Don't be shy.'

'You are nurses?' Michalis queried.

'That's right,' the man answered. 'I'm Gavin. And this is...'

'We met this morning,' Lucie jumped in. 'He's apparently also a butcher. Michalis.'

She had remembered his name.

'Well,' Gavin said. 'You must know *all* of the anatomy in that case.'

'I would not say that exactly,' Michalis replied.

'Well, don't let us hold you up,' Gavin said, passing him quite close and heading towards the front door. 'You have patients to see and we have dinner to prepare. Actually...' Gavin stopped walking and turned back to face him. 'Why don't you join us for a drink when you've finished? We have this mysterious bottle of alcohol on a bookshelf Lucie wouldn't let me try last night. But with you being a local and hopefully knowing it won't kill us, maybe she'll let me pop the top off under supervision.'

'I'm going for a shower,' Lucie said, slipping past them both.

Michalis watched her go. She might have remembered his name, but she seemed annoyed that he was here. He would need to tell Melina that this studio wouldn't do while guests were staying at the house. It wasn't fair.

'Stay for a drink,' Gavin said again. 'Reassure me it's not bottled goat piss again.'

'Perhaps,' Michalis answered. 'If this does not take all night.' He wouldn't stay. He had intruded enough already.

'Good!' Gavin said, clapping his hands together. 'Then I will definitely slip into something more comfortable.' He skipped to the door and Michalis was left with the expectant looks of villagers with ailments. He offered them a smile then checked his watch. Would his father, the one he was really doing all this for, actually turn up?

Twenty-One

'If you keep looking over your shoulder like that you're going to ruin your neck.'

'If he's gay I'll ruin more than my neck for him. Have you seen him, Luce? I mean, look at him!'

Lucie couldn't look at Michalis because Michalis was inside the studio with possibly his thirty-fifth patient of the evening. The throng had depleted over the last two hours, was a thinning line last time she looked, but just as she thought that was it, another figure would come out of the shadows and shuffle into place.

'Perhaps we could check the charcoal again now?' Lucie asked. They had lit it over an hour ago and Gavin seemed more interested in creating pressure points in his spine than he did on beginning to cook the *souvlakia* the doctor himself had prepared earlier.

Gavin waved a hand over the coals and shook his head. 'Not quite ready yet. Shall we get some more crisps?'

Lucie didn't want more crisps. She wanted something with a whole lot more substance to soak up the delicious beer with the hilarious name – Vergina. Gavin had joked it was giving him reminders of senior school when he had been desperate to fit in…

'I'll cook,' Lucie said, standing up. 'If it takes ages I'll finish them off in the microwave or something.'

'Maybe the good doctor will want a skewer,' Gavin suggested with a wink. 'Is there a portion for him?'

Lucie began to unwrap the parcel of meat. They did look delicious and her stomach gave a moan of appreciation even from them in their raw state. 'I suspect he'll want to get home having spent all this time seeing patients without a break.'

'Or,' Gavin began. 'He'll want to have an immediate drink and some sustenance.'

Gavin had said 'sustenance' like he meant 'penis'. Perhaps it would be good if the doctor/butcher *was* attracted to men. Then maybe she would *never* have to tell Gavin that Simon wasn't. Except, selfishly, a tiny part of her was willing Michalis to be interested in women, purely for fantasy purposes obviously. Because holiday romances were purely made up for women's magazines… or happened long ago to Meg.

Gavin leapt out his chair then. 'That's the last patient!'

Lucie turned from placing the *souvlakia* on the grill. 'What?'

'The tiny little lady in grey is sashaying away up the path.' Gavin grinned. 'That means the doctor is free! Shall I go and grab him? Suggest he joins us for a meat feast?'

Lucie could see that it didn't matter what she replied to Gavin, he was going to bound up to the studio door and make the invitation anyway.

Despite Gavin's insistence that the coals weren't hot enough to begin cooking anything yet, the chicken was already starting to turn from flesh-coloured to white and a pleasant sizzling sound was accompanying a fragrant steam as she gently moved the kebabs with tongs. It was so gloriously peaceful here looking out over the property's garden as well as the width of blue sea, the sun beginning to lessen in intensity. In these moments, in this stillness, the everyday tension started to drop away and her mind began to free up. Her thoughts were starting to become hers again, instead of constantly fighting a losing battle with the wants, needs and opinions of others. She was never the biggest personality in the room, but she could admit here and now, if only to herself, that she had let her presence shrink even further this past year, adjusting her focus so much that what she wanted and needed had slid completely out of view. Other people had mattered much more. They had had to matter. Their struggles had been insurmountable, terrifying, bigger and more important than anything else. Perhaps Corfu could help address the balance a little now though.

'Lucie, crack open another vagina beer for the good doctor!'

Wow. That was quick work by Gavin. Lucie turned her head and there was her beaming best friend together with Michalis, trying to shrug off the white coat like it was a strait jacket.

'The beer. It is pronounced "ver-gey-na",' Michalis said, arriving on the terrace. 'Gey like key.'

'Oh,' Gavin said, words dripping with disappointment. 'That's not as fanny.' He laughed at his own joke and went about plucking up a can and a glass despite having asked Lucie to do it.

'I hope my patients did not spoil your evening,' Michalis asked. He was by the barbecue now, close enough that Lucie was worried her chicken-turning skills might be scrutinised.

'Well,' Gavin said. 'We did pay close attention when that man made a noise like a sex-starved owl.'

'I… did not hear this,' Michalis said, looking confused.

'What?!' Gavin exclaimed. 'It was so loud, even out here!' He giggled. 'Don't make me do the noises.' He grinned. 'Do you *want* to hear me do the noises?'

'No,' Lucie said quickly.

'I think what you heard might have been an actual owl,' Michalis told them.

'No!' Gavin said, following it up with ridiculous laughter. Her best friend's yearning for tasting the slow and individual undercurrents of wine obviously didn't extend to beer.

'On Corfu we have the scops owl,' Michalis said. 'It is a small owl but its noise, it is a deep-throated whistle.'

'Oh my,' Gavin said, slapping his hands to his beard while his eyes rested on the doctor. 'A deep-throated whistle is what most of my dreams are made of.'

'Am I doing this right?' Lucie interrupted, moving the skewers of meat over the grill sat across the hot coals with the tongs. 'Sorry, I really didn't mean for you to sell me the food then give advice on cooking it.'

'Really you should not be grilling outside in the summer,' Michalis said.

'What?!' Gavin exclaimed. 'When else does anyone barbecue?'

'In the summer the risk of fire is high here in Corfu. There is not to be any open fires outside from May until November,' Michalis informed.

'Oh God! Have we broken the law?' Lucie said, feeling all the stress come rolling back. 'Should I... put it out?' She really didn't want to extinguish it because her stomach was already protesting for making it wait so long for fulfilment. But rules were rules and who knew how the Greek authorities punished people? According to the press they had been heavy handed with Harry Maguire in Mykonos...

'No,' Michalis said. 'We will just be very careful.' He leaned over the coals. 'Perhaps the grill is a little too hot in the centre. I do not wish to interfere, but I would move the *souvlakia* a little to the edge.'

'Too hot?' Lucie said, sending Gavin a look that suggested they could have begun cooking a whole lot earlier.

'Shall I get some wine from the house?' Gavin asked. 'Lucie and I bought a flagon of white wine and haven't had one drop yet.'

'Please,' Michalis said. 'Do not open this for me. If my father stays in his bedroom all day tomorrow I will be needed to work at the butcher's early in the morning.'

'I'll open it for me then,' Gavin said, grinning. He passed Michalis his beer then proceeded to trot over the terrace towards the steps that led up to the house.

'Sorry about Gavin,' Lucie said, the sizzling on the chicken slightly lessening now they weren't being cooked quite so severely. 'He can get excitable after a few drinks. I hope you didn't feel obliged to join us. I mean... it's nice to have you here and you're very welcome but... maybe you have somewhere else you would rather be than... helping a law-breaking barbecue virgin with her meat sticks.'

If Lucie's face wasn't hot from the charcoal temperatures and the humidity of the night, it was now burning from the sheer ridiculousness of the sentence she had just uttered. Meat sticks! Barbecue virgin! She wanted to disappear down the mountain and hide in an old ruin.

'You have not had a barbecue before?' Michalis asked, one eyebrow raising.

'I've *eaten* barbecue before, and I've seen other people cook it. But... no, I've never actually taken control of the... apparatus.'

'You are a nurse, yes?' Michalis said, putting his drink down on the edge of the wall.

'Yes.'

'Then all you have to remember is to treat the meat the same way you would treat a patient.'

'What?'

'May I show you?' He got a little closer and offered out a hand. For a second she was blindsided until she realised he simply wanted to take the tongs.

'Oh, please, be my guest.' Inwardly she cringed. He was her guest. *Their* guest. Gavin's guest actually...

Lucie watched as Michalis wrapped the metal spoons around the flesh of the kebabs and gently lifted and turned in one smooth and gentle motion. She wasn't sure she had ever been that delicate with any of her patients on Abbington Ward. Most of her work required brute force and clicking all the buttons on the remote control for the beds.

'You want to look after them,' Michalis said, beckoning

her in with his free hand. 'But you should know that they will not break.'

'I beg to differ,' Lucie answered, watching him shift the next skewer over. 'One wrong move and we might lose a pepper to the embers. Or, you know, apparently set the whole island alight.'

He turned his head a little, smiling as those dark eyes held an intimate audience with hers. She swallowed, looking back.

'Lucie,' he said, smiling. 'It is OK for food and for patients to fall apart a little. Because they have us to put them back together, no?'

God, she was loving his bedside/grillside manner almost as much as she was loving his muscular forearms skilfully griddling her breasts – *chicken* breasts. She shook her head then and became painfully aware that her *Killing Eve* locks were no longer an asset she possessed...

'And,' he started again, 'the breaking always takes a lot more than we realise.'

She shivered. There was something to be said for that nugget of knowledge. She had been through such a great deal and she was still here, still surviving, her pieces mostly together. But perhaps that need for self-preservation was holding her back from asking the tough questions about her mum. Maybe being mostly together was simply an illusion she expertly sold.

He held the tongs out to her again and she shook her head. 'Honestly, if I do it we probably will burn down Kerkyra.'

'If you do not try you will never learn.' He waved

the tongs again. 'If it helps... you can pretend it is a speculum.'

Lucie laughed and took the tools from him. 'You might regret saying that.'

Twenty-Two

Gavin was asleep. After drinking three large glasses of the flagon wine and eating two full skewers with hardly a pause between them, he'd relaxed into the swinging egg chair on one corner of the terrace and rotated into an open-mouthed slumber. It was only his gentle snoring, the chirping of the crickets and the gentle lapping of the water in the pool amid the quiet. And Michalis was still here with Lucie, underneath a now inky starlit sky…

'I'm sorry,' Lucie said. 'About Gavin. What a poor host, falling asleep in front of a guest.'

Michalis shook his head. 'There is no need to apologise.' He checked his watch and Lucie found herself feeling disappointed. He had been good company, telling stories about the mad village and its characters and suggesting places she and Gavin might like to visit. He hadn't actually told her much about himself though. A mysterious *and* sexy-looking doctor…

'One more drink?' Lucie offered quickly, pulling the flagon of wine towards her across the table.

'You know there is a reason why that wine is such a good price.'

'I like it,' Lucie told him, struggling to lift the flagon. Despite Michalis saying he wouldn't partake in any wine, Gavin had literally force-fed him a full high-ball glass before he nodded off.

'Well, in that case, you might have enjoyed the goat urine.'

'Well,' Lucie said. 'If you're not enjoying it I'm not going to waste another glassful on you.'

Michalis smiled and lifted his glass in the air. 'I still have some here.'

Lucie put her now full glass to her lips and took a sip. Awful. But highly alcoholic. And, if she wanted to find out more about him, why didn't she just ask?

'So, where do you usually practice?' she began. 'Did something happen to your usual surgery? A rent hike or… arson… or something.' The rough wine was now not helping with her thought process. Arson! He was going to start believing she *did* have plans to scorch the earth here soon!

He smiled and shook his head. 'Nothing like that. No drama.'

Except there had been drama, and plenty of it. His shoulders moved in reaction to his lie. Michalis had known if he stayed here too long, if he reconnected with life, he would have to talk at some point. Although he hadn't exhausted *all* the tales he could recount about Sortilas and the people who lived here yet, he had also been careful to pick out everything that had very little to do with him personally. He was emotional today. Those constant sharp-yet-warming reminders of his mama, coupling with the ever-present fear that what and *who* he had left on the mainland was going to reappear in his life was a dense mix. But he was the one who had chosen not to quickly rush his drink, to stay, to converse, to, at least, *try*.

'I don't live here,' he breathed.

'Wait, I don't understand,' Lucie answered, leaning a little forward in her chair as a moth flew over the table. 'You work at a butcher's. You're seeing patients as a doctor. But… you don't live here?'

He shook his head. 'No. I live in Thessaloniki. On the mainland. I am… taking a holiday.'

'And that's where you practise? You have your surgery there?'

An uncomfortable feeling was already beginning to travel around inside him. 'No. I work at the hospital.'

'Oh, really. So, what's your specialism?'

Of course Lucie was going to ask that. She was a nurse. The hoot of an owl called out into the night before he could make his answer. 'I am… a pulmonologist.'

'Shit.'

He nodded as she got the connection. He worked with the lungs. The organs that had been all over the news, under intense scrutiny when it came to research into their function and needing the most help to work properly so they didn't give up when Covid-19 invaded. 'I have been busy this past year. Everybody's lungs were under attack.'

'Tell me about it.'

He froze. He wasn't ready to say much more. Where did you even begin? The start of the struggle? The success stories? The ones who weren't so lucky? He could not go there. Greece, everyone said, had been lucky. But how could any country be lucky under these circumstances? The number of deaths did not tell the full story. Infection rate graphs and hospital admissions for Coronavirus did not talk of the many lives lost because of other conditions. Postponed cancer treatments, people having symptoms of other life-threatening issues but not feeling they should come to the hospital. The whole period and its devastation had been about so much more than one virus.

'Sorry,' Lucie said quickly. 'When I said "tell me about it", I didn't mean "tell me about it". I meant it like...' She shrugged. 'I get it. I understand.' She sighed. 'Tough times.'

'Tough times,' Michalis agreed, nodding slowly.

'So... tell me, what did you do for fun?' Lucie asked, sipping at her wine. 'I mean, we could talk about how horrendous the PPE is. About how after only fifteen minutes or so you're basted in your own sweat and need windscreen wipers on the inside of your visor.'

A laugh left him then. Unexpected but welcome.

'But let's not talk about that. Let's talk about what you did to let off steam, to try and be normal for a few hours, before the next shift began.' She smiled, as if remembering. 'Gavin and I always went for a walk. We'd get out of the PPE, we'd shower and then we would walk out of that hospital and keep walking until one of us said something. Sometimes neither of us would say anything for ages. We'd just walk, breathe, and try to pretend we could do anything we wanted to.' She smiled. 'Gavin missed karaoke. I missed playing pool and putting cheesy tunes on the pub jukebox. Most of all I missed my Aunt Meg.' She sighed, looking out into the night. 'Then we made lists of all the things we wanted to do when life got back to somewhere near normal. And we ate buckets of fried chicken. Some of the takeaways nearest the hospital gave NHS workers free food. And I drank a lot of full-sugar Coke. It was the only thing that seemed to keep me hydrated.' She took another sip of wine. 'I've probably got diabetes now.'

Michalis smiled. 'It will be completely reversible if you act now.'

She batted away a mosquito. 'So, what did you do? To take your mind away from the hospital?'

He took a breath, a deep ache running across his shoulders as if he were still back there, in charge of so many cases with patients and staff looking to him for answers he couldn't give. Taking on more than he could handle. They never had enough equipment, they had to take cases from the islands whose hospitals' facilities weren't adequate to cope with the volume or complexity of the treatment. 'I… took out my paddleboard.'

He put both hands around the wine glass then and leaned into the table. 'Like you and Gavin with the walking, I would take my car and head off to the beach and just paddle out into the ocean.' He took another breath. 'It was best at night. No one around. Just me in the centre of the sea.' He inhaled and closed his eyes, feeling the weight lift a little. 'I liked being the smallest, most insignificant thing compared to the huge expanse of water. There were times when I did not only feel like the only person at *Agia Triada*.' He looked across at Lucie then. 'I felt like the only person in the whole world.'

Lucie swallowed as the air between them seemed to

thicken and all she could concentrate on was his eyes, like sexy warm chocolate pieces...

Then suddenly, frighteningly, her vision became disturbed and next her seat began to jolt. And then the entire table moved...

'What's happening?' she exclaimed. 'Is this just me? Am I having a stroke?' Lucie got to her feet, swaying and unbalanced, not knowing whether to put her hands to her head or clutch onto something. Everything seemed to be shifting in a way that felt terribly unnatural.

'It is OK,' Michalis said, getting to his feet and moving around to her side of the table. 'Sit back down.'

'What is it?' She drew in a shaky breath. 'I don't like it.'

'Lucie, please sit.'

It wasn't a stroke. She was sure of that now, because even the wine flagon was wobbling a bit on the table. But the fact she didn't know *what* it was terrified her even more. Her eyes went to Gavin, the egg chair rocking back and forth and still he carried on sleeping. Michalis's hands were on her shoulders now, guiding her into her seat. She felt giddy and disorientated. Michalis took her hands in his. 'Listen, it is going to be fine. It is just an earth tremor.'

'What?!' Lucie exclaimed. 'An earth tremor! Do you mean an earth*quake*?'

Already her mind was giving her movie-style scenarios where tall buildings were flattened and people were trapped for days, surviving on dust and excrement until rescue workers responded to their plight by picking up the vague vibrations of a well-known show tune knocked out on underground pipes...

'There,' Michalis said softly. 'See... it is over already.'

'Oh God,' Lucie said, taking a breath. 'Well... are you sure it's over? What if it comes back? I... don't know what to do.'

'Listen,' he said, gently squeezing her hands. 'There may be a small aftershock later tonight... or maybe tomorrow... but there is nothing to worry about.'

'In England earthquakes aren't really a thing. Well, you know, unless you live near Leighton Buzzard.' She gave a nervous sigh. 'We have the occasional sonic boom from aircraft... but, you know, not the ground actually quaking.'

'Lucie, I promise you, there is nothing to worry about,' Michalis told her.

'The house isn't going to fall down while we sleep?'

'The house isn't going to fall down while you sleep.' He hitched his head towards the egg chair. 'Gavin did not even wake up.'

'He's a very heavy sleeper,' Lucie remarked. 'I don't think even a hurricane sucking him into its vortex would actually get him to open his eyes. And he snores when he's on his back. I can hear him from my room upstairs.'

'Oh,' Michalis said, sounding surprised. 'You do not sleep together? In the same room?'

'No... well, not usually. Not unless we've both had too much to drink, or eat, and we've fallen asleep talking... or apparently cut each other's hair.' She took a breath and endeavoured to be clearer. 'Gavin and I aren't a couple. We're best friends. The very best of friends.'

And Michalis was holding her hands in his, protecting her from an earth tremor, looking like he could replace David Gandy on any advertising campaign...

'Loosely! Gaveen!'

Lucie raised her eyes to the sky as Michalis finally let her go. Bloody Miltos!

'Loosely, are you there? I have vehicle for you. Hey, did you feel the earth move just now?'

Lucie got to her feet with a sigh and took a second to appreciate the good doctor again. She couldn't help but wonder if perhaps the earth might have moved even more if Miltos had arrived a couple of minutes later…

Twenty-Three

Corfu Donkey Rescue, Doukades

'It's like one of those coco-taxis in Cuba. That's what it reminds me of.'

'I stand by my first comment. It's a go-kart with a larger engine,' Lucie answered, adjusting her sunglasses as they made their way to the paddock.

'Ah,' Gavin answered, jabbing his forefinger into the air. 'No, because it has a roof.'

Lucie shook her head. Their new mode of transport – provided by Miltos – was not the hire car Lucie had envisaged. Yes, it might have four wheels and an engine and it could seat four people. But, apart from the metal framework and the canvas 'roof' that reminded her of a wagon from a western film, it was more dune buggy than automobile. And once Gavin's girdle bones had been shaken all the way back over the mountain again, Lucie was confident they would be swapping this lemon from the fruit van owner for a peach of a vehicle that included fully comprehensive insurance and actual doors.

'Aww! Look at the donkeys! Cuteness overload!' Gavin went bounding over towards the shelter, arms spread like he was either going to pick up one of the animals or was expecting an ass to embrace him…

There were lots of donkeys just ahead, under a canopy that didn't look so unlike the top of their vehicle. Shaded from the heat of the day, some were nibbling out of large green troughs, others were whipping their tails to relieve themselves of flies. They were all colours – brown, grey, black, white, a mixture of all four – and had varying degrees of hair. Some looked very fluffy, others had short, flat fuzz. All of them were cute, just like Gavin had said.

'Anyway,' Gavin said, turning his attention briefly away from a mule he was stroking as Lucie entered the enclosure. 'Never mind your issue with our car, which was almost as cheap as free. I want to know what I missed last night with Dr Delish!'

'What you missed?' Lucie asked. She was trying to pretend that all her senses hadn't started to jump to attention quicker than an exploding R rate. Nothing had happened. Michalis might have held her hands and it might have felt warm and protective and *she* might have had a whole lot of lustful thoughts momentarily but… it had been so long since she had felt anything remotely like it she wasn't sure she was able to recognise the signposts.

'I believe,' Gavin began, fingers stroking the mule again, 'that I was asleep at least an hour before Miltos span the egg chair around like it was part of a funfair and it propelled me into the day bed in a move worthy of an Ashley Banjo performance.'

'We just talked. And I drank more of the flagon wine.'

'Talked about what?'

'Stuff.'

'You are holding out on me.'

'I'm not.' She was. A bit. And although Gavin was her best friend, if she let on that perhaps she might find Michalis ever-so-slightly-a-little-bit-attractive, then *he* would take the lead on what happened next. And Gavin was as subtle as the absence of his eyebrows…

'He likes paddleboarding,' Lucie answered. She swallowed as a vision of the doctor in swimwear took a cruise around her brain.

'I can picture it,' Gavin said, an intake of breath whistling through his teeth.

It wasn't just Lucie having imagery then.

'Did you get round to discussing his relationship status?' Gavin asked, preening the donkey with a brush he had plucked from the fence. 'Boys? Girls? Either? Or both?'

'I didn't,' Lucie admitted. 'I thought "what's your sexual preference" might be a touch too much for polite after-dinner conversation.'

Gavin scoffed. 'After dinner is usually when we crack out Cards Against Humanity.'

'And I am so so glad you slept,' Lucie answered.

She turned her attention to a pretty white donkey with a long fringe, stroking her fingers down its mane. 'But I did tell him we weren't a couple. So he knows that "we" doesn't constitute an "us".'

'And how did he respond to that?' Gavin asked.

'What d'you mean?'

'Well,' Gavin began, dropping kisses on his donkey's long

nose. 'Did he look longingly at me while I was swaying in the breeze and gently snoring?'

'*Gently* snoring?' Lucie said, with a snort of her own.

'Or… did he look at *you*?' Gavin asked.

Her best friend raised his eyes from his new four-legged friend then and looked directly at her. And the heat really began to get to her. It was true, last night, with Michalis, had been the first time her heart had thrummed a different beat. Its rhythm had suggested that she was ready to consider more than nights out and evenings in with Gavin, more than Texas Hold 'Em with Meg, more than bedpans and observations on Abbington Ward. Romance… maybe.

'My God!' Gavin breathed. 'You don't have to say a word! I can see it all over your face! Whether he's gay or not… *you* like him.'

'I… like him, of course. I mean… he did us a good deal on the chicken and he's… polite and I—'

'Imagined him in pleather shorts dancing to Katy Perry?'

'No, that's only you.' Lucie took a breath. 'I don't know. Maybe, if any of my senses still work in relation to attraction, then… perhaps there was a small moment, after the earthquake, when he was holding my hands, that… maybe I felt something.'

'What?!' Gavin exclaimed. 'What did you just say?!'

'I know! I know! Me, the girl who never finds anyone even visually appealing in the pub, is getting moderately warm under the bra straps after two nights in Greece.'

'Did you say *earthquake*?'

'Oh, yes, that,' she sighed. 'It was quite scary at first, because everything felt wobbly and then *I* felt wobbly, but

Michalis assured me it would be OK. He said they get tremors quite often in Corfu.'

'And then he gave you tremors of a different kind.' Gavin grinned. 'I cannot believe I slept through my first earthquake. I mean... how?'

Lucie began stroking the little white donkey again, fingers swirling in its coat, enjoying the stillness of the animal and the peaceful time to reflect here in the quiet of the sanctuary. She couldn't help but think this was a gentle pursuit Meg would definitely have approved of.

Gavin let out a sigh. 'I'm not mad if that's what you're worried about. I mean, all the great, gorgeous guys with to-die-for cheekbones and lush eyelashes and muscles busting the sleeves of their doctor's coats can't be into men, can they? Or into men and not into me.' He shuddered like that was close to an impossibility. 'And what sort of a bestie would I be if I kept flaunting my none-too-shabby booty at someone who's made my sister-from-another-mister imagine an earthquake.'

'Well, Gavin, there really was a—'

'No!' Gavin interrupted. 'Don't say any more. We are taking you off the waiting list right now! This is going to be a literal surgical procedure.' He patted the donkey like it was going to turn around and bray its approval. 'We are going to irrigate your usual thought process and abort your misconceptions about relationships.' He closed his eyes and drew in a breath. 'Let's think of Michalis as a barium enema, to help you evacuate the ones that weren't good enough for you out of your psyche for good.'

Lucie winced at his nursing analogy and put her hands over her donkey's ears. She didn't really want to hear it either.

'Besides,' Gavin breathed, smiling. 'Even if I don't pick up in Corfu. I've always got Simon and his hot Colombian back at home. I will be absolutely even more irresistible with a tan.'

Shit.

Twenty-Four

Villa Psomi, Sortilas

'Is there anything more, Mrs Spatoulas?'

'There will be *more* warts?'

'If you use the cream I have prescribed, in the way I have described, then no.'

'I tried to tie a string around it. The string got caught on the door handle. I put a hole in my favourite dress.'

It was all Michalis could do to suppress a laugh. It had been a long surgery session. Longer than the hours he had written on a notice and pinned to the door. He knew the villagers were taking advantage, but he had expected that for the first few sessions. He was hoping it would tail off.

'Hello! Hello! Am I in time?!'

As Mrs Spatoulas stood up from the chair, Michalis's eyes went to the door of the studio and to Nyx, arriving in the room.

'I have warts,' Mrs Spatoulas announced to his sister like it was an accomplishment. 'But the doctor says I will be cured.'

'Are they infectious?' Nyx asked, backing up against the wall a little so the woman had more room to pass. 'Please say no.'

'Not from two metres away,' Michalis said, standing up himself. 'Good afternoon, Mrs Spatoulas. It was nice to see you.' He looked at Nyx. 'What are you doing here?'

'Not catching a lumpy virus, I hope.' She pulled a face. 'Listen, I know I am late. I know that we did not get to talk last night but…'

Nyx had left the sentence hanging in the air and Michalis had no idea what was coming next. What was this even about?

'He is in your car.'

Still, Michalis was at a loss. He looked at his sister, confusion reigning. 'Who is in my car?'

'Papa!' Nyx gasped. 'What is wrong with your brain? I know we are a day late. I know we are not at the allotted time but… we are here.'

His father had agreed to the examination and tests? Perhaps Michalis's pause outside the church that morning, a hand on the effigy of the golden tortoise, the memories of his mama insisting on a Sunday visit to worship, had worked a miracle. And then his initial pleasure evaporated. 'Why is he waiting in the car?' Michalis asked. 'Why is he not here with you?'

'*Ela!* Come!' Nyx beckoned, now backing out of the studio and onto the courtyard.

Getting up and following his sister, Michalis walked out into the sunshine. It was another hot day and while he had been seeing patients he had also wondered what Lucie's plans were. Before Miltos had arrived last night with some sort of half-car, there had been a moment, when he had been holding her hands, when something inside him had shifted. It was hard to describe, but those few short minutes of connection had felt warm and exciting and maybe like a sprinkling of opportunity...

Dodging a large, fat four-line rat snake that shot across his path and slithered off into the garden, Michalis followed Nyx to his car. 'Why did you drive my car? Could Papa not walk?'

Nyx didn't reply, just carried on striding forward and as Michalis rounded the raised bed of herbs, two grasshoppers leaping to another resting place, he realised that his dad wasn't in the car. He knew this news had been too good to be true.

'Hey, Nyx,' Michalis began. 'I do not want you falling out with Papa over this. You did your best, but he is so stubborn and he does not realise that we are only trying to help him.'

'What are you talking about now?' Nyx asked, flapping her hands in the air.

'Well,' Michalis began. 'He has left. Got out of the car and walked back to the apartment.'

Nyx snorted. 'What is wrong with you? He would not get in the car at all. He is not gone.' She sighed and reached forward. 'He is in the boot.'

Nyx pulled the lever and the back of the car opened. Dimitri was lying there, his hands tied together with, what looked like, latex gloves. And there was an apple in his mouth as if he were a roasted pig on display. There was also a very angry expression on his face. And Michalis didn't blame his father at all.

'Nyx! What have you done?' Michalis yelled. He reached for his father then and, putting his arms underneath his body, Dimitri attempted to sit up.

'What do you mean "what have I done"?' Nyx scowled now. 'You ask me to bring Papa here last night. He would not come. I had to resort to special measures today, like I said I would.'

'He looks drowsy,' Michalis said, as his father tipped forward, attempting to get out of the confines of the vehicle. 'Did you give him something?' He plucked the apple from Dimitri's mouth and waited for a well-deserved onslaught of expletives. Nothing was forthcoming and Dimitri's breathing was shallow.

When Nyx didn't immediately reply Michalis knew the answer. 'Nyx, what did you give him?!'

'Just a mild sedative.'

'In God's name!'

'I do not know what you are getting angry about. This was *your* idea!' Nyx folded her arms over her chest.

'It was my idea for him to see a doctor. It was not my idea to drug him!'

Nyx hissed a reply as Michalis aided his father to his feet and carefully walked him away from the car towards his surgery, untying the bindings around his wrists.

'How are you feeling now?'

Michalis put a hand to his father's forehead, observing the movement of his pupils. Dimitri slapped his hand away. A sure sign the man was feeling more like himself.

'I am feeling like I wish I did not have children.' Dimitri

sent a glare across the studio to Nyx. Michalis saw his sister shrink further into the cushion on the cane chair. Her fingernails were in her mouth and she was chewing like she had when she was a child.

'Papa, I am worried about you,' Michalis stated.

'Huh! Me! I would save your worrying for the person who drugged me, tied me up and put me in the boot of your car!'

Nyx got to her feet then, pointing a finger at Dimitri. '*You* should not have resisted! All you had to do was turn up for an appointment with the doctor, your own son, and there would have been no force necessary!'

'I do not need an appointment with a doctor!'

'No?!' Nyx screamed. 'Well, what is it with the night rides on your moped, the not turning up for work and the eating fish?!'

Dimitri scowled. 'Eating fish is a life choice, not a medicine.'

'Ha!' Nyx said, turning to face Michalis then. 'There it is! Did you hear it, Micha? Our papa saying the words "life choice". There is definitely something wrong!'

'Nyx,' Michalis said firmly. 'Please wait outside.'

'I will not. Always I am treated like the baby. I am not a baby!'

'Well stop acting like one!' Michalis blasted. As anger got the better of him he stood, feeling his own blood pressure rising. He bit his lip. He shouldn't have shouted at his little sister. This wasn't her fault. *He* had started this. He took a deep breath.

Taking a step towards Nyx, he placed a hand on her shoulder. 'Please, Nyx, I am sorry. Just, give me a moment with Papa.'

Feeling the reluctance through her skin, Michalis dropped his head a little and tried to meet her eyes. Finally, she engaged, gave a small nod and shuffled through the doorway and out onto the courtyard. Michalis pushed the door closed and turned to face his father.

'Do not look at me like that!' Dimitri ordered, throwing his hands up in the air. 'I should leave right now after what that crazy girl has done to me.'

Michalis nodded. 'Yes,' he responded. 'That is what you could do.'

'Right,' Dimitri answered. 'Yes.' He nodded and began to get to his feet.

'But you could instead stay,' Michalis suggested. 'I could run a few checks and then Nyx will be off your back.' He sighed. 'And I will be off your back too.'

Dimitri shook his head. 'Why do younger people always think they know more than people who have actually lived three quarters of their life already? Do you think we go around with our heads under a bucket, not seeing, not listening?'

Michalis shook his head. 'I do not think that. But I do think that if there was something going on with your health you would not listen to your body and you *would* bury your head into a bucket.'

'That is not true,' Dimitri responded, his tone set to aggravated.

'Come on, Papa!'

'Come on what?'

'When was the last time you had a check-up?'

'I do not need a check-up. Everything I own is in perfect working order.'

'Everything?' Michalis asked. 'No aching in your limbs if you stand for too long? No pins and needles in your hands? No rapid heart rate?'

'Only when your sister is being particularly annoying.'

Michalis shook his head. 'You are not taking this seriously!'

'I cannot believe you think, after what happened to your mother, that I would not take care of my health!'

Watching Dimitri drop his head a little, his dark hair lightly speckled with silver catching the sunlight streaming through the open window, Michalis felt his father's reverie fill the space. They had never discussed their loss, never laid out their grief, they had simply put it to one side and moved forward. Perhaps that was the biggest mistake and one they had both equally contributed to. Michalis had seen so much grief last year he knew categorically that most people reacted with an outpouring of some sort. But the Andinos just battened up the hatches.

'I still miss her,' Michalis whispered. He hadn't meant to speak, to say what he was churning up internally, but there it was, the words spiralling around the room amid the humidity.

Dimitri lifted his head, his eyes moist, and gave a brief nod that seemed to signal his agreement. Then, he used his fingers to touch the corners of his eyes, as if spilling feelings you could clearly see would be a slight on his patriarchy.

'So,' Dimitri began. He stopped to clear his throat before continuing. 'You really think if I let you do a few checks and make a few tests, Nyx will stop behaving like madness is in control of her actions?'

Michalis smiled then. 'Well, I do not promise that her

unique ways will completely disappear. But, I am sure it will give her one less thing to complain to you about.'

Dimitri nodded. 'OK.'

'OK?' Michalis checked, a little taken aback. His fingers were itching to reach for the stethoscope…

'If it will make you happy, son. And if it will quieten your sister, then let us waste no more time.'

Michalis smiled at his father and put the ends of the stethoscope in his ears. 'OK, first let me listen to your chest. The blood tests might have to wait until whatever Nyx gave you is out of your system.' He waited for his father to unbutton his shirt, then placed the metal circle on his chest. 'Just breathe normally.'

Twenty-Five

Fuego Beach Bar, Acharavi

'Are you at a nightclub?'

A niggle of annoyance bled into Lucie's subconscious. Meg had said 'nightclub' but it had come across as 'dangerous fire pit'. She pressed the phone closer to her ear and crunched across the stones on the beach to put a little more space between herself and the music of an amazing bar almost right on the shoreline that Gavin had already declared 'more lit than an episode of *Dynasty*'.

'It's a bar,' Lucie answered, eyes going to the now inky sky, then the sea rushing back and forth over the pebbles. 'A really lovely bar with great music and low lighting, and in Greece they always seem to bring you free snacks whenever you order a drink.' Despite having a delicious lamb gastra – lamb cooked in a pot with aubergines, courgettes, carrots and potatoes – at a restaurant called Maistro, she had still managed to eat a small bowl of roasted peanuts and some oregano-flavoured crisps.

'Greece has always led the way with hospitality, exactly

like I told you,' Meg answered. 'So, is this music real musicians with *bouzoukis* and mandolins?'

'Um...' At the moment it was definitely more The Weeknd and Clean Bandit, just how Gavin liked it. 'Well, it's definitely music we can dance to.'

'Oh, Lucie, make sure you go and see some traditional musicians while you're there. I remember I went to so many festivals when I was in Greece. Every village has a special night every year.'

The Day of the Not Dead. Immediately that poster with their buff resident doctor was in the forefront of Lucie's mind. As were the feelings that had rippled through her when Michalis had held onto her during the earth tremor. She really did need to think about putting a tentative foot on the dating carousel before Gavin started pushing potential suitors at her again. It hadn't been a great success the last time, although she did now have mates' rates at the Holistic Emporium if she wanted to see Laurence again.

'We have a doctor staying with us.' Lucie cringed. Why hadn't she just told Meg about the donkey sanctuary or the fantastic meal at Maistro? She definitely couldn't tell her about the half-car that looked like it was held together with fraying string.

'A doctor? Is everything OK? Has something happened?' Meg's anxious tones gathered pace. She might have known that would be her aunt's first reaction. Lucie kicked a stone towards the sea and watched it disappear under the foaming surf.

'Everything's fine,' she breathed. 'He's started a surgery. In the little studio opposite our house.'

'Goodness,' Meg said. 'Greece really hasn't changed at

all. It's all or nothing. Things either happen lightning fast or after years of tomorrows.'

'He's… called Michalis and he's… you know… quite nice.' She closed her eyes and willed the tide to her toes. Why was she sharing this? She never shared potential boyfriend talk with Meg anymore, not after the leavers' dance date with Jason. Poor Jason. Meg had taken the leather jacket he had worn over his tuxedo as a sign that he was going to put Lucie on the back of a motorbike without a helmet and drive like all the highways led to hell. It had killed the mood right off the bat.

'I like him,' she finally committed. 'I mean, I don't know him very well yet but… I like his exterior very much and, from what I *do* know about him, well, that's attractive too. And, you know, I'm saying that… he's attractive to me.' Ugh! Why did she sound like she was fresh out of college all over again?

'Thank God!' Meg exclaimed. 'I thought you were only ever going to hold a torch for Cormoran Strike.'

'Meg!'

'Well, there's nothing wrong with a televisual fantasy – I am testament to the delights of that myself – but it's one thing to put them on the screen for a little daydreaming and it's another to start avoiding social interaction in favour of them.'

'I don't do that,' Lucie immediately replied.

'Lucie-Lou!'

'I don't do that *all* the time.' And some of the reason she had retreated from the romance circle was because she was worried if the relationship progressed past a couple of drinks and a dinner she would feel she had to introduce the guy to Meg, and Meg would find something to disapprove of…

'Oh, Lucie, is that the sea I can hear in the background?' Meg asked, her voice thick with excitement now.

Lucie stepped closer to the water. It really was another gorgeous night and here by the sea there was a gentle breeze to divide the humidity. Lights twinkled from the other tavernas and bars along the beachfront and further away from the neighbouring resort. Loungers had been put neatly back into place, parasols folded down and wrapped up for the night, children, who could only be local as they were dressed in jeans, ran around, trainers crunching over the stones…

'It *is* the sea,' Lucie answered her aunt. 'And it's quite wavy tonight. I'm not sure about riding a banana boat in waves like this.'

'A banana boat!' Meg exclaimed. 'What do you mean, a banana boat?'

'Well, it's an inflatable, shaped like a banana and…' Lucie stopped talking. If she said words like 'throttling across the water' or 'being flung into the sky' this would turn into a warning lecture…

'And?'

'And Gavin's waving at me from the bar. Waving frantically actually. I'd really better go and see what trouble he's got himself into and—'

'Lucie Britney Burrows!'

Lucie cringed at the use of her middle name. That was one decision straight from her mum that had stuck with her. She often wondered whether her mum had actually liked the name or if it had been some kind of rebellion, knowing that her parents would have disapproved of a baby being named after a sometimes mentally unstable popstar. It was another question she'd never had the guts to ask Meg about. 'Got to go now. I'll call you tomorrow! Bye!'

She pocketed her phone and turned to head back to the bar. But, all of a sudden, a shooting pain in her neck stopped her dead.

Twenty-Six

'What is in this?' Michalis asked.

He was looking at a long drink in a tall cocktail glass, the liquid the colour of a Greek sunset under an intense Instagram filter. It was orange and pink with a hint of yellow, with ice cubes, a purple paper umbrella and two neon-coloured straws.

Nyx swayed back down into the beach chair, the straw in her drink already inside her mouth. 'It's called "The Flirt". It is meant to be served in one of those teeny tiny cocktail glasses, but I say to Milo, I will have to come up and down, up and down for more so... just triple the measures.'

Michalis put the straw to his lips and sucked. Wow. It was strong but not unpleasant. He took another drink. He remembered the very last time he'd had a drink like this. It had been with his ex-girlfriend, Thekli. Just thinking about her now brought a whole cocktail of emotions to the fore. They had been together a few weeks when they'd spent the day on the beach, ending up at a bar called Riveria. Things were at that new, exciting, let's-just-see-how-this-goes stage but it had been good, simple, fun. He'd liked Thekli. He'd liked her a lot, possibly more than he'd liked any girlfriend. But, quite early on, he'd sensed a seriousness about her, a need for some kind of commitment. And it wasn't something he could give when he needed to be wholly committed to his career. In the end, when the pandemic had hit and there weren't enough hours in the day to even sleep, he had had to call time on the relationship. And Thekli had taken it badly. The end of their romance had been the beginning of the downfall of everything else.

'It's good, right?' Nyx said with a satisfied grin.

'I think I asked what was in it,' Michalis reminded her.

Nyx whisked a hand through the air in dismissal. 'All the strongest stuff. We are from Sortilas. Nothing can touch us now we have the golden tortoise.'

'Don't say that,' Michalis said, the flavours on his tongue turning sour. And that flippancy was not the health message he had given the village back in March 2020.

'I was joking! Stop being so serious! We are celebrating,' Nyx said, putting her drink on the table and toying with the two pigtails she had hanging in tight corkscrew spirals. 'You wanted Papa to take the tests. He took the tests.'

It was true. Their father had stayed in the studio surgery that afternoon and Michalis had checked everything it was possible to check with the limited equipment he had. He had even agreed to have his blood taken the next day.

'And, you said, everything looked fine. That he was in good health,' Nyx continued, raising her glass.

'I did say that,' Michalis answered. And, going on what he had deduced from blood pressure, heart rate, reflexes and a urine sample given grumpily from behind a screen made of a semi-transparent shower curtain and a couple of bamboo canes Michalis had found outside the house, everything *was* fine. But there was still the blood test to go and until he had the results of that in his hands he couldn't completely rule out this niggling feeling that something was amiss with Dimitri.

'So, it is time you relaxed,' Nyx ordered. 'I have not seen you relaxed since you came back.'

Immediately, Michalis felt a throb in his temple. He tried to settle himself in his seat, all too aware of the tension he was holding, and the facts about his leaving the mainland. But he could never confess any of it to Nyx. He would always try to protect her at all costs. That's what big brothers did. 'I have spent a little time on the beach and in the water.'

'You have spent more time with me in the butcher's arranging shelves that do not need to be arranged. And now you are back working. That is not a holiday.'

He sighed. 'I know. But, it is a change.' And perhaps a change really was as good as a rest.

'So, tonight we relax,' Nyx continued. 'We drink and we dance and we forget about... warts and... Papa's health and... everyone else and...'

Suddenly Michalis found himself sitting forward on his chair and everything tightened up again. He focussed his attention on the white stone beach and the person trying to walk away from the shoreline. There was something that didn't look right about their motion.

'Are you listening to me?' Nyx snapped crossly.

'Sorry. I...' Michalis got to his feet. 'Just give me a minute.' He hurried out from behind the table and rushed down onto the beach.

Lucie had said all the swear words and some of them she wasn't even sure were actual swear words. All of them Meg would have definitely disapproved of. Walking was hurting. Even breathing was hurting. And she didn't know how to make the pain stop. She was not going to cry, but she might have to phone Gavin for help. If he was going to be able to hear his ringtone over all things Charlie Puth and Kygo...

'Lucie?'

She looked up at the sound of the greeting, then straight away regretted it as her neck reacted with a pulsing that rocked all the way through her core.

'For-mother-tucking-piss-sake!' And now she had said some ridiculous cobbled together expletives in front of Michalis.

'You are in pain?' he asked, all deep soft tones and concern.

'Mmm-hmm,' Lucie hummed out, doing a half-nod that ripped through her neck tendons.

'Here,' Michalis said. 'Let me help you.'

Lucie opened her mouth to bleat that she was fine, but another fizz of discomfort took the words away. She wasn't fine. And here was a doctor talking all calm and controlled and offering her aid. She might be heading for a CT scan if she turned this down.

'Slowly,' he whispered, his body leaning into hers, bearing her weight as her arm found its way around his shoulders. 'There is no hurry.'

'But... the bar is... that way,' Lucie said, not daring to turn her head in the opposite direction. Each footstep felt as if a rhino was sitting on each of her shoulders.

'We are not going to the bar,' Michalis told her. 'We are going… just here.'

Lucie felt him move away from her then and watched, without twitching her head, as Michalis began arranging a sun lounger, putting its back flat down, making sure it was secure on the pebbles beneath it. And then he was back by her side again, gently helping her reach the sunbed and encouraging her down onto it.

'There's no sun,' Lucie whispered. 'And I'm pretty sure… you can't get a tan from the moon.'

'You still have humour,' Michalis answered. 'This is good. Lie down.'

'Lie down?' Lucie swallowed, feeling like her own personal humidity had just reached high altitude. 'It hurts. I don't know if I can.' And what was he planning to do? Put his hands on her? She closed her eyes. She had to remember he was a *doctor*. And she needed to get her telephone conversation with Meg out of her mind. TV boyfriends were absolutely fine. Uncomplicated and everything you wanted them to be…

'Please,' Michalis said. 'Lie on your front. Let me help you.'

'You should know that… I chickened out of visiting a chiropractor after my… "friend" … that's "friend" said in the very loosest sense of the word… told me a horror story about never knowing her hip joints could move apart like Tower Bridge when tall ships pass under it until she visited one.' Lucie took a deep breath, debating between sitting and lying, her bottom on the edge of the sunbed. 'I really don't want to move like Tower Bridge.'

'You do not have to move at all,' Michalis reassured her. 'Just lie down and I will… see if I can find out what is going on.'

'Well, I—'

'A little less talking and a little more lying still,' he ordered.

Lucie eased her body around and slowly got into a prostrate position. What was the worst that could happen? Michalis was a professional. Maybe his focus was lungs but it was still highly unlikely that he was going to pull or push something that would sever her spinal cord. It was more possible that he was going to help. She just had to try to relax, not tighten her neck muscles and not get too hot under the cervix about the thought of Michalis's hands on her…

Michalis paused above her. There was that feeling again, the same rise inside of him he'd had when he'd taken Lucie's hands during the earth tremor. There was no getting away from the fact she was a beautiful woman and here she was, the creamy skin on her shoulders bare to him in the light gauzy sundress she was wearing. He shook himself and refocussed. What was he thinking? She was in pain and he needed to help. He could not let any feelings of attraction override his professional oath.

'OK,' he began. 'I am going to touch in certain places and you tell me if it hurts.'

'It *will* hurt,' Lucie said, her voice a little muffled from where her face was pressed into the sunbed. 'I've twisted something or pulled something somehow.'

He put his hands to her shoulders and closed his eyes, feeling his way over her skin and, in his mind, referring to the parts of the body – particular muscles, tendons and bones. 'Do you have pain in your back all the time? Or is this the first time?'

'I… do suffer from back pain every now and then.'

'Every now and then?'

'Well… a lot of the time I suppose.'

'You have seen the doctor in England?'

'It's been a difficult year. I don't like to make a fuss. Not when… oww… other people… oww… are a lot worse off than me. Oww!'

'It hurts there?' Michalis asked. He strengthened the pinching of his fingers in the area on her shoulders where his examination had stopped and opened his eyes.

'Yes, it hurts there! Don't touch it! Oww!'

'How about if I do this?' He pinched again, this time a little deeper into the tissue of the muscles between neck and shoulder.

'Yes! Stop! Stop!'

He watched her wriggle her body, attempting to rise from the lounger. He lay a flat hand on her back and encouraged her to stop moving. 'Hold still for only one moment.'

'Don't touch there again!'

He was definitely going to touch there. He was going to touch *exactly* there. It was a move taught to him not by any training he had received as a doctor, but by his mother. This was a classic case of displacement. Something had got swiftly misaligned and it simply needed to be quickly put back where it was meant to be. Exactly like Mrs Baros falling out of the olive tree and onto her pet sheep…

'Tell me... what did you have for lunch three days ago?'

'What? I... have no idea... I don't even... what day was it three days ago? Was I here? Or in the UK?' I don't—'

While Lucie and her brain were distracted with trying to locate a meaningless memory it had pushed to the very back of its filing cabinet, Michalis acted. Putting his hand to the bunch of muscle, engaging with everything he remembered about that incident when he was boy, he gave it a hard twist and then a flick.

'Argh! For-godding-bloody-hell-ness!' Lucie shrieked.

Had it worked? Or had he got it wrong and made things worse? Maybe it had been a flick first and *then* a twist...

'Oh,' Lucie said, beginning to stir with a lot less anger in her voice and a great deal more movement in her body. 'Oh... wow... I can move.'

Michalis smiled, watching as Lucie got up from lying down, sat on the edge of the lounger then rolled upwards, sandals meeting the stones, appearing rejuvenated.

'How did you do that?' Lucie asked him, eyes wide and shining almost as brightly as the stars in the sky above them. 'The pain, it's gone.' She shrugged her shoulders up and down like she was expecting the agony to arrive again at any minute. 'I mean, it still feels a little bit tense but nothing like it was and—'

She stopped talking suddenly and looked him straight in the eye. And straight away those feelings started returning to him, and fast. Her short dark hair and petite features, the plump blush of her lips, her strong energy yet gentle manner...

'Who exactly are you, Dr Michalis?' she questioned.

And then an uneasiness marched in and the feelings that

had been building inside him began to crumble like a Greek ruin.

'I... do not understand,' he replied.

'Well, when I first met you, you were a butcher. Then you were a doctor and now...'

'Now?'

'Well, now, after curing my neck pain, I'm thinking you're a magician.' She smiled. 'Or... a shaman. There's something I can't quite put my finger on about you.'

He shook his head. 'I am not someone who performs magic.'

'But you are the poster boy for the Day of the Not Dead. Why is that?'

'I believe that none of the cast of *The Avengers* were available.'

'Hmm,' Lucie said. 'I'm not so sure.'

'Listen,' Michalis began. 'If the pain in your neck returns, you really should take something anti-inflammatory.'

'You're changing the subject. *Definitely* mysterious.'

He smiled. 'I could prescribe some medication for you.'

Lucie shook her head. 'I'll be fine.'

'But if the pain comes back then...'

'I don't need tablets.' The words came out in an angry rush and her expression had clouded over.

'Well,' he began again. 'I believe you should consider—'

'Really, Doctor, I appreciate what you've done but I can take it from here.'

What had happened? What had he said to cause the change in her humour? One moment she was teasing him about his dual job and depiction on posters all over town and the next she was dismissive and withdrawn.

All he knew was he wanted to find out…

'Lucie, I—'

'There you are!'

It was Gavin. Arriving on the scene before Michalis could say any more. His chance to ask anything else had disappeared.

'And the doctor's in the house. Well, the sand! Prescribing good times I hope?' Gavin said with a smile.

'We should get back to the bar,' Lucie said, linking her arm with Gavin's. 'The barman told me there's a whole Cher section they play before midnight.'

'Well, what are we waiting for?' Gavin squealed. 'Come on, Michalis, you *have* to join us!'

'I… am here with someone,' he answered, his eyes going over to the outside table where Nyx was head down looking at her phone.

'Well bring them too! I've ordered snacks!' Gavin exclaimed, slapping an arm around Michalis's shoulders.

It didn't seem like he was going to be able to say no.

Twenty-Seven

'You are like my brother!' Nyx shouted, thumping Gavin on the shoulder and laughing louder than the pumping disco track funnelling through the bar. 'I am thinking the two of you were switched at birth and *you* are the Greek one.'

'I have to admit,' Gavin replied. 'It's not the first time I've been compared to a Greek.' He turned his face to side profile. 'Some say I have a look of George Michael.'

Lucie was trying her best not to feel awkward but there was no denying it, she *did* feel awkward. Michalis had cured her back pain and not only had she not said 'thank you' she had snipped at him because he had mentioned taking pills.

When they had first been introduced to Nyx, apart from thinking she was the kind of naturally stunning that naturally stunning people seemed oblivious to, Lucie thought this was Michalis's girlfriend. And her heart had sunk to the floor of the bar. She only hoped, after the sibling connection had been explained, that her relief hadn't been physically noticeable.

'George was sooo cute, wasn't he? I miss him,' Nyx said,

bottom lip poking out and her expression set like the singer had been a close family friend.

Gavin let out a yelp as the music changed and the track 'Amazing' began to pound out. 'It's a sign! From George himself! And we must heed his instructions!' He stuck a hand out to Nyx. 'Come and dance!'

'You might not be my brother,' Nyx announced, scraping back her chair and standing up. 'But you are my new best friend.'

They were going. Leaving Lucie alone with Michalis. It was either about to get even more uncomfortable, or she could take the initiative and smooth things over. Because with his surgery a few steps across from the front door of Villa Psomi, they would definitely be in each other's orbit while she was on Corfu.

'Michalis,' Lucie began, sitting forward in her chair. 'I'm sorry if I was a bit... abrupt earlier.' What did she say next? Would this apology do? Or should she try to explain? How did she even begin with that? Because, if she was going to be fully truthful, it had to start with the story of what had happened to her mum. And she didn't want to see the pity in Michalis's beautiful eyes once that knowledge was out there between them.

'I am sorry,' Michalis answered, leaning forward too.

'Oh,' Lucie said. 'No, really, you don't have anything to be sorry about. I—'

'I am sorry,' Michalis spoke a little louder. 'Because I cannot hear you.' He put his hand to his ear.

'Oh.'

'Shall we go outside?' He indicated the glass doors that led back out to the beach.

A quick glance over to Gavin and Nyx throwing shapes in the centre of the room and not caring for anything but the music made Lucie's decision. 'OK,' she nodded, picking up her cocktail glass.

Following Michalis, she stepped out of the bar leaving the music and the chatter of patrons behind for the gentle sea sounds and light breeze. He pulled out a chair for her and she sat down at the table. There were less people here outside now. Restaurants were clearing more tables than seating tourists at them and the sky was a rich expanse of dark. Lucie breathed in that soft salty aroma coming off the water... and then remembered she was meant to be apologising.

'I wanted to say sorry,' she began. 'For being short with you earlier.'

'Short?' he asked.

She nodded. 'You were trying to help me. Help my back. And I was a bit rude and...'

He was looking at her so intently, like he really cared about what she was saying and wanted to know what was going to come next.

'You do not have to say any more,' Michalis said, his fingers wrapped around his bottle of Fix beer.

'Oh.' He had given her an out. Was that because she had really annoyed him? Or because she hadn't? So much for thinking she might confide...

'Now I am the one who is sorry,' Michalis followed up. 'Forgive me. It is simply... I do not know... sometimes in life we are made to feel we must explain everything in the smallest of details and share this with everyone.'

'Well...'

'My sister,' he began, 'would tell you the colour of her underwear if you asked her.' He smiled, shaking his head. 'She would most probably show you also.'

Lucie laughed then. 'She's nice. And Gavin already adores her.'

'I adore her,' Michalis admitted with a nod. 'She has that fire, you know. The kind of spirit that people have when they have not had the goodness sucked out of them.'

Gosh. That was a statement right there. Lucie stilled, watching Michalis put his beer to his lips and sip some back. What was his story? This gorgeous clever man, who everyone seemed to respect and want to worship at a ceremonial festival, definitely held some secrets underneath that taut olive skin…

'Sorry! Here I am talking about the lack of need for sharing small details and—'

'No,' Lucie said immediately. 'I understand what you mean.'

'I *know* you understand what I mean,' he answered. 'Because from the moment you tell me that you are a nurse, I know that you have been through something similar to me this past year.'

She nodded. 'Yes.'

'And it was horrific, right?'

She shuddered involuntarily as the sounds came back to her more vividly than any of the visions. The machinery working hard to keep people alive, the desperate rasping breaths, the sobbing from her colleagues in those bleakest, darkest times…

'It was… something no one was prepared for. *No one.*' She took a breath, gaze finding the mid-distance. 'I remember not even really acknowledging it when I first heard it on the news. A virus in China, I mean, it was so far away, it was awful, but it was happening somewhere else. And then it got worse so quickly. It seemed as if one minute we were getting our first case and the next everything was closing up around us, masks were everywhere, death was everywhere and *we* were being embodied by drawings of rainbows.'

'Greece had hard lockdowns,' Michalis said. 'At the worst time we had to send an SMS if we needed to go out for shopping or exercise or other necessary things.'

'Well, in England, for the people that weren't dealing with the loss of a loved one, it was the differing rules that upset them the most.' She sighed. 'If you were in tier three you could only see some of your extended family outside in a public place, and if you were in tier one all the pubs were still open. The inequality of it all just shattered the idea that we were all in this together.' She sighed again. 'It was almost better when we started the third lockdown. We were all in the same storm again and vaccines were being rolled out.'

'How were you for tests and equipment?'

'Never enough,' Lucie answered. 'Of anything.'

'I would always ask, all the time, and it was like you had to fight and those in power were blind to what was going on around them. And I cannot think about it now without getting angry all over again.' He leaned forward then, putting his bottle on the table. 'Why did this happen? Can we make sure that it never happens again?'

'That is where we're different,' Lucie replied, dipping a finger into her cocktail then sucking the liquid from the end. 'It's probably why you're a doctor and I'm a nurse.'

'What do you mean?'

'I mean that I could only deal with things, *think* about things, on a day-to-day level… well, sometimes it was on an hour-by-hour basis.' She sighed. 'If I stopped and thought about the bigger picture, the whole world and all those millions of people, I don't think I would have been able to go on. I think the terrifying vastness of it would have made me question how much effect I was truly having. Not whether it was all worth it, because of course it was, it *is*. But I focussed on one ward full of patients on one day, those families that day… I couldn't dare to think deeper than that.'

'I questioned everything,' Michalis admitted. 'I still question everything. I really wanted to make a difference.'

'You *will* have made a difference,' Lucie told him. 'How could you not? But, I always thought it was a bit like… ants.'

'Ants?'

She nodded. 'You think you've got rid of all of them, that everything's OK again, and then one comes back… and then another and another and soon you have more than you had in the beginning and you have to start all over again. That's what it felt like. Always waiting for it to come back.'

'I cannot relax the way I want to,' he admitted.

'I was almost too scared to come on holiday,' Lucie said before she thought too much about it.

'Too scared?' Michalis queried.

'That routine. The hospital. Everyone staying at home. The first time Gavin said about getting away I thought he was mad. The idea that we could get on a plane and actually leave the country and travel and experience a holiday like people used to. I mean, I know tourism was open a bit last year but in the UK the second wave was much much worse. I didn't know how it would be with any restrictions or, even without the restrictions, how I would feel about being away.' She sighed. 'Millions of people have died. Most of them died suddenly, unexpectedly, never thinking for a moment that they might not have long left in this world.' She shook her head. 'And we've all spent so long staying at home, reducing our social contacts, sanitising our hands almost every time we even touched outside air... shielding our vulnerable... I thought about, what if I travelled on a plane and picked up the virus and then passed it on to my aunt before she'd had her second shot from AstraZeneca. I mean, nothing's guaranteed with these new variants, is it?'

'And how do you feel now you have made the decision and you are here in Greece?' Michalis asked her.

Lucie inhaled, feeling the complete sense of relaxation and joy bopping around like her insides were the dance space for all her emotions. 'I've never been anywhere that makes me feel so chilled. I mean, elements of it are crazy. Goat wee. Wedding dress making. Fruit vans. A go-kart car hybrid. A tortoise living in the house—'

'And a doctor moving in across the terrace,' Michalis added.

'Yes! That is very mad!' Lucie answered with a smile. 'But...'

'But?'

'But I think it's all exactly what I needed.'

'Lucie,' Michalis said softly.

'Yes,' she replied.

'Would you...'

She was holding her breath, waiting for him to say more. What was he going to say? What did she *want* him to say?

'Would you... like another drink?'

He stood up, motioning to her glass and her heart sank more than it really had a right to. She forced a smile and nodded. 'Yes, please, that would be nice.'

She watched him move towards the glass doors that led from the decked terrace area they were sitting on to the party going on inside. That divinely-shaped body presenting those jeans and T-shirt in perfect order. His dark hair, not too long or too short... and the way he thought so deeply, with such feeling.

And then he turned around and it was all Lucie could do to stop the train of her thoughts and change her expression from 'full-on leering' to 'resting affable'. He was coming back to the table. He'd probably forgotten what she was drinking. It was apparently called 'The Flirt' and Nyx had insisted they all try them...

'Lucie,' Michalis said, pressing his palms flat to the table and angling his body to hers.

'Yes,' she replied, trying not to fixate on his toned forearms or imagine him doing press-ups.

'The waiters... they come over if you want another drink,' he told her. 'So that was not what I really wanted to ask you.'

Suddenly she realised he looked a little nervous. 'No?' She was holding her breath again and pressing her back teeth together.

'No,' he answered. 'I wanted to ask you. If you would like to... go on a date. With me.' He let out a nervous sigh. 'Go on a date with me.'

It felt like her heart valves had opened like the Hoover Dam and now blood was flooding her whole body and all the platelets and cells were dancing like it was carnival time in Notting Hill. Her body was telling her there was only one answer. Even Meg might not suggest exercising caution in this scenario. But… but… were there any buts?

'Yes,' Lucie answered. 'I would like that.'

She knew she was blushing, could feel the heat on her cheeks creating a greater warmth than any candles on the table, but she still had enough control to see his reaction to her agreement. Michalis looked surprised, definitely pleased, but absolutely surprised. How could this gorgeous Greek doctor poster guy be almost shocked that she had accepted?

'OK,' he answered, taking his hands from the table and not seeming to know what to do with them. He settled them on his hips. 'OK. Good. I will… think of somewhere for us to go and… I will tell the waiter to get us some more drinks.'

'OK,' Lucie said with the biggest smile on her face.

Twenty-Eight

Sidari

'**G**avin, we really don't have to do this today.'

She wrinkled her toes, enjoying the heat of the sun on her skin and the lapping of the water as it glided up the golden sand of Sidari's beach. Now this was a holiday *resort*, nothing like the traditional Greek-ness at Sortilas, but extremely pleasant nonetheless. There were bars all along the beachfront serving beers and *gyros* to families and couples alike and the vibe was chilled and laidback.

'Sshh!' Gavin hissed. 'You're shouting again.'

Lucie looked at her best friend prostrate on his purple-bedded sun lounger outside Calypso Bar. He was under a parasol, wearing sunglasses with thick silver frames and a straw hat he had been given last night as a tip, having climbed on a bar to regale the patrons with a drunken version of Cher's 'Walking in Memphis'. She was actually surprised he had made it out of bed and into the go-kart car to drive over here. But getting on a banana boat... Lucie couldn't see how he was going to manage that in the next couple of hours.

'What time did you book it for?' Lucie asked, glancing at her watch.

'Twelve,' Gavin mumbled.

'Gav, that's only half an hour. Do you want me to go and see the guy and change the time?'

'No! I'm fine!'

'You're not fine,' Lucie stated. 'You never sit in the shade if there's a flicker of sunlight to be found and you keep sighing like you're trying to stop the vomit coming out.'

'Thank you! Thank you so much!' Gavin yelled, hurriedly turning onto his side and leaning his head over the edge of the sun lounger.

'Well, I'm just saying that we might have made a list of things to do, but we don't have to whip through them all today.'

'We aren't whipping through them today. We have the wine tasting later in the week. You have another wedding dress fitting on Thursday. And today it's the… banana…'

Gavin didn't even get to say the word 'boat' before he was dry-retching over the sand.

'Gavin, did you say I have another wedding dress fitting?!' Lucie sat bolt upright.

'Miltos sent me a text,' Gavin said, coughing. 'Said Mary and Ariana were going to come to the villa.'

'Our villa?' Lucie exclaimed. 'Oh God. I mean, I thought… they're old and I thought being measured and everything was a way of saying thank you for the lovely dinner. I thought they'd forget, you know, be sizing up another tourist for bridalwear the next day.'

'Elders who aren't afflicted by dementia remember everything. Or are you forgetting literally every person we care for over eighty on Abbington Ward?' Gavin let out a burp. 'That's better.' He sat up. 'Anyway, now you've got a date lined up with a Greek god there might actually be a big, fat Greek wedding to wear a dress to!'

'Oh,' Lucie said. 'You remembered what I told you last night.'

She had told Gavin about Michalis asking her on a date just seconds before he face-planted on the rug in the oven bedroom and started snoring.

'I don't have dementia either,' he said, clambering up into a sitting position and picking up his beer. 'So, tell me more. I remember you saying "he's so gorgeous" and "do you think he's too gorgeous for me?" and "I haven't been on a date since... Gav, when was the last time I went on a date?".'

Why *did* Gavin remember everything when he was drunk? It was a total skill.

'So... where's he taking you?' Gavin asked, reaching for his phone on the small table between their loungers.

'I don't know,' Lucie admitted. 'Should I have asked?' Just how bad was she at this?

'No! Absolutely not! He asked you. Let him be in charge. If all goes well, you can take control of the second date.'

Second date? She had almost been outwardly catatonic in accepting the first one...

'When is it?' Gavin asked.

'I... don't know.'

'Well, there's letting him be in charge and then there's not having a freaking clue about any of it.' Gavin raised his eyebrow space. 'Are you sure he really asked you?'

'The cocktails were strong, Gavin, I admit. But it wasn't me who fell asleep on my bedroom floor.'

'OK. OK. No need to get personal about it.'

'Shall I get us another drink before I cancel the banana?' Lucie suggested.

'We are *not* cancelling!' Gavin insisted. 'This holiday is all about embracing new opportunities and being fearless and fierce and... I've made a life decision.'

'Oh, Gavin, I'm not sure making those when you're hungover is such a good plan.'

Gavin just grinned. 'I've decided, when we get back to England, I'm not going to dance around the issue anymore.' He seemed to nod in defiance of life itself. 'I'm going to be as straight as I've ever been about anything.' He grinned. 'I'm going to ask Simon out.'

Twenty-Nine

Sfakera

This little *cafeneon* in the heart of the village of Sfakera was a short drive away from Sortilas and somewhere his mother and father used to take Michalis as a young boy. With its plaka stone outside seating area, leading to a larger dining space and well-stocked bar, it immediately gave rise to all the nostalgia. And it had been Dimitri's idea to come here for a drink. Nyx was at the butcher's shop and in a few hours it would be time for siesta and that period of rest before work began again and continued long into the evening. It was a reaching out from his father that hadn't happened since Michalis had got back to the island.

But here they were, the small wooden table between them, two green bottles of Alfa beer glazed with condensation, saying nothing at all. Michalis had earlier made comment on the newly-renovated white-and-grey house across the road, an ancient millstone a feature in the wall, bright pink climbing bougainvillea a beautiful contrast to the whitewash, and Dimitri had given a grunt and a nod. Michalis had thought, after yesterday, there might have been a breakthrough in communication…

'So, my tests, they are OK?' Dimitri asked, wrapping his fingers around his bottle of beer and drawing it closer.

'Well,' Michalis began. 'We took the blood this morning. We will have to wait a few days for the hospital to process this but…'

'But?' Dimitri's thick greying eyebrows dipped a little.

'Papa, I think you are in good health. There was no abnormality I could find.'

Michalis heard the slow hiss of relief leave his father's lips. Then he watched Dimitri take a large swig of the beer. 'You are surprised?' Michalis asked him.

Dimitri shook his head and put his bottle down. 'No, I am not surprised. I did not think there was anything wrong with me but… a man gets to a certain age and he begins to think about what comes next.'

'Papa,' Michalis said with a smile. 'In Sortilas? Where everyone is living longer than just about anywhere else in the world?'

'Except your mother,' Dimitri replied in sober tones.

His father's comment stung and it was Michalis's turn to take a drink. He turned his head away from the table, instead focussing his attention on a black-and-white kitten chasing a bright green cricket across the road outside. And Dimitri was right. Of all the residents of Sortilas living a long and prosperous life, there was still the rare exception and why had that had to be Lola?

'She would be proud of what you have achieved, Michalis. You know that, do you not?'

Michalis shrugged. 'The only thing I do know is that I do not know exactly *what* I have achieved. What have I really changed? Would the world be any different if I had stayed here and been a butcher?'

Dimitri snorted. 'You would never have made a good butcher, I know that much. It is a very good thing that you do not often cut people open in your work. And it is good that your sister was born with more skill with knives than I ever had. Have you seen her dissect a goat? It is like a work of artistry.'

Michalis smiled, feeling every ounce of love and affection he held for Nyx jump up as he thought about her behind that counter.

'She still scares the customers, I know, but I am working on her service techniques.'

Michalis nodded. 'They do need some work.'

'And you?' Dimitri asked. 'You are feeling that your work in Thessaloniki is somehow inadequate?'

'I don't know,' Michalis breathed. 'I guess.'

His father had never seen him battle weary from his work on the wards during the pandemic. Drenched in sweat, running on adrenaline, eyes forced open by sheer determination – desperate to close so his body could shut down and rest. A good outcome was always rapidly followed by the worst of ends, before anyone had a second to rejoice over a small victory. And even now, here, away from the hospital, the cases diminishing, there was still his phone resting in his pocket that had the potential to blow his world apart with just one call or message. It was incredibly difficult to live like that.

'And that is why you are hiding here on Corfu?'

He shook his head quickly. 'I am not hiding.'

'You can call it anything you like,' Dimitri told him. 'A holiday. A break. It all amounts to "running away".'

'I'm… not running away.' Pinpricks tapped on the back of his neck. Was he that transparent? But also, hadn't he earned the right to do a little backing off? How much could one person absorb before they were irrevocably broken?

'I cannot believe that you would give up the wage of a doctor in Thessaloniki for nothing but donation money from the village fund. That you would rather treat eyes and arses and fungal feet than investigate diseases of the lungs.'

'There has been a pandemic,' Michalis blurted out. 'I know that Sortilas was virtually untouched by this, but it happened everywhere else. Being an expert on the lungs was…'

'Fortunate?'

'I was going to say "the hardest of responsibilities". And it's not about the money… or the fungal feet.' He put his hands around his beer bottle, shifting the small wooden chair forward with his body weight.

'Then what is it about?'

Michalis sighed so deeply it made his own ribs ache. 'It's about… not being able to save everyone.' There. It was out. And he felt no better.

'Michalis,' Dimitri scolded.

'What? It is true.'

'Of course it is true!' Dimitri answered.

'There were far too many,' Michalis continued, feeling his agony taking a hold. 'Too many people that should still be here now.'

'Everyone knows this,' Dimitri stated. 'We are not blind and deaf in Sortilas. We see the television and the newspapers. And we have the rules of restrictions too.'

'Yet I should have had the skills to stop it from happening to the extent that it did!'

Michalis hadn't meant to raise his voice. Even the kitten skittered away from the *cafeneon*, deciding to go back to the cricket pursuit.

'Michalis, listen to me,' Dimitri began in soft tones. 'You cannot persecute yourself for not being able to eradicate something that the entire globe was at a loss over. You know what your mother would always say when anything went wrong.'

Michalis looked up at his father then and gave another shake of his head.

'What did she say?' Dimitri encouraged again.

Michalis sighed. 'That it was God's work.'

'Exactly.'

'And we are to believe that God wanted so many people to lose their lives?'

'No,' Dimitri said, sitting forward and putting a hand on Michalis's arm. 'Your mother had faith because she believed God gave her the strength to carry on after bad things had happened.'

'But if God is meant to be in charge of everything, all seeing, all knowing, then he could stop things from happening at the very start.'

'Michalis,' Dimitri said, softer still. 'No one knows His plan. But surely, not even God can save everyone.' He squeezed Michalis's arm. 'But, I do believe that God has helped to create a doctor with passion and commitment, one who has always worked tirelessly, often to his own detriment so that he can save as many people as he can, no?'

'I am so tired,' Michalis breathed, the words making his lips quiver.

'I know, my son. I see it,' Dimitri whispered. 'But you are never on your own, please know that. Your sister and me, we are always here for you. Perhaps we are not as good with the guidance as your mother was but... we love you and... you can come to us and...'

Michalis looked into his father's eyes as he stopped talking and saw the thick emotion settling there. He knew the tears would not fall here in public, that at any second Dimitri would clear his throat and moisten his lips with beer. But he felt deeply the comforting weight of reassurance and support being passed on.

'*Yassas*, Dimitri.'

It was a woman's voice now breaking the quiet of the *cafeneon*, where before only the hum of the large refrigerator had been audible. Michalis smiled at her as she stopped at their table. She was perhaps sixty years old with long grey hair, tied into a neat plait at the back of her head. She was wearing a colourful light blue dress covered in bright red and pink flowers.

'Oh, hello, Amalia. How are you?' Dimitri answered.

Immediately Michalis sensed something change in his father. Was there a stiffness to his tone? An awkward balance to his shoulders all of a sudden?

'I am very well,' Amalia informed. She turned her body towards Michalis and smiled a greeting. 'Hello. You must be Dimitri's son.'

'Amalia,' Dimitri said. 'This is Michalis.'

Michalis got to his feet and kissed each of Amalia's cheeks in turn. 'It is nice to meet you.'

'You too,' Amalia answered. 'Your father has told me much about you.'

'Well... I have not shared many details. Just that... you exist and that you do not live here.'

Michalis watched his father's desperate show of nervousness. Who was this woman? Dimitri was flushed in the face and keen to direct his gaze anywhere other than on this new arrival to the *cafeneon*.

'You live here?' Michalis asked her. 'In Sfakera?'

'Yes,' she replied. 'I have a small house not far from the *cafeneon* and an even smaller artist's studio.'

'And, I am sure, that you must get back there before your paints go dry,' Dimitri said in a rush.

It sounded so rude, Michalis felt compelled to apologise. 'I am very sorry for the rudeness of my father. Would you like to join us for a drink?'

'Oh, thank you very much, but no.' Amalia smiled at Dimitri. 'Your father is right. I should get back to my paints.' She turned her attention to Michalis, smiling again. 'It was nice to meet you, Michalis.'

'You too,' Michalis replied.

'Dimitri,' Amalia said in goodbye, nodding her head.

Dimitri waved a hand, turning his body to the roadside and almost knocking the kitten with his foot. It was like his father was shrinking into himself before Michalis's eyes.

'Papa—'

'That woman!' Dimitri exclaimed, sounding exasperated. 'Always unhappy with something!'

Michalis frowned. 'I thought she seemed nice.'

'Nice?' Dimitri snapped back. 'She is an *artist*!'

As if that statement answered everything, Dimitri folded his arms across his chest and the conversation was over.

Thirty

Sidari

'Gavin, are you *sure* you want to do this? There's still time to back out.'

'There's no time to back out,' Gavin replied. 'We have life jackets on and there's four other people on this double banana thing with us.'

That was true. But the watersports man had said they were just waiting for another couple to arrive and then it would be 'rumpy bumpy time'. Lucie knew she wasn't feeling anywhere near as bad as Gavin and *her* stomach already felt like it was researching the fastest route to her mouth. She was also worrying a little bit because Meg hadn't picked up when she'd called her before they came to get on board. It wasn't a day her aunt was scheduled to go to physio and, as far as Lucie remembered, it wasn't a day for her cribbage lunch or ceramics class. She was trying to tell her brain not to overreact. Wasn't she always wishing Meg worried a little less about her? She would try her again when this hell-ride was over. If she survived...

'We go! Rumpy bumpy time everybody!' The watersports man clapped his hands together and began heading towards the boat that was going to pull them along.

Lucie leaned forward in her 'seat', legs astride the inflatable, and put her chin to Gavin's back. 'Last chance to change your mind.'

'No,' Gavin said decisively. 'Gavin Gale does not do indecision anymore. I told you. I am ready to commit to what I want and not let anxiety about the outcome of everything get the better of me.'

'That's a fantastic life mantra, Gavin and I'm all in with that, but, right now, I'm more worried about *my* anxiety. I'm literally silently doing a risk assessment as to the likelihood of you spewing up last night's Flirts and the trajectory of any blowback!'

'Did you *have* to say that?!'

The powerboat roared into life and Lucie clamped her fingers around the hand-holds. Gavin let out a scream and every other body on board shot forward in their positions as the banana propelled ahead.

'Oh my God!' Gavin shouted above the noise of the speedboat engine. 'This is horrific! I feel… like… my bones are going to shatter!'

'I did say!' Lucie yelled back. She was gripping the handles so hard her knuckles were already turning white. And despite the hot temperature again today, the wind from their speed was like standing in front of an industrial-size fan that, on the Beaufort scale, probably had the ability to tear your clothes off.

'Tell me something nice!' Gavin demanded.

'It all ends soon?' Lucie gritted her teeth. She had seen

a group before them go out and although falling off was meant to be part of the ride, it seemed terribly hard to get back on. She was going to avoid the depths of the sea if she could.

'They said fifteen minutes and I thought it was going to feel like no time at all but... ow! Argh! Lucie!'

Lucie closed her eyes as a ferocious wave rode over the banana, dousing them in salt water. The sea was calm, it was the boat, weaving around ahead, sending them this way and that, forcing the banana to traverse its wake that was making the white water extravaganza.

'Tell me... I'm going to find someone nice,' Gavin continued, not seeming to care that he was shouting louder than the opposition leader at Prime Minister's Question Time and the full length and breadth of the yellow fruit could hear him.

'Gavin... I don't think now's the right time for... gosh... bloody hell... the right time for heartfelt pleas.'

'I feel close to death!' Gavin shrieked, highlighted streaks of hair gusting up from his head. 'That's exactly the right time for a heartfelt plea! Give it to me! Tell me that, one day, I'm going to meet Cher!'

Lucie opened her eyes again, bracing her body against the vessel as it bucked and slammed into water that felt as solid as concrete. 'You're going to meet Cher.'

'That didn't sound convincing!'

'Gavin! We're riding a banana!'

'I am well aware! Ouch! Oof! My parts that could facilitate a meaningful relationship feel like they're coming off!'

Lucie dared to turn her head slightly and saw their

nearest fellow passenger was smirking. 'Gavin, you are going to meet someone. Someone lovely.'

'And ripped... like... Chris Pratt.'

This jolting was undoing all the good the hands of Michalis had done last night. Lucie's neck was as full of tension as it had ever been and her shoulders felt as if they had accepted a flatshare with her ears. A tortoise! Yes! She felt like the tortoise who had appeared out of one of the kitchen cupboards this morning and nonchalantly swaggered across the striped marble floor back to Gavin's bedroom...

'And ripped like Chris Pratt!'

'I heard you the first time!' Lucie bellowed, another flash of white water slapping her cheeks. 'But I'm afraid it won't be Simon! Because... he's... not into men.' What had she said?!

There wasn't time to think because suddenly the banana hit the crest of the powerboat's wake and the whole inflatable took flight like a lightweight Boeing, sailing skyward and turning upside down. As Lucie clung on, her fingertips began to loosen, almost one by one, and all she could hear was Gavin wailing. With her thoughts desperately trying to decipher if staying on was less dangerous than falling off now they were in the air, upside down and dropping like Isaac Newton's apple, she could barely breathe. And then all choices were ripped away from her as the banana hit the water and she was bounced up and off the inflatable and into the sea.

The crash landing took her breath away and Lucie pumped her legs to bring herself back to the surface, gasping for air. Despite the life jacket she was wearing, it still felt somehow hard to stay afloat and in one position as the wake still carried on delivering a fierce rolling current her way.

Blinking water from her eyes she saw the banana, back upright, just to her right, occupants spattered around it, all laughing or shrieking. Only one person wasn't laughing or shrieking. Gavin was a few metres ahead, arm resting on the bottom of the banana like it was a life raft, his face pale. Lucie swam towards him, hoping the pallor was to do with his hangover but knowing it really wasn't.

'Are you OK?' Lucie asked when she had reached their transport, where people were beginning to help each other get back aboard.

'No,' Gavin stated simply. 'My innards are up there somewhere, on their way to Paxos!' He pointed skywards. 'And my best friend has been lying to me!'

'Gavin,' Lucie said softly. 'I haven't been lying to you. I promise I haven't. Simon said—'

'And there it is!' Gavin said, bobbing up and down with the sway of the water. 'The fact that Simon said something to you about me... about the potential of us... and you didn't say anything.'

Lucie swallowed. 'I didn't know what to say.'

'Oh really?' Gavin said with a snort. 'How about... "Gavin, Simon isn't into guys"? You know, nicely, not when we're on a banana!'

'Well, I'm not making excuses but—'

'Here comes the excuse!'

'Well, the thing is, I was so taken aback when he said it that it took me a while to process it and, he had, you know, all the usual hallmarks...'

'Because we're all so stereotypical, right?'

'No! No, of course not,' Lucie said, noticing it was nearly her turn to get hauled back on. 'But, you know, from my very little and limited experience I don't know many straight men who colour coordinate the way Simon does and... I don't know...there was Carson Kressley and, well... *you* were the one going on about "queer" jeans!'

'And he told you he was straight, did he?' Gavin asked, sweeping back his wet hair with his hand. 'Just like that.'

'Well...' Lucie thought back to that moment in the canteen. Now was the time to be completely honest. 'I asked him for his phone number for you and... well, he thought I was asking for me and—'

Gavin raised a palm and pushed it towards Lucie in a show of 'stop'. He shook his head. 'That's it! That's actually it! As if 2020 wasn't enough of a pile of shite!'

'Give to me your hand!' It was the watersports guy standing atop the banana and leaning down over Lucie.

'One second,' Lucie said, ignoring the trailing hand held out for her. 'Gavin, I'm sorry. Please don't let my mistake ruin the day.'

'Please, Mr Watersports Man, could I sit on the other side of the banana?' Gavin asked, swimming past Lucie and no longer engaging with her. 'This part's gone a bit rotten.'

Thirty-One

The Andino Apartment, Sortilas

'What are you doing?' Nyx leaned in over Michalis's shoulder, doughnut hair nudging his ear as he studied the computer on the balcony table.

'Nothing.' Michalis closed the lid of his laptop and smiled up at his sister. 'What are *you* doing?'

'I am trying to work out what my doctor brother would need to hide from me!' Nyx whipped the lid upwards before Michalis could react to her fast fingers. 'What is this? You are sending a message to Lucie?'

Michalis sighed, knowing exactly what he was in for now. He waited, watching the wide grin form on Nyx's face.

'Maybe *I* should type,' Nyx said, snatching the laptop up and plumping down in another seat with the computer on her lap. 'Lucie… I do not know the words to say how much I would like to tear at your clothes with my teeth and… taste what lies beneath and—'

Michalis stood, grabbing the computer back and shaking

his head at his sister. He *had* been trying to compose a message to Lucie, but it had been nothing like that. It was only asking if tonight would be acceptable for their date. Except everything he typed sounded juvenile or not enough or, stupidly, too much. He didn't think he would be in this position again. He had told himself *not* to be. It was his talk with his father, his encouragement that he was a good, solid person, that was spurring him to act. But a few kind words didn't fill the void in his heart or repair any of the damage rattling around in there. Perhaps this was all a mistake…

'What?!' Nyx asked, all wild eyes and flailing arms. 'Isn't that what you want? Were your hands not all over her last night?'

'Nyx, she had hurt her back. I was helping her. As a doctor.'

'Relax!' Nyx ordered, slapping him on the back. 'It was not a criticism. I think everyone should be more open in expressing themselves. So, you like her?'

'I… like her,' Michalis admitted. 'But—'

'So, eat her!' Nyx said, laughing hysterically as she made loud smacking noises with her lips.

'Stop that,' Michalis told her. 'You sound like a horse.'

'And you sound like you have never had a moment of fun in your life! When was the last time you were with a girl?'

Michalis headed for the door now. He did not want to get into this conversation. He had never discussed his love life with his sister and he wasn't about to start. He would continue trying to get this message right from the comfort of his bedroom.

'Oh no you do not!' Nyx said, sprinting ahead of him and blocking his path to the rest of the apartment.

'Nyx,' Michalis said with a heavy sigh. 'Please, when do I ask you about partners?'

Nyx folded her arms across her chest and stood firm. 'Well, ask me. Go on. I have nothing to hide.'

Michalis really didn't want to know the details of whether Nyx was dating or not. She was his little sister. The only time he might feel he needed to be involved was if the partner was behaving without respect. Then both he and Dimitri would most probably step in.

Nyx groaned in annoyance. 'Fine. I will tell you. I had sex last Friday. It was shit. He had no idea what he was doing and I will never see him again.' She pulled a face. 'He wanted to do weird things with my hair. Crazy man. English. On a flight back to somewhere called "midlands" now.' She sighed. 'What is "midlands"?'

Michalis closed his eyes and dropped his head, wanting to unhear all he had just heard.

'Sex does not mean marriage,' Nyx stated so loudly Michalis was certain everyone in the square below could hear them through the open balcony doors. 'I think of it as a workout. With more endorphins than you can get from battle ropes.'

'I think I will go and see how Papa is getting on.' He made to side-step Nyx.

'He is fine. It does him good to be in charge on his own sometimes. If he is always helped he will not remember how hard it is to run the shop and he will not give me the pay rise I certainly deserve.' Nyx smiled, determined to press on. 'So, tell me about the last time you had sex.'

'No. Not now. Not ever.'

'You do not have to tell me *all* the details. That would be disgusting. What kind of person do you think I am?'

'Sometimes I really have no idea,' Michalis admitted.

'There has been no one, has there?' Nyx asked. 'No one in Thessaloniki.'

He swallowed and nodded. It was much much easier to lie. Because if he started to tell Nyx about Thekli where would he stop the story? At the break-up? Or with all the tragedy that came after with Anastasia, Thekli's younger sister? 'That's right. No one at all. Your brother has been living like a monk.'

'Wow,' Nyx said. 'I know we laughed when Melina talked about breeding, but shit you must need some practise.' She held a finger in the air. 'That is what you should type to Lucie. Dear Lucie, before my penis goes into retirement I think we should—'

'Do you know someone called Amalia?' Michalis broke in, to stop her ending the sentence.

'Amalia, who?' Nyx shook her head at him. 'There is someone else as well as Lucie? Preparing to go big this summer, my brother?'

'No, she is, older, maybe near Papa's age. She lives in Sfakera. She paints.'

'And what is there in Sfakera for me? It is a village where they think a cocktail is a bottle of beer with a straw inside it. Why do you ask me about this woman?'

'I do not know. Yet.'

'I do not understand! Is this about your penis or not?'

'Definitely not,' Michalis replied.

'Then what are you talking about?' Nyx shouted.

'Nothing,' he answered. 'Ignore me.'

'Happily,' Nyx answered. 'You are *sooo* boring!'

Thirty-Two

There were as many butterflies in her stomach as there were grazing on the blue plumbago and pomegranate bushes next to the vine-covered pergola as Lucie stood looking out over the serene sea. Michalis was coming to pick her up in a few minutes time… and Gavin still wasn't talking to her properly.

She sighed, stretching her arms to the sky and trying to rid her shoulders of her usual tension, plus the after-effects of being catapulted from the banana another two times. A fifteen-minute experience had definitely been enough. But, after her admission about Simon, not even three *biftekis* – Greek burgers – had calmed Gavin's obvious annoyance with her. He was currently draped over one of the sofas in the large upper sitting room, Beats headphones on, devouring a packet of oregano-flavoured crisps.

As she drank in the tranquillity Lucie wondered what advice her mum would give her now if she was still around. Rita had obviously been into boys – Lucie was living proof of that – but what would an older Rita have said about Lucie preparing to go on a date with a Greek doctor? And what would she think about her predicament with Gavin? Lucie sighed. Being a good friend was often a road full of potholes – one wrong move and you ended up covered in rainwater or breaking an ankle. She didn't want to seem ungrateful for the nurturing she'd had, but sometimes Meg's advice on love and life was a little too black-and-white. From what little information Lucie had, her mum had definitely liked to explore the grey and bleed those boundaries as far as possible. But she'd been denied that take on things. Who knew what kind of mum Rita could have been if she'd made different choices...

Lucie pulled her phone from her bag and checked the screen. There was still no response from her aunt yet either. Three text messages Lucie had sent now and another couple of calls. In the end Lucie had ended up leaving a voicemail and a message on Meg's home answerphone. If she had heard nothing by the morning she was definitely going to have to raise the alarm. She would probably be raising the alarm now if she had anyone else to contact but The Other Sharon Osbourne...

'Loosely! You are ready?'

She put the phone back in her bag and turned at the sound of Miltos's voice. She shivered when she saw he was accompanied by his grandmother and great-aunt. Both were walking very gingerly down the slope towards her position on the terrace. Miltos appeared to be wearing a giant backpack that wouldn't look out of place belonging to a Royal Marine on exercise...

'Oh, Miltos, I... didn't know Mary and Ariana were

coming tonight.' She was *sure* Gavin had said something about Thursday.

'No?' Miltos asked, helping the two old ladies to navigate the drop from path to patio. 'Gaveen, he telephone me. He say tonight, not Thursday. So here we are!'

Lucie felt her temperature rise and irritation scorch her cheeks. Of course Gavin had done that. Because Gavin was pissed at her, and he might be her best friend, but he could also be an absolute bitch when he put his mind to it. This was his payback for her keeping Simon's sexuality from him, trying to interfere with her date with Michalis.

'Oh, well, I hate to disappoint you, but I'm actually going out in a minute and—'

'You can go out later,' Miltos told her, beaming as he hauled the rucksack from his shoulder and set about opening it.

The old ladies were already in Lucie's space, attaching some sort of callipers to her wrists and ankles. How had they managed that without her even realising? And how much measuring did your joints need for a wedding dress?

'I can't. I can't go later,' Lucie said, still feeling flushed. 'Because someone is picking me up.'

'Who is picking you up?' Miltos demanded to know, eyebrows meeting in the middle and expression darkening. 'You have a relationship with another taxi driver?'

'No,' Lucie gasped. 'No, of course not. I… it's… someone else.'

'Who?' Miltos asked. 'I know everybody.'

Of course he did. And who didn't seem to know the doctor-cum-butcher around here? His face and anime version of his body were on posters…

The women had stopped bustling now. Miltos was presumably translating their conversation into Greek. But Lucie's hands were still in the grip of metal and her skin was starting to turn grey. 'Could I take these off now?'

'You can take them off when you have told us where you go.' Miltos sounded completely uncompromising, part father figure and part prison warden.

Lucie sighed, the eyes of Ariana and Mary fixed on her. 'I'm just meeting up with Dr Michalis.'

Mary and Ariana sighed dramatically, exactly in sync, hands going to their mouths. Lucie guessed they didn't need the name 'Michalis' translated at all.

'Dr Andino,' Miltos said, mouth stretching into a wide smile that was wholly better than his fierce face. 'Meeting up with him? What does this mean?'

Lucie wet her lips, feeling rather like she was being put through an ancient Greek version of a polygraph test. And all she could think about was the contents of that backpack she was really hoping didn't contain a blancmange of a wedding dress. 'I... well... we are getting together to discuss—'

'Medical techniques of the twenty-first century.'

Lucie looked past Miltos, shielding her eyes from the sun, and saw Michalis was standing next to the hedge of rosemary. God, he looked more attractive than ever! He was wearing a pair of navy trousers with a white shirt – two buttons open – and a very pale blue linen jacket. His hair looked freshly washed and was brushed back from his face, tendrils tucked behind each ear. *And* he had saved her from answering their fruit van friend's question. That was a true act of heroism.

'Hi,' Lucie said quickly, side-stepping Ariana and getting ready to leave the terrace.

'Hi,' Michalis replied.

'You cannot go anywhere yet!' Miltos ordered.

'Well, the questions about modern medicine *do* need answering,' Lucie informed him as she joined Michalis by the earthenware pots of bright orange chrysanthemum.

'Pah! Modern medicine!' Miltos scoffed as Ariana and Mary scurried around him and the huge bag. 'It was not modern medicine we turned to in Sortilas when the Coronavirus hit. Was it Dr Andino?'

Michalis had been enjoying admiring the beauty of Lucie in the little dress she was wearing. It was light blue, like the jacket he had chosen to wear, but embellished with small white daisies. Its thin straps showed off the curve of her shoulders and that perfect back he had got to help give relief to last night. But now Miltos was talking about last year and expecting him to elaborate. He definitely wasn't going to.

'I have disturbed something,' Michalis found himself saying, perhaps a little too loudly. 'What were you getting started with before I arrived?'

'Oh, nothing,' Lucie answered. She took hold of his arm and angled her body towards his. 'Please get me out of here.'

'Lucie,' he said softly. 'Is this a fitting for your wedding dress?' He couldn't keep the grin off his face. He knew all too well how persistent the twins could be.

'With no wedding in my future,' Lucie reminded. 'And no

firm dates for parties because most people are still worried about the rule of six.'

Michalis took her hands in his then. 'When I was thirteen,' he began, 'Ariana and Mary made me a costume for a party on *Ochi* Day.'

'What's *Ochi* Day?'

'It is a national holiday in Greece,' Michalis continued. 'It means the celebration of "no". It commemorates the time in our history where our prime minister said "no" and declared that he would not give in to the demands of Mussolini during the Second World War.'

'Greeks do not like to be bullied!' Miltos called. 'We are a proud nation.'

'We celebrate this every year, in October, and there are parades in the streets with marching bands and the waving of flags and then there is family time, parties and dancing.' Michalis lowered his voice then, so Miltos, Ariana and Mary could not hear him. 'My costume was made up of glue, wire and the wool of sheep.' He smiled. 'I would have given anything to be offered a wedding dress.'

He watched Lucie look over her shoulder at the others. Ariana and Mary were bending over the backpack now, taking out bits and pieces of fabric and there was a thick wad of rope on the ground. Neither of them were taking notice of the swarms of mosquitos congregating under the vines.

'We have time,' Michalis told her. 'If you want to make two old ladies very happy.'

Lucie swallowed. 'I'm a horrible person and you... aren't.'

'Well,' Michalis mused. 'Perhaps I am being a little selfish wanting to watch them dress you up.'

'I'll do it,' Lucie agreed. 'But on the condition that you realise I am very, very hungry and very, very thirsty and I see absolutely no driving in my near future.'

'The place we are going is not far and it does the best swordfish.' He smiled. 'And my donkey is waiting just around the corner, so neither of us has to drive.'

He waited for the talk of animal transportation to sink in and then he laughed. 'Relax, Lucie, I have a car.'

She let out a sigh of relief and then screamed, fingers plucking at a metal device on her wrist. 'Oh my God! If I hadn't remembered that was on there, my hand would have gone black!' She turned towards Mary and Ariana, squaring her shoulders. 'OK, I'm ready.'

Thirty-Three

Harry's Taverna, Perithia

She was in Perithia. The very village Meg had told her she stayed at when she had visited Corfu all those years ago. Lucie sipped at the sweet white wine Michalis had ordered for them and took a moment to gaze through the tumbling flowers that decorated the outside of this traditional taverna. Across the road was a *cafeneon*-cum-post office, its paved outside area full of wooden tables and chairs occupied mainly by men enjoying a chat or playing some sort of game involving a board and counters. A curly-haired white dog meandered between the *cafeneon* and the taverna, and cats sought scraps or stray crumbs being brushed from laps. A little further along the road was a glass-fronted restaurant called Jelatis and a mini-market they had passed on the way. Lucie tried to imagine a much younger Meg, long hair blowing in the breeze, tanned skin, holding hands with someone called Petros. It was difficult to envisage that version of the woman who had basically raised her. Meg was, and had always been, this organised and measured adult with the strongest sense of what was right and wrong. Delivering advice and cautionary tales along with money for college and home-cooked meals...

'What are you thinking about?' Michalis asked her.

Lucie smiled, turning back to face him. 'Sorry, it's just, my aunt has talked about this village. She stayed here once and she said it was one of the best times of her life.'

'It is the place I like best apart from Sortilas,' Michalis admitted. 'I feel at home here.' He smiled. 'That sounds so stupid, does it not? Corfu *is* my home. Perithia is only ten minutes to drive from my village but—'

'But there's a difference between familiarity and feeling at home,' Lucie interrupted. She gave a nod. 'I understand completely.'

'You do?'

She nodded again. 'I haven't had the most traditional upbringing. That's why I'm so close to my aunt. She brought me up, her and my grandparents, after...' The sentiment caught in her throat and she forced a swallow. 'After my mother passed away.'

'Oh, Lucie,' Michalis said, reaching for her hands and holding them tight.

She swallowed again as she felt her eyes begin to well with tears. A first date was not the moment to go blubbing about things she should have grieved for long ago. But when had she really let it come out? Could it be that it was always simmering away, locked in a pressure cooker inside her, ready and waiting for someone to knock off the lid?

'It was a long time ago now,' she replied, feeling a little more steady in the potential weeping department. 'But, I do get the sentiment about feeling at home.' She smiled.

'Sometimes, even though I had the best, most wonderful loving family, it felt like I was... I don't know... a bit of a jigsaw puzzle whose edges had been shaped wrong. A piece that didn't quite fit.'

'How so?'

'I don't know, it's hard to explain. Just like, I wasn't exactly the same as my nan or my grandad or my aunt I suppose.'

'I do not think we are always replicas of our family members. Look at my sister,' Michalis said, smiling.

'I know, but although our feelings for each other were always strong... I wonder if it was more by design than it was by real connection.' She bit her lip, feeling that this admission was something akin to a betrayal of everything her aunt and grandparents had tried to do for her. It can't have been easy, especially for her grandparents. Having a toddler suddenly your full responsibility when you saw retirement on your horizon. Losing your daughter so suddenly...

'You are talking about the spirit now,' Michalis said, letting go of her hands to pick up the wine carafe and add a little to her glass.

'Too deep for an evening of olives, breads and feta cheese dip?' Lucie asked. And the swordfish was to come...

'No,' Michalis said, shaking his head and leaning back in his chair a touch. 'Greece is all about the spirit. Most of our heritage relates to mythology and gods.' He seemed to pause before his fingers found the rim of his glass. 'And *my* mother believed she could tell a great deal about someone by simply laying her hand on theirs and tuning in to their energy.'

Michalis had used the word 'believed'. Like his mother wasn't here anymore either. Should she ask? Or was he going to tell her? She watched him inhale.

'My mother has passed away too,' he admitted.

'She has? Oh, Michalis, I am so sorry.' His hands were now out of reach to her so there was no opportunity to comfort him other than with her condolences.

'In Sortilas,' he said, sighing. 'Where people live for almost forever.'

Michalis shook his head as the anger he still felt about his mother's passing threatened to be exposed. He took a breath and looked back to Lucie. 'I am sorry. I should not have said that. I love that everyone lives for a long time.'

'No, I get it,' Lucie said, nodding. 'My mum died when she was eighteen. I was really young, so I didn't know exactly what was going on at the time, but now I'm older I think "how can that be allowed to happen".'

He blew out a breath, the wind taken out of his sails by this revelation, his own feelings dropping into an immediate back seat. 'Eighteen,' he said. 'She was so young.' And how *had* that happened? Had she been sick? An accident? He wanted to know, to understand a little of Lucie's history. But perhaps the way to get her to open up was to open up himself…

'Yes,' Lucie answered, nodding. 'She was.'

'My mother,' Michalis began. 'She had a rare condition. A form of vasculitis that she was not aware of.' He sighed. 'She would often have a cough and a bad chest that, sometimes, would develop into a pneumonia. But being Greek and being equally as stubborn as everyone else in my family, she would never rest and she would wave away the idea that she was sick.'

'That's why you work with the lungs,' Lucie said in understanding, leaning a little closer into the table.

Michalis nodded. 'That is why I work with lungs.' He took a breath. 'The last time she had pneumonia she refused to go to the hospital. She was too weak to even make the journey. And that was... the end. Nyx was one year old. I was just ten.'

'You must miss her very much.'

'I miss her for Nyx more,' Michalis admitted. 'Like you with your mother, Nyx, she was so very young. She will only know who our mother was from the stories we tell her.'

'But I bet you have some wonderful stories,' Lucie said.

'We do but, you know how it is, there can never be too many memories made. You always long for another. More time, one more day, another week... another always.'

'*Xiphias.*' A voice speaking Greek interrupted their conversation.

Two large platters containing large steaming swordfish steaks, complete with thick homemade chips and a fresh-looking salad of bright red tomatoes, oblongs of cucumber and red onion rings were delivered to the table.

Lucie gasped. 'Gosh, this looks incredible!'

'It really is incredible,' Michalis said, smiling at her enthusiastic reception to the food.

'I'm so hungry after riding a giant fruit around Sidari.'

'And I want to hear about it,' Michalis told her.

Thirty-Four

Ice Dream, Perithia

'So, what I really want to know now is...' Lucie deliberately stopped talking and waited for Michalis's dark eyes to meet hers over the gigantic portion of waffles and ice cream they were sharing. They had devoured the moist and tender swordfish steaks, finished the wine and then Michalis had said she had to indulge in the Ice Dream experience. They left the car in Perithia and took the short walk to the gelateria that was apparently known for having the best ice cream on the island. And there were flavours right the way through the taste spectrum. Taking ten minutes to select a few difference choices had enabled Lucie's dinner to settle in her stomach and they had eventually opted for the *baklava* and mint chocolate chip flavours after much debate.

'Yes?' Michalis replied, spoon poised near his lips. Delectable lips that somehow looked even more delectable when he was eating ice cream. He had taken off the jacket earlier and Lucie was very much enjoying the body contouring shirt...

'Are there any photos of you in this costume made of sheep's wool?' She laughed then, but it tailed off as she felt the vibration of her mobile phone. It had been going off periodically for the last twenty minutes or so and after she had checked it in the toilets and seen it was Gavin, she knew exactly what it was about. Gavin was ready to make up. Her best friend never held a grudge for long. Probably the longest falling-out they had ever had was around twelve hours and that had been during a Netflix marathon and had all started with a 'discussion' about the hotness of Penn Badgley. But Lucie wasn't going to let Gavin's need to move on interrupt her date with Michalis. Her phone was on silent now and that's how it was going to stay.

'There may be,' he answered, digging his spoon into the spongy waffles. 'But I will never allow you to see them.'

'Well,' Lucie began. 'The next time I am in the butcher's I will ask your sister about them.'

'Please do not do that,' Michalis said with a good-natured groan. 'I can see the expression on her face now. She lives to find ways to humiliate me.'

Lucie smiled. 'You seem to get on well.'

'We do,' he agreed. 'And we get on even better when I live in Thessaloniki.'

'Will you go back there soon?' Lucie asked.

He looked up. 'Am I boring you?' There was an eyebrow raise of epically hot proportions that sent a shot of sauna through her.

'No... not at all. I just... didn't know what your plans were. Now you have a surgery at my holiday accommodation.'

'That was… not planned but, here, sometimes it is better to give a little when you can. I am meant to be on holiday but—'

'You decided you would carry on treating the sick and needy instead of relaxing by a pool and drinking cocktails. That's true dedication to your Hippocratic oath. And that's probably why I'm only a nurse.'

'Only a nurse?' Michalis queried.

His eyes were back on her again and Lucie concentrated on spooning up more dessert and shovelling it into her mouth so she didn't have to respond straight away.

'I believe the job of a nurse is far more complicated than the job of a doctor.'

Lucie swallowed. 'You do?'

'Nurses have to make quick and important decisions far more often than doctors. At least, that is the case within *my* hospital.' He mused for a moment before carrying on. 'A patient is struggling to breathe and in pain and there is no doctor. The nurses have to make the choices in those moments and deal with the consequences if things do not work out well.' He focussed on her again. 'There must have been times like that this past year. Times when you had to think quickly and make an even more rapid response.'

He wasn't wrong. At all. With staff shortages at her and Gavin's hospital, there had been times when she had made a call that really a consultant should have been there to make. What else could you do when someone was dying right in front of you and their loved ones were waiting for hope that might not ever come.

'You're right,' Lucie told him, nodding. 'And if things do

go wrong I'm pretty sure our backs might not be covered like a doctor's would be.' There was one time Sharon had almost administered penicillin to a patient with an allergy to it. Lucie put down her spoon and sat back in the neon orange chair. 'Have you always wanted to be a doctor?'

'You mean, did I dress up in a white coat and line up my sister's dolls for consultations.'

Lucie laughed. 'Well, did you?'

He smiled, shaking his head. 'No. But I also didn't want to be a butcher like my father. In Greece, most people they will stay within a family business if one exists. I did not see my future doing that and, after my mother died, I focussed on my studies and decided to try to see if I could avoid what happened to our family from happening to anyone else.'

'That's a really great reason,' Lucie said.

'What was your reason for becoming a nurse?'

'Well,' Lucie began. 'I lined up my nanna's creepy dolls...'

'Come on,' Michalis said, laughing. 'I am being serious. What made you want to care for people?'

Lucie swallowed, picking up her spoon again and toying with a piece of waffle. 'Well,' she began. 'I've always liked helping people. And when I wound a sling around my grandad's arm when he fell over his cucumber frame, Meg called me Florence Nightingale for a week.' She took a breath. 'And, maybe a little selfishly, I wanted a career where I felt needed. Nursing is something I'm good at and it's also something that makes me feel a part of something. For some reason, I fit there. It might not be life-saving all the time, but it's definitely life enhancing. And the most important part of what I do, the most vital thing that *all* nurses do, is care.' She smiled. 'Just that. Care.'

Her phone started rumbling again and this time when it was past the very first set of vibrations it started going again immediately after. Gavin was probably wishing they had more in their Greek cupboards than flagon wine and bread with slices that weren't exactly Hovis size...

'That's beautiful,' Michalis told her softly.

Their eyes connected and Lucie knew she wasn't going to look away...

But next her spoon started to rattle against the plate and the floor began to tremble *exactly* like it had at the villa.

'Is that—?' Lucie said. She recognised it. And it wasn't quite as terrifying as the first time. It would be OK because Michalis said this might happen and he was here with her again.

'Another tremor,' Michalis concurred, his voice remaining calm. 'It is unusual to get another one on another day this soon after the first.'

'What does that mean?' The intensity was wearing off a little now, the ground becoming still.

'Nothing,' Michalis said, reaching across the table for her hand. 'Everything is OK.'

Michalis's hand in hers felt so *right*. She closed her fingers around his.

Then Lucie's phone started wobbling again and she had to let him go to reach her bag. This time she pulled her bag up onto her lap and unzipped it.

'Something is wrong?' Michalis asked her.

'Oh, no, not really. It's just Gavin. He's been calling for a while and it's only to ease his conscience really but... he didn't feel the earth tremor the other night even when the egg chair was basically spinning like a lottery ball, and I think it will freak him out so I'd better... oh!'

Lucie looked at her phone screen. There were apparently at least a zillion calls from Gavin but there were also a couple of missed calls from Meg.

'Is everything OK?' Michalis asked.

'I hope so,' she breathed. She unlocked her screen and squinted at a message, also from her aunt.

On my way!

Lucie screwed up her nose up in confusion. *On my way*. What did that mean? She shook her head. Perhaps Meg had sent the text to the wrong person. That had happened a few times. Once there had been an awkward chat about marrows Lucie hadn't understood at all until it became apparent the message was destined for the head of the horticultural society... Still, she now knew Meg was alive and well and had obviously got all her panicked messages.

'I'll just give Gavin a quick call back,' Lucie said, pressing the screen of her phone. 'Don't finish the ice cream.' She smiled at Michalis and waited for the call to connect.

'Lucie?!'

It was Gavin sounding all breathy and panicky. It wasn't Gavin sounding all mew-y and sugar sweet wanting to get their friendship back on an even keel. This wasn't good. Perhaps she should have picked up sooner. Maybe there was a real emergency.

'Gavin, what's wrong?' Lucie asked, her eyes flashing

over to Michalis. He wasn't eating their ice cream. He was looking at her. And if she wasn't having a best friend crisis right now, she would be allowing herself to wallow a little deeper in that sexy, dark gaze...

'You weren't lying about the earthquake. It came back!' Gavin wailed.

'I know,' Lucie said. 'But it's stopped now and it's fine.'

'And there are three tortoises in the house now! I don't know which one the pet is!'

'Oh, OK, that sounds like a bit of an issue.' How did you identify a tortoise? Didn't they all look basically the same? She risked a glance at Michalis now. He knew Corfu. Maybe tortoises appeared like that all the time here.

'The egg chair's in the swimming pool too! I put it on the edge to see if I could dip my feet into the water while I was swinging and then the ground started shaking!'

'OK, well, have you not got it out?' Lucie asked. Honestly, now it sounded like Gavin was five years old and incapable of wiping a bogey off his finger. 'The cushions will get soaked through otherwise and you don't want the metal to rust either.' And how much were egg chairs to replace? She didn't really want to have a debt to clear after the holiday expense...

'I was going to,' Gavin said. 'But...'

'But what?'

'Well...'

'Gavin! What's going on?!'

There was a shuffling sound and a breaking up of their conversation and Lucie wondered if the phone lines had been affected by the earth's shifting. Until...

'Oh, Lucie-Lou, this house is absolutely fabulous! It's so

beautiful and rustic and very Greek! *And* I experienced my second ever earthquake!'

'Meg! What... how... you're... here?!'

'Surprise!' Meg answered. 'Although I did send a sneaky text telling you I was on my way.'

Thirty-Five

Villa Psomi, Sortilas

'Oh, Lucie-Lou, your face when you arrived back here was an absolute picture!'

Meg had a bottle of ouzo in her hand, half the contents gone. And, despite the alcohol ingestion, her usual slight limp when she walked was virtually non-existent. Her aunt was practically gliding across the striped marble floor looking twenty years younger. Her hair was loose too, gently tumbling over bare shoulders that were peeking out from a short-sleeved sundress Lucie didn't remember seeing before. It obviously *was* her aunt in the kitchen of Villa Psomi but this model was a definite upgrade in the mobility and relaxation realms.

'And I'll tell you who else is a picture,' Meg continued, grinning as she took glasses out of cabinets and filled them. 'Michalis.'

Lucie didn't even know there were glasses in that cupboard and it was *her* holiday house. She shook herself. Only earlier today she had been imagining her aunt clinging to life having fallen over the edge of the hideous patchwork rug that had been in the hallway Lucie's whole life, and which should be consigned to the dump. Now, Meg was vibrant and zinging with energy like it was the year 2000 all over again.

'He is *delicious*, Lucie!' Meg continued, slugging at an ouzo like it was water. 'Mouth-watering. Like those strawberries I bought from the man who collected me from the airport. He had a whole van full of them.'

Lucie shook her head. Miltos had picked Meg up from the airport and Lucie hadn't even known she was coming. She needed to start saying something now and hope Gavin could keep Michalis entertained in the garden while she found out how this impromptu trip had come about.

'Meg, it's lovely to see you but... what are you doing here?'

'Well, I... it was... your descriptions of this house and the sunshine and the... nature and...'

Lucie watched on as Meg stopped floating effortlessly and began to stiffen up, until finally she stood completely still and there were tears seeping out of her aunt's eyes.

'Oh, Meg! What's wrong? What's happened?' Lucie was over to her in one stride, arms encircling Meg's body.

'Nothing,' Meg breathed, holding herself a little out of Lucie's embrace she noticed.

'Meg, you're crying,' Lucie said with a swallow. She could count on one hand the number of times Meg had cried this way in front of her. Before her stroke, Meg had been someone who shrugged her shoulders in the face of adversity, pulled on big girl pants and got on with things.

She always told the story of having come out of her divorce with everything she had put in, plus two sets of golf clubs she could have sold but decided to burn – along with all John's AC/DC CD collection.

'Let's blame the ouzo, Lucie-Lou,' Meg said, giving a sniff that sounded like the beginnings of recovery. 'And the travel. When you get to my age it really can take it out of you.'

'Meg,' Lucie said, relinquishing her grip just a little. 'You don't like going to Lidl without someone going with you because the checkout operators are fierce. And now you've travelled to the airport and got on a plane and... somehow summoned the same fruit taxi that brought Gavin and me here and...'

'I haven't come to ruin your adventure,' Meg breathed, eyes still watery. 'That's the very last thing I want to do.'

Lucie tensed a little, worried what was coming next. But surely her aunt wouldn't have travelled all these miles to check up on her. Would she?

'And I have my own accommodation,' Meg informed. 'I've booked that very same apartment in Perithia I stayed in before. But I was so excited when I got here, I just wanted to see you... so I asked to come here first and... the house, it's so beautiful and... well it brought back all the memories of that perfect summer I spent here all those moons ago.'

Lucie felt relief as Meg smiled and gave a giggle that was definitely down to the ouzo consumption. Then, quickly, there was seriousness again.

'Oh, Lucie, I don't want to wake up one day and find I

can't get out of my chair at all,' Meg admitted. 'Even if the travelling was exhausting and, yes, perhaps I should have booked special assistance, but I want to *live again*. And I've been putting it off. Everything has been shrinking, my world getting smaller and smaller every day. And I don't mean just because of that seemingly never-ending period of restrictions with all the tiers I could never understand, but because I've allowed myself to be defined by what life has thrown at me and how the stroke has left me. *How* have I done that? And why?' Meg took a breath. 'Your grandparents, their whole lives they did the right thing and that's how they brought me up but then it got worse because—'

Meg stopped abruptly and Lucie saw the expression that only clouded her aunt's face for one unique reason.

'Because of what happened to my mum,' Lucie finished softly. 'And then, because you got stuck with me.'

'No!' Meg responded immediately. 'No... I didn't mean that, my darling. I didn't mean that at all. Oh, I'm such an idiot.'

Lucie swallowed. 'It's OK. Honestly. I can't imagine what I would do if I ended up in charge of someone else's child right now.'

'Lucie-Lou, that really wasn't what I meant.' She sighed and shook her head, closing her eyes. 'I just meant, when I was little, my mum treated me like one of her scary-faced dolls who were never allowed out of their boxes to be played with in case their dresses got dirty or one of their porcelain arms snapped off,' Meg said in a rush. She heaved a long breath that made her boobs shake a little.

'And, when your mum came along, instead of doing as she was told like I did because I had been scared by the Bible stories, the "doing the right thing" was simply too stifling for Rita's vigorous spirit.'

Spirit. Wasn't that exactly what Lucie had been talking about with Michalis over dinner? She wet her lips and hung onto every snippet of this opening up that was so incredibly rare.

'I want to get my dress a little dirty,' Meg admitted sadly. 'And step outside of my box before it's too late. And... I worry that perhaps while I've been keeping my own not-porcelain arms by my side, I've been responsible for stifling *your* spirit, Lucie-Lou.'

A powerful rush shot through Lucie's core then and she immediately thought about Michalis. From her position in the kitchen she could just see the terrace outside through the window. Gavin was stood up, silver hot pants over the barest minimum of flesh without flouting a nudity clause, performing a dance routine he'd perfected from watching *Little Mix: The Search*. And there was Michalis, looking at her mad best friend but not really watching. Instead, his eyes were on the house and then, as if he knew, suddenly that gaze was on Lucie. As Meg continued to talk about her arrival and her dress getting caught on the luggage carousel at the airport, Lucie could feel herself zoning out, her attention focussing on the gorgeous man outside on her patio. *He* was the one she wanted to play with...

*

Michalis was standing even before Lucie came rushing out of the door. He watched her feet moving quickly over the courtyard until she was down on the terrace.

'Lucie,' he said, not really knowing why he had felt the need to say her name.

'Luce! Come on! Show Michalis that thing we do when we—'

Lucie was taking hold of his hand now and grasping tight. 'Come with me.'

As his heart picked up pace, Michalis sensed it wasn't the time to ask where they were going or, in fact, to say anything at all. She was guiding him now, urging him to move off the terrace and away from the gyrating Gavin. And he was more than happy to leave the dance show behind.

She led them up the incline, past his parked car and the go-kart hybrid, onto the track that eventually wound its way down into the main square of Sortilas. And then she stopped. Surrounded by the mountainous terrain, overlooking the expanse of dark sea, Lucie turned away from the view and instead locked her eyes with his, still clutching his hand.

'I don't want to be a porcelain doll,' she whispered, as if it made all the sense in the world.

'OK,' he answered, wetting his lips.

'Because Meg said it a minute ago and when she said it I realised she was completely right. It's not just her who's ageing behind a flimsy see-through window in a box that smells of 1980. That's exactly where I've been for... probably forever. And yes, Meg is overprotective and sometimes that's really irritating but I've been giving in to it. I've *let* my spirit be stifled. Until now.'

She was smiling at him and he thought she had never looked more beautiful. Her eyes were alive and there was a glow to her skin. He took a breath, rubbing his thumb over the skin on the back of her hand.

'I really like you,' Lucie admitted. '*Really* like you. More than I've *liked* anyone in a very, very long time.'

They were so close now he could smell the light scent of her perfume and it was doing all kinds of crazy to his libido. 'Lucie…' He should be cautious. He knew how any kind of romantic attachment could end. But…

'Sshh,' she ordered, putting a finger to his lips.

He longed to taste her skin and her finger was right there, resting on his top lip. He kept holding onto his breath.

'So… I feel… that this is the right thing to do,' Lucie continued. 'The right thing to do *right* now.'

Before Michalis even had time to think any further, Lucie had dropped her finger from his lips and replaced it with her mouth. It took him less than a second to catch up.

All thoughts that this might one day hurt were whisked away and he matched her passion completely, wrapping an arm around her waist and drawing her in close. He leaned into the way she controlled the kiss, next playfully surrendering, before then ensuring she was in charge again. It was the sweetest, most honest kiss, but also the sexiest, and when they finally parted Michalis couldn't help but long for it to begin all over again.

'Wow,' Lucie said, smiling and putting her own fingers to her lips. 'I'm… so glad I did that.'

Michalis sent a smile straight back. 'Me too.'

'So, Dr Andino,' Lucie began. 'Do you think we might,

you know, go on another date while I'm in Corfu?'

'Is tomorrow too soon?'

He took Lucie in his arms again, kissing the top of her head and relishing how good it felt to hold her under the moonlight and a star-scattered sky.

Thirty-Six

Sortilas Square

'It's very early, isn't it?'

Lucie looked at her watch in response to Meg's remark. It was half past seven in the morning and at just after seven they had all been rudely awoken by a gong being hit outside the front door of Villa Psomi. Next there had been the shouting of Greek words that Meg had looked up in the dictionary she had brought with her and translated to mean 'village meeting' and the word '*epikindynos*', which meant 'dangerous'. Now they were here in the square, in front of the church, joined by what looked like the whole population of Sortilas. Greeks and holidaymakers alike all had confused expressions on their faces.

'It's half past five in the morning in the UK,' Gavin commented. He was still wearing the silver hot pants and Lucie just knew he had slept in them. Despite not having a chance to really discuss or make up, things were pretty level between them. This meant that although she hadn't yet told Gavin about her hot kiss with Michalis, she would as soon as there was an opportunity... and she would maybe say she was sorry for not telling him about Simon's sexual preferences sooner.

'That's a pointless remark,' Meg said, putting thumb and forefinger to her straw-hat-covered head. 'You're on Greek time now.'

'And I need to be back in my Greek oven bedroom,' Gavin said with a sigh.

'The bed in the little yellow room was a bit soft,' Meg said. 'Not that I'm complaining. Thank you for putting me up last night.' She drew in a breath. 'But I am looking forward to seeing my apartment in Perithia and finding out what hasn't changed.'

'I'm sure this will just be about this Day of the Not Dead festival they have going on soon,' Lucie said, shielding her eyes against the first rays of sun. 'The village president seems to think that event is more important than a general election.'

'I hope it's going to be a lot more fun than that,' Gavin moaned.

Lucie noticed the door of the butcher's shop opening and she began fiddling with her short crop of hair. She wished it would grow a tiny bit quicker so she could do more things with it. If she'd had her semi-afro Sandra Oh-esque do she would be pulling all the weaving, plaiting, straightening, curling and crimping tricks to look her most desirable. The best she had managed this morning was pinching a little product into it before they were basically evacuated from the house. And there Michalis was...

He looked tousled in all the good ways. Hair slightly wavy and falling a little over his face, wearing a plain white T-shirt and black jeans, trainers on his feet. She closed her mouth up as she realised she was in danger of looking a bit too fan-girl... Nyx was next to come out, hair in space buns, a long tapered blade in her hand, apron on over jeans and feet in high wedged sandals. And there was an older man too, presumably Michalis and Nyx's father.

Then everyone was reaching for their ears as an air raid siren sound filled the square and even the cats lounging outside the church pricked up their ears and put disdainful looks on their furry faces.

Melina Hatzi swept into the square, carrying a wooden pallet in one hand and a megaphone in the other, and everyone seemed to move to give her space. Apparently her authority continued unabated even when she was wearing a dressing gown and slippers... Lucie watched her put down the pallet and stand on it like it was a stage at a music festival.

She began to talk in Greek and suddenly a hush descended and people began to look at each other with concern.

'What's she saying?' Gavin asked Lucie as if she were suddenly fluent in the native tongue.

'I don't know,' Lucie said, continuing to watch people's body language and hoping she could garner information that way.

'I got the words "this morning",' Meg offered. 'And then, I think, the word for "road" but nothing after that.'

This was mad. People were making noises of alarm now, then followed a low hubbub that suggested the main headline news had already been imparted. She was going to find them a translator.

'All I really want to know is... when do you think we can go back to bed?' Gavin asked.

★

Michalis saw Lucie approaching and he couldn't help but smile. Last night, holding her in his arms had been the antidote to everything he had endured over the last year. The whole date had been a reminder of how beautiful and simple life could be if you let yourself embrace it. He had checked his phone last night after he had climbed into bed, all the places he used to hang out online and... nothing. Was it possible it could really all be over? He thought about texting Chico, getting him to check his locker at the hospital. But that would involve opening up and right now, while things were quiet and balanced, he didn't want to tempt fate.

'Good morning,' Lucie said, arriving in front of them.

'Oh hey!' Nyx greeted enthusiastically. 'This is the excitement you get when you decide to take your holidays halfway up a mountain, right?!'

'Well,' Lucie began. 'We still aren't quite sure why we were woken up so early and made to come to the square but—'

'There has been a big collapse!' Nyx told her. 'Huge boulders of rock have rolled down from the top of Pantokrator and blocked the main road!'

'What?!' Lucie exclaimed, a hand going to her chest. That sounded really serious! 'Was anybody hurt?'

'I don't know!' Nyx exclaimed. 'No one asked that!' She punched Michalis in the shoulder. 'Why did you not ask that? You are the village doctor!'

'It is not as bad as my sister is saying,' Michalis said in reassuring tones, his eyes still on Lucie.

'How do you know this?' Dimitri asked. 'Have you seen the road for yourself?'

'No, Papa,' Michalis replied. 'We have only just woken up.'

'Speak for yourself,' Dimitri groaned. 'I am going with the others to see with my own eyes.' He sauntered off towards a group of village men who seemed to be contemplating their next course of action in front of the taverna, with plenty of cigarette smoke circling between them.

'If we are locked down people will need meat,' Nyx announced excitedly. 'I have been wanting to get rid of a couple of elderly cows for a while.'

'Locked down!' Lucie exclaimed.

Michalis drew her closer to him and spoke softly. 'I am sure Nyx is exaggerating. In all the years I have lived here, the village has never been locked down in this way. Sure, there have been a few landslips, but the road has always been passable.'

'But… what if it is worse this time?' Lucie asked. 'Nyx said "boulders". Boulders aren't little stones, they're slabs that barricade things. What if they've barricaded the village and there's no longer any connection to anywhere else?'

Michalis could see Lucie was close to panicking and he sensed this reaction wasn't just to the fact there was something blocking the road. He knew it was the word 'lockdown' and what that meant to literally everyone on the planet. It spoke of fear and isolation and not knowing when it would truly end. But it was especially poignant to them as medical workers… It was a word that had signalled all the horrific things that followed for months and months.

'Listen,' he told her. 'Whatever has happened, we Greeks are very resourceful. And, unlike a real lockdown, without government rules telling us to stay where we are, we will simply set about making this blockage disappear and all will be well.'

'OK,' Lucie said, taking a deep breath. 'Because, as much as Meg likes Villa Psomi, she really wants to get to her rental apartment in Perithia and I want that too and—'

'Lucie,' Michalis said, reaching out and rubbing his thumb against her cheek. 'Everything will be OK. I promise.'

Promise. The last word stuck in his throat and his insides suddenly stung, making him drop his hand from Lucie's cheek and withdraw a step. He shouldn't have said that. He quickly smiled to hide the real emotion he was feeling and was grateful when Gavin and Meg arrived outside the butcher's.

'Is it true we're going into lockdown?' Gavin asked, his face a little pale. 'We came to Greece to get well away from all that.' He shuddered and stood close to Lucie. 'I got a flashback of that weedy Grant Shapps talking about travel corridors and quarantine. And, what I want to know is, does Corfu have to do what the rest of Greece says, or is it like England, Scotland, Ireland and Wales, where everyone made things up as they went along and did something ever so slightly different?'

'Gavin,' Meg said. 'A road has been blocked. It's not another deadly wave and more "hands, face, space".'

'Knees and toes. Knees and toes,' Gavin chanted in a sing-song way.

'Meg,' Lucie said. 'I know you really, really want to get down to Perithia today.'

'Lucie-Lou, what will be will be,' Meg said, putting an arm around her shoulders.

Michalis felt his phone buzz in the pocket of his jeans and he drew it out as Lucie, Meg and Gavin left him for Melina and a group of villagers surrounding the president. There wasn't a name on the display, just a number, but he knew exactly who had sent it. His heart dropped to the floor. So much for being in the clear. It was going to start all over again.

Thirty-Seven

Villa Psomi, Sortilas

'**R**ight,' Gavin said, clapping his hands together. 'Let's look at our options.'

Thankfully Gavin had changed out of the silver hot pants and was now wearing some slightly more substantial shorts with a watermelon print as he, Lucie and Meg sat at the large table on the terrace overlooking the pool. It was another beautifully clear day with the fragrant scent from the flowers in the garden adding a pleasing tinge to the gentle breeze.

'I don't think we have that many,' Lucie admitted with a sigh. She had taken her own eyes to look at the boulders blocking the main road out of Sortilas and they weren't the kind of stones even a team of professional strongmen could shift with ease. This was going to need machinery and Melina hadn't seemed too optimistic as to when this help would arrive. OK, so it wasn't a lockdown where everything was closed and bars had a curfew, but their Corfu world *had* just got a bit smaller.

'Positivity, Luce!' Gavin insisted. 'Our options are a lot more varied than any kind of lockdown in the UK. There you were grateful for a "cheers mate" with an Amazon delivery dude and a scotch egg with your beer.' He softened his tone a little. 'And no one is ill here. And if anyone *is* ill it's not our responsibility, there's a village doctor to take care of it.' He took a deep breath. 'Anyway, I've emailed the wine tasting people and shifted our session and I've gone through my case and assessed all the toys I brought with me.'

Toys? Those golf balls that probably weren't for golf…

'I'm so dreadfully sorry you're going to have to put up with me,' Meg stated with a sigh. 'But as soon as the road is unblocked again, I will be out of your hair.'

It did feel a little bit odd having Meg here without any warning and Lucie really hoped her sudden need for adventure *was* all the 'taking life by the scruff of the neck' she'd spoken about last night and not a ruse to keep tabs on what she was doing. At Lucie's age, if she couldn't be trusted to keep herself from harm now, when could she be?

'Speaking of hair,' Meg carried on. 'I think the new short style on you is growing on me.'

Lucie sighed. 'Well, I wish it was growing on me… literally.'

'At least you don't have eyebrow issues that no amount of searching on YouTube can really help with,' Gavin said, a finger slicking over the bare skin above his eyes.

'You could pencil them in,' Meg suggested, turning to scrutinise Gavin's forehead. 'We always added some pencil to them when I was younger.'

'Oh no,' Gavin said immediately. 'YouTube *did* show me

all about what *not* to do with eyebrows. You should have seen some of the results.'

'Well,' Meg said, closing the guidebook she had been reading and paying full attention. 'What toys do you have for us to play with?'

Lucie baulked, nudging the table with her knees and almost sending the jug of iced water into a wobbling frenzy. She really hoped this was a PEGI 12 conversation coming up.

'Well,' Gavin said, producing his bright flight bag and putting it onto the table. 'I've narrowed it down to Throw Throw Burrito or Stress Bingo.'

'Gavin, I'm not sure those are games Meg would enjoy.' If she was honest, Throw Throw Burrito stressed her out more than Stress Bingo.

'I have no idea what a game suggesting you hurl around Mexican food would achieve… but I'm ready to embrace new experiences and challenges I ordinarily wouldn't contemplate, so…' Meg said.

'And I also have a drone,' Gavin announced.

From his bag came a rather large device with rotor blades that looked like it might be capable of Yodel delivery if the packaging wasn't too over-the-top.

'Wow,' Lucie said. It was all she could manage. In truth her mind was still working over her last interaction with Michalis. He had seemed so pleased to see her in the square initially and then, when they had gone back to him with more news from Melina, it was like something had changed. He'd seemed distracted, a little cool even, and Lucie was left wondering if he had had a change of heart about a second date. Not that they could actually leave the village and go anywhere now…

'I've always wanted to have a go with one of these,' Meg announced, standing up and moving closer to Gavin. 'They did a video using drone footage at our last summer party at rehab. The results were fantastic and you would never have guessed the camera had spent half of its flight crashing into the hydrangeas or Mrs Lafferty's grandson.'

'Well, come hither, Meg. Let's take it for a little flight and see if we can find out what other people are getting up to around here,' Gavin suggested, plucking up the device and galloping away from the table and down into the garden.

'Gavin,' Lucie called. 'That sounds very much like spying! You can't spy on people!'

Thirty-Eight

Sortilas Village Square

Michalis hadn't ridden for at least two years, but right now it was exactly what he needed. Aboard the large black stallion, the leather reins felt good between his fingers and the strength of the animal he had to be in control of was both scary and adrenaline-fuelled.

'What are you doing?!'

It was Nyx, barrelling out of the butcher's, a heavy-looking carrier bag swinging from her fingers.

'I am going for a ride. Do you need anything from town?'

'What are you talking about? The road is blocked! We are locked down! Have you hit your head somewhere? I would say you should see a doctor but…'

'You do not ride horses on the road, Nyx.'

'Do you remember how far it is down the mountain on the tracks, and how hard?' She squinted at the animal he was astride. 'Is this Bambis? Micha, he is still a beast to ride. And last month he bit the cheek of Mavros. It looked like the face of a butchered pig.'

Michalis shrugged. Right now he didn't care how hard or how far. In fact, the further and harder the better. He needed to be doing something that wasn't practising medicine or waiting for his phone to vibrate again. This was how it always started and he couldn't deal with it again. He just couldn't.

'Micha,' Nyx said. 'What has happened?' She dipped her voice further still. 'Has Lucie dumped you already?'

Lucie. Beautiful Lucie. She had no idea about any of this. Perhaps relief would never come. Maybe it would always be this way. The second he let his guard down and thought there was a chance for something brighter, the reminders returned.

'There is nothing you want? Good,' Michalis said, avoiding all the questions. He rubbed the horse's neck, fingers digging deep into its coat.

'Micha, you are not acting like yourself,' Nyx said, looking like she wanted to find a safe space to put the carrier bag down. 'I am… going to get Papa.'

'Why would you do that?' Michalis asked her, annoyed now.

'Because you are being crazy. And you are the sensible one in our family. You have all the brains in your head and… I have all the brains in this bag.' Nyx held the carrier aloft but then quickly put it down again. 'Mrs Pappas is making grotesque lollipops for the Day of the Not Dead festival.'

'And you think *I* am being crazy?' Michalis mocked.

'Do you have surgery today?'

'No.'

'Come and help me in the shop.'

'You do not need my help.'

'Well, I know I said it was good for him but... Papa is getting a little slow.'

'Please do not tell him that before I get back.'

'Micha! I won't let you go anywhere on that... wild thing!'

Right on cue, Bambis let out a bloodcurdling whinny, rearing up on his back legs. But then, as Michalis tightened his hold and made the horse snatch on the bit, Bambis finished his attempt at dominance with a steam-riddled snort. This was what he needed. Bambis to take him for a ride that would ease his anxiety just for a few hours, two raging individuals warring with each other for supremacy.

'See!' Nyx said, stumbling back from stray hooves and fiery eyes.

'Your concern is appreciated but it is not necessary.'

'Micha, please stay here.'

Now his sister really did look concerned for his welfare. He softened his tone. 'Nyx, I will be fine. I have ridden Bambis many times.'

'But, I swear to you, he has become more psychotic with age,' Nyx replied.

'Well,' Michalis began, thighs gripping the brute of an animal. 'So have you, but we deal with this.' He dug his heels into the horse's girth. '*Ela, Bambis!*'

Thirty-Nine

Villa Psomi, Sortilas

Lucie powered up and down the pool, feeling the movement of every single muscle as she swam length after length. This holiday was already doing wonders for her energy and mental well-being. Who wouldn't feel that little bit more relaxed amid a seascape and undulating mountains, eating the freshest local food and soaking up all the sunshine? She stood as she reached the shallow end of the pool, smoothing her hair down and looking over at Gavin and Meg, who were poring over Gavin's mobile phone, which both controlled the drone and sent back the images from the camera.

'Lucie,' Meg shouted across the terrace. 'This is quite remarkable.'

'I can almost see what book that woman is reading on the beach!' Gavin said delightedly.

Lucie shook her head as she strode up the pool steps, then walked to the sun lounger where she had left her towel. 'I thought we agreed no spying.'

'We haven't been spying,' Meg insisted.

Lucie slipped on sliders and walked over to join them again.

'We've gone all the way along the coast from Almyros to Acharavi and now we've got to Roda,' Gavin informed. 'It's crazy good. Come and see.'

Lucie shook her head. 'I'll pass.' She sat down in the egg chair that was finally dry from its expedition in the pool. 'What's the range on that thing? You've been at this for over half an hour and the battery can't last forever.'

'Fuck!' Gavin exclaimed.

'You're not too unrelated to me that I wouldn't wash your mouth out, young man,' Meg warned.

'Sorry, Meg. But Luce is right. We're probably touching on the five kilometre limit and I think the box said forty minutes' flight time. We need to turn this baby around and get it back here. Oh!'

'What is it?' Meg asked. 'Another idiot on water skis?'

Lucie looked over at Gavin and saw her friend was holding his hand to his chest like it might be concealing a fatal poisoned dart. The last time she had seen that expression was when the hospital canteen had completely run out of coffee. She swung out of the egg chair and went to join them.

'No... it's... but it can't be... I...'

'Gavin, what is it?' Lucie asked, looking over his shoulder.

Gavin shook his phone up and down as the screen began to fail, the picture distorting. 'Oh bloody hell! Now I can't see at all!'

'Is the battery going?' Meg asked, looking intently too. 'What if it just runs out? Will the drone fall out of the sky like the one at my rehab centre did?'

'I don't know,' Gavin admitted. 'This is the first time I've flown it anywhere other than around my communal garden.'

'Perhaps it wasn't wise to steer it so far away,' Lucie suggested.

'It's a bit late to say that now!'

'Well, good luck, dear,' Meg said, getting to her feet. 'I think it's high time I had a dip in that pool.'

Lucie waited for Meg to leave the terrace, then she watched Gavin begin to perspire, fingers pressing at his phone screen as intermittently the drone's footage started to come back. 'Will you get it back here?' she asked softly.

'I don't know,' he admitted. 'I got carried away and then… I thought I saw someone I knew on the beach.'

'It wasn't Cher, was it?' Lucie asked, smiling.

'No,' Gavin said. 'I could have sworn it was Simon.' He took a breath. 'But that's impossible, right? Because, why would Simon be in Corfu?'

'You and Meg have been looking at that screen too much,' Lucie told him. 'It's boggled your eyes.'

'Yeah, probably,' Gavin said with a sigh. 'But you know what they say about imagining people, right?'

Was there a wise old saying for mistaken identity? She looked at Gavin quizzically. 'I don't think I do know.'

'Well, if I was ready to forget him and move on I would be moving on, wouldn't I? I would be looking at all the hot Greek-ness on the beach, not thinking I've seen Simon. I mean, there was this one guy Meg pointed out who was actually nude and honed like an artist had sculpted him that way, but apart from that…'

'Gavin,' Lucie said as the drone gave them pictures of an

olive grove rich with trees and those silvery green leaves, gnarly trunks aged by decades of growth. 'I am sorry about not telling you about Simon. I really am.'

Gavin shrugged. 'S'alright. I shouldn't have reacted like a queen bitch.'

'So we're good now?' Lucie asked. 'Even with Meg turning up and moving in?'

'I've always liked Meg,' Gavin admitted. 'I just have to watch my swearing, not be too overtly gay and remember that she still thinks make-up is only for girls.'

'Gavin!' Lucie exclaimed. 'She was the one suggesting eyebrow pencil.'

'Oh shit,' Gavin said, eyes on stalks as he surveyed the drone's progress. 'I'm not sure it *is* going to make it back. We might have to go and retrieve it.'

'Well, how are we going to do that?' Lucie asked him. 'The road's blocked.'

'Gaveen! Loosely! Someone tell me that you need transport to Perithia!'

Lucie turned her head to the approach to Villa Psomi. It was Miltos. With a fluffy friend...

Forty

'This is amazing!' Meg said happily, arm sweeping through the air like she was caressing the very existence of sunlight. 'The Greeks are so resourceful! I mean, I know everyone jokes about *avrio*, but you, Miltos, are a nation of unstoppable people. If there's a problem you think *around* it.' Meg sighed. 'In England we would be consulting health and safety guidelines before we even dared to consider another route out of the village.'

Meg was aboard the donkey Miltos had acquired from who-knew-where, riding side-saddle like she was one of those elegant Victorian ladies. It had taken a little persuasion for Meg to get up onto the animal. She said she hadn't been on the scales for a few months, but last time she had looked at the numbers she was still too weighty for some of the Amazon value stepladders. But Miltos had insisted the donkey was a working animal used to service of this kind and was well-treated by his owners. And then he had winked and told Meg that she was the perfect size in his opinion. Ever the charmer...

However, Lucie still wasn't on board with the whole idea. The main road out of the village was impassable and Melina had been insistent that they were locked down until such a time that help arrived. Melina had looked a lot less than her usual confident self as villagers and tourists alike threw questions at her. *Would essential supplies still get in? Was the trip to Corfu Town and the fortresses cancelled?* So, why then, was her aunt now on a mule and why were she and Gavin, with their most substantial shoes on, picking their way through the mountain tracks following Miltos's lead? Was it because Meg wanted her own space in the apartment in Perithia? Or was it more that Lucie was keen to have her Greek life back *sans* her aunt? Now she felt a bit guilty.

'Well, I think this is a wonderful idea,' Gavin said, sucking in a deep breath. 'I was going a bit stir-crazy back at the house.'

Despite having trainers on his feet, Gavin was still wearing the watermelon shorts and a tiny tank top as he carried Meg's suitcase. Lucie hoped he was suitably sun-creamed because this track – all rocks, grass and impassable to vehicles except maybe a mountain bike – was permanently right in line with the scorching sun.

'We've only known about the road being blocked for a few hours,' Lucie reminded him. 'Ordinarily you wouldn't have even been out of bed by now.'

'Well, I still remember the Christmas-that-wasn't-really-Christmas when we all wished we'd made a move a bit sooner. Five days to see family, wait, no, one day only but not if you live in tier four. I'm still a bit wary now. That BBC Breaking News tone comes on my phone and I'm out the door and heading to Sainsbury's just in case there's an EU embargo on booze.'

Lucie had worked every day over last Christmas and chosen not to see Meg indoors at all. The first time around with the lockdown, everything had been the new different. It had been scary, but everyone was in a similar position – staying at home, finding new indoor hobbies or buying a bike. The second forms of lockdown segregated people and when the third lockdown had come in it had led to overwhelming and total desperation. During the tough times of the winter when hospital admissions had risen all over again, the free food had stopped being offered to NHS staff and no one clapped them from their doorstep anymore. Lucie shivered and tried to rearrange her thoughts. Sortilas wasn't in a lockdown like that. Everyone was well. No one was going to die...

'What's his name, Miltos?' Meg called, somehow her body naturally poised on the animal like she had been born to take this ride down mountain. Lucie watched her aunt reach forward and stroke its ears.

'Tonika,' Miltos informed. 'And he is a she.'

'Oh, how wonderful!' Meg answered.

Everything was wonderful to Meg here on Corfu. The weather was wonderful. The food was wonderful. The smell of the cypress trees was wonderful. Lucie couldn't deny that as every day passed she felt somewhere near the same, but what *wasn't* wonderful was the fact she had texted Michalis to tell him they were being escorted down the mountain to Perithia and he had yet to respond. Something was definitely off and she didn't know what. Had she done something wrong? Was she putting too much energy into this chance of a holiday romance?

'Does this happen often?' Lucie asked their guide, taking care where to put her feet on the next section of rough, barely-there track.

'You think I take beautiful ladies on rides with donkeys every day?' Miltos inquired.

'No,' Lucie said. He probably would, given half the chance. 'I mean the road getting blocked like that.'

'Most years we have one or two slips of the land,' Miltos informed. 'Corfu is a green and beautiful island because of the rain. In the winter it rains and rains, and it rains so much parts of the island come away and fall down. This time it is because of the tremor.' He stilled and then... 'Crack!'

Lucie jumped at the last blasted word and almost slipped up on a smooth shiny stone when her trainers lost traction. Taking a breath, she regrouped. Miltos had given them a pep talk about potential wildlife on their trek down into the bigger village and snakes had been mentioned. It was OK for Meg, high up on her saddle and Tonika's hooves taking the fallout of any slithering creatures arriving in close proximity. Gavin had missed the talk, needing the loo, and Lucie was glad. He screamed every time the grass shifted.

'I remember one particularly fierce storm,' Meg reminisced, flapping heat away from her face like her fingers were a fan. 'Petros and I were caught out in the woods.'

'Oh really, Meg!' Gavin exclaimed. 'And what were you doing in the woods with a hot Greek?'

'Petros knew all about wildflowers,' she began. 'He had brought me to see this particular field that was awash with cyclamen. I still remember it now, it was the most gorgeous pinky purple colour.'

'Get to the storm bit. I'm sensing a seeking of shelter,' Gavin answered, tramping hard and disturbing two butterflies.

'Well,' Meg continued. 'The heavens just opened. It had been such a calm, blue-sky day and then it was exactly like someone had turned on a fire hose and directed it right at us.'

'That actually sounds divine right now,' Gavin sighed, fanning his tank top out a little.

'What happened then?' Lucie wanted to know. She hadn't heard this story before. Just like she hadn't heard anything about this love affair her aunt had had in her youth. But perhaps it was going to shed a little light on the psyche of Greek men to help her understand Michalis.

'Don't tell me you huddled under an olive tree, because even *I* know you should never shelter under a tree during a thunderstorm. Was there thunder?' Gavin inquired.

'There was,' Meg said, nodding. 'And Petros led us under the branches of this fat, wide, olive tree that seemed quite spooky in the fading light. Neither of us had coats.'

'What?' Lucie said. 'But, like Gavin just said, everyone knows you don't get under a tree in a thunderstorm. *You've* told me that so many times yourself.' Lucie actually had a list in her head of all the things she must or mustn't do – not walk under ladders, always salute magpies, throw salt over her shoulder, never take drugs...

'Pah!' Miltos scoffed. 'What is this fairy tale of not standing beneath a tree? In Greece, when it is raining or there is a storm, we stand anywhere we will not get wet. It is as simple as that.'

'I'm getting to love the Greeks,' Gavin announced. 'There are some things they really don't give a shit about. I totally respect that.'

'What happened then?' Lucie asked, brushing a mosquito off her leg before it could suck.

'Oh my God, Lucie, I don't think we need Meg to go any further,' Gavin began. 'Use your imagination.'

'Petros was a gentleman,' Meg replied.

'Oh, that's boring!' Gavin chimed.

'There was passion, but... we both kept our clothes on just in case any goat herders came along,' Meg finished off.

Gavin squealed in delight and Lucie just shook her head. She was smiling a little at Meg's tale of youth, but she was beginning to realise that there really was a lot more to her aunt than only the steadying solid influence she had always been. Why did that side of Meg never come to the fore now? And, if Meg remembered how it felt to have a Greek adventure, did she need to be quite such a stickler for safety in her holiday advice when it came to Lucie? Because, as far as Lucie knew, no one had ever died from not wearing a cardigan when there was a cool breeze. She sighed, then took a second to admire the rocky terrain as it wound down and around towards the village that still wasn't yet in sight. Peaks and troughs, bumps and plateaus. Just like life. It made her think about her mum again. Her long, glossy dark hair she always wore loose according to the photos – until she'd cut it all off. Wide eyes that spoke of innocence, kohled with thick black liner that spoke of anything but. School uniform skirt a little shorter than it should be. Meg only offered up stories from Rita's childhood, the times before Rita began to defy rules. Two sisters bonding over ice cream, farm animals and arcade games on a summer trip. But these stories were almost worthless to Lucie. It was like they had been fabricated by a film studio only dealing in happy-ever-afters. The rest of the tales came as intense warnings about the risks Rita took, her carefree, reckless nature that had led to her downfall. But people were always multifaceted, like Lucie was finding about Meg. And *those* were still the stories she was missing. That was the detail she needed if she wanted to find out who her mum had really been.

'What was the last name of this man Petros?' Miltos asked, one hand on the rope he was gently leading the donkey with.

'Oh, I have no idea,' Meg answered with a breathy sigh. 'In those days I wasn't so much about the details.'

'Just about the pecs and the mane of hair – like me, I bet.' Gavin gave a sigh of longing. 'I might have to change my criteria soon. Men with good hair seem to be cruel.'

Suddenly Tonika stopped dead in her tracks and Meg rocked in her position on its back, hands coming down onto the donkey's body to aid balance. She stroked its mane and whispered a platitude.

'Whoa! Tonika, what is the problem?' Miltos asked, stroking the donkey's neck and observing its expression as if he could read its thoughts. The donkey didn't appear to want to walk any further. That was bad news considering Lucie calculated they were only about halfway and the heat of the day was dehydrating them fast. Luckily they had been sensible and packed plenty of water and snacks for them and for Tonika.

'Come on,' Gavin urged the animal, giving its bottom a little pat. 'I saw this happen once at a village fair when I was six. This poor donkey had been giving rides to this terribly large child at my school called Rafe Beesley. Rafe Beesley's family were rich, so basically they just kept paying for him to have ride after ride after ride and no one else – no one lighter – got a turn. And the donkey had just had enough. It planted its hooves in the field and refused to budge. Four men had to pick it up and carry it to the horsebox.'

Miltos let out a snort of annoyance. 'Four men? They could not be Greeks.' He patted Meg's hand. 'You must know that if Tonika does not move, I will carry you to Perithia myself and then I will come back for the donkey.'

Lucie walked a few steps away from them, a little further down the path. 'What's that?' Straining her eyes and shielding her face from the bright sunlight, she tried to look through and past the bushes outlining their path as the track weaved around the base of Mount Pantokrator. And then there was a sound, a stamping, and an expelling of air. It was some kind of animal.

'Oh, fuck! That sounds like a bull!' Gavin screamed. 'Can I get on the donkey with you? What was her weight limit again?'

'Gaveen,' Miltos interrupted. '*You* need to be more Greek. And there are no bulls on this mountain. Although... there was the time Mr Leonardis had one of his breakdowns and let his animals loose. We still look for one of the cows.'

Lucie didn't think it was a bull. She took a few more steps, cautious but inquisitive to find out what was there.

'Lucie,' Meg called. 'Please be careful.'

She gave an eye roll, knowing her aunt couldn't see. She was going to be careful. She was *always* careful. But she also wasn't going to stand there and wait until the donkey decided if it was going to start to move again. She was going to find out what had spooked it and what sounded like it was waiting just around the corner...

Forty-One

What sort of idiot was he? He was a doctor! And he had come out here, to a wilderness, in the heat of the day, riding an animal he knew had the potential to be dangerous if his wits were not with him. And now here Michalis was, propped up against the trunk of a tree, examining himself for the worst of his injuries. He had no water and Bambis had run off. This was bad. This was exactly how people died. Maybe this was his karma for ignoring the messages and calls from Thekli. He closed his eyes. To begin with, when the contact had begun all those weeks ago, he had called his ex-girlfriend and tried to reason with her. But he had soon realised that no matter what he said, Thekli was going to hold him responsible for what had happened at the hospital. She was not someone who could see any other alternative conclusions. Her grief was completely entangled with her loathing for him, like they were one and the same thing. She'd hated him for calling time on their relationship no matter that it was for good reason. And she hated him all the more for failing her family when they had needed him most.

He took a long, slow breath. He shouldn't think about that now. He had to focus on keeping himself alert to his surroundings and find out where the worst bleeding was coming from. He unfastened his shirt with a shaking hand, trying to halt the panicked feelings that always kicked in as the body's natural response. Adrenaline, fight, close down…

A branch had caught him in the midriff and had torn away a section of flesh that was bleeding profusely. He quickly bunched up his shirt and used it to plug the gap. He guessed any more analysis of his injuries would have to wait. He simply had to hope that he found the strength to get up and that his hurting ankle could stand the walk either back to Sortilas or down to Perithia, because his mobile phone was where he'd left it, face down on his bed.

'Hello! Er, what's the word for "hello"… er… *yassas*! *Yassas* is anyone there?'

Now Michalis was *really* concerned. His mind was imagining the one other person who had kept filling his head the whole time during his hack through the Corfu countryside. There had been all those unwelcome rewinds of what Thekli had engineered and then there had been the moments he had spent with Lucie. Lucie's voice was coming to him now like a mirage for the ears. He closed his eyes and pressed the shirt to his wound, attempting to slow his heart rate.

'Oh my God! Oh!'

Michalis snapped open his eyes then as the voice grew louder. Could it really be? His vision started to blur but he thought he could also see Bambis again.

'Michalis!'

And then he wasn't only hearing Lucie, but smelling her too. It was that gentle fragrance that reminded him of summer. A light sun cream, cherries, skin…

'What's happened?' Lucie asked, knees hitting the ground next to him. 'Were you on this horse?'

'He is here?' Michalis asked. 'He is mainly wild. He will run again.' His side ached as he attempted to shift position.

'I have tied him to a tree with knots I scored badges for in Guides,' Lucie informed. 'And Miltos, Meg and Gavin will be here any second.'

Michalis didn't understand. 'What are you doing here?' Had Nyx raised an alarm? He had not been gone all that long. He knew his sister had not wanted him to ride, but had she really been that concerned she had taken action already?

'We have a donkey,' Lucie told him, as if that went all the way towards a full explanation.

Now he wondered if he had hit his head in the fall. He leaned left and then right. No, he didn't think so. As he wasn't wearing a helmet, he probably wouldn't be here at all if he had fallen on that part of himself.

'I'm going to have a look at that injury,' Lucie told him.

'It needs stitches, but it is OK,' Michalis replied right away.

'I know you're the doctor but you're also the patient and I'm not sure you should be making the decisions right now.'

'Lucie…'

'No,' she said with authority. 'I'm having a look right now.'

Before he could say anything else, Lucie had whipped away his shirt, made a quick assessment and jammed the material back on the wound, replacing his hand to maintain the pressure.

'Well, it can't carry on bleeding like that and yes it needs stitches. Where's the nearest hospital?'

He couldn't help it. Despite the pain and his light-headedness, he laughed. 'Corfu Town.'

'Where I flew in to?' She shook her head, looking dissatisfied with his answer. 'Anywhere nearer that can deal with it?'

He nodded. 'Yes, my surgery.'

'Michalis!'

'What?' he queried. 'You are a nurse. You can do the stitches.'

'I want a doctor's opinion on it first,' Lucie stated.

She was holding his shoulder, tilting him to the right a little so as to keep his body in the best position for his wound. She was so beautiful and he saw that deep genuine concern for him reflected in her eyes…

'You *have* a doctor's opinion,' Michalis answered. 'Mine.'

'You know that's not what I meant.'

'And… we had a conversation about nurses being the real decision makers when it counts,' he reminded her. 'When the consultants are… too busy at their meetings or… are delayed saving the lives of others. That's what you do every… day of your life.'

'Michalis, I…'

'I am not going to the hospital,' he said. 'Please know that.'

Lucie saw he definitely meant it and the tone of his voice also told her the discussion was over. But how was she going to get him back to Sortilas?

'Loosely!'

Miltos's shout broke into her thought pattern. They were coming now, Tonika obviously finally moving, and between them they would think of something to do. Wouldn't they?

'Over here!' she called.

'Does he have the fruit van... somewhere?' Michalis asked, the beginnings of a wry grin on his lips.

'That thing?' Lucie said, adjusting his position again as gently as she could. 'I'm unsure of its suitability as a vehicle on proper tarmac, let alone on a track like this. On parts of it, it was barely wide enough for the donkey.'

'You really have a donkey?' Michalis asked, with half a laugh.

'Did you think I was making it up?' She saw sweat was beading on his forehead now and she was concerned it wasn't because of the summer temperatures. She hoped she hadn't missed anything. She had taken his word for it that he wasn't hurt anywhere else...

'Oh, good heavens!' Meg announced as the donkey – still a little hesitant – arrived at the scene.

'What's happened? Shall we call an ambulance? I know the Greek number for that. I memorised it before we came,' Gavin gasped.

'It is three digits,' Miltos remarked, looking bemused.

'No... ambulances,' Michalis spoke up.

It looked like talking was taking considerable effort now and Lucie turned away from her patient for a second and looked to Gavin, who was stripping himself of his tangerine flight bag. 'Gavin, can you bring over the water?'

'I am on it,' Gavin stated, pulling out an unopened two-litre bottle of Zagori and hurrying over.

'An ambulance would never get up here,' Miltos said

rather unhelpfully. 'It sometimes takes hours for one to arrive in Sortilas by the main road.'

'I don't suppose you have a first aid kit?' Lucie asked Gavin.

'Of course I do. I never go anywhere without a first aid kit and a golf ball.'

Lucie swallowed. He was her best friend and she really didn't know where these balls fitted into things... then again, perhaps it was best not to know exactly where they fitted into things.

'You get him drinking and I'll get the pack,' Gavin said. He passed Lucie the bottle of water and headed back to Tonika.

She unscrewed the lid on the bottle and proffered it towards Michalis. He looked very pale now and he either needed to get into the shade or move out of here and back to the village. 'Here, drink some of this.'

He moved his mouth over the bottle as Lucie slowly tipped. She watched him ingest some, but a little spilled out over his lips. Before she had thought about it she caught the droplets on her finger, touching his bottom lip as she did so. Those hot lips together with the bare torso would ordinarily be ticking all the lust boxes. But he was her patient now...

'Miltos, help me get down from this donkey,' Meg ordered.

'No, Meg,' Lucie countered, refastening the lid of the bottle and turning to look at her aunt. Meg was rocking frustratedly, attempting to shuffle herself off the mule who was starting to pad at the ground, its eyes on the black horse who thankfully currently seemed to be more snort than buck. 'You're going to Perithia, like we planned. Stay where you are.'

Lucie was working things out in her head. Michalis. The first aid kit. How far it was back up the mountain. If Michalis was alert enough to guide them...

'Gavin,' she called, decided. 'Once we've dressed this wound as much as we can, I want you to take half the water supplies and go with Miltos and Meg to Perithia.'

'O-K,' Gavin said, scurrying back over with a zip-up pouch. 'And what are you going to do?'

Lucie took a deep breath and eyed the tied-up horse. 'I'm going to ride Michalis back to Sortilas.'

Forty-Two

'I want you to tell me if you start to exhibit any of the signs of shock,' Lucie ordered. She couldn't quite believe she was in this position, but she and Michalis were on the back of a so-far-behaving Bambis, her in front and Michalis behind, his arm around her waist, his body weight leaning against her. She knew nothing about riding, could count on one thumb the number of times she had been on a horse, but her focus was on getting Michalis to the surgery conscious and not too dehydrated.

'I have no chest pain. I am not confused. I am sweating profusely only because it is warm today,' Michalis answered, his voice so very close to her ear, his breath was tickling the skin. He was still shirtless, body slathered in sun cream, a procedure that Gavin had insisted he helped with. If they weren't in the absolute midst of a crisis it would be almost holiday romance goals.

'How is your pain everywhere else?' Lucie asked. She was digging her heels into the horse a little, urging him to move a bit faster. She didn't really want him to take off like he was a steed under Oisin Murphy, but this plodding was taking much longer than she was comfortable with with an injured person behind her.

'Manageable,' came the answer.

'That's doctor-speak for "it hurts like hell but I'm damned if I'm going to admit it". I think if I asked what your pain level was from one to ten, you would probably say something like "four".'

'Maybe a three and a half,' he answered with a jagged breath.

Lucie shook the reins a little. Yes, the terrain was rocky and clumpy but didn't horses thrive on that sort of land? Weren't they clever? Knowing exactly where to plant their hooves?

'You do not need Bambis to go any faster,' Michalis whispered.

'I do,' she replied, knowing a little fear was creeping into her voice. 'Because you've had the maximum amount of ibuprofen and paracetamol and we need to get that wound properly cleaned and sewn up.'

'I actually had one more of each tablet when your back was turned,' Michalis told her.

'What?!' Her whole spinal cord reacted to that statement and set off a concoction of emotions she seemed to have no control over. Before Lucie even realised it, tears were springing out of her eyes and her hands started to tremble. 'Why... why would you do that?'

'Because, you are right, it hurts more than a three-point-five and I knew the recommended dose on your English medicines was too low.'

'What are you talking about? You... can't go taking more

pills than the packets tell you. And you're a doctor!' Her heart was thumping against her rib cage now, like someone was playing basketball with it, throwing it against the wall time after time.

'Lucie,' he breathed close. 'An extra two hundred and fifty micrograms of each tablet is not going to kill me.'

She closed her eyes then. Not a sensible move when she was in charge of a horse she had been told could turn into a marauding monster at the flick of a grass blade. She opened them again and tried to concentrate on the task in hand. 'You shouldn't have done that. You're *my* patient.' She sniffed, attempting to conceal the depth of feeling that was leaking out and wetting Bambis's mane. 'You said I was making the decisions.'

'And... you are,' Michalis responded. 'What is wrong?'

'Nothing.'

'I can tell you are crying.'

'Nope.'

'Lucie...'

'No.'

'Does this have something to do with the pain in your back? The fact that you do not take medication.'

Lucie sighed, pulling the rein back a little so Bambis could navigate a tricky ascent to the next section of track. Michalis had remembered what she'd said on the beach outside Fuego Bar and somehow he was putting two and two together. Thoughts of her mum were flooding her mind now. All the grief she had witnessed but was too young to understand, the sketchy explanations even now, being torn between asking for details and clinging onto the sugar-spun reality Meg continued to always feed her...

'Just because I work with medicine,' she said to Michalis. 'It doesn't mean I don't believe there are alternative ways to heal.'

'I agree.'

'I would rather… lie on my acupressure mat for twenty minutes and relieve pain that way.'

'I agree. But… Gavin did not seem to have one of those in his orange bag.'

His comment drew a smile from her and she gave a short laugh. 'Gavin has literally *everything* else in that orange bag, believe me.'

'And I am grateful,' Michalis told her, his body somehow moving even closer into her.

The heat from him, coupled with the heat rising up from Bambis's saddle and the sunlight shining down on her shoulders, gave rise to an internal quiver that made Lucie have to swallow. Could she tell him about her mum? Was that the sort of thing you shared with a holiday romance? Columns in women's magazines did seem to think that sharing worries with a stranger did wonders for the soul…

'Pass to me the reins,' Michalis said.

'No way.'

'We can go a little faster, but Bambis is strong.'

Lucie held onto the leather straps, making tight fists and steeling herself for greater motion. 'Yes,' she breathed with renewed determination. 'But so am I.'

Forty-Three

Villa Psomi, Sortilas

'I don't know how to get you down.'

Lucie had descended from Bambis, secured him to the fence outside the property and she was now looking up at Michalis like the bottom could, at any moment, drop out of her world. Michalis stilled, putting a hand to his side where thankfully the dressing was holding its own. He had seen that look before. Many times. But, yes, that one time had been the most haunting. It was the expression that had hurt him the most, the one that stayed with him and was present during every procedure. The one he saw when he got those text messages from Thekli.

'I can get down,' Michalis insisted quickly. He shifted around and onto his good side. OK, so it wasn't going to be as easy as he had hoped. Bambis was not a small horse and the animal was currently stamping on the courtyard and blowing steam from his nose as if he was inviting the grasshoppers into a duel.

'Don't be stupid, Michalis. Let me help you.'

Perhaps now was not the time for being brave. He didn't want to risk injuring himself further for the sake of needing to be like that poster image of himself he loathed. He shook his head. 'OK.'

'OK,' Lucie said, arriving at his side. 'Just gently ease yourself over and I'll catch you. Well... you know... I'll grab you... by the jeans or something and... we'll see what happens next.'

Michalis didn't doubt her inner strength, but he knew once he was sliding off this animal the only way was down and he didn't expect there to be the greatest outcome if he couldn't find his balance when he hit the floor. But, he had to get off the horse to get himself repaired and, as much as he hated to admit it, he was feeling weakened.

'OK... go,' Lucie directed.

The pain ripped through him as he tried to slow his slide, but the horse's coat and his bare flesh slick with perspiration was not the best combination. He landed, feet meeting cobbles, and then listed, preparing to feel the ground on every single other part of his body. But then he stopped leaning, his balance catching up and Lucie, as she had promised, captured him.

He was suckered to her, her petite form wound around him tight, softening the jarring, stopping the toppling and easing his body into a safe and secure dismount. She looked up at him then, a smile forming on her lips and, despite the agony that was currently rolling through him, he couldn't help but mirror her expression.

'Caught, like a boss,' she told him.

God, he liked her. He liked her so very much it was crippling him on the inside. But Thekli catching up with him again, taunting him, wanting to hurt him and punish him, it was surely proof that, when you got attached to someone, the price you paid in the end was always some form of heartache. Was it worth taking the chance?

'Do you have the spare key for my surgery?' he asked, shifting from her embrace and hobbling across the courtyard to the white wooden door.

'Yes,' Lucie answered. 'I will go in and get it.'

Lucie had put Michalis on a wobbly and frankly archaic-looking 'examination table' with the plastic covering coming away from the foam on some of the edges, and then she had looked in the cupboard he had directed her to for the things she needed to inspect this wound, sterilise it and close up.

'Michalis,' she said, raising her head from the supplies. 'There's barely anything in here. I don't know if we have enough—'

'I did stitches on a goat bite the other day. There are suture kits and sterilising wipes... and there is ouzo.'

She looked back in and located the alcohol. 'You said there are sterilising wipes.' She came back up, bottle in hand.

'Sure,' he answered. 'The ouzo is not to sterilise, it is for me to drink. And for you, if you are going to panic about this.'

Why was she panicking? This was all in a day's work for her. She was good at stitching, *really* good, much better than Gavin and he freely admitted it. Except her patients never usually made her weak under the PPE. But there *was* no adequate PPE here, only a box of large-sized gloves that looked like they were going to be gigantic on her hands. She drew them out anyway.

'The gloves will be too big for your hands,' Michalis said, as if reading her mind. 'All my health screening is up to date.'

The words 'health screening' reminded her of the welcome goat excretions on their first day here. 'Mine too,' she answered.

'Then just wash your hands and let's get this done.' He held his hand out for the ouzo bottle.

'Please don't look at me doing this,' Lucie begged. Her hands were shaking as she worked with the needle driver and toothed tweezers, drawing the silk through his skin. The studio room was exceedingly hot and this wound was deeper than it had first looked. But, on the plus side, it didn't appear there was anything inside the tear and she had cleaned it to within an inch of its life while Michalis gritted his teeth and kept silent with the pain. 'There's a fantastic view from that window over there and it's so much nicer than watching your skin being sewn together.'

'You are doing very neat work,' Michalis told her.

'I know,' Lucie answered. 'I am very good at this.'

'I can see.'

He was smiling now and she knew those extra tablets he had popped, plus the amount of ouzo he had ingested since she handed him the bottle, had gone some way to stabilising him. She would feel happier if he had at least another litre of water when she had finished though.

'But there is something you are not so good at,' Michalis continued.

'Oh, there's a whole list of things I'm not so good at and apparently now I can add riding a banana to it.'

'Sharing,' Michalis said, putting the ouzo bottle to his lips again and taking a swig.

'I think you might want to swap that spirit for water. I shared a whole horse with you down a very unsuitable track for what felt like hours.' It had been over an hour but hadn't quite reached two. She had had confirmation from Gavin that he, Meg, Miltos and Tonika had reached Perithia without incident and they were now all receiving refreshments from the *cafeneon*. And, once they had found somewhere for Tonika to rest up for the evening, Gavin and Miltos had been offered a ride back up to the village by rickshaw. She could only imagine how bone-shakingly tough that was going to be on all of them. And would it really fit along some of those narrower sections of the path?

'Why do you not take pills?' Michalis asked. 'Will you tell me the real reason for that?'

Lucie paused in her stitching. The Greek aperitif seemed to be making Michalis very forward. And his directness was unavoidable as there was nowhere for her to go. You couldn't exactly run away with stitching implements in your hands...

'I've never taken them,' Lucie admitted.

'Never?'

'Never.'

'But... if you get a fever then—'

'Cold flannel. Get in a lukewarm bath. Suck on ice pops. Drink water.'

'A headache?'

'Cold compress. Magnesium. More water.' She sighed. 'I could do this for hours if you want to name another ailment.'

'But why?'

There really was no backing out now. And perhaps it would do her good to be unburdened. How could she criticise Meg for never talking about her mum if she couldn't open up herself?

'My grandparents and my aunt kept all medication in a locked cupboard in our house,' she began, refocussing on drawing the thread through Michalis's skin. 'They had to have *some* tablets for certain ongoing conditions they suffered from, but apart from that, no one in our house took painkillers and definitely nothing *more* than painkillers.'

He didn't say anything and Lucie knew that it wasn't because he had nothing to say, but that he was giving her space to continue if she wanted to.

'My mum,' she began. 'Died from a drug overdose.'

There. It was said. Out loud. The words were in the room, big, fat, grey and packing a trunk. Did she feel better about it or worse? Would it change the dynamic between them? Suddenly it was *her* who felt like the injured one…

Michalis turned his body closer and she flinched, worried for her implements and the stitches she was still knitting together. 'Michalis,' she breathed. 'You have to keep still.'

He shook his head, reaching out a hand to gently cup her face. 'No, Lucie. *You* have to be still.'

Somehow she knew exactly what he meant. She hadn't settled with her mum's death at all. It wasn't a case of coming to terms with it, it was still a case of barely acknowledging it had happened. At two years old, how could you be expected to get over anything except fear of having to start using a potty?

'I didn't know her,' Lucie whispered. 'I still don't know her now.'

'It is OK to not feel OK about it,' he told her.

The driver and tweezers still in her hands, she closed her eyes and let herself be comforted by the way Michalis was stroking her scalp so tenderly. She had spent so long being strong, keeping things together for the sake of harmony for a family who had been through so much. Externally she had given off all the right noises about coping, getting on with life, but in reality she had buried her loss like she was unaffected by it. And it had been harder to hide going through 2020 as a nurse surrounded by people losing their fight for life, family a Zoom call away shedding desperate painful tears. Lucie had cried too. So many times. For everyone she couldn't save and a little bit for her mum who would never know who she had grown to be...

'To lose someone in those circumstances... I cannot imagine,' Michalis whispered. 'Did she... was it...'

Lucie opened her eyes then. He didn't seem to be able to finish his sentence and she wasn't quite sure what he had been going to say to conclude.

'Did she... do it to herself?' Michalis asked.

'What?' What exactly was he saying? Her mind started to whirl and think back to all the times she had tried to force Meg to give her more information about her mum's death.

'I mean... was it an accident or did she... *mean* to die?'

Michalis elaborating on the question sent her whole self into a spiral. Did he mean... *suicide*? Suddenly Lucie felt sick, her stomach rising up into her throat, full of raw acidity and heartache. The implements in her hands turned to leaden weights and she struggled to keep them still, fingers trembling. She had never thought that before. Never. Never? *Had* she thought it and blotted it out of her mind along with everything else that didn't fit the vague wild-child-off-the-rails-let's-only-remember-the-good-stuff memories Meg and her grandparents had always sold her?

'Lucie,' Michalis said, quietly but firmly. 'Give me the tweezers.'

'I'm OK.'

'I *can* stitch this myself.'

'No.'

Her voice didn't sound familiar at all. It was all out-of-sorts and she didn't want to be out-of-sorts. It meant there were more unanswered questions and now they were staring her in the face, uncovered and bare. A shaft of sunlight trickled through the open studio window, falling on them, calling to Lucie that this was an opening in time she needed to step through.

Michalis put his hands over hers, warm, steady, calming, and she felt her bottom lip turn to jelly.

'I am stupid,' Michalis told her, the proximity of him forcing her to look up into his eyes.

'No... you're not,' Lucie whispered.

'I do not know the circumstances,' he carried on.

'Neither do I,' she replied. 'And that's most of the problem.'

'Please forget what I said,' Michalis said, his hands still in hers, the medical equipment almost insignificant apart from the fact it was still attached to him.

'No,' she said, shaking her head. 'I don't want to forget it. I need to face it. I need to ask things I haven't ever asked. Things I should have asked ten, fifteen years ago.'

'Lucie,' Michalis said, finally moving his hands from hers but laying them on her shoulders, soft yet supportive.

Lucie forced a smile. 'I know you want to say all the right things and… I appreciate it. But this is something I need to sort out on my own.' She firmed up her grip on the tools of her trade. 'But, first of all, I need to show you exactly how good my stitching really is and get this wound sealed. So… stop moving and… no more of that ouzo.'

As Michalis repositioned himself slightly, giving her a better access to his injury, Lucie refocussed. The person she really needed to speak to was Meg.

Forty-Four

Andino Butcher's, Sortilas

'I need to borrow your moped,' Michalis stated the evening of the following day as he walked into the shop from the apartment upstairs.

'Oh, please, do not interrupt me! I am in the centre of a difficult procedure with the tongue of a sheep.'

Nyx had plastic glasses over her eyes that seemed to have a microscopic attachment set inside them. They were almost exactly like something a surgeon would wear for an operation. The mid-sixties male customer who had been in for rabbit and steak mince was watching his sister intently as she made incisions.

'What are you doing to it?' Michalis wanted to know.

The customer looked to him. 'She tells me that the most minute cuts in certain places of the tongue will ensure a fuller flavour and more tender tasting experience.'

'My sister is a craftsman when it comes to dead animals,' Michalis confirmed with a nod.

'This I no longer doubt,' he agreed. 'Despite the condition of so-angry-itis.'

Michalis gave him a smile. 'Indeed.'

'Do not make fun of me while I am doing the most delicate type of Greek butchery,' Nyx warned.

'The keys to your moped?' Michalis asked.

'Where are you taking it?' Nyx wanted to know. 'You know that only one boulder has been removed from the road. It is still impassable to anything more than—'

'A moped,' Michalis agreed with a nod.

Suddenly the door of the butcher's burst open and Dimitri swept in, Melina hot on his heels. Both were looking panicked.

'The news, it is all over the village! You were skewered by a tree! Yesterday! You need the hospital!' Dimitri exclaimed, rushing behind the counter and pulling at the hem of Michalis's shirt.

'No… Papa… stop.' He backed away, swatting at his father's attempts to inspect him.

'People need to know if you are able to keep their appointments this week and we need to start rehearsals for the Day of the Not Dead festival. The guest of honour has to not be dead for it to be a success,' Melina announced, looking like she very much wanted to lift his shirt too. 'I tell the workers to not have breaks for cigarettes and get the blockage moved as quickly as they can. If days turn to weeks then it will impact on everything! Our new tourists will not be able to get here, and we might have to keep the old ones for longer and they will want free accommodation until they can leave and—'

A mallet was slammed down on the wooden butcher's

block and Nyx faced them all. 'Shut up!' she directed at the president. Then she turned to her brother. 'Michalis! What is going on? Did you fall from Bambis yesterday?! I said that animal was not to be trusted!'

Michalis just wanted to escape now. But he could clearly see he wasn't going to be able to get out of the shop without giving them all reassurance that he was OK. It wasn't unlike the last time he had been injured and Chico had found him on the sofa pressing arnica to his wounds.

He lifted up his shirt, displaying the rather neat knit of stitches Lucie had delivered on his side. 'I am fine.'

Everyone gasped, including the customer waiting for his tongue.

'Micha!' Nyx exclaimed, microscope glasses facing the wound like she needed to know the intricacies of it. 'It looks like someone has tried to carve a steak from you!'

'Son, we need to take you to the hospital!'

'This is not the picture of health we need for the festival!' Melina declared.

'Melina, this is my son. He is a person, not an advertisement!'

'Enough!' Michalis roared, dropping his shirt down again and spreading his arms wide. 'Please, stop this. Remember who the doctor in Sortilas is.'

Nobody said anything.

'I have been assessed, by myself. I have been repaired, by a fully qualified nurse. I am rehydrated, I took things easy last night and I am feeling almost back to normal. And Bambis is happy in his field breathing rage at the goats.' He looked directly at Dimitri then. 'I also need *your* moped and please, let the answer only be yes.'

'You cannot drive two mopeds together,' Nyx stated. 'Not even a stubborn doctor can manage that.'

'One is to be ridden by someone else.'

'It is still dangerous to pass out of the village,' Melina told him. 'This is why I order a lockdown. This is why I have the men working with floodlights tonight. If things do not open up soon everyone will be raiding Ajax's supplies for the apocalypse he has predicted.'

'Mrs Hatzi,' Michalis said. 'I know you wish to keep the village as safe as possible, but you cannot lock people down for no reason. It is an inconvenience, larger vehicles cannot get in and out, yes, but—'

'There could be another quake at any moment, or the rain will come and cause another land slip or—'

'Remember what I told you last year?' Michalis asked her.

Melina nodded a little soberly. 'You told me that if the villagers all took the elixir you made then…'

'Not that,' Michalis said hurriedly. 'The most important things.'

'Taking precautions. Being vigilant. Looking after one another,' Melina parroted like it was a holy mantra.

'I will take precautions with the mopeds. We will drive slowly and we will wear helmets… on our heads.' He looked to his father and his sister. 'I know that you both wear them around your arm for the purposes of appeasing the police and do not think about the consequences should you fall off.'

'It does not fit my hair,' Nyx moaned.

'It makes what hair I have look thinner,' Dimitri added.

'*You* must not die,' Melina told him, pointing a finger. 'It would be a very bad look for the first Day of the Not Dead.'

'I promise,' Michalis said. 'I will try not to die.'

Dimitri reached into the pocket of his trousers, produced his keys, and plonked them into Michalis's palm.

'Do not ride my moped any way like you ride that horse,' Nyx ordered. She offered forward the pocket of her apron. 'They are in there.'

Michalis slipped his hand inside and hoped to find only the keys, not a mousetrap, as she had once caught him with when they were younger. He drew out the keyring and smiled at his sister. 'Thank you.'

'Excuse me,' the customer called to them all. 'I know you must think I come here for the family drama but... I really do come here for the meat.'

'And,' Nyx said, turning to her customer, 'my prices do not reflect the putting up with the impatience of my patrons!'

'Michalis,' Dimitri said, as Michalis made for the door.

He stopped and turned back to his father.

'Yes?'

'Be careful,' Dimitri said firmly, but the words were coated with as much love as anything he had ever said to him before.

Michalis nodded. 'I will.'

'And,' Melina said, pointing again, 'no more injuries. Your costume is going to be made entirely of wood and feathers and there is only so much magic I can do with make-up.'

He couldn't listen to any more.

Forty-Five

'I'm not sure what I'm more excited about... the road being passable – just – or karaoke with Meg.'

While Lucie was sitting, Gavin was sashaying around the upper lounge in a silk robe he had found in one of the wardrobes, dust motes floating into the air as he moved around and over the ancient cypress wood floorboards you could see right the way through to downstairs. The city of Sarandë was visible across the water in Albania from the large windows. Lucie could even make out the shapes of buildings, grey/white structures en masse, contrasting with the undulating mountainous landscape amid the rest of the scene. Michalis had asked her out on another date and she had accepted somewhen between the outpouring of emotion about her mother and the finishing of his stitching procedure. Thankfully, despite all the warnings of no one being able to fix the road for weeks at best, some village men, together with a digger that looked like it was older than Ariana and Mary put together, had managed to safely shift one of the stones barring the road. Motorcycles, mountain bikes and walkers could now access Perithia and the other towns below. If they had only waited a day, none of them would have had to be caught up in the donkey drama. Whether or not Michalis would still have been out on the horse, well, Lucie would have to ask him. Except it was Meg she really wanted to be asking things of now. And she probably would be if Gavin hadn't arranged a karaoke date as soon as he found out lively bars were again accessible.

'What's her favourite croon?' Gavin asked. 'Is she a "Somewhere Over The Rainbow" kind of girl or more an Elvis fan?'

'I have no idea,' Lucie admitted, shrugging. She didn't even know if her aunt really knew what karaoke was all about. And therein lay the problem. She had always thought that she and Meg shared this unbreakable bond, that she knew everything about her. But she was beginning to realise she only knew the person who had been the stoic, controlled and in some ways, controlling, mother figure. That person was nothing like this total free spirit that seemed to be lying beneath.

'Is Michalis really alright?' Gavin asked, turning in a circle and wafting the silk robe about. 'I mean, it was quite the wound he had there. I'm not sure riding a moped is the best form of recovery plan.'

'I did stitch it up. I know what it was like,' Lucie snipped.

'Whoa! OK! No need to get your Brazilian in a twist. I was only asking.'

'How's your drone?' Lucie asked. 'Seen any more apparitions of men from back home?'

She closed her lips then. She was sounding like a

super-bitch and Gavin hadn't done anything wrong. This angst was a long time brewing though and she did feel like a bottle of ginger beer ripe for the popping.

'OK,' Gavin said, sauntering over to the sofa Lucie was sitting on in this magnificently large room with a vaulted beamed ceiling. 'We are now going to make time to deal with whatever's going on with you. Because even I know this isn't about my unmanned aerial vehicle.' He plumped down next to her, folding the cape around his body. 'What's going on?'

'Nothing,' Lucie answered. 'I'm fine.'

'And that's a great British reflex answer if ever I heard one. Are we talking about the weather next or biscuits?'

Lucie shook her head and then she made a noise that sounded similar to one that had come from Tonika yesterday. It was a sound of frustration and annoyance. All she wanted to do was relax on this holiday, not think about all the hideous things she had had to deal with last year, but here she was suddenly delving deep into exactly how fragile life was and wanting to know exactly what had happened to her mum *all* those years ago. It was like her brain was cursing her. No, you can't switch off. Are you crazy? If you take your eye off the ball things tumble down. So, here's something else to churn over...

'Is it Michalis?' Gavin asked. 'Is he one of those Romeos who seems all wide-dark-eyes and innocence but really he's a player?'

Lucie shook her head. At least, she didn't think so. Not unless he was really *really* good at pulling the wool over people's eyes, or if she wasn't in the best place for making judgements because she was focussed on other things...

'Then what is it?' Gavin wanted to know. He took a breath and fixed her with a thoughtful expression. 'Is it... you know... like that time we both locked ourselves in the supplies cupboard and bawled like babies because Mrs Pernice never got to see her grandson? Because...' Gavin paused before carrying on. 'Because I still have nightmares about that.'

She put her arms around her best friend and hugged him tight. Gavin had been her strength at work, always keeping an upbeat attitude no matter what they were faced with, but that day it had been his turn to break down. She had held him close and they had both cried for the loss of an elderly patient who had been trying to hang on until her grandson arrived from Northern Ireland.

'No,' Lucie breathed, still hugging Gavin tight. 'It isn't quite like that.' But it was about a death. One that should have been avoided. She swallowed. 'Do you think I should find out more about what happened to my mum?'

Gavin sat back from their embrace and looked at her. She could instantly read his expression. It was that dark topic again. Almost like a dirty secret that no one wanted to discuss. Except Lucie couldn't carry on feeling ashamed. For one, it wasn't her fault. And secondly, she couldn't feel shame for something she knew none of the details of.

'I just... think... if I knew more about... the situation... it might help change my outlook on life.' Lucie gave a shrug. 'I don't know.'

'Well, what do you want to change?' Gavin asked.

'What?'

'Well, all I'm saying is, what's wrong with your outlook on life right now?'

'Gavin, I risk assess everything,' Lucie stated. 'I organise everything. The only thing I haven't organised lately is this holiday.'

Gavin gave a soft smile. 'And I did a fantastic job. You have to admit that.'

Lucie sighed. 'Although Meg has taught me to keep safe… she's also made me look at things through a very narrow lens without really giving me all the reasons why. And… I want things to be… bigger and… fatter and… fuller.' She shook herself. 'For one of the first times I really want to… gorge on life like it's an… overloaded plate of Greek meze. And I don't think I can properly move forward unless I address the past.'

'That makes sense,' Gavin said with a nod.

'But, you know, it's hard. Every time I start a conversation with Meg about my mum, she either tells me some cosy tale about the time they visited a lighthouse or she shuts me down with creepy doll analogies.'

'Maybe *you* should take her to karaoke and I'll go on a date with the doctor,' Gavin suggested, waggling his forehead at her.

'No… I'm… not quite ready yet,' she answered. The thought of confronting her aunt was uncomfortable and she needed just a little more time to settle herself with it. 'And I really want to have another date with Michalis where we don't talk about our dead mothers and just… I don't know… be in the moment… and do spontaneous things.'

'You say "spontaneous things". I'm hearing "sex on the beach",' Gavin chortled.

'Gavin,' Lucie said seriously. 'Don't say anything to Meg

tonight, will you? I mean, I just wanted you to hear me out and for you to hopefully tell me I'm not crazy and—'

'Process,' Gavin interrupted. 'We all need to process.' He sighed. 'I'm still processing Simon not being gay, if I'm really honest.'

Lucie slipped an arm around her friend's shoulders again. 'Me too,' she agreed. 'How did we call it so wrong?'

'How did I get so hung up on someone for so long when there was zero chance? If I'd got my game together and asked him out like you kept telling me to do, I would have known before now. God knows how many opportunities I let pass me by.'

'But now you know,' Lucie reminded him, pulling him into her. 'And you can move on.'

Gavin checked his watch. 'What time is Michalis coming with our transport?'

'About fifteen minutes,' Lucie said.

'Time for a glass of flagon wine?' Gavin asked, leaping up from the cushions.

'Absolutely.'

Forty-Six

Lafki

This little village was straight out of a book about authentic Greece. From its beautiful stone square, complete with archaic swings and roundabout set around a large olive tree, to the simple taverna they were sitting outside of, complete with stunning sea view. Colourful petals spilled from urns around the outside eating area and a collection of tabby cats alternated in humour between disinterested to ravenous depending on the dishes that were being brought out to diners.

Lucie turned her head towards the view and let the peace it instantly brought move from her mind, down into her shoulders. The nagging ache that almost permanently lay there was easing with every second of gazing over such a staggering landscape. 'It's beautiful here.'

She hadn't realised she was going to say anything until the sentence tumbled out of her mouth and she looked back to Michalis like she had been caught with her thoughts on pudding before she had even eaten the entrée.

He smiled at her. 'It *is* beautiful.'

Just like you, Lucie thought. God, it seemed her talk about spontaneity with Gavin included possibly X-rated thoughts. But this was what she was missing, she was sure of it. She hadn't let loose in her youth at all. She had been too worried about the consequences if she made bad decisions and equally worried about Meg's reaction to those consequences. Here was her chance to try and redress the balance.

'How's your side?' Lucie asked him, reaching for her glass of wine.

'You are doubting the strength of your closing abilities?' Michalis asked with a wry grin.

'Not in the slightest,' she answered. 'But… it was… quite bad. I think we need to acknowledge that.'

She watched him sigh but then he nodded. 'It was quite bad for a moment. But only for a moment. And tonight we are having much nicer moments here, no?'

'We are,' Lucie agreed. 'And I don't want tonight to be about anything other than… relaxation… having fun… We're both on holiday from our jobs and our lives not in Corfu and we should be… spontaneous.'

That bloody 's' word! And now all she could think about was Gavin's comment about sex on the beach. She followed it up with a hopeful smile, praying that Michalis wouldn't now think she was a complete idiot.

'Tell me something about you, Lucie,' Michalis said to her, leaning forward in his chair.

'Like what?'

'I do not know. That is why I am asking.'

'Well…' This was the moment she should think of something super-exciting that would make her sound like the kind of person worthy of dating a gorgeous Greek doctor. She swallowed and immediately she was thinking she wasn't worthy. That lack of self-confidence was also knotted up in the root of her problems. She *was* worthy. She needed to believe that. She took a deep breath.

'OK so… my middle name is Britney. Say nothing. And, up until a few weeks ago, I used to have really long hair.'

'No,' Michalis said, shaking his head. 'You are playing with me. I do not believe this.'

'Which one? I can get you my passport if you need proof about Britney. And as for the hair… I can show you right now.'

She reached into her bag and pulled out her phone. There was a text waiting on her lock screen from Gavin asking:

Banged him in the sand yet?

She quickly flicked it away before finding an appropriate picture where she thought she looked attractive and handing her phone to Michalis.

'Wow,' he said, eyes on the screen.

'I know,' Lucie breathed. 'I look different, don't I?'

Michalis shook his head. 'Your hair is different. You are not.' He was still looking at the phone screen. 'Your eyes are very much the same… and your smile.'

Little sparks began to fire in the pit of her belly. He was describing her with so much thought and feeling. She wasn't used to it and it felt so nice.

'Why did you decide to have it shorter?' Michalis asked, passing the phone back.

And that's why she should have thought of something

better to say. How could she admit she hadn't decided anything? That she – or Gavin, or maybe Sharon Osbourne – had cut it all off when they were drunk.

'Oh, you know,' Lucie stated. 'Practical reasons.' So much for being a whole lot less 'crisis management' and much more 'living on the edge'.

Michalis nodded. 'My hair was shorter in Thessaloniki. All the tying back and the heat of it from the coverings. It made sense to keep it manageable.'

And, for him, it had been a conscious change to grow it again. It represented the him he had been when his mother had been alive, as well as the person he wanted to be while he was back in Corfu. He didn't want to look how he had looked the day he left the hospital and came here. The greater distance he could put between the him he was trying to restore and the desperate person who had arrived back on his father's doorstep, the better. He knew the outward appearance wouldn't really alter the feelings he was still harbouring inside him but he had to start somewhere.

'Well, I think I need to see a photo of you with short hair,' Lucie told him. 'It's only fair.'

'Oh no,' he said, sitting back in his seat.

'Why not?'

'You must trust that this look is better for me.' He edged his hair back with his hands, tucking it behind his ears and feeling a little self-conscious now.

'I think I should be the one to judge.'

'You are not going to stop asking, are you?'

'Literally only the arrival of the greens and *bifteki* we ordered will shut me up.'

He took his phone from his pocket and pressed onto the

photos icon. There had not been much time for photo-taking in the past year when things had been so difficult. But here was one, taken by a colleague – Roberto – during a rare night out prior to lockdown conditions. He had a bottle of beer in his hand and he was smiling, almost relaxed.

He passed the phone over to Lucie. 'You can say all the bad things. I am over it.'

He watched her look at the picture and he wondered if this simplicity could last. Here in Corfu, with the good wholesome food and sweet wine and his people, there was a peace he felt flowing through him he could never seem to recapture on the mainland. Was his destiny being a village doctor in Sortilas? Or would he have to look further than Greece to start again? Suddenly there was a loud crash from inside the taverna and he jumped a little in his seat. There might be peace in the surroundings here but there was still that tinge of anxiety nestled in his subconscious. Lucie hadn't seemed to notice. He took a second, catching his breath and calming his breathing.

'Michalis,' she said on an intake of breath. 'Your... eyes.'

'I was a little thinner then. Too much working. Not enough time to eat or to visit the gym.'

'You look so... tired and... maybe... a little defeated.'

She had seen behind the smile so completely. She had been perceptive from the moment they had met. He tried to shrug it off. 'All this from one photo of me with my hair cut short?' He sipped at his wine.

'Aw, you worked with babies too!' Lucie remarked. 'Sorry, I flicked to the next photo out of habit. I hope that's OK.'

What did he say? That it *wasn't* OK? He felt the unease spirit through him and tried to mentally push it away. That's what you had to do when you were moving on. Show inner strength, not let that façade crack or crumble.

'Yes,' he answered softly. 'Mainly the premature babies whose lungs needed help.'

'Is this… a girlfriend?' Lucie asked.

He reached for the phone back then and his eyes settled on Thekli. She looked happy there. They both did. He didn't know he had even kept that photo. But he was nodding before he realised it. 'Sorry… to talk of someone else is…'

'Don't be silly,' Lucie told him. 'Unless… you're still together. I mean, not that we have clarified the nature of our friendship by any means, but I would feel terrible if I had kissed someone who was in a relationship with someone else and I would then have to leave before the food arrived.' She took a breath. 'So please say you aren't together anymore. Because as well as all that, I'm not sure I can drive a moped.'

'We are not together any longer,' Michalis answered and he watched for Lucie's reaction. She had talked of their kissing but had said the word 'friendship'. Did she doubt his romantic feelings towards her? Or perhaps she was second-guessing what *she* felt. Either way his heart took another dive.

'What happened between you?' Lucie asked. 'If it's OK to ask.'

Immediately that burning sensation in the back of his throat was there, the stress reaction that was always testing his resolve. He shook his head and put down his wine glass. 'She… wanted a commitment that I could not give her.' He took a breath. 'The virus hit, it was fast, it was mayhem and… I started sleeping at the hospital. I had to commit to my job and she did not understand that.' He gave a nod that he hoped would signal the end to the explanation. He hadn't lied, but he hadn't opened up completely. It was still too sore. He took back control. 'Do you have a boyfriend?'

'*Do* I have one?' Lucie gasped. 'Gosh, no. I wouldn't be… doing this with you if I did. I know these days people are freer with their relationship statuses but… I couldn't do that.'

'For the record,' Michalis said with a smile. 'I could not do that also.'

'Good,' Lucie breathed. 'That's good to hear.'

He reached across the table, fingers dodging the olive oil and vinegar between them until he was holding her hand. 'But, there was someone special in your life at some time?'

He felt her fingers knit together with his, but her body language told him she was feeling a little ill at ease about his question. He waited, gently caressing her fingers.

'This is going to sound really bad but I don't think I've ever had someone special in my life in quite that way.' She paused for a beat. 'You know, romantically.'

'No?' he queried.

She let out a breath and he felt a little of her tension dissipate in the handhold.

'I've had a few boyfriends but… I don't know… none of the relationships ever felt like… "it".'

'It?' Michalis asked.

'I know, I'm not making any sense. I should probably stop talking completely now.'

'No,' Michalis urged. 'Do not stop talking. I like to listen to you talk.'

'See!' Lucie said, squeezing his hand. 'None of them would ever have said something like that to me. Ever.'

Michalis frowned. 'I do not understand.'

Lucie tightened her hold on his hand then. 'I know that life isn't like the movies but... I want to meet someone who gets inside my head as well as my heart. Someone who wants to know how I think and why I think it. Someone who supports me and encourages me even if they have an opposing opinion.'

'These men did not want to know your thoughts?' Michalis asked, baffled.

Lucie smiled a little. 'One of them said he loved me, but he was just saying the words because he thought he ought to say them. Because he thought that's what I wanted to hear.'

'And what you really wanted to hear was someone telling you... I know you.'

Lucie swallowed as Michalis's eyes met hers. As clichéd as it might sound, holding the hand of her holiday romance, everything so new and uncharted territory for her, he had nailed perfectly what she dreamed of from a partner. She didn't want to hear words people often said because they fitted an expected love remit. She wanted to feel the depth of their emotion, know it in her heart and her mind, hold it tight and then share it right back.

'I feel,' Michalis began softly, 'that there is much to know about you, Lucie.'

'I should definitely stop talking now,' Lucie answered, her cheeks a little flushed. 'Spontaneity and fun is what we are supposed to be going for.'

He squeezed her hand, then slowly brought it to his lips,

dropping a sensual kiss on her skin that made her shiver.

'I think it will be fun to find out your thoughts,' Michalis told her.

Lucie smiled, her mind spinning in a frenzy of sun, sea, sand and removing Michalis's clothes. 'Be careful what you wish for.'

Forty-Seven

Oscar's Bar, Roda

'Do you sing?' Michalis asked.

'God, no… well, only when Gavin needs someone to play the other parts of ABBA.'

After their delicious meal in Lafki, Lucie and Michalis had ridden to meet up with Gavin and Meg at Oscar's Bar in the resort of Roda. Currently Meg was on stage singing a rendition of Kate Bush's 'Wuthering Heights' – with all the loose hair and hand movements – and Gavin was getting rather cosy at the bar with a guy wearing a neon green T-shirt. She and Michalis were sitting at a table on the edge of the bar – more outside than in – just able to hear each other speak over the music.

'Do *you* sing?' Lucie asked him, leaning in a little and loving the way she felt so comfortable doing that.

'You want to sing with me?' Michalis replied.

'No!' Lucie exclaimed.

He got to his feet. 'They must have a book of songs. We will find something.'

'No!' Lucie said, grabbing his arm and pulling him back down into his chair. She watched him laugh and shake his head.

'I see your thoughts now,' Michalis said, still laughing. 'And they are scared of being spontaneous.'

'Oh really?' Lucie said, feeling a challenge was being laid down.

'Really,' he countered, eyebrows raising.

'OK then. Let's sing.'

'What?' Michalis asked, hand on his chest and looking concerned. 'You are not serious?'

'Michalis, suddenly you look terrified.'

'No,' he insisted, rearranging his expression quickly. 'Terrifying is… seeing your image on posters all around the area and to know that villagers of Sortilas are building something out of bamboo and vines to carry you into the village square.'

'That *is* terrifying,' Lucie agreed. 'But not quite as scary as two elderly ladies making you a wedding dress when there is no wedding to wear it to.'

'But there maybe one day, no?'

Lucie swallowed, feeling her heart beat a little faster. How would it feel to be so connected to someone you wanted to spend every single day with them? 'I don't know.'

'You do not believe in marriage?'

'I… don't know what I feel about it. I guess you learn about things like that from seeing how other people fare with it.' She smiled. 'My nan and grandad were married forever, but I can't say that a relationship based around a lot of "pottering" and disputes over who ate the last dark chocolate digestive really fills me with excitement.' She picked up her cocktail and took a sip. 'Meg's marriage ended in divorce and my colleague, Sharon, has been through several marriages without much success, well, unless you count the fact she's never short of cash for the newest iPhone as success.'

Michalis nodded. He had always assumed he would get married one day. But, here he was, older, attached only to his career, not knowing what happened next. Would things have been any different if he had committed to his relationship with Thekli? Would she have coped with his living at the hospital for a year? Or would having someone waiting at home for him have changed his priorities? He knew, deep in his heart, the answer to that was no. He also knew that not committing to Thekli would not have changed the outcome of the tragedy that made him leave Thessaloniki.

'Do you believe in marriage?' Lucie asked. 'You know, theoretically. As a concept.'

She was blushing furiously now, dropping her gaze to her glass. He adored her complete lack of awareness about what a beautiful person she was and he took a moment to let that sink in as he watched her. Yes, physically she was attractive to him, but what he loved the most was the sheer gentleness about her. She carried this tone, this feeling, a calmness that somehow formed a bubble around you and... lifted you up. To be able to give off that ease and serenity so naturally, without even knowing, that was a true gift.

'My parents had a very good marriage,' Michalis finally answered. 'I never once doubted how much they loved each other.'

'That's so nice.'

'I think,' Michalis began, 'that marriage only works if both people keep trying every single day. Because life, it is difficult. We know that already, from our jobs, from what has happened to the world. But, even when my mother started to be sick, my father would do small things, romantic things, each and every day to make her smile.'

'Like what?' Lucie asked.

Michalis smiled, remembering. 'He made traditional Greek cookies that almost burned down the apartment. My father may be a butcher but he is not a baker.'

'That is sweet.'

'It might have been sweeter if he had used sugar instead of salt.'

Michalis let the laugh leave his lips as he recalled the effort Dimitri had put into giving Lola the biscuits she craved. His father had sweated and toiled, getting flour all over himself as well as all over the kitchen, and he would not let Michalis assist. 'My mother put the cookie in her mouth and said it was the best she had ever tasted.'

'But...'

'I know,' Michalis said as around him the audience began to clap and Meg descended from the stage in a waft of chiffon. 'She knew how hard he had tried to please her, to make her happy. She told me not to eat the cookies, to get rid of them and say that she had eaten them all.' He smiled. 'To me, that is the mark of a marriage working.'

'Did your father ever realise?'

Michalis laughed again. 'Of course. He tried one before I could throw them away. And, after he had worried about making my mother's condition worse with the salt, he realised that it did not matter that he had made a mistake with the recipe. It only mattered that he had tried and my mother had loved it, and loved him for it.'

He took in his own words and settled a little in his skin. People made mistakes. But most mistakes were not because people did not care. Sometimes it was a case of people caring a little too much... He wanted to believe that, he really did.

'Oh goodness!' Meg exclaimed, throwing herself into her seat and fanning her face with her hand. 'I don't think my vocal cords have been exercised that much since the typing pool's Christmas party of 1984.'

'Why don't you have a drink?' Lucie said, pushing her glass towards her aunt. She did look very hot. It was another humid night and inside a busy bar where dancing was the order of the evening, the temperature was rising even more.

'What is it?' Meg asked, eyeing the liquid like it might have been spiked.

'It's a Mediterranean Manhattan!' Gavin announced, bounding back into their circle all eyes and teeth and... was that a love bite on his neck?

'What does it consist of?' Meg asked, still not touching the glass and peering at the contents like it could contain a tiny yet very potent poisonous jellyfish that was going to leap out and sucker to her throat.

'Mainly raki,' Gavin said. 'I made that one a double too.'

'Gavin!' Meg exclaimed, the joy of Kate Bush leaving her expression as well as her demeanour. 'You shouldn't do that!'

'Do what?' Gavin asked. He slapped a hand to his neck. 'Oh gosh... has Barak made his mark?'

'Barak?' Lucie queried. 'His name can't be Barak.'

'It is not like the president. It is a Greek name,' Michalis informed. 'It means "lightning".'

'Well! That completely explains why he has all the flashy moves,' Gavin said, grinning.

'I'm going to get rid of this and get us some water. It's incredibly hot in here.' Meg got to her feet, her gait a little unsteady.

'Wait, what?' Lucie said, jumping up. 'What d'you mean you're getting rid of it? It's *my* drink!' There it was again. Meg's need to be in control of what Lucie did. And all those questions she wanted to ask about her mum were hammering on her mind. Meg was much older than her mum. Had she been like this with her? With strict parents *and* a strict sister, was that the reason Rita went looking for an outlet?

'Oh, Lucie, it's literally all alcohol. Double measures. You'll thank me in the morning.' Meg made to leave with the glass held tight in her hand.

'No!' Lucie said, reaching out and clasping fingers to the stem, pinkie wrapping around the straw. 'Don't do that! *You* said, in our kitchen, when you were practically *wasted* on ouzo, that we had to... get our dresses dirty and embrace everything!'

'I know I did, darling, but everything in moderation, remember?' Meg continued, smiling yet still very much trying to get the glass out of Lucie's grasp.

'Why? Why "everything in moderation"?'

Lucie could feel herself losing control. She didn't want to have a confrontation with her aunt. She had told Gavin not to say anything about the way she was feeling at the moment, that she needed space and wanted to get the timing right, yet here she was, in the middle of a rowdy bar, calling Meg out, almost daring her to spit some kind of truth to the background of a being-badly-tortured Alanis Morissette number. And right about now she simply wanted to shriek 'I'm not my mother'.

'It's just a silly little drink,' Meg said, her eyes going to Gavin and Michalis, the look insinuating that Lucie was making a fuss out of nothing.

'Well,' Lucie said. 'If that's all it is, then why can't I drink it?' She was almost goading her aunt now, she knew it. And as unsavoury as this whole moment felt, she couldn't stop herself.

She didn't let Meg say anything else. Tearing the glass from her aunt's hand, she dispensed with the straw and swallowed the contents like it was a drinking challenge. God, it was strong and it was making her throat wince a little, but she was not going to give in to showing any of that on her face.

'Well, that was childish,' Meg remarked, folding her arms across her chest.

'Well,' Lucie yelled. 'Maybe if you stopped treating me like a child I'd stop having to act like one!' She picked up Gavin's glass and drank the contents of that too. '*Yamas!*'

'OK,' Michalis said, arriving at her side. 'I think it is time we go.'

That last drink hadn't tasted very nice at all and Lucie's stomach began to feel like the mixture inside it wasn't happy to cohabit for much longer. 'I think I need some fresh air.'

She bolted for the outside.

Forty-Eight

Villa Psomi, Sortilas

'I am such an idiot! Why did I do that?' Lucie asked herself as much as Michalis as she marched circuits around the swimming pool glowing from the lights inside the water. 'I shouldn't have looked for the perfect moment. Because do they actually even exist?! No, I should have been brave and sat Meg down and asked her all the questions about my mum tonight. Instead, I drank all the spirits and made myself look stupid.' Two espressos and a glass of water meant the temporary alcohol high had been alleviated, if not the crazy combination of liquids in her stomach.

'You did not look stupid,' Michalis told her.

'You don't have to be nice to me.'

'You would like me to be not nice?'

She stopped walking then, adjacent to the rattan sofa he was sitting on. 'No, of course not. I just wanted tonight to be about making my own decisions and living this holiday to the full.' She sighed. 'Lafki was so beautiful. We should have stayed there. But I was wondering about Gavin and Meg – mainly Meg – and...'

'Putting others first,' Michalis said. 'That is a very Greek quality you know.'

'*Philoxenia*,' Lucie said, her breathing slowing a little now she had come to a stop.

'You know of this?'

'Miltos told us about it when we went to see my wedding dress makers the very first night we were here.'

'Come sit with me,' Michalis encouraged, patting the space on the cushion next to him.

'You shouldn't want to sit with me,' Lucie said, plumping down next to him. 'You should be running the other way and finding a new tourist to have fun with. Apparently I can't have a good time like a normal person. Apparently I shout at relatives in public and scare taxi drivers.'

'The taxi driver at Roda was not scared,' Michalis reassured, putting his arm around her shoulders and drawing her close to him. 'I have seen taxi drivers look much worse when they have encountered tourists behind the wheel of a car forgetting what side of the road they should be driving on.'

'There's still time to run,' Lucie said. Although his body next to hers, sitting underneath another star-filled sky, the lights from Albania twinkling across the short stretch of sea separating the two countries, was doing all kinds of internal massage on her.

'I think running could pull my stitches,' he admitted. 'And, Lucie, you should know, I do not want to find another tourist to have fun with.'

'No?'

'No,' he said so forcefully that it made her shiver.

Perhaps *now* was her time to act. Make the first move and dare to take a chance. She got to her feet and wound her fingers around the thin straps of her sundress. 'No running then,' she whispered. 'But how about swimming?'

Michalis watched her ease the spaghetti straps down over her shoulders and couldn't stop the instant reaction within him. It was a feeling he hadn't experienced for so long he was almost second-guessing its existence here and now. Except he *did* know how he felt about her. It had been an instant hum of sexual attraction from the outset, but then it had quickly deepened and was deepening still. But was this too soon? Casual wasn't his style but he hadn't been able to commit to Thekli because of his job. Had anything changed? The fierceness of the pandemic was hopefully behind them but there were also many decisions he needed to make about his future. And Thekli was back in his life again, a spectre from the past reminding him that moving on wasn't an option for everyone...

'I should not get my stitches wet,' he answered, hating himself.

'Oh,' Lucie said, the dress loose but still holding up over whatever lay beneath. 'I... didn't think.'

And now he had made her feel worse than she already did over her fight with her aunt. He got to his feet and stood directly in front of her. 'Lucie,' he whispered, reaching out to touch her short hair. 'I do not think you were talking about swimming. Am I right?'

He heard her intake of breath as his fingers caressed her skin. What he would not give to trace a trail under that cotton dress, discovering her curves and dips...

'If you were not talking about swimming,' he began again. 'If you were talking about… taking off our clothes and… sliding into the pool and… making love then…'

'Stop,' Lucie begged. 'You can't say all that and turn me down. Stitches or no stitches.'

'Lucie,' he breathed, his fingers running along her collarbone. 'I am not turning you down.'

'No?'

'No,' he whispered. 'There is nothing I want more at this moment but…'

But he was not worthy of her. He had made mistakes, whether they were intentional or not, no matter if he had tried his hardest. It was fact that he could hurt people, *had* hurt people. And he did not want to hurt her. But how could he ever move on if he never tried? Wasn't that what second chances and forgiveness were all about? He shook his head, trying to straighten his thoughts. Was it safe to give in to this? Or should he still be looking over his shoulder?

'But?' Lucie asked, putting a hand on his shoulder and connecting their torsos.

'But… if we come together like this, even if it is fun or… spontaneous… know that it will mean something to me.' He swallowed.

'It will mean something to me too,' Lucie whispered. 'I don't think even I know how much yet.'

He kissed her lips gently, perhaps a little teasingly, then held her away a little. 'If we take off our clothes and we get into the water and be together then… you should know I will want to see you, for all of your time here.'

'O-K.'

'I will want to… kiss you in the village square and… hold

you closer if the earth moves again and… listen to you tell me your thoughts.'

His desire was flowing fast now, like the waterfall at nearby Nymfes, and he didn't want to stop it. All he could see was Lucie's perfect lips and the pure, soft, powerful peace in her eyes. It felt like she was this beacon of sanctuary calling him back from all his despair.

'I feel the same,' she answered. 'It doesn't have to be goodbye until easyJet closes the gate for boarding.'

With that said, he ripped at the buttons of his shirt and threw it to the tiles, pulling her towards him. Instantly a shard of pain echoed through his wound as his body bumped her rib cage, but he wasn't about to call a halt. Now Lucie's dress fell to the floor and quickly afterwards, her underwear. With eager hands, she helped him out of his jeans until they were both standing next to the water, completely naked, breathing ragged.

Despite the heat of the night air, Lucie was shaking. This man, this doctor, was perfectly formed in every which way. His physique really was a feast for the eyes and it was taking every bit of self-restraint to stop herself from indulging in a banquet right there and then.

'You are so beautiful, Lucie,' he told her, stepping forward and lowering his mouth to her neck.

She closed her eyes and wriggled closer, wanting to feel every part of him. This was what living in the moment with no regrets was totally about.

'Let us get in the water,' Michalis whispered, his lips finding her mouth, his hands outlining the curve of her waist.

'But... what about your stitches?'

He raised his head and looked deep into her eyes then. 'It was never really about the stitches,' he told her. 'I just... wanted us both to be certain.'

She smiled then and stepped forward to the very edge of the pool. 'Last one in—'

Before she could finish her sentence, she was scooped up into Michalis's arms, his muscular chest hard against her body as he strode them to the steps into the pool.

'What will happen between us,' Michalis told her, first foot landing in the water. 'It will begin and end together. No first one. No last one. Always together.'

Lucie liked the sound of that. And, as her bare bottom hit the water, she let out a squeal of pleasure and hoped there would be many more of those to come.

Forty-Nine

'Oh God, don't stop! Don't stop!'
      'That is good, yes?'
   'Oh, Michalis, yes, right there! Right there!'
   'Harder? Slower?'
   'Both! No... harder! Harder!'
   Michalis smiled, his fingers on Lucie's shoulders, easing the muscles that were still far too tight for his liking. He dropped a kiss on the back of her head, inhaling the scent of her wet hair, just like he had done when they'd made love the first time. He dropped his hands and turned her around to face him, water splashing up with the motion.
   'That was so good,' Lucie breathed, looping her arms around his neck and pressing her body against his again.
   'Only the massage?' he asked with a raise of his eyebrow.
   'You know not only the massage,' she answered, flicking at one of his pecs.
   He held her still, looking into her eyes the way he had when she had cried out his name. 'You make me feel... how I used to feel,' he told her. 'You make me feel like me again.'

He felt her take a deep breath, her chest rising and falling with his.

'Well… you make me feel I can start to try and find out who I really am. And who I'm meant to be,' she answered.

'Then this is good,' he stated. 'For both of us.'

'It is,' Lucie agreed. 'It really *really* is.' She put her mouth to his and he closed his eyes, relishing the taste of strong coffee, strong cocktails and a little chlorine. It was the story of their evening that had ended with the sweetest and most passionate connection.

'Well! Cover me in glitter and feed me to the Pit Crew! Are you… naked?!'

Michalis felt Lucie grab hold of him, burrowing herself into his body until she had all but disappeared. He put his arms around her, shielding her from the arrival of Gavin and another man at the side of the pool.

'*Yassas*, Gavin,' Michalis said, turning them both into deeper water to maintain some form of dignity.

'Hello, Doctor!' Gavin greeted, a crazy grin on his face. 'Performing a deep internal examination were you?'

'Gavin, go away!' Lucie screeched. Then quieter, so only Michalis could hear – 'Meg's not with him, is she?'

'No,' Michalis said. 'But there is someone else. Another man.'

'The man from the bar? In the green T-shirt?' Lucie queried. 'Barak?'

'*Ochi*,' Michalis said. 'Someone new.'

Lucie gently unfurled herself a little, being careful not to show off bits Gavin hopefully had never seen before, despite his *own* carefree way about nudity. With her chin on Michalis's shoulder and her eyes on the figures at the edge of the pool, the next word left her mouth like a projectile.

'Simon!'

She couldn't believe the hospital canteen barista from back home was standing poolside here in Corfu. And *why*? Why was he here? It had to be some kind of coincidence, didn't it?

'Hi, Lucie,' Simon answered, giving her a miniscule and slightly bashful wave.

It was then Lucie re-remembered she was naked and drew herself into Michalis again. 'What are you—'

'Doing here? I know!' Gavin interrupted. 'It's like the craziest thing ever, right? And I will never ever doubt drone footage again!'

'So…' Lucie said, deliberately leaving the word hanging in the air with the mosquitos.

'So…' Gavin responded, pulling a face.

'Well…' Lucie continued.

'Well…'

'I was just going to have a coffee,' Simon said. 'After Gavin's steering of the moped I think I need something to settle my nerves.'

'It wasn't my fault!' Gavin exclaimed. 'We are actually in lockdown here. I took Meg back to Perithia first then I went back for Simon and, Lucie, you know, the gap between those rocks is very *very* small. I was breathing in and channelling my inner Cher in one of her tight corset numbers just so I didn't snag my leg hairs.'

'We should maybe get out of the water?' Michalis suggested.

It was then Lucie realised she was shivering. It might be a balmy night but standing still, half her body out of the water, was still giving her goosebumps.

'Don't mind us, Doctor,' Gavin responded with a giggle.

'Gavin!' Lucie yelled. 'Take Simon inside.' She thought about that sentence for a second and rephrased. 'I mean, go into the house and make coffee.'

'Fine, fine. Are you staying for coffee, Michalis? Or did you... already get what you came for?'

'What I came for?' Michalis answered, sounding confused.

'Do not listen to him! Shoo!' Lucie ordered, brave enough to brandish a hand into the night air.

'Come on, Simon,' Gavin said, turning a one-eighty. 'But watch out for tortoises. The house seems to be breeding them faster than a David Attenborough documentary.'

Lucie left it a few beats and then let out a breath. 'I am so sorry.' She let Michalis go and dipped down into the water again to warm herself up.

'Why sorry?' Michalis wanted to know.

'Gavin and his... ogling and... well, Gavin.'

Michalis laughed. 'I like Gavin. He is a person who knows who he is.'

Lucie nodded. 'Yes, he certainly does know who he is.'

'And he is happy. All of the time.'

'Yes,' Lucie agreed. 'He is generally very upbeat.' She swallowed, oaring her arms through the water. 'And, you know, don't listen to what he said about... getting what you came for. That's a real Gavin-ism.'

'You would like me to go now?' Michalis asked her.

She looked at him, drinking in every nuance of the physique she had smoothed her fingertips over time and time again, his wet hair dripping droplets of water down that chiselled jaw. 'Do you *want* to go now?'

He shook his head. 'No.'

'Then stay,' Lucie whispered, reaching for him under the water. 'And let's see what happens on dry land.'

Fifty

Lucie had opened the shutters, but not the insect nets, and sunlight was now streaming into the bedroom, rays of brightness illuminating the bare boards. Looking out over the thick, lush garden, a lone cypress towering above the dozen or so olive trees, to the sea beyond, she watched a ferry boat slowly and silently cruising its way across the water. Unlike Southampton, where there was the dull hum of traffic pretty much all the time, here the only sound was a cockerel greeting the morning and the trickling of water from the pool. *The pool.* Lucie smiled as she remembered the first time with Michalis. It had been hot and feverishly passionate, both of them desperately seeking a sexual high. Fingers had explored and mouths had followed and Lucie had really truly let go more than ever before. She'd taken control, then given that control to Michalis and then snatched it back again. And it had felt so good.

She turned away from the window, looking to the bed. And there Michalis was, long legs stretching the length of it, feet dangling over the end, under the gauze of a mosquito net, still very much naked. Lucie smiled. Under that netting, it had been like they were the only ones in the world, secretly ensconced in a special hideaway. The lovemaking here in the bedroom had been different to the pool. It was languid and luxurious, taking time for tenderness and whispered wants.

With her thoughts reliving those moments, Michalis began to stir and she watched him stretch out an arm to the space where she had been. Finding her absent he turned, lifting his torso a little and looking into the room.

'Good morning,' she said, stepping away from the window and moving back to the bed.

'*Kalimera*,' he answered.

'Did you sleep OK?' Lucie asked, sitting down on the mattress and trailing a hand over his back as he propped his head up under a pillow.

'We had sleep?' he queried with half a smile.

'A little,' Lucie answered.

'I do not remember this,' Michalis said, dragging his body into a sitting position, his eyes meeting hers.

'No?' Lucie asked, enjoying the ab display and having a quick regard of his wound. The stitches were still good.

'But I remember many other things,' Michalis told her, leaning close and placing his lips on hers.

'Oh really,' Lucie breathed as his mouth shifted from her lips to the lobe of her ear, then down her neck, her skin fizzing with each tiny contact.

'I remember you made a special noise when I touched you… here.'

'Don't do it! Don't do it!'

Too late! She made a sound she hadn't even known it was possible to make until last night. It was Michalis's fingers, gliding over some kind of sweet spot on the back of her hand, not quite her wrist... It felt so good to be touched when touching – even platonic touching – had been outlawed last year. The gloves were off here and it felt wonderful.

'What time is it?' Michalis asked, kissing the one exposed shoulder peeking out from under his shirt she was wearing.

'So *now* you have what you came for?' Lucie joked.

'No, now I am checking if we have more time to come for,' he answered.

'Doctor Andino! So forward!' She looked at her watch. 'Well, it's... eight-thirty.'

'No!' Michalis exclaimed. 'It is not. Please tell me it is not.'

'Well, I could tell you that it wasn't but... it is.'

He was up and off the bed, eyes scanning the room. 'I have my surgery this morning. People will be lining up around your house and... the swimming pool and... I do not have my white coat... or...' He turned back to face her. 'My shirt.'

Lucie smiled. 'I can take it off right now.'

'I would like to watch,' he stated, stepping towards her again. 'But if I do that I will most definitely not make it downstairs in time.'

'Then turn around,' Lucie told him. 'I'll grab a T-shirt and then I'll make some coffee.'

'Morning! There's coffee in the pot if you want to rehydrate yourself!'

Gavin was fully dressed when Lucie entered the kitchen,

an anomaly of large proportions at eight-thirty in the morning. And he didn't look hungover at all – another rarity for this holiday and, in fact, most of Gavin's adult life since she had known him.

'Morning,' Lucie answered. 'Is everything OK?'

'Of course everything's OK! The sun is shining! The drone is happily charging! The coffee is perfectly percolated! What more could a guy like me want... apart from Sam Smith's T-shirt on the floor of my bedroom? Actually, scratch that, I'm going to take that off my bucket list.'

'O-K. Now I know something's wrong.' She crossed the striped marble floor and reached for the full pot of simmering dark liquid.

'Nothing's wrong,' Gavin insisted. 'But maybe something's changed.'

'Is it the tortoises?' Lucie asked as she filled a cup.

'No,' Gavin said, still smiling like he had the time they'd finished watching all six seasons of *Glee*... twice.

Then Lucie realised the last time she had seen this expression and super-perky morning attitude from Gavin before. It had been when he'd got a parking ticket outside the hospital and burst into tears in front of the warden because they had actually illegally parked to rush into the hospital a boy they had seen knocked off his bike en route to their shift. Once Gavin had stopped crying, and the warden had cancelled the ticket, there had been a swapping of phone numbers followed by at least four months of heavy dating before Guido had to return to his motherland.

'Simon stayed the night!'

Gavin's whisper was full-on rasp but with volume that could raise the dead. Lucie's eyes bulged and her mind began doing all kinds of expansion akin to creating a loft conversion in her head. She needed more and opened her mouth to say exactly that until…

'On the sofa,' Gavin said in more normal tones. Then he pointed skywards. 'He's in the upstairs lounge.'

Lucie was still trying to figure out what that meant, if it meant anything. 'Did you get too drunk to moped him back to wherever he's staying? Or… is his accommodation not so good? Or—'

'None of those,' Gavin answered. He was back to beaming and there was hip movement suggesting some kind of twerking might occur very soon.

'You're going to have to give me something else,' Lucie said as outside the kitchen window she could see that Michalis was right about his patients. There was a small group gathered around the clematis bush.

'I don't think you're ready!' Gavin half-sang, leaping from one Adidas trainer to the other.

'I really am!' Lucie assured swigging back some coffee then reaching into the cupboard for a mug for Michalis.

'He's gay!'

Gavin had said the words like he was announcing a Grammy winner and then proceeded to roll his fists in the air while simultaneously hair-flicking and gyrating his hips. It was a total mood.

'I don't quite understand,' Lucie said, filling the second mug with coffee as, outside, a man carrying a bird-filled cage arrived at the studio queue.

'No, I know,' Gavin said, calming considerably. 'And neither does Simon, you know, not quite yet. And I shouldn't actually have said "he's gay" because he doesn't fully understand *what* he feels yet except that... well... he knows he feels something for me!'

'Oh, Gavin!' Lucie exclaimed, hands going to the sides of her face. 'I'm so excited for you. Is it... OK to be excited for you?'

'Yes!' Gavin insisted. 'We had this gorgeous heart-to-heart on the upper terrace, under the stars, you know, when you and the doctor had got dry, dressed, drank coffee and picked up where you left off... those floorboards are not soundproof by the way.' He sighed, happily. 'And he was just so wholesomely honest that my heart turned to butter and almost dripped right out of my chest.'

Lucie winced a little at the vision his words had conjured up, but she could see a very thoughtful, gentler and more considerate Gavin than perhaps she had ever seen before.

'And he came to Corfu to see me,' Gavin said, slapping a flat hand against his chest and intaking breath. 'He said that the thought of me thinking that he didn't feel something because he'd said he didn't feel something was eating away at him. And he couldn't wait until our trip was up to act. He also said he didn't want me to throw myself into something else – and by "something" I think he definitely meant "someone". Isn't that the most romantic thing you've ever heard?'

Possibly it wasn't *the* most romantic thing Lucie had ever heard but it was pretty impressive. 'Gavin, that's so lovely. Honestly, I'm really thrilled for you.'

'Me too!' Gavin exclaimed, coming closer and throwing an arm around her shoulders, perhaps squeezing a little too tight for someone with neck and shoulder issues. 'And I know, I mustn't get too excited because he's at this scary junction in his life where everything's a little bit confusing and judgement is literally everywhere but... I'm going to give him all the time and space he needs to, you know, eventually realise that he wants to fully commit to me!'

Lucie tried to escape the tight cuddle by whipping around to the left in a move she'd once seen Jason Statham do in a film. Once free she smiled again at her best friend. Now was definitely not the right time to suggest that the result of Simon's soul-searching might not be a happy-forever-after with Gavin. That would have to come later, once his elevator had dropped a few clouds down from nine.

'There is one little thing we need to discuss before he wakes up though,' Gavin said, back to whispering.

'What?' Lucie asked.

'Well, as you probably saw at Oscar's Bar, I was getting a little friendly with Barak and... this!' Gavin pointed at the mark at the bottom of his neck.

'O-K,' Lucie said. 'But you're single and on holiday and if you're going to think about starting a relationship with Simon, or at the very least be his supportive soul as he transitions to a new stage in his life, then you should begin that journey with nothing but the truth.'

'Hmm, there is that,' Gavin mused, fingers grazing the mark.

'But you haven't gone for the truth, have you, Gavin?'

'Well...'

Lucie sighed. 'What have you told him?'

'I might have said – under intense pressure and those cocktails Meg thought were a second cousin of antifreeze – that you did it.'

'What?!' Lucie exploded, coffee sloshing from her mug to the floor. 'You didn't! Well, what sort of message is that sending out to someone who isn't quite sure if they feel one thing, or another, or all the things?!'

'Oh, don't worry about that,' Gavin said, flapping a hand. 'Your cis woman hetero status is intact. I said we were singing Annie Lennox's "Love Song for a Vampire" and you got a bit carried away.'

Lucie didn't have time to say anything before Michalis was bounding down the wooden staircase that led from her bedroom to the kitchen, his hair still as tousled as it had been prior to his redressing. As his feet met the pink-and-cream marble, Lucie held out the mug of coffee to him.

'I do not have time to drink this now,' he said, tucking his shirt into his jeans, causing a midriff reveal that wasn't unwelcome. 'There is a man with birds in a cage waiting to see me like I am a vet.'

'Well, Doctor,' Gavin jumped in. 'I suspect he's heard how accomplished you are at ruffling a few feathers or… giving good beak or—'

'Go,' Lucie said. 'His jokes will only get worse. But take the coffee with you.' She pressed the mug into his hands.

'*Efharisto*,' Michalis said. 'Thank you.'

He leaned in to kiss her lips and Lucie revelled in the display of affection. This might be only for the time she was here in Corfu, but it meant something to both of them.

Michalis waved a hand at Gavin, then seemed to brace himself before opening the front door. The second the light flooded into the space there was a cacophony of sound, each person's voice fighting for priority over the other.

'God,' Gavin stated. 'It's like a Tesco car park during a lockdown Click-and-Collect.'

Lucie looked to the window and watched her handsome man friend talking patiently with the waiting crowd on the courtyard, while attempting to get into the studio and close the door on them until their appointment times. Then she was distracted by the lighting up of her phone screen, charging next to the toaster. There were many notifications but the most recent one was from Meg.

Can we meet for lunch? I think it's time we really talked.

Fifty-One

Andino Butcher's, Sortilas

'Whoa! Be careful! I am carrying the livers of calves!' Nyx braced the large metal tray, containing meat that looked like it was marinating in its own blood, against her midriff. They were in the inner hall at the back of the shop, just before the foot of the stairs. It was where coats were hung on thick old abattoir hooks and shoes were stacked in a rack made from an old pallet. 'Where is the fire?' she asked Michalis.

'You do know that Melina outlawed jokes about fires five years ago because Little Spiros's one comment in the village square prompted the calling of the spotter planes,' Michalis answered.

'I remember,' Nyx told him. 'In fact, *I* told *you* that! You were not even in Sortilas at the time.'

He smiled at his sister, then reached out, pinching her cheek.

'Ow! What are you doing?! What is wrong with you today? Rushing around and being weird! Both you and

Papa are being strange and I do not like it!'

'Papa is being strange?' Michalis queried. He had rushed back here after surgery to tell his father the good news. All his blood tests had come back perfectly normal. Michalis was relieved and he knew his father would be too. Although Dimitri would likely not admit that he had ever been concerned.

'He has been here in the shop since before five a.m.,' Nyx informed, stepping back a little to give Michalis an uninterrupted view of behind the counter. 'He has sliced things he has not sliced in over a year. I realise we have a large order for the Day of the Not Dead festival, but we are not at preparation stage for this yet.' Nyx took a breath. 'And we need the road to be open! The meat will not last forever and some of the villagers are stockpiling. Miltos bought five kilos of chicken yesterday. Five. I am going to start making limits soon.'

Michalis watched his father caressing a carcass tenderly, fingers massaging the flesh... then bringing the machete down hard. 'Maybe there is something else he is preparing for?'

'Like what?'

'Like something to do with going off on his moped at night and his mobile phone?'

Michalis watched Nyx mull over this information, studying their father afresh.

'He told me he was going to Sfakera this afternoon,' Nyx said. 'That he would not be home for dinner.'

'OK,' Michalis stated.

'This woman called Amalia,' Nyx began. 'You think something is going on?'

'I don't know,' he replied. 'Do *you* think it is possible that Papa could be… dating?'

'What?!' Nyx burst out, fingers nearly losing their grip on the large metal tray. 'Dating?! No! Of course not! He is so old!'

'Then what do you think is going on?'

'Well, there are a few things it could be,' Nyx whispered, huddling into him as tightly as the tray would allow. 'I worry that maybe this woman is trying to get money from him. I read this article on the internet that spoke about these people creating all kinds of fake social media accounts to lure old men like Papa. First they pretend to be nice and then, suddenly, they have no money to pay for the operation for their sick grandchild or sick dog or sick self. Then hundreds of euro becomes thousands of euro and the next thing that will happen is there will be no butcher shop and I will have nothing!'

Michalis was almost too scared to ask what other thoughts Nyx had on the subject. But he did. 'What are the other things?'

'That he has an embarrassing hobby,' Nyx said. 'Like pilates or hula-hooping. Or that… he is interviewing other people to work in the shop because he thinks I am not good enough to take over when he dies.'

His heart squeezed for his sister then. She couldn't really believe that was what Dimitri thought, could she? Nyx had been running the shop alongside their father since she was sixteen. Now she was only a few years older it was obvious that she was the one in day-to-day charge and that Dimitri, experienced as he was, had taken a back step to something more like a figurehead.

'Nyx, I can assure you it is definitely not the last one. Why would Papa need another butcher working here when he has the best one on Corfu?'

Nyx shrugged, calves' livers sloshing in their 'sauce'. 'Because I am not a boy?'

'Nyx!'

'What?! Do not give me that "everyone is equal now" bullshit. This is Sortilas. I am surprised that women do not have to take an extra kind of driving test to prove they are capable of passing through the village.'

Michalis shook his head. 'It was Yiannis trying to get his flock of sheep down the path past the *cafeneon* that took plaster off the wall, remember, not any woman in a car.'

'You know what I mean,' Nyx said. 'You know how things are.'

'Papa values you, Nyx. So much. Why do you think he criticises you all the time?'

'Because I cannot do anything right? Or as good as him? Or as good as someone with baby nipples and a penis?'

Michalis shook his head. 'No. He criticises because he knows you are even *better* than him. It is... a backward way of giving his approval. Come on, you know how he is. Insults are like medals of honour.'

'So,' Nyx whispered. 'You are saying he is not interviewing other butchers. So, that means, this woman from Sfakera must be going to try and get Papa's money from him. With her sick child and... a fake Facebook account and many different profiles?'

'I don't think so,' Michalis stated.

'Then, that only leaves...'

He watched Nyx look from him to their father and the meat-slicing and back again.

'Dating,' Michalis told her.

His sister shook her head. 'That is the most disgusting thing I have ever heard.'

How his father having a relationship with someone was worse than Dimitri being embezzled or trying to replace Nyx in the family business, Michalis wasn't quite sure.

'It has been a long time since Mama passed away,' Michalis said softly.

'Oh, so, now it is an acceptable time for Papa to get us a new mother?'

'Nyx...'

'What?!' she asked, her body language suggesting that if she wasn't holding a tray of meat products she would be throwing her hands in the air. 'Why cannot he be satisfied with joining a team for darts... or doing what other old men do? You know... drink ouzo and play *tavli*... and groan about the holes in the road and the broken streetlights?'

'Nyx, Papa is not that old. And perhaps it is his decision how he wants to spend the rest of his life and who with, no?'

Nyx was already shaking her head. He understood how she felt. She was so much younger than him, already feeling she had dipped out in the mother stakes, being so young when Lola died. She had none of the memories of who Lola had been. If there was someone new in their father's life, someone Nyx had time to get to know better, then maybe his sister worried she would eradicate Lola completely.

'Listen,' Michalis began gently. 'I think maybe one of us should bring up the subject and see what happens. Perhaps

Papa is keeping this a secret because he is worried what we might think.'

'He should be worried,' Nyx stated, shaking the tray. 'I will not like her.' And there we had it.

'We don't know it is the woman from Sfakera,' Michalis said. At the moment it *was* just a hunch.

'I will not like any old woman,' Nyx reasserted.

'Will you do one favour for me?' Michalis asked, putting a hand on Nyx's shoulder.

'Oh, not again!' Nyx said. 'And where is my moped? I did not hear you come in last night.'

'Will you keep calm with Papa until we find out what's going on?'

'I am not asking him about partnerships unless they involve making offal into coffin-shaped burgers for the Not Dead festival,' Nyx stated with a foot stamp.

'You don't have to ask him,' Michalis said. 'I will.'

'You will?'

'With caution,' Michalis told her.

'And my moped?' Nyx questioned.

He drew the keys from the pocket of his jeans. 'Around the back. I am on my way to collect Papa's now. And the reason you did not hear me come home last night,' Michalis said with a smile. 'Was because… I did not.'

Now Nyx's eyes popped out of her head. 'My brother! Spending the whole night with a girl!' She screwed her nose up then. 'It was a girl, right?'

'Yes,' Michalis breathed, his brain bringing him all the hot, wet, naked images from the pool with Lucie. 'It was Lucie.'

'You must be careful, Micha. If Melina finds out she will

enrol you in the new Sortilas breeding programme.' Nyx turned away from him and began walking towards the door leading to the shop.

'That is not a real thing, is it?' Michalis asked. 'I thought it was a joke.'

'Ha!' Nyx said, turning back to face him. 'Everyone thought Little Spiros's dream of building a cable car down to Acharavi was a joke. And now look at us. Waiting for more boulders to be removed from the road!'

Fifty-Two

This little taverna, only a short walk away from Sortilas, was as traditional as they came. Up stone steps to a terraced outside sitting area were tables spread with cotton cloths, below fresh paper covers. Wooden chairs were set around circular tables under a fabric canopy. Then, to the right, was another seating area, open to the air and under nothing but curling green vines. Meg was already there, sitting at a table under the pergola, a large bottle of water and a half-full glass in front of her.

Lucie took a deep breath and put her hands into the pockets of her lemon-coloured trousers. She couldn't help but remember her mad display the other evening *and* there was also the fact that instead of talking things out like an adult, she had run away. Still, that's what this get-together was for, wasn't it? To talk like grown-ups.

'Lucie!' Meg greeted, waving a hand.

Lucie watched her aunt get to her feet, looking a little more unsteady than she had when she was impersonating an Eighties icon at the karaoke session. Maybe Lucie had overreacted in the moment but, on the other hand, she was well aware a reaction had been building for some time. She gave Meg a smile and stepped towards the table.

'The weather is being so wonderful, isn't it?' Meg gasped, palms splayed upwards as if she could catch the sunbeams. 'I haven't seen a cloud since I got here. Greece is still as super as it always was.'

'I wish you'd told me all about Greece before,' Lucie stated, slipping down into a chair. 'Sorry.' She took a breath as she realised her words had sounded a bit like an accusation. 'I didn't mean that quite how it came out. I just meant that—'

'It's OK, Lucie-Lou,' Meg said with a sigh. 'I know what you meant. Would you like a glass of water?'

'What I'd really like is a glass of wine,' Lucie blurted, knotting her hands together on the paper cloth covering the table. She was nervous here in this situation, under the sun and the vines, a little white-and-tan-coloured dog bounding down the steps from inside the taverna. She couldn't remember ever feeling this nervous with Meg before. Maybe it was because she knew something was about to change, for better or for worse, there were things that had to be addressed.

'Then have one,' Meg said. 'I'll have one too. And I won't say a thing about it being too early or… well, you know.' She swallowed. 'I won't be how I was the other night.'

Before Lucie could make any reply, Meg beckoned a lady who was coming out of the building with a plate of *meze* for another customer.

'*Miso litro lefko krasi, parakalo*,' Meg said, sounding almost like a native.

'*Amesos*,' the woman answered with a nod.

'I still can't believe you can speak Greek like that,' Lucie said.

'I still can't believe I can remember it after all these years,' Meg answered, softly smiling.

The conversation stilled and Lucie waited.

'Oh, Lucie-Lou, this feels so awkward and I don't want it to feel awkward.'

'Neither do I,' Lucie admitted. 'And I am sorry for how I behaved at the bar. I shouldn't have raised my voice to you and I shouldn't have run off like that. And I probably shouldn't have drunk those cocktails.'

Meg was shaking her head before Lucie could even finish the sentence and the quick arrival of the jug of white wine, covered in condensation, plus two short tumblers, was well-timed.

'I'm glad you left,' Meg said, her voice shaking almost as much as her hands as she began to fill both their glasses with the sweet-smelling amber-coloured liquid. 'It meant I had to stop talking. That there was no further opportunity for me to keep being... stifling.'

Lucie swallowed. She wanted to tell Meg that it was OK, to make up and keep this uncomfortable feeling to the bare minimum. But she also knew this was a chance. One they should have both reached out for before now.

'You don't have to tell me that I was speaking to you like you were... a naughty girl who had just been caught eating strawberries straight from the plant at a pick-your-own farm.'

Lucie took a long, slow sip from her glass of wine.

'I said all the *right* things on my very first night here, under the influence of alcohol myself, when I said about not being a boxed-up doll, getting out of our confines and living life to the full.' Meg sighed, fingers wrapping around her glass. 'And I said all that when one of the purposes of my trip was to... check up on you.'

Lucie bit her lip. It wasn't what she wanted to hear but she knew it was the truth.

'I can't help myself, can I?' Meg gasped. 'I told you to have a Greek adventure and then, at home on my own, I was envisaging all the things that might go wrong and before I'd thought it through I'd booked a flight. I kept telling myself this was about me revisiting my youth and not about making sure you were alright, but that wasn't altogether true. I was worrying more about you here in Corfu than I did all those months you were working fighting the virus.' She took a breath. 'But perhaps the worst thing of all...'

Lucie watched her aunt take a large breath, her bosom rising almost up into her neck and then dropping southwards again.

'Was knowing I was treating you like you are your mum.' She swallowed. 'I know, in my heart, that you are completely different people and I also know, although it's so hard to accept, that my time for steering your course for you is... over.'

There were tears in Meg's eyes now and Lucie watched her aunt try to blink them away. Any second now she would blame it on the sunlight or cataracts like she did every other time talk took an emotional turn. Except this time, she didn't.

'I don't know why I do it,' Meg continued, a finger wiping the condensation from her glass. 'There are just times when I see so much of Rita in you. Physically I mean. I think that's why seeing you with your shorter hair was such a shock. You look even more like her now than you ever did.' She smiled. 'She had that beautiful long hair like you did and then she chopped it all off. Of course your mum cut her hair and had her nose pierced to be rebellious. Whereas you—'

'Don't know if *I* cut it or Gavin cut it or if Sharon cut it, but we were all drunk on a coconut-flavoured liqueur,' Lucie informed with a sigh.

'And that's the sort of thing you should be doing,' Meg said. 'I mean it.'

'No,' Lucie said, shaking her head. 'This isn't about alcohol or not taking painkillers. This is about barriers.' She took a breath. 'It's about constantly feeling that I have to second-guess everything until the choice I have to make isn't *my* choice at all.' She sighed. 'It was Nan or Grandad's choice in my head when I was younger, and now it's *your* choice. Meg, I don't feel as if I have any free will. I just have an ongoing battle to take charge of my own thoughts and make my own decisions, and at my age that's really rather sad.'

Meg gave a sober nod. 'And that's all *my* fault. I over-swaddled you. If you were a baby you would have been running a temperature and screaming for a window to be opened.'

'Well,' Lucie said softly. 'Maybe it's time to take off a layer or two and let in some air.'

'I should have started doing that a long time ago,' Meg admitted. 'Made it much breezier.'

They both seemed to be on the same page, but this had to

go deeper or it would keep being an issue going forward. It was time for Lucie to be really *brave*. Her eyes went to the little dog, turning circles on the terrace. It was time for *her* to stop spinning and get some clarity.

'There's something else we should have started doing a long time ago.' Lucie paused for a moment. 'You... you don't speak about my mum enough.'

She made sure her eyes met with Meg's as she delivered the sentence. This statement was years in the making and she had to keep the dialogue going.

'I mean, yes, you talk about how she was when she was growing up. The singing along to the radio and the dressing up, the family picnics and her drawing being displayed in the town hall when she was seven... but there's never anything else. There's no substance. There's nothing about what she did when she hit senior school or who she was as a person. There's only talk about these "bad decisions" and "unsuitable crowds". Was she black all the way through, from the moment she hit Year Seven? Surely there were other things in her life then apart from the mistakes?' She swallowed and braced herself against the solidity of the tabletop. 'What about... my father?'

'You know about your father,' Meg said quickly.

'I know nothing about him. I don't even know who he is.'

'And, I promise you, Lucie, that is all I know too.' Meg put hands to her face and gasped. 'Did you think that I knew who he was? That I would keep this from you?'

Lucie shrugged. 'I don't know. I hoped not.' She took a deep slow breath. 'But, you do shield me from things that I really should experience myself, even if they might hurt me a little bit.'

'But, Lucie, I would never have kept your father from you,' Meg insisted.

Lucie blew out the breath she had been holding onto and pressed her fingertips into the paper cloth on the table. Had she really thought Meg knew more than she had ever said about her father? Maybe not. But she did find it hard to believe that *no one* knew.

'Was there *no one* special in my mum's life? Someone from school or... I don't know... someone older?' Lucie asked. 'Someone... *anyone*... who might have made me.'

'Lucie,' Meg said, reaching for Lucie's hands now and cupping them gently in her own. 'Your mum... she got so secretive. And no, it didn't happen overnight. It crept up on us all over months and weeks, little things at first. She wouldn't want to watch TV with us anymore, preferring to listen to music in her bedroom. She started to stay up late and she didn't sleep. She stopped communicating with us in an everyday way and there was just... nothing we could do.' Meg sighed. 'Mum and Dad, they tried. They made doctor's appointments Rita just never turned up for, they got her a private counsellor so she had someone not in the family to unburden to, they talked to the school and later the college. But, it didn't matter what we tried, Rita just didn't want to be the person she used to be. She wanted this new version of herself that was eating her up from the inside out.'

Lucie nodded. She had heard this before. And that wasn't what she needed now. She needed to feel she knew her mum as much as everyone else had. Mums were meant to be so close to their daughters, it couldn't be right that she felt so little.

'If there was a boyfriend, Lucie, I promise we didn't know

about him. A few college people came to the funeral but, I don't know, even when I tried to speak to them about what class they had been in with Rita, or what things they had in common, it was as if *none* of them really knew who she was at all. But, she wasn't actually there much, was she?'

Lucie bristled as a shaft of sunlight hit her shoulders. 'I can't live in her shadow.' Her voice sounded confident and determined. 'And that's what's happened. Whether you meant that to happen, whether *I* meant that to happen... that's how it's been and... I don't want to let it hold me back any longer.'

'I understand,' Meg said. 'I understand completely. And I know I haven't helped.'

'Meg,' Lucie breathed. 'You've been there for me constantly. *You* brought me up! You fed and clothed me and taught me everything I know about the world. If it wasn't for you I would have been in care or... worse. I will *forever* be grateful.'

'It's been nothing but the greatest pleasure,' Meg said, her voice wavering. 'And I know it hasn't been perfect and I have made many, many mistakes and—'

'Meg,' Lucie whispered. 'You were right when you said you needed to start living more and... get your dress dirty. You totally should.' She gave a wistful smile. 'And... it's OK. You can let me go now.'

She watched Meg's expression crack a little.

'I'm not my mum and I promise, I'm not going to make the same mistakes she did. And you have to trust me with that.' She sighed. 'I will always come to you for advice and I will always take your wisdom on board. But my choices have to be mine to make and you have to let me work things out on my own, even if the next consequence might be difficult or not quite perfect.'

Meg was nodding as tears began to fall with force. 'I know. And I will.'

'And it's your time too now.' She squeezed Meg's hands again, memories of all the handholding from the past – a grazed knee, someone being cruel at school or not scoring as high as she'd wanted on a test paper – flooding back. 'You've been my real mum and I don't want to completely sack you from the position but… maybe you should have a little furlough.'

Meg smiled then, dashing the tears away from her eyes with a finger. 'Is there any government incentive package?'

'Well, I don't know about Rishi Sunak, but Lucie Burrows doesn't want to stop having an excuse to buy chocolate-covered pretzels to go with our tea on Saturday mornings,' Lucie said.

'Phew!' Meg said, pretend-wiping her forehead.

Lucie plucked a napkin from the table and held it out to Meg. 'There is one other thing I wanted to ask.'

'Anything, Lucie-Lou, I promise,' Meg said, taking the tissue and wiping her eyes.

Lucie looked to the mountain foreground, peaks stretching high and wide across the blue sky, and wondered, as the warm sun hit her cheeks, whether it *was* important to know the answer to this particular question. What would it change? Rita was still gone. Lucie would never know who her father was, if Rita herself had even known. And did Meg even hold any puzzle pieces to make the picture any clearer?

'Was it an accident?' Lucie blurted. 'Did Mum's drug

addiction and recklessness mean she just took too much or...' She swallowed, remembering how hurt she had felt when Michalis had brought up this subject.

'Or?' Meg asked, looking a little bit unsure what was coming next.

'Did she... *mean* to die?' Lucie breathed. 'Did she think there was no way back to any kind of bearable living? Was she so unhappy because she was so young, with a baby she didn't want, that she thought checking out was the only answer?'

Meg answered instantly. 'No.'

It sounded so definite, a statement with no compromise or flicker of any uncertainty in her aunt's eyes. 'Absolutely not,' Meg added, leaving no doubt.

'But... you said she was lost. That she didn't seem to have many real friends. And she had me... and that can't have been easy no matter how much support you gave her. Especially when Nan and Grandad would have been so shocked and upset and disapproving, even if they didn't mean to be.'

'Lucie-Lou,' Meg said, holding both her hands tight again and looking directly at her. 'The very last time I saw your mum happy she was holding you in her arms.' She smiled. 'She was... singing some awful pop song to you, dancing you around her bedroom to the beat and kissing your little nose. Lucie, she loved you, very much, and you must never ever doubt that.'

'I know that's what you say but—'

'I've *always* told you the truth I knew, Lucie. That's why you've felt so penned in with warnings about misadventure. I've never hidden what happened to your mum. As soon as I thought you were old enough to understand I told you.'

Meg squeezed her hands tighter. 'It was an *accident*. There was absolutely nothing to suggest that she had ever thought about harming herself. She just got herself caught up in an impossible situation she couldn't break free from and… she went too far that one night.' Meg inhaled sharply. 'One mistake. Many lives shattered. And… all of us changed.'

Lucie inched off her chair until she was hovering in the space between them. And then she put her arms around Meg and held her close as they both began to cry.

Fifty-Three

Vouni

Lucie spread her arms wide and tried to channel her inner Arctic Circle. She was standing in the centre of Ariana and Mary's terrace wearing what felt like at least forty-five layers of petticoats and the day was too hot for clothes *at all*, let alone a bespoke Greek wedding dress...

'You look amazing,' Gavin said, dropping a handful of olives into his mouth from the little pots on the rustic table, the cats looking on. 'Doesn't she look amazing, Miltos?'

'We will find you a groom!' Miltos said, clapping his hands together like he meant business.

'No,' Lucie breathed. 'I don't... I mean... I'm not really getting married. I did say that from the outset.'

Gavin started laughing until he realised the olives he had palmed contained stones and he began to splutter a little. The cats lifted their heads as if in amusement and the black-and-white one made a mew that definitely sounded like a laugh.

It had been a few days since her heart-to-heart with Meg

and, feeling a little more centred, she had relaxed into the holiday vibe with Gavin and Simon. They'd hired bicycles so they could leave Sortilas and meet up with Simon and together they'd hit the beach at Agios Spyridon, hiring a pedalo and trying pints of Corfu Beer. *And* Lucie had spent another perfect date night with Michalis. He had cooked a delectable meal of roasted figs, Greek cheese and fresh bread and they had taken it in a picnic basket to a wrought iron bench a short walk away from the village in Anapaftiria. The view there was even more spectacular than the views from Villa Psomi, the ocean stretching out ahead of them like a skein of the most luxurious blue silk ... The delicious food and Michalis's company – as well as his kisses – had made the night simply perfection.

The road out of Sortilas was at last almost fully open. You could now get to and from the village by car, but anything bigger than a Skoda Citigo had to pull in its wing mirrors and bigger vehicles like Miltos's fruit van were still unable to pass. Melina Hatzi had called a village meeting to enlist more people to help with the removal of the final boulders blocking the road. She had looked highly stressed, had had to lean on her *mati*-topped staff for support at one point and then had dropped her megaphone on the head of a little boy called Spiros who seemed to be drawing a picture of cable cars. Coaches were coming up to deliver and collect tourists, but not all of the holidaymakers were happy with the final mile of the journey being made on foot or in the back of a wooden wagon. Just this morning, Lucie had caught sight of the president bowing to the golden tortoise on the church and whispering a prayer. The rumours were that the Day of the

Not Dead festival might have to be postponed if supplies could not get through.

'The village knows about you and the doctor,' Miltos said firmly.

Lucie caught his eye and suddenly felt guilty of something. *The village knows.* It felt like there was something close to threat behind the statement. Before she had a chance to say anything in reply, Miltos had spoken again.

'But you cannot marry him,' Miltos stated.

'What?' Gavin spluttered, olive bits hitting his chin. One of the cats stuck out a paw and snagged a flying scrap.

'Dr Andino is Greek Orthodox,' Miltos said matter-of-factly.

Was he? Michalis had never mentioned religion to her when they had had that conversation about marriage and he'd told her the story of his dad making salt-infused cookies. But then, why would he mention it? They were having a holiday romance, not coupling up for forever...

'I know you'll hate me for it,' Gavin began. 'But I'm now imagining him in one of those long black papa robes, a string of beads and a crucifix around his neck.' He drew in a breath and fanned his face. 'Like the Madonna "Like A Prayer" video.'

'So,' Lucie began as Ariana and Mary carried on circling her, one with pins, both with ribbon. 'If you're Greek Orthodox does it mean you can't marry someone who isn't Greek Orthodox?'

'No,' Miltos said immediately.

'Oh,' Lucie answered. Then what was the problem? You know, if she was going to be envisaging this marrying scenario that was never actually going to happen...

'But the marriage must take place in a Greek Orthodox church. And the bride would have to be Christian.' Miltos nodded. 'If you are not Christian then you cannot be married.'

'Well, that doesn't seem fair,' Gavin said. 'What about "love is love" and "all love is equal"?'

Miltos scoffed. 'Fairy tales.'

'Well,' Lucie breathed. 'We don't have to worry about any of that, do we?'

'You are Christian?' Miltos wanted to know, one eyebrow raising.

'I'm not getting married!' Lucie said aloud.

Such was her shout that Ariana and Mary both took a step back as if they thought they had jabbed her with a pin.

'Sorry,' Lucie breathed. 'But, you know, one day I might get married and wear this lovely dress.'

'You could always become Orthodox,' Miltos suggested.

His mobile phone began to ring and he plucked it from the table and shouted a greeting:

'*Ne!*'

'Don't listen to him about marriage to Michalis,' Gavin said, getting up and standing next to Lucie as Ariana and Mary carried on busying around like worker bees.

'I'm not listening to anyone about that,' Lucie said. 'Because we're enjoying each other's company while I'm here and then when I'm not here, well…' She stopped because she didn't know what else to say. What did happen then? Did it all just come to a natural conclusion?

'Please keep in touch,' Gavin told her. 'Because otherwise I'll have to go through all that finding new friendship groups and membership to the Southampton Socialites stuff with you again and the only thing I got out of that was the plot of *Dark* explained to me and a recipe for chocolate salami.'

'We must go!' Miltos announced. '*Ela! Tora!*' He whisked his arms around in the air like he was a human KitchenAid. Even the cats got scared and sprung from their seat at the table to the sanctuary of behind a large watering can.

'Go?' Lucie asked, looking down at her layers of tulle and lace and patchwork pieces of who-knew-what. 'Go where?'

'There is an emergency in Sortilas,' Miltos said. He spoke fast in Greek then to his grandmother and great-aunt. Lucie watched as the women's eyes widened and suddenly they were stripping the frock from her as fast as their aged, oddly nimble fingers could go.

'What sort of emergency?' Gavin gabbled. 'Oh, God, it's Simon, isn't it? He said he was going to catch up on some reading at his hotel, but what if he got bored and he tried to come and see me and I wasn't there and what if there was another landslide? Has there been another landslide? Is he part-crushed under a boulder before we've even had a chance to figure things out?'

'Who is Simon?' Miltos asked, somehow sounding accusing.

'Miltos, what's happened?' Lucie demanded to know.

'Maria, she is having the babies,' Miltos said, suddenly stepping in and also helping to remove Lucie's dress.

'Phew,' Gavin said. 'Now please tell me Maria is a cat.' He grabbed another fistful of olives.

'Maria is not a cat.'

'I can take this off myself, Miltos,' Lucie said, wriggling her arms out of the confines of rather tight lacy cuffs.

'Good,' Miltos said. 'Because we must go.' He produced

the keys to the go-kart car they had come here in. 'Dr Andino cannot be found so... you two need to deliver the babies.'

'What?!' Lucie exclaimed, as finally her body was released from the steamy confines of material and she was back in just her shorts and vest.

'Ha!' Gavin said. 'This is one of your jokes, isn't it, Miltos?' He folded his arms across his chest. 'Maria's a dog, isn't she? We're going to squeeze back into the go-kart and you're going to insist you drive – too fast by the way – and then we're going to get back to Sortilas and—'

'*Kane isychia!*'

Lucie had no idea what Miltos had roared, but the words had rolled like thunder.

'Maria is a woman,' Miltos explained. 'She is pregnant... with twins... and you are going to help her get the babies out. Now, let's go!'

Lucie swallowed and pulled a pin out of the bottom of her vest. There didn't seem to be anything else to say. This was happening.

Fifty-Four

En route to Sortilas

'I feel sick,' Gavin announced as they bumped up and down in the go-kart en route to the village.

'Please don't criticise Miltos's driving again,' Lucie begged. 'If you make him mad, it's only going to get worse.' And it wasn't really Miltos's crazy steering that was the worst thing about this ride. It was Gavin's body pressure, taking up his seat *and* hers. It almost felt like she was wearing his deodorant… She attempted to sit a little forward to speak to their pilot.

'Where is she?' Lucie yelled against the rushing humid air as the kart whipped around another hairpin bend on two of its wheels. 'Maria… and the babies.'

'And, more importantly, why isn't there an ambulance coming?!' Gavin screamed.

'You think an ambulance could get into the village when my fruit van cannot?' Miltos shouted back over the roar of the engine.

'Well, you could bring her down the mountain to the

health centre. I saw one in Roda the other day,' Gavin suggested. 'They must do more than treat sunburn.' He touched one of his red shoulders.

Miltos threw the steering wheel around to the left. 'You want to put a pregnant woman in the back of this thing?!'

'*We're* in the back of this thing!' Lucie reminded as Gavin's elbow hit her kidney.

'And that wasn't how you pitched this vehicle when you hired it to me!' added Gavin. 'You specifically sold the safety features!'

'What are you so scared of?' Miltos wanted to know. 'You tell me you are a nurse, Loosely and Gaveen, he is a doctor.'

'Yes,' Lucie called back, foliage coming through the open 'window' and scraping her arm. 'I mean, no. Gavin's not a doctor, remember?'

'Only when you're needing to lie to your gran and auntie for sexist reasons,' Gavin grumbled.

'What?' Miltos shouted, apparently not hearing. He did that quite a lot when he didn't want to listen.

Lucie shifted slightly in her seat and drew her phone out of the pocket of her shorts. Michalis hadn't replied to any of her texts yet today. But that wasn't unusual. When he was helping at the butcher's he didn't seem to check his phone, nor when he was seeing patients at the studio surgery. He was conscientious to a fault. But she had also now called him several times. You would think, unless his mobile was on silent, that the noise might have alerted someone near his phone – Nyx or one of his patients. She pressed on his number and tried again. This time it went straight to voicemail.

'Where did people look for Michalis?' Lucie asked Miltos, as she re-pocketed her phone.

'The butcher's. The surgery. His apartment. We also sent Little Spiros on his tricycle to see if he was at the bench where you ate picnic food,' Miltos answered.

What? Everyone knew they had had a picnic at Anapaftiria? It was a good job they had kept their clothes on in that case... Now Lucie was concerned that she and Gavin were *really* going to have to deliver these babies.

'Have you delivered a baby before?' Lucie asked him.

'Oh yes!' Gavin exclaimed. 'Many times!' He rolled his eyes. 'Just like I perform open heart surgery and tonsillectomies... OK, the last one I may have *thought* I'd performed previously with a couple of boyfriends, but never under anaesthesia.'

'Gavin, this is serious!'

'I am well aware but, Luce, we've been through everything at work together. When have you seen me with my fingers anywhere near the business end of a woman? And *do not* mention Madame Viceroy, because that "lady" was forced to go private after the episode with the hydrocortisone cream.'

Lucie took a deep breath. She knew she would know if Gavin had delivered a baby *at work* but she thought perhaps he may have aided a labouring shopper in an Aldi car park... but then again, if Gavin *had* done something like that, it would have been headline news and he would have presented himself with an honorary lanyard.

'Please tell me *you've* delivered one,' Gavin said, seeming now to bump up and down with nerves as well as the rough ride. 'Because if *I* haven't then *you* must have. You and half a dozen taxi drivers, right?'

'I haven't,' Lucie breathed. 'The closest I've got to birth is a guinea pig I looked after once.' She sighed heavily. 'And she ate one of them.'

'Oh, Jesus!' Gavin exclaimed. 'Right, that's it!' He drew his phone from his pocket and began tapping as the go-kart neared the boulders still part-blocking their way into the village.

'What are you doing?'

'I'm googling how to deliver babies. I mean, there is a YouTube video on everything, remember? Like my make-up tutorials. There's guitar lessons and… unpacking the box of every laptop ever made and… BTS's best eating moments… so there must be something about this!'

'And what if that's not enough?' Lucie breathed.

'I'm going to call Sharon. Surely, if neither of *us* have delivered before, you can guarantee *she* will have. Failing that, she's bound to have the mobile number of a midwife or… wasn't she almost married to Mr Tuck the gynae guy?'

'Don't forget it's twins,' Lucie breathed. 'I think everything is different for twins.'

Fifty-Five

Michalis had taken the SIM card from his phone and was holding it between his fingers. This tiny, slightly weird-shaped chip needed to be thrown away, there was just one more call he had to make before he did that. He slipped it back into his phone and watched the screen reset.

It wasn't the first time he'd done this, but this time he really wanted it to be the last. Three more texts from Thekli had arrived over the last couple of days and the harshness of the one he had received that morning had been the final straw:

You killed Jonas. I hope you rot.

He had borrowed Nyx's moped and headed out, winding around the mountain and then down to here, Kalami Bay. If there was one place guaranteed to settle his soul it was here. So many family times had been spent here, his mum and dad sharing a carafe of wine at this very taverna while he had his first taste of paddleboarding before it became so current. He'd had a bodyboard and a bamboo cane back then and it had sometimes taken him thirty minutes to even get on it and balanced. But once he'd been up there, centred, he'd glided out into the blue relishing the quiet to look for fish.

Now he was sitting at a table overlooking the pebble beach, a glass of ice-cold lemon-flavoured Fanta in front of him... a new SIM card waiting to be inserted in his phone. A brand-new number always felt like a fresh start. And it halted the messages for a while... but somehow never for good. This time though he had to do something additional, something more courageous. It was an action he had been too scared to consider as an option before. He pressed on a name, starting the call to Anastasia. Looking out at the gently rippling water ahead of him, he closed his eyes and prayed she would pick up.

'Hello.'

As soon as he heard the voice of Thekli's sister, Michalis was flooded with hard-to-handle memories that stopped him from immediately speaking. Thekli was so close to her sister. Thekli had told him how the two of them had grown up together in a tiny flat in Athens, sharing a single bed, because it was the only apartment their parents could afford. And that physical closeness had led to an unbreakable sisterhood. The family moved to Thessaloniki when Thekli was fifteen and it was only a few months after that when Anastasia met her now husband, Nikos. The bedroom sharing might have changed but the sisters had remained as close as ever during his relationship with Thekli. Anastasia was the first person Thekli had introduced him to and Michalis had liked her very much. It was clear from the outset what a big role Thekli's sister played in her life and when Anastasia found out she was pregnant, Thekli was almost as excited as the mother-to-be.

'Hello?' Anastasia said again.

'Hello,' he responded, shifting his position in his seat. 'Hello, Anastasia. It's... Michalis... Andino.'

There was a loaded pause he should have expected, and then he realised he really should say more before she had the chance to end the conversation before it began. 'Please, I know that you do not want to speak to me but...'

'I do not think I am allowed to speak to you,' Anastasia replied. 'I am sure it was a requirement of the document I signed when the hospital paid me money.'

Her words were hollow. If he had thought there would be anger or sadness, or a combination of the two, he had been wrong. There was no emotion at all. Was that what happened? Did the devastation turn you numb?

'Anastasia,' Michalis breathed. 'I know that saying how sorry I am again will not make things right. I know that things will never be right for you anymore but—'

'What do you want, Michalis?'

The reply was firm, not quite brutal, but hard enough to remind him that he was at the edge of a precipice.

'I have... heard from Thekli,' Michalis said.

Another heavy sigh came next and he wondered if the ending of the call would happen now. He held his nerve and tried to focus on the swimmers in the bay and the family drifting out from the shore aboard a pedalo. But still no response came. Michalis adjusted the phone next to his ear. 'Anastasia?'

'Thekli... she is not well,' Anastasia stated. 'I have tried to get her to... see someone. But, you know, she has lost her faith in the medical profession.'

Michalis closed his eyes. It was *not* his fault. He had to remember that. He might take responsibility for an element of exhaustion hindering his performance last year, but he had not actually made any clinical mistakes in baby Jonas's care. The hospital had paid out because they were scared of a scandal, worried a court case would show them in a negative light no matter if there was blame or not. Thekli had been the one to appoint her sister a lawyer. She had also been the one to be horrified at Anastasia taking a deal.

'What has she said to you?' Anastasia wanted to know.

'The details do not matter.'

'It must matter,' Anastasia answered. 'Or you would not be calling me.'

He nodded like she could see him. 'It is... not for the first time.' He swallowed as all the words Thekli had sent him washed over his shoulders like the water of the bay had earlier. 'She has been sending messages and leaving voicemails for the past six months.' He sighed. 'To begin with they were regretful words, sad messages full of grief but... then they changed. There was anger. Calls in the middle of the night.' He swallowed. 'Threats.'

'Michalis, I do not know what you expect me to say.'

He winced, the injury from his fall from Bambis reminding him of something else equally painful. The cuts and bruises he had treated with arnica. It was the reason he jumped when there was an unexpected noise. The cause of his searching the shadows, scared of what might be waiting for him.

'Two months ago, three men attacked me in the hospital car park.' He waited a beat before carrying on. 'The next day Thekli, she sent me a video of it and… she said there was more to come.'

He closed his eyes and held his nerve. He wasn't expecting sympathy. That wasn't what this call was about. It was about letting a sister know that her sister was struggling more than she probably realised. And it was about trying to make this stop for all of them.

'Michalis,' Anastasia breathed. 'You know I never blamed you for what happened to Jonas.' There was a pause. 'For what happened to my son.'

He blinked away rapidly appearing tears. He wanted to believe Anastasia's words, but the buck *had* stopped with him whether there was intention and negligence or not. He had been over and over this again since that horrifying night, not sleeping, then when sleep had finally arrived he would wake shivering wondering if any of it was real.

'And, I think, if Thekli is honest with herself she does not think you are really to blame either.'

Michalis blew out a breath and shook his head a little. 'I hurt her.'

'You broke up with her because you were fighting the virus,' Anastasia reminded. 'You were exhausted, barely living, I *do* remember.'

'Thekli deserved someone who could give her more time.'

'She knows that. Maybe she does not accept it yet, but she does know.'

'Anastasia,' Michalis said. 'I want you both to be able to try to find happiness.'

There was a sigh down the phone that sounded like her whole heart was deflating. Perhaps this had been the wrong call...

'You deserve that too, Michalis,' Anastasia breathed. 'And I am so sorry Thekli has been doing this to you.'

He didn't know what to say next. There was so much he could say, but nothing seemed right or felt quite enough. He didn't want to make this about his absolution. Anastasia had lost so much more than him. A baby. A son. Someone who wasn't coming back. 'I am sorry, Anastasia. Every day... I am so sorry for what happened to Jonas.' His voice broke at the end of the sentence.

'Thank you, Michalis,' Anastasia said softly. 'I think, no matter how hard it is, it is maybe time we all realised that, for whatever reason, it was God's will that Jonas was called back to Him.'

He hated to believe that. Just like with his own mother and all those millions of people who had died last year – God's will had a lot to answer for. One of the reasons he had gone into medicine was so he could do something when it was thought all hope was lost. How did you sit with the fact that things might really be out of your hands when you were a doctor?

'You did the best you could,' Anastasia whispered. 'That is all anyone can do.'

Michalis closed his eyes again and took a deep inhale of the sea air.

'I will speak to Thekli and I will make sure she does not contact you again. Please, Michalis, I am sorry those men hurt you but... please could you consider not reporting this to the police. I hate to ask you this, but my sister...' Her voice trailed off and Michalis felt the raw sound of emotion over the connection.

He opened his eyes. 'I haven't,' he whispered. 'And... I won't.'

The blows the thugs had delivered that night, as painful as they had been, he'd seen as some kind of deliverance. When fighting back hadn't been an option, because he was outnumbered, he had simply let it happen and waited until they'd reached exhaustion. Somehow, even as it happened, he had felt it wasn't random. And afterwards, when Thekli threatened him with more, his thoughts had never been to make a report. It had always been about escaping. Except, as he was trying to find his peace in Corfu, there had always been this fear in the back of his mind that Thekli knew where his family lived. That it might happen again. This phone call would hopefully change things for the both of them.

He spoke again. 'I just... want to try and find a way through what happened. And I wish that you can find a way through this too. No one deserves to be punished anymore.'

He heard Anastasia's relief in her breathing. 'You are a good doctor, Michalis. And people, they will always need good doctors.'

'I do not know,' Michalis said. 'There is only so much we can do and sometimes it simply isn't enough.'

'But, the one thing you did achieve was... you gave Jonas time,' Anastasia said strongly. 'And you gave *me* time with him.' She paused. 'I know you pushed for medication others thought would make no difference. You did all you could for my son.'

He held onto that simple truth and gripped tight.

'Goodbye, Michalis,' Anastasia said. 'And good luck.'

'Goodbye, Anastasia,' he whispered.

Fifty-Six

Villa Psomi, Sortilas

'No wonder he wouldn't bloody tell us where she was!' Gavin exclaimed as they rushed down the short slope then dropped down the steps to the pool and terrace area. 'She's here! By *our* pool! I hope she isn't expecting a water birth!'

Lucie's legs were quaking like all her nursing training was dribbling out of her with every step she took. When she had worked in accident and emergency she had never known what to expect when someone was pushed through the door. It couldn't be that hard to deliver a baby, could it? Except she only had TV dramas to go on. She'd never actually even been present at a birth before. Why would she have been?!

'Do we need to get water and towels?' Lucie asked Gavin.

'Was that a joke?' Gavin said, turning his head to her as they made their way across the *plaka* flagstones. 'The very first thing we need to do is get rid of all these people.

There's almost a village here and... is that a priest?'

Lucie gulped. She couldn't even see a pregnant woman for all the bystanders at the side of the water. Were they all really expecting experts to arrive and sort out this medical emergency? Pressure grew like a prevalent fungus inside her belly. What if she wasn't up to the job? Where was the *actual* doctor? Why hadn't Michalis answered her messages and calls? She drew her phone out and checked the screen again. Nothing.

'Right!' Gavin shouted, holding his hand in the air like he could be signalling to the pilot of an Airbus. With no one really taking any notice of him, he snatched the *mati*-topped staff from Melina and raised it as if he was commanding seas to part. 'Listen to me!'

Even Lucie stifled her breathing a bit in case the noise punctured the now still atmosphere. Finally, as people seemed to retreat a little, she could see Maria. The soon-to-be mother was pacing strongly, her hands at the bottom of her very rotund stomach, lips moving like she was talking to herself. Her long dark hair was loose and her beautiful complexion looked a little dewy – probably from the exertion of contractions. They should definitely find out how far apart they were. If things hadn't progressed too much then there was time for a doctor to get here. Even if the ambulance couldn't get into the village, paramedics could surely bail out at the blockage and walk the rest of the way like the tourists had to.

'Right, all of you, you need to leave, right now!' Gavin insisted. Then he seemed to have a change of heart. 'Not you,' he said, one hand on Maria's shoulder. 'You're the most important person here. You and your precious babies.' He surveyed the others. 'You, go! You, go! You… you stay.' He was addressing Melina now. 'You can boss people around and get us anything we need. I'll start off the requests. There's a flagon of wine inside the house. You can get that.'

'For sterilisation?' Melina wanted to know.

'No, for me to drink. Steady nerves are required during labour.' He looked to Lucie then. 'I've left The Other Sharon Osbourne an urgent message.' His attention seemed to be drawn to a man stood close to Maria whose manner was giving off all the 'scared to death'. 'Who are you and why do you need to be here?'

'I am Damocles,' he replied. 'I am the father.'

'Hmm,' Gavin mused, eyes roving up and over him. 'I'm not sure I believe you. You look very young to be her father.'

'I am the father of the babies,' Damocles added.

It was then Maria let out a scream like she was being disembowelled by wolves and clutched her stomach as if the babies were imminently going to burst out of the tight giant beach ball shape under her dress.

'Time check!' Gavin shouted and Lucie looked at her watch, ready to calculate what was going on.

'What are we going to need?' Gavin asked more of himself than anyone else. 'Cloths, blankets, gloves…'

Maria's wailing seemed to calm a little.

'I have knives.'

Lucie looked up to see Nyx standing a short way away from them. 'Nyx… where's your brother?'

She shrugged. 'He left early this morning. He did not say where he was going. I have tried to call him… but there is no answer.'

'Is it like him to do that?' Lucie asked. Perhaps she didn't know Michalis as well as she hoped she did. 'To not let people know where he's going and not take calls?'

'He is a man,' Nyx said, like it gave all the answers. 'And he is stupid.'

'OK, Maria,' Gavin said gently. 'Where would you like to get comfy so we can examine you and see when these babies are going to come along?'

'We need... to wait for the doctor,' Maria breathed, seeming to be struggling with pain again.

'Well, lucky for you, *I'm* a doctor,' Gavin stated, looking only at his patient. 'I've got...'

He stopped talking as his eyes went away from the soon-to-be-mother and it was then Lucie noticed five tortoises in single file, strutting along the edge of the pool and demanding the space to walk unheeded into the grounds. She shook her head like it might be a mirage.

Gavin seemed to refocus. 'I've got a golden doctorate from the world renowned... Tur-tell Institute in the UK.'

'You are a real doctor?' Maria asked again, her face scrunching up and teeth biting together.

'Is that another pain?' Gavin asked, shooting a look that Lucie caught immediately.

'*Ne!* Damocles!' Maria screeched in a tone that could have called dolphins home.

'How long was it between the pains?' Gavin whispered to Lucie.

She shook her watch like she really wanted it to be faulty due to a dunk in sea water earlier in the week. But it clearly wasn't. 'Barely two minutes.'

'OK,' Gavin said, sounding unnaturally calm. 'Once

this one is over we need to examine her and get her settled somewhere, quickly.'

'I will call Michalis again,' Nyx said, reaching into her apron for her phone.

Fifty-Seven

Andino Butcher's, Sortilas

What was it with this village? Every time Michalis left it something happened. His father had told him about the emergency the second he got through the door of the butcher's and, after his initial reaction – which was to head straight to his surgery at Villa Psomi – his next thought was... a baby. *Babies* plural. Hadn't he just been talking about the loss of one little life that had been in his hands? It was possibly the worst timing ever.

'What are you doing?' Dimitri wanted to know.

Michalis looked down at his hands as he loitered in the hallway. His fingers were wound around a set of worry beads he seemed to have taken down from the coat hooks without realising it. *His mother's worry beads*. Made from olive wood, they had never been far from Lola's hands. She had used them for prayer and contemplation right up until the end. And he wished she was here for guidance right now.

'Michalis?' Dimitri said, coming closer. 'Is there something wrong? Did you not hear what I said? About Maria and the babies?'

Michalis nodded. 'I… know. I heard what you said but… it might be better if we go to get a doctor from Acharavi.'

'The road is still blocked for cars bigger than the smallest models,' Dimitri reminded him.

'I could go… on your moped. Bring someone to the villa.'

'Michalis,' Dimitri said seriously. 'You are the doctor in Sortilas. You are right here. Right now.'

He wet his lips, trying to stop the panic from rising up and turning into beads of sweat on his forehead. 'I know, but—'

'Listen,' Dimitri said, his tone a little stern. 'This is not the time for a crisis of confidence. You went to school with Maria and Damocles. They are depending on you.'

People depending on him. Him letting people down. But then there was Anastasia, practically pardoning him for his role in what had happened in Thessaloniki. *You did all you could.* He wasn't doing all he could running olive wood spheres over his fingers.

'OK,' Michalis said, forcing himself to take a deep breath.

'Whatever is on your mind,' Dimitri said, 'we can talk about it.'

'We can?' Michalis asked. It wasn't like his father to offer counsel. That had always been his mother's job. Dimitri was nothing if not traditional in his ways. The bread winner, well, the meat seller who provides financial support. Lola had always given emotionally and spiritually.

'You were the one who stopped talking, Michalis,' Dimitri told him. 'I never wanted to stop listening.'

The words were potent and it was the kick he needed.

He gave a nod and slipped the beads into the pocket of his jeans. 'OK.'

'You want me to come with you?' Dimitri asked, much softer now.

He shook his head. 'No, Papa, I will be OK.' Michalis smiled at his father. 'Thank you.'

Fifty-Eight

Villa Psomi, Sortilas

'Has anyone given birth in an egg chair before?' Gavin asked Lucie as Maria screamed and they observed things from the business end. Damocles was alternating between holding his wife's hand and steadying the egg chair when Maria was pushing instead of trying to get something therapeutic from the swinging sensation.

'I don't know,' Lucie breathed. 'Probably not... and we don't have time to google it, right now.'

They had pulled the chair into the shade before Maria had settled into labouring, but it still felt warmer than a greenhouse set next to Venus. Lucie had on the too-big gloves from Michalis's surgery, but they were sweaty and slippery and she was considering ditching them. The last thing she wanted was for the babies to come flying out and for her to drop them because of these inadequate floppy fingers.

'What's happening? You've propped me where I can see mostly her authentic Greek dress and only a whiff of the bearded clam!'

It was The Other Sharon Osbourne shouting via FaceTime. Lucie used her elbow to readjust the position of Gavin's phone that was balancing between the rim of a terracotta planter, filled with a fragrant mint plant, and a stack of classic novels Melina had pulled from the shelves of the lower living room when shouted at to do so by Gavin.

'Is that better?' Lucie asked Sharon, before sending a reassuring smile to Maria. 'You're doing so so well.'

'Looks like she's fully patulous to me! I can see hair... that *is* the baby's hair, isn't it?'

'Another one is coming! I want to push!' Maria screeched mid-swing.

'Don't let her push!' Sharon's voice yelled. 'She shouldn't push until she gets the *really* strong urge that she *needs* to push. She can't be pushing if it's just to get it over with.'

'I want to get it over with! It hurts!' Maria screamed as Damocles whispered platitudes in her ear.

'Drink this!' Melina said, holding out a small vial of creamy liquid with a tiny cork in the top of it.

'What is that?' Lucie asked. She was pretty sure that Maria ingesting anything right now was a bad idea.

'It is a simple... potion,' Melina answered, pulling out the cork and re-offering it to the patient.

'Well,' Lucie began. 'Whatever it is you can't give it to her now. She's about to deliver babies!'

'And this will ensure that they are anointed with the life-preserving spirit of Sortilas and are birthed with all the health benefits.'

Lucie eyed up the tiny test-tube Melina was holding carefully like it contained tears of a dragon. Did this teeny amount of liquid really give *all* the health benefits? What on earth was in it? And why wasn't it being added to cereals already?

'I... do not want to wait! I want to push!' Maria demanded, eyes large and full of fire now.

'But, Maria, this man is a doctor and we should...' Damocles began, clamping the egg chair still as Maria braced her back into the cushions, dragging her knees up into her chest.

'Who's a doctor?' Sharon's voice bellowed into proceedings again. 'If you have a doctor there why was I summoned?'

'Shut up, Sharon!' Gavin demanded, hands in a very delicate position. 'I knew I should have brought my head torch instead of the golf balls.'

Lucie winced, then turned her focus back to their gasping patient. This was putting her right off the idea of having children. It looked agonising. Perhaps *she* should drink the test-tube, unless... 'That's not more goat pee, is it?'

'No!' Melina insisted. 'It is—'

'*Ya.*'

Lucie turned around at the sound of Michalis's voice. He was here. Finally, he was here! And he looked ready to help them, an apron over his clothes, his sleeves pulled up over his elbows, hands looking scrubbed. She opened her mouth to say something but Melina beat her to it...

'There is a complication with the babies. No one is saying anything apart from a loud woman on a little screen who tells Maria not to push. I suggest the elixir you gave to everyone last year.' Melina brandished the test-tube.

Michalis looked at the vial and then his eyes found Lucie. *The magic formula.* He had hoped he could avoid talking about that and he certainly did not expect to be faced with it here amid the labour.

'I said that Maria should have nothing to drink while she's in the middle of a delivery of twins,' Lucie answered.

'And you are right,' he stated. 'Let us see how you are getting on, Maria.'

He kept his voice calm and even, the way he always did with patients before he knew the extent of their issues. There was no reason to be fearful until there was something to be fearful of.

'I am wishing I had not let Damocles anywhere near me nine months ago! Arrrrgggghhh!'

'Why is she in this chair?' Michalis wanted to know as he started to make his examination.

'Don't look at me,' Gavin said, taking a step back. 'It was where she wanted to be. And as there's no birthing suite provided in Villa Psomi and there are tortoises all over the house, we thought out in the open, in the shade, with no near neighbours to overlook proceedings, was the best thing.'

'We wanted to keep Maria comfortable,' Lucie added. 'I tried to call you. I sent several text messages saying how urgent it was.'

And he had thrown away the old SIM card, delayed his arrival by questioning his competence, not been here for her when she needed him most. 'I am here now.' He looked at Maria. 'Maria, keep taking slow, steady breaths, OK? Try to control the breath. Damocles, you will help her. I want you to inhale a long, slow breath, to hold it for a second and then I want you to blow it out and make it sound like... the coffee machine at the *cafeneon*.'

'The new one or the old one?' Melina asked.

'They have a new one?'

Michalis turned at the sound of his sister's voice now. 'Nyx, what are you doing here?'

'I have made drinks for everyone and I have experience. I once helped cut a baby from a sheep. So I am here, with my knives, if I am needed.'

'Damocles! I do not want the babies cut out by the butcher!'

'No one is cutting anything,' Michalis reassured softly. 'Apart from the cord when both your babies are safely born.'

He swallowed. He had got in trouble when he had made promises he couldn't keep before. But there was a difference between a promise and giving his patient the optimism she needed to get her through what came next.

'OK, Maria,' Michalis said. 'I am going to touch your stomach now.'

'Let's do the coffee breathing,' Damocles suggested to his wife.

'Can someone end the video call now?' Sharon's voice screeched.

Tears were flowing down Lucie's face now as she looked at new mother, emotional father and two beautifully perfect boys she and Gavin had helped ease into the world. The newborns were both squawking like angry hungry birds, mouths eager to latch onto something Maria was a little too exhausted to immediately offer. All of them were well. They had successfully delivered twins while the mother sat in an egg chair overlooking the glistening water and the mountain range of another country.

'I'm going to get that mystery bottle of booze right now and do not even try to stop me,' Gavin said, wiping sweat from his brow with the back of his arm.

'I'm not stopping you,' Lucie answered with a sniff.

The birth had been the most frightening yet compelling event she had ever witnessed. But it had also been beautiful, and Michalis had been so composed, so sure and definite in his actions, so in control of how it had all played out.

'I am also not stopping you,' Nyx said. 'I will come to help.'

With Melina fussing around Maria, Damocles and the babies, Lucie was left with just Michalis.

'I don't know what we would have done if you hadn't arrived,' she told him.

'You would have delivered the babies,' he told her. 'You did most of the hard work here, not me.'

'That's not true,' Lucie said at once. It had been Michalis's steady hands ensuring safe passage for the babies' heads and then the rest of their squirming bodies, one a whole fifteen minutes after the other. He had been *amazing*.

'Lucie, people always think that the babies are the most important things in a birth,' he told her. 'But the babies, they cannot do anything. They are there. That is all. The most important person is the mother. She and nature have to do all the work. And you helped her, keeping her calm, encouraging her, saying all the correct things.'

'Gavin sang two verses of Cher's "Just Like Jesse James".'

'And that was neither calming nor encouraging,' Michalis said with a smile. 'Maria looked to *you* for advice. You helped her control her breathing and her pushing and—'

'And now I know exactly what the coffee machine at the *cafeneon* sounds like.'

'Unless they really have a new one,' Michalis said. 'You may never experience the exact sound but, trust me, Damocles had it so right.'

Lucie let out a breath of relief that even took herself by surprise. 'This place... it's crazy. Earlier I was tangled up in the latest version of my no-wedding wedding dress and now I've helped to bring two new little boys into the world.'

'What do you want me to say?' Michalis asked. 'This is Greece.'

Lucie smiled. 'Well, Dr Andino, what I'd really like you to tell me is what is in that test-tube Melina was trying to get Maria to drink.'

Michalis sighed. 'I think that will have to be something we talk about at another time.'

Well, that was mysterious...

'And there is...' Michalis began again. 'There is something else that I need to speak with you about.'

'Oh?' His tone was serious and she started to worry that their holiday romance was going to end up being postcard-sized rather than the at least C5-sized notebook she had hoped for.

'Here we are! Still no idea what it is but Nyx has tried to tell me it's made from trees!'

Gavin was back on the terrace holding the neck of the large glass bottle in the fist of his right hand.

'It *is* made from trees!' Nyx insisted. 'It is *mastika*.'

'I'm going to call it tree juice,' Gavin replied.

'Why are there tortoises in your house?' Nyx wanted to know.

'I don't know,' Gavin admitted. 'There was nothing about them in the email information I was sent. And they eat for England. One of them – the biggest one – brazenly picked grapes off my plate this morning.'

'Oh, Gavin,' Nyx exclaimed with a laugh. 'You do know we have wild tortoises in Corfu, no? They must have come in from the garden.'

'What?!' Gavin said, taking the top off the bottle. 'You mean… they're not pets?'

'They are invading your home. You must remove them. I will help you.'

'You won't cook them, will you?' he asked. 'Because, although they're annoying, I couldn't condone that.'

'I should clean up,' Michalis said, indicating the carnage around them. 'I will get some things from the surgery.'

Lucie nodded and as she watched him head away from the terrace, she couldn't help feeling that something was about to change between them.

Fifty-Nine

Syki Bay

'I'm really not sure this is a good idea,' Lucie began. 'My balance is all about not eating too many biscuits from the ward share tin rather than, you know, actual balancing.'

Michalis smiled at her as she put her feet on the paddleboard and immediately her bikini-clad frame began to wobble, even though the fiberglass was anchored on the pebble beach. Today had been a good day. Earlier he had helped Maria, Damocles and the new twins to get settled at home and now, this evening, the road in and out of Sortilas was finally able to be passed by full-sized cars and minibuses. Meat was on its way to the Andino Butcher's shop and the news had put a smile back on Melina's face for five minutes... until she started shouting on the phone to coordinate the delivery of a stage. Perhaps while all was harmonious in the village, he should have left it there, called it a win and given himself some breathing space, but he knew Lucie wasn't going to be on the island for much longer and he wanted to settle himself with the truth... and share that with her, no matter how things might turn out for them. So, he had put his paddleboard on the roof of his car and driven them down the mountain to this beautiful little cove nestled below the road between Perithia and Kassiopi.

'I will teach you,' Michalis told her. 'But first we have to get the board into the water.'

'Is it deep here?' Lucie asked. 'It looks deep.'

'It is peaceful,' Michalis said. 'That is why I like it.'

He took a second to let his eyes rest on the water ahead of them, then track over to the right and the rocks and greenery sheltering the bay.

'We could just sit on the beach,' Lucie said. 'Or swim.'

He looked back to her then, a smile growing on his lips. 'You are scared to try this?'

'No!' Lucie said immediately. 'Of course I'm not scared. I have helped to deliver babies and... I've ridden a banana and survived several trips with Miltos at the wheel of the go-kart car and I've been a human pin cushion while I've been literally mummified with lace.'

'Then this will be easy,' Michalis reassured. 'OK, the first thing you have to do is strap yourself to the board.' He bent down and fastened the Velcro around her ankle.

'Is that so we don't lose the board? Or so I don't get swept out to sea?' Lucie asked.

'No one is getting lost today,' he told her. Except that might not be true. It would depend on how Lucie reacted when he told her exactly what had happened in Thessaloniki. It might be that he ended up being cast adrift from her.

'OK,' she answered, shrugging as if she was readying

herself for an Olympic event. 'OK, I'm listening. What do I do next?'

'OK, so we are going to pick up the board, there, by the handle and we are going to take it into the water.'

He helped Lucie to turn the board up on its rail then let her put her grip around the handle and lift it up.

'How long have you been doing this?' Lucie wanted to know.

'A long time,' he answered. 'Before half the world was trying to do it… and dogs. There are a lot of dogs doing it on the internet.' He paused before continuing as the water rose up around knees then quickly reached mid-thigh. 'I was perhaps eight. I did not have a real board like this. I had a bodyboard and no paddle, just a long stick of bamboo.'

'So, you're basically a professional,' Lucie said shaking her head. 'Born into it.'

'No,' he breathed. 'I still fall off sometimes.'

'Oh, great! There really is no hope for me!'

Despite the drama in her reply she was laughing and it was then it really struck Michalis exactly how much he would miss her if this was going to be the conclusion of what they had begun together.

'OK,' he said gently. 'So, put your knees up on the board, one each side.'

'You said that like it's as easy as getting out of bed.'

Her body was up close to his now, the board bobbing alongside them. He took a moment to revel in having her next to him. 'It is easier than getting out of bed when you are there in the room wearing nothing but my shirt.'

He felt himself blush. Perhaps it had been wrong to say that now when he knew what he had to tell her.

But before he could think any more about it, she had planted a kiss on his lips. She tasted of salt water and sunshine and he indulged in the sensation in case it never came again.

He watched her grab the board and hoist herself onto it. 'Good!' he told her.

'God, I'm on it! Look at me! Ha!' Lucie said.

'OK,' Michalis said. 'Now, here, you take the paddle.'

'OK, alright, that feels slightly less secure now,' Lucie answered, wavering a little and trying to maintain equilibrium.

'You are doing great,' Michalis reassured her. 'Now, take a few strokes.'

'Are we still talking about paddleboarding?' She grinned at him and then shrieked as she almost toppled to her left. 'Sorry, mind out of the sexy now. Concentrating. This isn't so bad.'

'You are on your knees,' Michalis reminded her.

'I'm only a beginner. Just because you have a black belt in this doesn't mean you get to showboat.'

'Want to try standing up?'

'Well...'

'The answer of course is "yes",' Michalis said with a smile. The water was deeper now so he needed to swim a little. 'So, put the oar down across the board. Then put both your hands around it and keep a balance.'

'Help,' Lucie breathed. 'I don't think this is going to work.'

Her *everything* was shaking and she hadn't realised just how incredibly weak her core was. How could standing up straight be so difficult? Granted, she was on the water, but still, she was young and she could hold her own on the dancefloor with Gavin. She willed her limbs to comply but as she drew her feet up from behind her the board began to gain momentum in its sideways motion and she could feel herself begin to panic.

'Hold the balance, Lucie,' Michalis instructed. 'You're in control of the board. Hold it... hold it—'

'Not happening!' Lucie squealed and she tipped over into the water with a splash.

Water filled her nose and ears and she resurfaced with a frustrated grunt. 'I almost had it!'

'Yes, you did,' Michalis agreed, rescuing the paddle. 'Shall we try again?'

He was already moving the board back to shore a little to aid Lucie getting back onto her knees.

'OK?' he asked her.

She nodded and remembered how she had got centred the last time. *New experiences, here we go!* Settled back on her knees, she gave a few strokes forward and then rolled herself up onto her feet, focussing on keeping her weight over the middle of the board.

'That's it! That is it!' Michalis cheered as Lucie rose to her feet. 'Now, take another few strokes, keep your chin up, looking forward.'

She was doing it! She was actually doing it and it felt wonderful. There was nothing but her and the calling of the empty sea ahead. Lucie dipped the paddle into the water and gently propelled herself along. This was possibly the most relaxing thing she had ever done.

'This is... fantastic,' she breathed to herself. Then,

realising she had barely whispered the sentiment, she said it louder into the quiet. 'This is fantastic!'

'Hey, not too fast! Wait for me!' Michalis shouted from behind her.

Sixty

Michalis was on the paddleboard too now, taking control and sailing them around the bay. His wound was really starting to heal and Lucie's great work with the closure was going to mean only the faintest of scars. He looked down at her then. Lucie was lying out, body absorbing the sunshine, eyes on the view as they drifted quietly, enjoying the serenity this mode of transport brought.

'I can get why you would want to do this,' Lucie said to him. 'Straight away after a shift at the hospital.'

'You can?'

'Completely,' she answered. 'If Southampton was a little bit more like Greece I might invest in a board and do it too. It's so gentle and relaxing. I think this might be the closest I'll ever get to feeling like... a swan.'

'A swan?' Michalis queried.

'Yes! Don't you feel that way too? It feels majestic and regal and not at all like that hideous banana I sat on in Sidari.'

He smiled, stroking the paddle once more through the

water before he carefully put it down across the board and lowered himself to a sitting position to join her.

'We should have brought a picnic,' Lucie said, carefully turning herself around so she was facing him. 'Because did you know there's no privacy at the little bench you took me to?'

'Lucie,' Michalis breathed. 'There is something I have to tell you.'

'Oh,' she answered, her expression changing from a bright summer's day to an afternoon expecting a thunderstorm. 'I was hoping you'd decided whatever it is wasn't important or, if it *was* important, that you had changed your mind. Because... I don't want something to ruin what we have together.'

He took a breath and met her eyes. 'I... do not know if things will change after I tell you. But... I just know... that I *have* to tell you. Because, if I do not, I can never be free of how keeping it inside makes me feel.'

'Oh, Michalis,' Lucie said, reaching forward and taking his hand in hers.

He shook his head, not wanting to let himself give in to the enjoyment of the sensation of her touch. 'I have held this back from you when I could have... when I *should* have told you much sooner ago. When you told me, about your mother and all your fears about living your life in the right way... that is when I should have been saying this.'

'Then tell me now,' Lucie said gently. 'I'm ready to listen. No matter what it is.'

He nodded soberly, knowing there was no turning around on this now. 'Well... the truth is... I left Thessaloniki because I lost a patient.'

Lucie gave a nod but said nothing further, squeezing his hand as if in encouragement.

'He... Jonas... was only a few weeks old. He was born prematurely so his lungs, they were not fully developed. He was... so very small and so very weak that nobody thought that he had a chance.'

'Oh, Michalis,' Lucie breathed. 'That must have been so devastating.'

He shook his head. 'I see death every day,' he began again. 'Just like you do. And, last year, you know there was more death than ever before... but this little boy... he *fought*.'

Michalis could feel his throat tightening as his body reacted to the grief he still held tightly enveloped inside. He swallowed. 'He improved. He bought himself some time. And next I managed to secure a new drug for him to try. Only a very few days later there was such hope that he was going to get well again, to be able to breathe on his own.' He closed his eyes, seeing the tiny form of Jonas in the incubator attached to monitors and wires, his tiny chest being made to sucker in and out.

'Then, one morning, that was it,' Michalis stated. 'The alarms sounded and... by the time I was called... when I got to the neonatal intensive care... the consultant paediatrician had already... well... Jonas... he was gone.'

'Michalis,' she began. 'I don't know much about premature babies, but I do know that sometimes they are so tiny they simply aren't equipped to survive, no matter what care they get.'

'I know that, Lucie,' Michalis answered. 'I am a doctor.' He sighed. 'And that was what it was. Exactly as you say. It was not Covid-19 or pneumonia. He was just too small, not ready enough to be born and to survive.'

'Then you know that there was nothing else you could have done.'

'I should have been there. I should not have left him.'

'It's not your job to spend twenty-four hours with individual patients. I have had to say that to myself and to Gavin so many times over this past year. We aren't machines. We're humans. And we need rest, otherwise giving our best isn't going to be our best.'

'I know that but... there was a little more to it.'

'What was it? You can tell me.'

Michalis dipped a hand into the sea, scooping up a little water and sprinkling it down onto the board. 'I told you... about Thekli.'

Lucie nodded and then she gasped and let go of his hand. 'Oh, Michalis, was Thekli Jonas's mother?' A hand was at her throat now. 'Was he your... son?'

'Oh, no,' Michalis stated quickly. 'No, Thekli... she was... she was Jonas's aunt.' He shook his head. 'And when we broke up, she did not take it so well.'

'Tell me,' Lucie said.

'We had separated and she did not want that. She would call me in the middle of the night and she would cry and scream and nothing I said would calm her down. And then her sister, Anastasia, had Jonas... and all I did was my job. I tried to do what I always try to do... help people... cure people... make the sick get better. But I could not help him.'

Lucie reached for his hand again but this time he didn't let her take it. He swallowed. 'When Jonas died, Thekli broke even further and now she had something to really blame me for. She holds me entirely responsible for her nephew's death and she has been harassing me every day since it happened. Text messages, calls, she paid people to attack me. I have had many different SIM cards because... somehow she finds a way to know my new number.'

'Michalis,' Lucie said. 'You have to go to the police.'

He shook his head. 'Thekli needs help. And, today, I found the courage to speak to Anastasia. It was... one of the hardest things I have ever had to do... to call the mother of a child I let slip through my fingers like that.' He took a breath. 'And she found it in her heart to forgive me. She even said there was nothing to forgive and that she understood I had tried to do everything I could and that she would try to make sure Thekli did not contact me again.'

This time, Lucie wasn't going to let him shy away from contact. She gingerly rolled up onto her knees and crawled the short distance to where he was sitting, putting her arms around him and drawing him in tight, the board bobbing a little with the motion. 'That's why you didn't get my calls or messages about Maria having the twins.' She traced her fingers over his bare back, outlining his muscles.

'And Jonas is why I did not come straight away when I *did* find out what was happening,' he admitted, his voice close to her ear. 'It was... newborns... two babies and their lives relying on me. I did not know if I could do it.'

Lucie sat back, keeping her eyes on him. 'What made you realise that you could?'

He looked at her so deeply then that it pinched at her heart.

'I spoke to my father. And then I realised in that moment,

that what would be worse than doing something wrong or making a mistake would be to run away. And I did not want to let Maria and Damocles down. And I did not want to let my mother down. But most of all, I did not want to let *you* down.'

'Michalis,' Lucie breathed, reaching out and running a hand through his hair.

'That is why I am telling you all this, Lucie,' he began again. 'Because... I want you to know exactly what happened to make me feel as adrift as we are right now on this paddleboard and to say that... perhaps I am not the man you think I am.'

'Michalis, do you think I like you because you're a doctor?'

'I do not know why you like me at all, if I am truly honest,' he said, sighing. 'You are so warm and caring and bright and funny and... so very beautiful. I cannot give to you anything you do not already possess.'

Lucie shook her head. 'And that's where you're completely wrong. In the short time we've known each other you have given me everything I was missing.' She laced their fingers together. 'You gave me the strength to really face what happened to my mum and to ask Meg the tough questions about it. You've pretty much cured my shoulder tension. And you've shown me exactly what sex is meant to be like.' She smiled. 'And usually I would get all red-faced and embarrassed about feeling so good about that... but I'm not embarrassed at all. I feel empowered and rich with endorphins over it.' She palmed his face. 'You did that,' she whispered. 'And, from what I remember, you weren't wearing a stethoscope then.'

'Lucie,' he breathed, their faces close. 'Sweet, sweet, Lucie.'

'I don't think who we are is written through us without the opportunity to make an edit,' she told him. 'We don't have to be who we've always been. And I'm learning very quickly, right here in Greece, that the only person I have to prove anything to is myself. And I also don't think I've discovered the true depths of Lucie Burrows just yet.'

Michalis smiled at her. 'I think Lucie Burrows is a very beautiful mystery.'

'And I think,' Lucie began. 'That you might be the person I most want to start puzzling it out with.'

She reached for him again then, connecting their lips without a care for their stability in the sea. And the way he kissed her back in response, told her that their staying afloat was also the last thing on his mind.

Hitting the water, Lucie straightaway kicked for the surface then wasted no time reconnecting his lips with hers as they both trod water. The fizzing salt water on his lips speckled her own and the sensation only heightened her desire to give in completely to this closeness they were sharing.

'Lucie,' he breathed.

'I could look at you forever,' she breathed.

As her words worked their way into her mind, planting romantic saplings, she began to think about exactly what 'forever' meant. One thing it definitely didn't mean was saying goodbye at the end of this holiday…

Michalis said no more, but used his free arm to loop around her waist and drag her into him as they both kept kicking to keep afloat.

'Will you,' Lucie began as the water lapped around her.

'Come to the wine tasting with me?'

More time. She just wanted more and more time with him while she could.

'I would say there is nothing more I would rather do but...'

She felt a thrill run through her as his already sexy eyes turned sexier still and his mouth dropped to her neck.

'*Ne*,' he breathed into her skin. 'Yes.'

Sixty-One

Sortilas Square

Two days later

'You are terrifying!'

Nyx screamed out a laugh, bending double as she looked at Michalis in front of her. They were standing in the square in front of the lemon-painted domed church, where all manner of preparations were taking place for the Day of the Not Dead Festival.

'I am a warrior tortoise,' Michalis replied with a straight face, pumping a fist in the air. Immediately one of his really heavy, hand-carved wooden arm cuts fell off and onto the concrete with a clatter.

'You cannot move!' Melina immediately shouted. 'This is the very last dress rehearsal before the festival.'

'The last dress rehearsal?' Nyx queried. 'When were the others?'

'I am not complaining that there is only one,' Michalis answered, trying to remain motionless.

'Did you not notice that we were in lockdown? All my arrangements had to be changed!' Melina said. 'This is the first time everyone has been able to get into the village with the artwork and the pieces for the stage and everything we need to make this festival a success. And it *will* be a success.'

The hope and desperation in the village president's voice sounded on the very verge of menace and, with pins between her fingers, Michalis hoped they were not going to be jabbed anywhere near the very short leatherette skirt he had been tied into.

'Melina!' a shout came from across the space. 'We need to know where the children should congregate for the Dance of Defiance. And, we are three rattle drums short!'

Melina tutted and suddenly thrust a handful of pins at Nyx. 'You can continue. The edging needs to be pinned into place on the waistcoat before it is sewn.' She turned away and shouted, 'I am coming!'

'I am supposed to be folding pastry around beef chunks for the tortoise pies. They are going to look amazing. I am using black olives for their beady eyes.' She plunged a pin into the material and caught Michalis's side.

'Ow! Nyx! Be careful!'

'Such a baby!' Nyx answered. 'I cannot believe you survived being skewered by a tree branch if this is how you react to a little pin.'

Michalis's gaze went back to the other side of the area where Lucie was being as prodded and poked as he was. Layers upon layers of lace and material were being added to the dress she was wearing, Miltos there, directing his grandmother and great-aunt like he was an orchestra conductor and they were reaching the final overture.

'I see you looking at Lucie,' Nyx remarked, pinning a little more gently now.

Michalis smiled.

'When is she going back to the UK?'

'Saturday,' Michalis answered. 'After the festival.'

'Is she going to be one of those clinging people?' Nyx asked with a shudder.

'What?'

'You know, someone who wants your phone number and to "stay in touch". I had one of those once. He was from somewhere called "Silly Isles". Who calls a place "Silly Isles". Ugh!'

Michalis swallowed. 'Lucie already has my phone number.'

'The new one?' Nyx wanted to know. 'Because I had only just got used to the old one. I do not know why you have to change them so often.'

Michalis was glad Nyx didn't know. 'You do not think we should stay in touch when she leaves?'

'What is the point? She lives in UK. You do not.'

'But—'

'I am glad you are here,' Nyx blurted out.

Something in the tone of his sister's voice made him look away from Lucie and back to her. 'I am glad I am here too,' he answered.

'Are you going to stay?' Nyx asked bluntly, still hiding her eyes from him.

He took a deep breath that made the waistband of the skirt tighter still. 'Oh, Nyx, I don't know.'

'I know I can be annoying. Sometimes. And Papa can be annoying. Much more often than me. And I know you hate the shop and—'

'I don't hate the shop,' Michalis insisted. 'I'm just not a butcher like you.'

'I have... liked having you back here,' Nyx admitted. 'There. I have said it. You can feel smug and superior and...'

Despite how difficult it was to manoeuvre himself in this tortoise homage, Michalis put an arm around his sister and pulled her close. For a very brief second she gave in to the emotion until:

'Oh, God, you are half naked and you smell of chickens! Ugh! I hate the smell of feathers. Plucking is my least favourite job!'

'I am a tortoise warrior with wings,' Michalis answered. 'What can you say to that?'

'Ugh,' Nyx said again. 'Ugh, so disgusting.'

'You said that already.'

'I am saying it again! Ugh!'

'Nyx,' he whispered.

'What?'

'If I do not stay in Corfu,' he began. 'I will visit far more often than I used to.'

'Really?' Nyx asked, eyes lighting up like inside she was still that little girl he had left behind to pursue his studies.

'I promise,' he told her.

Gavin fanned at his face. 'Is it me or has the heat level risen a good few degrees today?'

'Oh my God, Gavin!' Lucie exclaimed, wafting out her

arms. 'You're stood there in shorts and a vest. I'm blanketed up like a burrito!'

'And look at your man across the way there,' Gavin said, nodding towards the plinth Michalis was standing on.

Lucie smiled. Michalis was being fitted into a rather odd-looking costume that somehow still managed to show off his best physical attributes. It seemed to be made of coconut shells, wood, feathers, leather and not a lot else...

'I so wish he was bi,' Gavin stated, sighing.

Lucie slapped his arm. 'Put your eyes back in your head. He's not.'

'You don't know he's not. Has he explicitly told you he's *only* into girls? There's so much putting into convenient boxes these days and we don't all fit the same shape, you know.'

'I haven't asked him,' Lucie replied. 'But *you* are with Simon!'

'Well,' Gavin breathed. 'Not exactly "with".' He made the quote marks in the air.

'Come on, Gavin, what happened to being supportive and helping him on his journey wherever it may lead? It's only been a few days and you've pined over him for the best part of a year.'

'I know.'

'And you remember how hard it was for you at the beginning? When we joined the hospital you were worried about fitting in.'

'Everyone made their own assumptions about me,' Gavin stated.

'And what did you do?'

'Dressed as Freddie Mercury at the very first social opportunity there was.'

'Exactly! And you have tons more confidence than Simon,' Lucie told him. 'Simon's softer and more cautious about everything. He literally caresses that coffee machine at work. Unlike Jez, who goes at it like he wants it to bleed.'

'I really like him,' Gavin stated, hands on hips.

'I know you do. But you've played the long game already. You just have to play it a little bit longer, this time knowing that possibly there's going to be this terrific reward at the end.'

'Now you're making Simon sound like an Amazon gift card.'

'Loosely!' Miltos shouted, even though he was only a few steps away. 'My grandmother says you have to keep still. You do not have to move your whole body to talk.'

As he said this, Miltos's arms were flailing around expressing himself like they always were. He flattened them to his sides quickly and frowned. '*You* are not Greek,' he said by way of explanation.

'So… what's going to happen with the good doctor when we go home?' Gavin asked, plumping his bottom down on the edge of a wooden cart stacked full of watermelons.

'I don't know,' Lucie breathed. 'And I almost messed up the day he took me paddleboarding.'

'What do you mean?'

'I said the "f" word.'

'Darling, we all say the "f" word.'

'Forever,' Lucie said on an out breath. 'I said "forever" and, when we made love in the water, I almost *almost* said I loved him.'

'Fuck!' Gavin's gaze then went to the two Greek women

still buzzing around Lucie's dress. 'Sorry, ladies. What was it again… *signomi*.' He lowered his voice. '*Do* you love him?'

'I can't, can I?' Lucie said. 'It's too soon. Who falls in love this quickly?'

'Most romantic comedy heroines are in *lust* in the first five minutes of the movie and in the *deepest* love known to Hallmark by the end.'

A gentle voice broke in. 'And I was definitely in love with Petros.'

Sixty-Two

L ucie turned around.

'Meg! You're here! I was worried when you didn't call me back. We were going to come and pick you up.'

'Stop worrying about me, Lucie-Lou. I've been getting out and about to some of my old haunts from when I was here before,' Meg said. 'I've ridden a bicycle for the first time in years and I've spent time listening to the anecdotes of a real life man from the mountains. Oh! Don't you look so beautiful in that dress?'

'Well,' Gavin began. 'It's not quite Valentina but it does have a certain *je ne sais quoi* I guess.'

'Do you mean Valentino?' Meg inquired.

'No, he doesn't,' Lucie replied.

'Right, time for more refreshments,' Gavin said, clapping his hands together. 'Is this going to take all day do you think? Or are we going to have time to meet Simon at the beach?'

'I'm not standing in this dress all day,' Lucie told him.

'Frappe?' he asked her. 'One for you too, Meg?'

'That sounds divine,' Meg answered.

'Sit down, Madame Meg,' Miltos ordered, arriving with a fold-up chair whose mechanisms were crusted with rust. 'Relax! Take in all that a Sortilas festival is going to offer. This is my grandmother and my great-aunt.'

'Goodness!' Meg exclaimed. '*Kalimera sas. Xero poli.*' She smiled at Lucie. 'I said "good morning" and "nice—"'

'Nice to meet you,' Lucie said. 'I've been learning a bit of Greek too.'

'From Michalis?' Meg asked, adjusting her sun hat.

'Yes,' Lucie replied.

'You sound a little sad,' Meg said. 'Is something wrong? I'm sorry if I butted into your conversation with Gavin.'

'I'm not sad,' Lucie replied. 'Just wondering, I suppose.'

'About your feelings for Michalis?'

She nodded, gaze going back over the square where Michalis was having an elaborate headpiece put in place. 'I came here to... clear my mind and try to move on from how hard last year was, and I *have* done that, but...'

'But?' Meg queried.

'But it's been so much more than that. This place,' she breathed. 'Greece, Corfu... Sortilas. It's got into me like nowhere I've been before. It's not a step back in time as such, it's... a giant leap away from how I've been living at home. Here I never know what time it is and that's such a good thing. I've read books, I've swum and I've eaten foods I never would have even thought of. And, I've met someone who makes me feel so comfortable with myself. I haven't ever had that before.'

'And that is exactly how I felt with Petros,' Meg admitted, nodding.

'And you never saw him again after your holiday.'

'And that was a mistake,' Meg said very definitely.

'Really?'

'Yes,' Meg concurred. 'I know that I never met another man who made me feel the way he did. I don't know how to explain it fully, but it was almost as if he instinctively saw things the way I saw them, thought the same way, breathed in life at the same pace somehow.'

'Oh, Meg... I don't know what to say. Do you think maybe you could find him again?'

Meg shook her head. 'I can't do that. Look at me, I'm nothing like the pretty young thing I used to be. And Petros, he was so handsome, someone more courageous than me will have snapped him up years ago.' She sighed. 'I imagine him bouncing grandbabies on his knee, singing and watching his wife dance around the kitchen.'

Lucie reached for her aunt's hand and held it tight. 'You are beautiful,' she insisted. 'I've always been a little jealous of your amazing skin. And... you don't know that Petros is living the perfect life. He might be miserable and alone and remembering a girl he loved and lost long ago.'

Meg shook her head. 'It just wasn't meant to be. Perhaps it was because I needed to be somewhere else so that someone else could take a chance on another Greek man years later.'

Lucie looked over at Michalis again. 'I'm not used to jumping into things without due consideration.'

'And I think during our conversations on this island we've both agreed that jumping should be... jumped at.'

'But... what if he doesn't feel the same?' Lucie asked. 'What if it's been a lovely holiday romance but that's all he wants?'

'Lucie-Lou,' Meg began. 'Don't be so scared of the answers that you never end up asking the questions.'

Lucie nodded. She felt better having asked Meg all about her mum. It hadn't taken away the fact that Rita was gone but it had helped to know that it was accidental, that Rita *had* loved her. Maybe that was all she ever really needed to be certain of.

'I don't want to be afraid anymore... and I have been. Without truly acknowledging it.'

'Then, my darling girl, you must ask the questions,' Meg told her.

Lucie drew in a deep breath, looking once more at the gorgeous man who had been ever-present during this Greek escape. 'I'll ask the questions,' she told Meg. 'And whatever the answers are, I'll accept them.'

'Oh no!' Meg interjected rapidly, swatting away a mosquito. 'I never said anything about *accepting* the answers. No matter what Michalis says, you must fight for what you want. Because sometimes, people answer with their head and not with their heart.'

'So, if he doesn't want me I have to force him to change his mind?' Lucie asked. 'That doesn't quite feel right.'

Meg shook her head. 'I'm not saying you try to force him to do anything he doesn't want to do. I mean, for example, if someone asks you to stay and live somewhere... let's say Corfu. Then, as well as considering the practicalities... like... what would people think? Where would I work? Or I'm too young to make a decision like that, what if I stay and it all goes wrong and I have to go home with egg on my face...' Meg took a breath. 'Instead, think about joy. And happiness. And what if things go *right*.' She smiled again.

'Ask the questions, hear the answers and then listen to both your hearts. Together.'

Lucie squeezed her aunt's hand. 'OK,' she agreed. 'I will.'

'Who knows,' Meg began. 'You might be wearing that beautiful traditional dress up a real aisle one day... not one adorned with fur and tortoise excrement.'

'Thank you, Meg,' Lucie breathed, putting her fingers to the lace and revelling in the texture.

'What are you thanking me for?' Meg asked.

'Well, from what you've just said, I think I'm most probably thanking you for not listening to your heart when Petros asked you to stay.'

Meg nodded and looked a little wistful. 'Well, that was my decision and I wouldn't have missed your growing up for the world.'

'But, if you had the chance again?' Lucie had a feeling she already knew the answer.

'I might know a lot more of the Greek language than I do now,' Meg whispered.

'Loosely!' Miltos called, coming back towards them. 'It is time for you to get into position for the dancing.'

'What?!' Lucie exclaimed. 'No... wait... dancing? I'm... not a part of the festival. I'm just here to be fitted for this dress... out of kindness to your—'

'Every year my grandmother and aunt make a traditional Corfiot dress that is worn in a parade at one of our festivals,' Miltos informed. 'And this year it is *this* new festival.' He grinned wide. 'And they have decided it is also *this* dress!'

'Of course they have,' Lucie said through gritted teeth and a smile to the old ladies.

'So, you need to learn your movements for the big evening. *Ela!* Come!'

'Meg,' Lucie said as Miltos prepared to drag her into the centre of what was about to become dance space. 'I'm not altogether sure about staying in Greece. It might move at a different pace to the UK, but your time is never ever your own unless you lock all the doors!'

Meg laughed as Lucie picked up her skirts and followed the fruit van man.

Sixty-Three

Theotoky Estate, Ropa Valley

'It says here,' Gavin began, reading from his phone, 'that the Theotoky family are one of the oldest families in Greece.' He smiled. 'I wonder if they come from Sortilas?'

'Sshh,' Lucie said as they made their way across the courtyard to a white-washed stone building, a brick archway surrounding the heavy-looking door, two iron benches set outside. It felt like so long since they had altered their visit to the winery due to the landslide on the Sortilas road and Lucie wanted to soak up every tiny bit of this visit and her last few days on this beautiful island.

Finally in a luxurious minibus they hadn't seen the like of since they'd left Corfu airport, they had been driven down the very centre of the island, then across almost to Paleokastritsa, passing near Doukades where they had visited the donkeys, until finally ending up here in the Ropa Valley. Unlike most of the rest of Corfu, this area was exceedingly flat. Grassy fields like cricket pitches stretched out, some containing flocks of grazing livestock, or, like here, row upon row of vines.

'You didn't mind me inviting Meg, did you?' Lucie whispered to Michalis as they were taken into a room containing large metal vats.

'No,' Michalis answered. 'Why should I mind?'

'Well, because it started out as being you and me and Gavin and Simon, and now Meg's here and Gavin asked Nyx too and—'

Michalis silenced her with a kiss and she melted like she always did when he touched her with any part of his anatomy. It was very difficult to keep her head straight when he was constantly giving her all the heart vibes…

'It is good my sister is not in the shop for a while. She works too hard,' Michalis replied.

Lucie looked ahead of them to where Gavin, Simon, Nyx and Meg were grouped around their guide who was shortly going to be explaining to them the process of converting grapes into their organic award-winning wine. It was so peaceful here and yet another step back to simpler times.

'But,' Michalis stated, 'Nyx will drink the wine like it is water. And sleep all the way back in the coach.'

Lucie laughed and it earned her a very stern shush from Gavin.

The tour had taken them from the room where the raw product was turned from fruit into wine, to the most magnificent cellar. Scores of dark glass bottles surrounded them, stacked side by side, corks facing outwards, kept at the most precise temperature. Everyone had marvelled at the room with its wooden beams and stone walls, taking photos of the mammoth stack of full bottles and being very careful not to knock into any of them. But it was the room they were in *now* that was the real spectacle. There were more rugged stone walls and beams, but this time huge wooden barrels sat the length of the long room and running down its centre were tables and chairs, each decorated with glowing candles and rings of olive branches.

'Oh, this is simply wonderful!' Meg announced, stepping into the room, camera already out and snapping.

'It's so cool!' Gavin said, fanning his T-shirt a little.

'I think it is very cool,' Nyx replied.

'I meant it's *actually* cool,' Gavin said. 'The temperature.'

'Yes, that is what I mean also,' Nyx answered.

'I have never been anywhere like this,' Simon said, standing close to Gavin.

Lucie swallowed as her mind conjured up visions of what this room could be used for if it wasn't hosting their wine tasting. It would make the best venue for a party or perhaps a murder mystery or even... a wedding. That dress had so much to answer for and now, tomorrow night she was going to be 'performing' in it. How had that happened?

'You do not like the room?' Michalis asked her.

'Oh, no,' Lucie began. 'The room is absolutely breathtaking. Really, really gorgeous.'

'But something is wrong?'

She shook her head. 'No, nothing is wrong.' Except for the fact that she was going back to the UK soon and she hadn't yet been brave enough to ask Michalis what happened next for them.

'I have never been here before,' Michalis told her.

'No?'

'People often think that people who live on Corfu have been everywhere there is to go. But, there is much to do here and we are always working. Plus, it is a much bigger island than some think… because of its many little places.'

Many little places. Yes, that was another plus point of this island. There were hundreds of tiny gems of villages tucked away around a tight bend or sprinkled down through narrow roads surrounded by olive groves and wildflowers.

'Shall we try some wine?' Michalis suggested.

Lucie nodded. Perhaps a little organic wine on her tongue would give her the kick she required to start an important conversation.

'This wine is the rosé from 2018,' their guide informed them.

'It smells wonderful,' Meg said, lifting the glass to her nose and inhaling like it might contain a fragrant spray of flowers.

'Perhaps *sip* this one?' Gavin suggested, giving Nyx a nudge in the ribs.

'I am sipping the water,' Nyx replied with a scowl.

'Don't let him boss you around,' Simon said to Nyx. 'He can be a bit like that sometimes.'

'Hey!' Gavin replied, but he sent Simon a smile and raised his glass to him.

'It has a very discreet nose,' the guide continued, finishing off the pouring.

'Unlike you, Michalis,' Gavin said.

'And there are notes of pink grapefruit,' the guide said. 'It should feel fresh, like crunching fruits but also with a beautiful thickness to it.'

Michalis looked to Lucie then and watched her as she slowly put the rim of the glass to her lips. The liquid finally met her mouth and Michalis continued to watch, imagining the sensation as it hit her tongue and rolled into her senses. She closed her eyes then and seemed to take a moment before opening them.

She smiled at him. 'Aren't you going to try some?'

'I was watching you try a little first.'

'It's so nice,' Lucie admitted. 'Refreshing and cool and light.'

Michalis drank a little and nodded. 'I like it.'

'We should buy some,' Lucie suggested. 'Maybe we could find somewhere private and have another picnic before I go home… you know, if you have time and… you want to.'

'This is the perfect wine to go with sausage,' their tasting expert interjected.

'Did you hear that, Simon?' Gavin asked loudly.

'I would like that very much,' Michalis said, leaning a little closer to Lucie. But, as he moved, something in his peripheral vision distracted him. It was someone coming into the entrance area. He couldn't see very well, but the shadow being cast had an odd air of familiarity about it…

'Would you?' Lucie asked softly. 'Because I have to leave soon and—'

She stopped talking when there was a crashing noise from outside the tasting room and Michalis got to his feet, hurrying to investigate. He pushed open the door and couldn't quite compute what he was seeing in front of him.

'Papa?' he said, as if he needed some sort of clarity that his eyes were not playing tricks on him.

There was another crash as Dimitri seemed to lose control of a large box he was carrying and the woman next to him, Amalia, hurried to help. Despite his surprise at his father being here, Michalis stepped forward too.

'I can do it,' Dimitri said gruffly.

'Papa, come on, let me help you,' Michalis said, putting hands either side of the rigid cardboard.

'Thank you, Michalis,' Amalia said. 'They are quite heavy.' She began to assemble the containers she was holding, pushing them back out of the way of the door.

Michalis could see the redness appearing on his father's cheeks and he knew this wasn't from the exertion of the lifting, but from feeling he had somehow been caught in a compromising position.

'What are you doing here?' Dimitri barked, still not meeting his son's eyes.

'We are here for a tour and a wine tasting.'

'How lovely!' Amalia said with a big smile. 'The wine is so delicious and I adore that special room in there.'

'You did not say this was where you were going,' Dimitri said, looking increasingly uncomfortable.

'You did not say you would be closing the shop today,' Michalis countered.

'What? Your sister is...'

As Dimitri began to join the dots that both his family members were present at the winery, the door to the wine-tasting room opened and Nyx barrelled out.

'What's going on? You are going to miss the olive oil

and bread. It's next and...' Nyx stopped talking the second she saw Dimitri. She scowled. 'Why are you not at the shop?'

'Because I am here,' Dimitri answered. 'You did not tell me you were coming here.'

'I did not know that you even knew this place was a place,' Nyx countered. 'But you seem to be... very intimate with it.'

Michalis watched his sister look from the boxes and containers to the woman their father was here with.

'Hello, Nyx,' Amalia greeted. 'It is wonderful to meet you.' She seemed to get caught between stepping forward and staying where she was and in the end she just sent them both another smile.

'Hello, lady-I-do-not-know,' Nyx said in sullen tones.

'Nyx,' Michalis said.

'What?' Nyx asked. 'My father is somewhere he should not be. Somewhere where I am. The one day that I leave the butcher's.' She tutted. 'And what is all this stuff?' She stepped forward and pulled something from the box.

'Put that down,' Dimitri ordered a little too late.

It was a canvas and Michalis watched his sister's expression as she looked at it.

'What is this?' Nyx asked. 'Things you have collected for a tabletop sale?'

'I said put it down,' Dimitri ordered again.

'Dimitri,' Amalia said softly. 'Perhaps it is time that you told your children what you have been doing in your spare hours, no?'

Michalis took a step towards his sister who was now gazing at the board in her hands anew. It was a painting.

A really *really* good painting in watercolours and Michalis recognised the view immediately. It was trees and mountains ending with the sea, the exact vista from the spot on the edge of Sortilas where his mother had always liked to walk to and sit in the sunshine.

'Did you... paint this?' Michalis asked him.

'I...' Dimitri began, as if ready to deny it. It was only when Nyx looked up from the artwork and met their father's eyes that his shoulders dropped in resignation that lying would be futile. He nodded. 'Yes.'

'And it is fantastic, no?' Amalia said quickly, discharging the muted energy. 'All of Dimitri's paintings are amazing. And that is why Theotoky Estate is displaying them here.'

'You did this?' Nyx queried, as if the 'yes' hadn't told a big enough story.

Dimitri nodded again. 'Yes.'

'And they are being displayed?' Nyx carried on. 'Here at this winery where people will come and admire them while they are not too-slowly sipping the wines?'

'Yes,' Dimitri answered, still sounding a little sober.

Not even Michalis had seen this coming. He had thought this was all about his father finding a new partner, but this was something else entirely. And he couldn't really work out why Dimitri seemed almost ashamed of it.

'I am hoping that people will buy some of the paintings,' Amalia told them. 'Dimitri is my most improved student. He has a wonderfully natural gift.'

'I do not understand,' Nyx stated. 'You chop so hard. Everything always slashed so rough. But, to create this picture, you must sit very still and be so very quiet and... gentle. I... do not know this person.'

'I know,' Dimitri said with a sigh. 'I know you don't.'

'I will leave you and… take some of these paintings into the area for the exhibition,' Amalia said, lifting one of the boxes back up and making her way towards another door up a short flight of steps.

'Papa,' Michalis said. 'These paintings are so good. You should be proud, not hiding away your talents.'

Dimitri shook his head. 'I do not know if I am good. All I know is that doing this… losing myself in these pictures helps me to remember your mother and… also to let her go a little more.'

Michalis swallowed. He hadn't realised exactly how much his father was still struggling with that loss all these years on.

'Oh, Papa,' Nyx said, throwing herself at him all octopus-like arms and over-enthusiasm. 'You are a stupid old man!'

The comment was made with deep affection and Michalis enjoyed seeing the embrace between his sister and their father.

'Michalis thought that you were having romantic relations with that funny woman,' Nyx continued. 'And all she was doing was teaching you how to paint.'

'Amalia and I,' Dimitri started as Nyx let him go. 'We have become very good friends.' He cleared his throat. '*Just* good friends,' he emphasised. And then added: 'For now.'

Nyx folded her arms across her chest. 'I do not like the end of that sentence.'

'Nyx,' Michalis said. 'We talked about this. Papa needs a new life too.'

'And now he has his painting! I think it is a fantastic hobby. So not hula-hooping.'

'Nyx,' Michalis said, shaking his head. 'I know that you could not really know this but... Mama would like Amalia. I am sure of it.'

'Well, the Mama I make in my head would think that her lipstick is too bright and that she is a little too cheery.'

Michalis felt for his sister then. Always having to create a version of their mother because her memories were so sparse. It was so much like Lucie with *her* mother. How could either of them form a full picture of who their parent really was out of old photographs and stories they weren't part of?

'Perhaps,' Dimitri began. 'We can have a meal all together and you can get to know Amalia a little better.' He directed his gaze at Nyx. 'I was thinking you might like someone else to try your lamb balls.'

Nyx immediately screwed up her face, but Michalis was quick to put a hand on her shoulder and slowly, very *very* slowly, his sister straightened out her annoyed wrinkles until her expression was changed to one of only mild irritation verging on maybe one day being open to the suggestion.

'No one is replacing Mama,' Michalis whispered to her. 'Say it will be nice.'

Nyx gritted her teeth. 'It will be nice.'

The door to the wine-tasting room swung open and Lucie appeared.

'Oh, sorry, I didn't mean to interrupt anything...' She smiled and stopped talking, taking a step backwards as if she might be about to disappear again.

'No, Lucie, wait,' Michalis said, leaving Nyx's side and stepping up to her. He caught her hand in his and then turned back towards Dimitri.

'Papa,' he began, taking a nervous breath. 'I would like you to meet Lucie.'

'Ah,' Dimitri said, stretching out a hand. 'This is who you have been spending time with. I was beginning to think Michalis had made you up.'

Lucie smiled and took his father's hand in hers, giving it a firm shake. 'It's nice to meet you. *Xero poli.*'

'You know Greek?' Dimitri asked, looking impressed.

'A little,' Lucie said.

Michalis watched her looking so cute and his heart soared. He couldn't imagine staying in Corfu without her here now. But where would he start over again when he knew his sister wanted so much for him to remain?

'Let me present our father,' Nyx said, splaying out a hand. 'The artist formerly known as the butcher.'

'*Xero poli*, Lucie,' Dimitri said.

Sixty-Four

Day of the Not Dead Festival, Sortilas

The village square had been turned into something that resembled New Orleans during Mardi Gras. Garlands and ribbons adorned the trees, and little stalls were packed with produce in a market-style bazaar that had been open from early morning. Now it was evening and the main festivities were set to begin. Before she got dragged into traditional dances, Lucie was making the most of a cold frappe and the shade of the largest olive tree, dressed rather like one of the old-fashioned doll toilet roll holders her nan had used in the downstairs toilet.

'I've bought too much,' Meg announced, arriving by Lucie's side and taking a moment to catch her breath. 'I've got three olive wood appetiser dishes, two embroidered cotton bags and a gorgeous pair of leather sandals the man made right in front of my eyes.'

'Goodness,' Lucie said. 'Did he? I might get myself a pair.'

'The only thing I haven't bought,' Meg began, 'is

something to eat. And I have to say I'm famished. Shopping takes it out of you.'

'Did someone say shopping?' Gavin asked, appearing with a large paper bag swinging from his hand.

'What have you got?' Lucie wanted to know.

'I think the question should really be "what hasn't he got",' Simon said.

'I keep telling you, you can never have too many balls.' Gavin grinned. 'I've got a set of hand-carved skittles for my niece. And… I got some massage balls.'

'Are they going to replace the golf balls?' Lucie asked him.

'Oh, God, no!' Gavin exclaimed in horror. 'I don't want to get the wooden ones wet.'

'I don't think I need to know any more,' Lucie said, regretting bringing up the sporting equipment.

Gavin put his hands on his hips. 'Luce, what do you think I use the golf balls for?'

'Well… I know it's not golf.'

'I take them with me whenever I go on holiday,' Gavin informed. 'Because most foreign hotels don't have plugs for the bath. It's a great hack.'

Lucie closed her eyes but then quickly opened them again. 'But… our bath at Villa Psomi *does* have a plug.'

'Yes, I know,' Gavin stated. 'So I've been putting them in the freezer and rubbing them on my eyebrow space. I finally found a helpful blog! Apparently it promotes growth.'

'I'm interested to know what Lucie thought you were using them for,' Simon said, nudging Gavin with his elbow.

'Yes, me too. Come on, Lucie, tell us what you thought I was up to.'

'Oh, look, there's Michalis,' Lucie rambled fast. 'I've got to go before he has to be carried to the front of the stage on a throne!'

His headdress was ridiculous. Looking at himself in the reflection of the butcher's shop window, Michalis realised he didn't represent a warrior king, which was the look he thought Melina was going for, but more a carcass of a large game bird before the plucking. Why was he even doing this? Except he knew the answer to that. To keep the village happy. But what of himself? What did he need to be happy going forward? He had received a Messenger message yesterday, from Anastasia. It had told him that she had spoken to Thekli and for the meantime, Thekli was going to be moving in with her. She promised again that she would ensure Thekli made no further contact with him. *He was free*. At least from the messages, calls and threat of attack. But how did he feel on the inside? With this clean slate, could he really begin to live again?

He turned around and there was Lucie, running across the square towards him. The traditional dress was ballooning out like a parachute, her fingers lifting it a little, presumably so she didn't trip, and she was smiling at him. Pleased to see him, despite the fact he looked like a crow that had been in a near-miss with the engine of a plane...

'Whoa!' Michalis said, catching Lucie as she all but ran into him. 'You are OK?'

'It's this dress,' Lucie breathed, holding onto his arms. 'It's completely changed my centre of gravity. At first I think I have a handle on it and then, no, it tips me up the other way.'

He smiled at her, remaining quiet and still, imprinting the moment on his heart. 'You look beautiful.'

'Really?' Lucie asked in a way that led him to believe perhaps no one had ever said this to her before.

'Lucie,' he breathed, putting a finger to her hair and tucking a short strand back behind her ear. 'When I say something to you, it always comes from the deepest place.' He kissed her then.

'Ow! Feather in the eye!' Lucie said, recoiling slightly.

'I am so sorry,' Michalis said, putting his hands to his headwear. 'It is this bird helmet! I cannot wait to take it off.'

'Don't wish the minutes away,' Lucie answered with a sigh. 'Because before we know it I'll be getting back in Miltos's fruit van, being pummelled by grapefruits, and on my way to the airport.'

'Oh, Lucie,' Michalis said, taking hold of her hands. 'Do you really think I would let you travel that way again? I can drive you to the airport. In my car. With no fruit.'

Lucie swallowed. She knew he meant that to be the loveliest of gestures, but really the thought of leaving him behind was making her sweatier than the fabrics she was currently taped into. Did he really not feel the same? Perhaps, right now, it didn't matter so much what he felt as long as she was true to herself.

'I've been thinking,' she began, trying her best to ignore the beginnings of Melina on a microphone that wasn't quite tuned to the right level.

'You have?'

She nodded. 'I have.' *Come on, Lucie, just spit it out.*

'And am I allowed to know what this thinking is about?' Michalis asked.

'I... know we said that we would... enjoy the time we have together *here*, in Corfu, and that maybe that time would simply be "that time" but—'

'You do not need to say any more,' Michalis interrupted.

'I don't?'

'*Ochi*,' Michalis said, shaking his head. 'I know it is that you have... decided that I am still a little messed up. And you would like us to say goodbye at the airport and for that to be... the end.'

'I... wasn't going to say that.'

'You were not?' he asked.

'No,' Lucie answered. She took a breath and ventured on. 'But, is that what *you* want? For this to have been a holidate and nothing more?'

She was holding her breath now, waiting, hoping as drums began to beat, followed by a melody played on stringed instruments. She recognised the song. It was the one before the one when she was involved in the dancing...

'Lucie,' Michalis said, squeezing her hands tight. 'I do not want this "holidate" you speak of. Because it sounds like something that holds your interest for a little while and then it is thrown away.'

She went to say something, but Michalis put a finger to her lips.

'I do not want to throw away anything that we have shared together,' he told her. 'This time with you has been some of the best moments of my whole life.'

'Really?' Lucie mumbled, her lips moving up and down against his finger.

'Why do you doubt so much?' Michalis said.

'I don't know,' Lucie breathed. 'Maybe because I'm

standing in uncharted territory... in a wedding dress... never having felt for someone what I feel for you.' She looked into his eyes. 'A man dressed as a gladiator of the avian world.'

'Are you mocking me?'

'Flocking you.' She laughed. 'Sorry, couldn't resist.'

He kissed her then. Hard. Passionate. No doubt of his intent. And, when he finally drew away, Lucie was lost for breath.

'I do not know where I will be,' Michalis told her. 'But wherever I am, whatever I am doing... I want to... call you and... see you... as many times as we can.'

'Re—'

'Do not ask the "really",' Michalis interrupted her.

She laughed. 'I want that too. So much.'

'Then we are agreed,' Michalis said. 'No goodbyes at the airport. Only *ta leme sindoma*.'

'I don't know what that means,' Lucie told him.

'It means "see you soon".'

'*Ta... lay-may... sin-doma*,' she copied. 'That might take a few goes to get perfect.'

'I am very happy to commit to practise with you,' Michalis said, pulling her close to him, wooden arm cuts digging into his skin.

'Are we still talking about Greek lessons or do you think we might have time for honing other skills?' Lucie flirted.

'Loosely! *Ela!* Come! My grandmother and Ariana need to fix the bonnet to your head now.' Suddenly Miltos was right beside them and within seconds he had locked her arm with his.

'Bonnet? No. No, no one said anything about a bonnet!' Lucie said as she was dragged away.

Michalis laughed. 'I would take a bonnet right now. Look at me! I have the head of an eagle and the body of a tortoise.'

Sixty-Five

Greek festivals were simply brilliant, Lucie had decided. Despite being dressed head-to-toe in materials that were ill-equipped for the July temperatures, wearing a bonnet covered in paper flowers and model bees made out of tiny yellow-and-black circles of wool and felt, the ambience was as laidback as it was electric. The villagers of Sortilas were dressed in their finest clothes, some in costume, all dancing and singing and enjoying hot lamb *souvlaki*, *loukoumades*, Mrs Pappas's gross lollipops and Andino Butcher's special beef tortoise-shaped pies. Even an actual tortoise had made a surprise visit in the village square, proving that they didn't only live in Villa Psomi.

Lucie's dance over, it was time for the main event. Sitting at a plastic table with Meg, Gavin and Simon, she watched as Michalis was helped into a wooden stretcher-cum-popemobile contraption that would definitely not have held up as being structurally sound under UK rules.

'Christ,' Gavin remarked. 'I can't look. He's a tall guy and he's wearing literally a whole olive tree on his body, not to mention enough feathers to coat one of Cher's headdresses. This is all going to end very badly.'

'Don't say that,' Lucie begged, looking through her fingers at the scene now. 'Not now we've just committed to keeping in touch when we go home.'

'What?!' Gavin exclaimed. 'Really?!'

Lucie nodded, her gaze going to Meg next to her. 'A very brilliant friend, as well as a lovely family member told me that life shouldn't wait any more. That sometimes you need to listen to your heart.'

Meg put her hand over Lucie's. 'I am so so happy for you, my Lucie-Lou.'

'I'm happy for you too, Lucie,' Simon told her. 'And I want to thank you.'

'You do?' Lucie said, shifting in her chair to face him and Gavin.

'Yes,' Simon said, sounding a little nervous. 'Because, back at the hospital, if you hadn't told me how Gavin felt about me then I think I would have carried on pushing my own feelings down.' He reached for his can of Vergina beer and took a quick swig. 'Because, I know that I told you... I'm not gay... and truthfully now, I don't know exactly what I am, or even if I need to define *how* I feel but... I should have been a bit more honest and... I shouldn't have asked for your phone number.' He gave a nervous smile. 'Not that you're not the greatest fun but... I really don't fancy you.' He shook his head. 'God, that sounded awful.'

'It really did,' Gavin agreed.

'Sshh, let me say this,' Simon begged.

Lucie watched as he turned in his seat and faced Gavin and her heart gave a little leap in anticipation.

'I'm not going to say I know the roadmap for where I'm going at the moment,' Simon started. 'But I do know that jumping on a plane and flying to Corfu was the best decision I've made in a very long time.'

Lucie looked at Gavin and she could see that her best friend was starting to tear up. *Hold it together, Gavin. Don't force out an inappropriate innuendo.*

'I have had the best time here on this island,' Simon carried on. 'And that's because of you.' With shaking fingers he reached for Gavin's hand. 'And... whatever journey I take next, I know already that I want you to be a part of it.'

Lucie desperately wanted to squeal and jump across the table to hug them both, but the cuteness of the scene in front of her made her stop and simply watch as Simon leaned in towards Gavin and planted the softest of kisses on his lips.

Now Lucie moved, jumping up, dress knocking the empty plastic chair next to her over onto the floor, and clapping excitedly. She watched Gavin's face glowing with happiness and she felt so ecstatic for both of them.

'And now I will speak in the English!' Melina's voice boomed over the sound system. 'It is time to welcome our village saviour! Last year, when the world imploded...'

A series of firecrackers suddenly fizzed into life and dramatic drumming commenced from the band of school children seated next to the stage – all wearing traditional Greek costume.

'A hero was born!' Melina shrieked and oddly everyone began clapping.

It was at this point that Michalis's bizarre transport – tied to chunky bamboo canes – was hoisted up onto the shoulders of six – hopefully strong enough – village men. Once balance had been achieved, they began a slow and sedate walk into the centre of the square and the performance area as balletic dancers swirled around, half their faces painted a ghastly green with one dark eye, the other half painted bright yellow with *that* eye decorated like a daisy.

'A man... who saved us from the virus!' Melina continued. 'A Greek god... who foresaw what was coming... and gave us the tools to fight it off!'

The whole village began to cheer, stamp their feet on the ground or bang tables with their hands.

'Goodness,' Meg exclaimed. 'What exactly did Michalis do?'

'I don't actually know,' Lucie admitted. 'Whenever I ask him he keeps brushing it off like whatever he *did* do was nothing. But look at this festival, this *new* festival, all for him.'

Her boyfriend. Her more-than-a-holidate. Encased in a wooden cage, dressed like a bad-ass bird who once mated with a tortoise. It was almost too much.

'Doctor Michalis Andino!' Melina announced. 'Tonight... and on this day for every year ever after... we will honour you with this festival!'

There were more cheers.

'And we will never forget how you saved Sortilas! And made it the ultimate health destination... as featured in *Travel Europe* magazine... one of our sponsors.'

Gavin burst out laughing. 'She's advertising! In the middle of a festival. This is class!'

'Light the flames!' Melina ordered. 'And may they burn throughout the night as a symbol of our resilience! And a sign of our appreciation for our new and first village saint. Step towards your throne to be ordained... Saint Doctor Michalis Andino.'

'Jesus Christ!' Gavin exclaimed, getting to his feet.

'Almost, I think,' Meg replied, dabbing her forehead with a serviette.

'Even Sir Sean Connery never got made a saint, God love him,' Gavin said.

'I'm not sure you can *make* someone a saint,' Lucie mused as she watched Michalis's cage being lowered precariously to the ground and then him emerge to cheers and back-slapping from the crowd around him. 'Don't you have to die first?'

'Well,' Gavin said, eyes still on the action. 'I was concerned when they mentioned flaming torches. I mean, there's quite a lot of wood around here.'

'And actually, when I visited Corfu the first time, you weren't allowed fires of any kind until November. Fires here can be deadly,' Meg added.

Lucie was still feeling guilty about their very first barbecue...

'Oh! Phew!' Gavin said, hand to his chest. 'Solar-powered fake flaming torches. We're all saved.'

Sixty-Six

'Please, remove my head! I cannot stand it any longer!'

Michalis bent forward in front of his sister, who was stationed behind the stall outside the butcher's shop as a continuation to their enterprise for this night only.

'Do you need to take it off now to make room for your halo, Saint Michalis?' Nyx asked with a snort. She put her hands around the headdress and wrenched hard.

'Ow!' Michalis said, standing up straight and rubbing the back of his neck as Nyx plonked the headdress on the end of her stall.

'I will put it here. It will discourage the flies and maybe scare the children so they do not keep picking up my tortoise pies.'

'Where is Papa?' Michalis asked.

'Ugh,' Nyx sighed. 'He is inside the shop with *Amalia*. She has persuaded him to put some of his paintings on the wall. He has taken down my poster of the inner workings of a cow and replaced it with a seascape of Apraos.'

'Nyx,' Michalis said. 'Please give Amalia a chance. Papa likes her.'

'I *am* giving her a chance,' she answered bullishly. 'I have not threatened her with any of my boning knives. What more do you want?'

'Would it be possible to buy some pork chops?'

The question came from the Greek man Michalis remembered buying rabbit, steak mince and the cow's tongue…

'You again?' Nyx greeted. 'What do you want pork chops for tonight? We are in the middle of a festival!'

'Nyx,' Michalis said warningly. 'How many chops would you like, sir?'

'I think two,' the man answered.

'No problem,' Michalis said. 'Let me take you into the shop and my father will be able to help you.' He led the way.

Nyx shook her head then simultaneously slapped the hand of a child about to pick up one of her tortoise pies.

'Nyx,' Lucie greeted. 'We'll have some lamb *souvlakia* and some tortoise pies.'

'I'm so hungry and it smells so wonderful,' Meg added.

'I will do you some big bags,' Nyx said with a smile. 'You can take some for Gavin and Simon. They are so cute together.'

'They are, aren't they?' Lucie answered with a contented sigh.

'Much cuter than you and my brother, the saint that looks like roadkill. Ha! I pull off his head!' Nyx indicated the feathered mohawk on her stall. 'But good hair style. I might try this.'

'Where is Michalis?' Lucie asked. She hadn't seen much of him after the ceremony. The whole village seemed to want to spend time in the company of their new honorary saint.

'He is taking an annoying customer just inside to the shop,' Nyx informed, putting sticks of slick and delicious-looking skewered lamb into insulated bags.

'Why annoying?' Lucie asked.

'Oh, he comes in and wants this and wants that and does not listen to my advice. Tonight he wants pork chops.'

'I love pork chops,' Meg replied. 'I remember one meal I ate here in Corfu.' She sighed. 'It was home-cooked by someone special. I'd told him how much I liked them – my mum used to make them with a honey and mustard glaze and—'

'Mashed potatoes… with all the butter.'

A male voice had broken into the conversation and suddenly her aunt was quivering next to her.

'I… don't believe it,' Meg whispered, her voice breaking.

A man was standing just outside the doorway of the butcher's shop, a plastic bag in his hand staring straight at Meg. 'Are my eyes broken?' he asked.

'This is him!' Nyx exclaimed. 'The one who complains. Is there something wrong with our pork chops now?'

Lucie looked back to Meg, not understanding at all what was going on. 'Meg, are you OK? Perhaps you should eat something? Or I'll get you some water.'

'Is it really you?' the man asked, almost tiptoeing closer to them like he was afraid to approach too swiftly.

'Is it really *you*?' Meg said, tears bouncing out of her eyes and down her cheeks.

'Meggie,' the man breathed, finally right there.

'I can't believe it,' Meg whispered. 'You look... just the same.'

'You look... even more beautiful than the picture I carry in my head,' the man replied.

And then the pieces started to fall into place for Lucie. There was only one person this could be...

'Oh, Petros... it's so wonderful to see you,' Meg said, beaming as she cried.

Sixty-Seven

'Melina wanted fireworks,' Michalis said. 'Like this new festival was more important than anything and we could suddenly forget that we live on an island that in the height of summer is almost as dry as a desert.'

Lucie laughed. They were sitting on the balcony of the Andino family apartment, alone at last, looking out over the festival still continuing in the square below them. She could see Gavin and Simon in the middle of the dancing, being taught traditional moves by the locals as the band played from the stage. They were both a little red-faced with the frenetic pace Mary and Ariana were setting, leading dancers holding handkerchiefs in a zig-zag formation around a little girl dressed as an effigy of a virus. Earlier there had been an interpretive dance with a troupe of schoolchildren in tortoise costumes battling against another group dressed as dark evil organisms...

And then there was Meg. Sitting at a table on the terrace of the taverna, eyes only for her dining companion, Petros,

446

looking like all the years were simply rolling back. There was a girlish expression on her aunt's face that Lucie had never seen before and it was starting to give her an insight into who Meg had been before she took on the responsibility of her sister's child.

'The solar-powered flickering flames were inspired,' Lucie answered him.

'Another drink?' Michalis asked, lifting the bottle up.

'This is *mastika*, isn't it? Like the bottle we found in Villa Psomi.'

He nodded. 'But, this one, it is a little different.'

Lucie sat forward in her seat, layers of lace coming with her... but at least she had been able to remove the bonnet. 'Different, how?'

Michalis poured them both another small measure of the cloudy liquid then sat back in his chair, picking up his glass and surveying it. 'It is usually clear.'

'And this one isn't because...'

'You asked me what I did for the village last year. To try to keep them safe,' he began.

'And you keep not answering me. As if you're the mastermind behind a vaccine that is one hundred per cent effective and the rest of the world knows nothing about it.'

He smiled. 'I wish for that.'

'Me too,' Lucie agreed. 'But if it's not that then...'

'Take a drink,' he encouraged.

Lucie looked at him with suspicion. 'You are being very mysterious, Dr Andino. Is this part of your role play for the flying tortoise king you're dressed as?'

'No,' he answered. 'This is me about to tell you the only

447

secret I have left to share.' He took a breath. 'Once you know this, you will know more about me than anyone else.' He smiled. 'Take another drink.'

Lucie picked up her glass and raised it to her lips. 'This is a bit like the wine tasting now. Do you want me to smell it?'

'If you like,' he answered. 'Tell me what you smell. Then, tell me what you taste.'

Lucie put her nose over the glass. 'It smells like trees, like the one we tried at the villa. Trees and earth.' She took a sip. 'And there's a little lemony aftertaste that's really quite nice.'

He smiled. 'There is, is there not?'

'Stop dragging this out! Tell me what this has to do with Sortilas having some gold health status and a tortoise to prove it!'

'If I tell you,' Michalis started, reaching across the table for her hand. 'You have to promise me you will never tell anyone else.'

'Anyone? Because sometimes, when I've had too much wine, Gavin deliberately leads me down a dark path to confessing anything I've previously held back from him.'

'You cannot tell *anyone*,' Michalis told her.

'OK,' Lucie breathed. 'I get it.' She swallowed. 'I promise.'

He picked up the bottle and caressed the glass as if he was stroking a much-loved pet. 'This… was all it was.'

Lucie waited a beat for him to carry on and actually do some explaining but when nothing else was forthcoming she jumped in. 'What was all it was?' She frowned.

'This drink,' he said with a smile. 'It is *mastika*, just as the villagers drink it, with a few small additions.'

'You… gave them all alcohol?' Lucie asked, still not fully getting it.

He sighed. 'You have seen how old some of Sortilas is. How old Ariana and Mary from Vouni are. This virus was attacking the elderly and the vulnerable more than anyone else and there was nothing I could do about that. Nothing other than reminding them to wash their hands, to sanitise, to wear a mask and to keep distance.' He took a large swig of his drink. 'But the other element of life the Coronavirus attacked… was in here.' He put his fingers to his temples. 'That fear, the mentality that the life they know was not accessible anymore. They had no hope. And I decided I *could* do something about that.'

'Go on,' Lucie urged.

'I made this vintage,' he informed. 'Bottles and bottles of it. Enough for the whole village to have a small shot of it every day over the last twelve months. It contains Vitamin D, basil, lemon, but mainly alcohol.' He drew in a breath. 'Some might say it was a placebo. But, it is proven that those ingredients can help the body fight off a virus and boost the immune system. The fact that *no one* in Sortilas contracted Covid-19 means that *something* worked and if Melina wants to believe it was my elixir, then who am I to make argument?'

'Dr Andino,' Lucie gasped. 'You *are* a shaman! I knew it!' She stood up. 'I am in love with a witch doctor!'

She stopped talking as she realised exactly what she had said. Her cheeks reddening, she was caught between sitting back down or perhaps running from the balcony and finding somewhere to hide.

'I—'

'Do not take it back,' Michalis begged her. He pulled her forward and onto his lap, the heavy skirts almost burying them both.

'Is it too soon?' Lucie asked, gazing up at him and enjoying sitting against his taut leather-clad body.

'I do not know what we are waiting for,' he said with a shrug 'I have known for some time now that I am in love with you.'

'You have?' Lucie said, swallowing as her heart took flight.

'Yes,' Michalis told her. 'I just apparently needed to be made a saint before I declared this to you.' He clasped her hand then cleared his throat. 'I love you, Lucie. And... I *know* you.'

It felt like her heart was filling with stardust-coated helium and she could float up onto a cloud. He'd remembered what she'd told him and how much it meant to her.

'I love you,' she breathed as she moved her lips towards his. 'And I want to know you. Completely.'

And then, to the music of the festival band, the chirruping of the crickets and the hubbub of this special Greek village, they held each other tight, knowing that this was a new beginning for them both. A beginning that would hopefully lead to many *many* tomorrows together.

Epilogue

Three months later

'You're carrying a bedpan with a smile on your face. What's happened? Won the lottery? Got an audition for *The Wall*?' Gavin questioned, ripping off gloves and dropping them in the disposal bin. 'Wait, wait... that radio competition to win a lifetime's supply of hot chocolate.'

'Nope,' Lucie answered, dealing with the detritus.

'What then?'

'Well... the new doctor starts today, doesn't he?' Lucie said, still grinning.

'And that's good because the last consultant we had was a total shitshow and this one can't possibly be worse?'

'Gavin!' Lucie said. 'Are you kidding me? Haven't you worked it out yet?' She led the way into the break room. She really wanted the tiniest bit of something fizzy and alcoholic for this moment, but she was going to have to make do with a nice strong cup of coffee to celebrate while she was on duty.

'You've lost me,' Gavin said, grabbing a biscuit from the open selection pack on the table. 'I've been finding that lately. Since I'm seeing slightly less of you now Simon and I are officially a couple, our best friend's telepathy needs a software update.'

'Well, we're getting a new consultant and Michalis has been *very* cloak-and-dagger about his career options on FaceTime. He's been very closed about interviews he's had and he wasn't like that at the beginning of his job search,' Lucie stated like it was all complete fact. 'He used to tell me every email he'd had from every hospital or care centre.'

'Maybe he's gone off you,' The Other Sharon Osbourne suggested, appearing from nowhere with two mugs in each hand, slamming them down on the worktop. 'My second husband was like that. He'd tell me exactly what he'd found underneath his toenails one minute and the next he wouldn't even tell me if he'd had an asthma attack... not that I really cared by that stage.'

'Wait a minute,' Gavin said, hand on hip. 'Are you telling me that you think the new consultant is Michalis?'

Lucie nodded, so excited she hadn't stopped grinning all morning. Michalis was doing this for her, for *them*, as a surprise. They had talked about being closer to each other and with Michalis deciding not to return to Thessaloniki, it was obvious, wasn't it? He was going to work here, at her hospital, on her ward sometimes. There was nothing she wanted more. She missed him so much. 'Yes,' she said. 'It's got to be.'

'But, Luce, surely he would tell you. I mean, you don't just decide to leap on a plane and apply for a job at your girlfriend's hospital without telling them, do you?'

'I'd batter someone if they did that,' Sharon concluded. 'Genuinely bash them up.' Then, under her breath, 'Or shave their eyebrows off.'

'It's not that crazy,' Lucie said, a flicker of doubt arriving. 'I mean we have talked about being together more and—'

'Well,' Sharon began. 'I heard the new consultant was called Mr Fox.' She sniffed. 'I'm hoping for the silver variety. I'm going through a new Hugh Grant phase now he's being mean and moody in that Sky series.'

Lucie's humour dropped and she picked the coffee jug up, disappointed to find it completely empty.

'Right,' Gavin said, putting an arm around Lucie's shoulders. 'This calls for a visit to *my* man.' Then he looked to Sharon. 'Did you just say you would shave someone's eyebrows off? I knew it was you! I *knew* it!'

Café Connexions was quite busy for a Monday and there was a queue to get to Simon's station. Lucie wasn't sure even the strongest bold Colombian was going to fix her mood now. She had been so certain. Perhaps she just should have asked Michalis outright, not made assumptions. Anyway, it had been a month since they had seen each other. She had managed another quick short break back in Corfu to take Meg to visit Petros. The two teenage-hood sweethearts were rekindling the romance of their youth and it was just beautiful to watch. Petros had been married, just like Meg, but his wife had passed away five years ago. It seemed that fate had put them in each other's paths at exactly the right time again. Lucie also didn't think it would be long before Meg was ready to box up her nan's dolls for auction and put a 'for sale' sign on the Southampton house. Part of Meg's heart had always been in Greece and Lucie hoped her aunt would embrace this second chance with everything she had.

'Have *you* heard that the new consultant is called Mr Fox?' Lucie asked Gavin. She looked at her watch. Whoever it was was meant to be making an appearance on Abbington Ward in thirty minutes.

'I haven't heard anything about him or her,' Gavin said. 'And I can't really believe Mrs O has either. We're far too low in the pecking order to get early information like that.'

Now Lucie's shoulders were starting to ache. Since she'd left the heat of Greece and Michalis's healing hands, the tension was back. She'd have to try and teach Gavin the flick technique…

'You should have bought some massage balls too,' Gavin said, picking up a plastic tray and moving along the queue. 'I can tell your back's aching. Your shoulders are up by your ears. You need to chill a bit. When's your next trip to our favourite Greek island booked for?'

That was another problem. She hadn't got anything booked yet. Because Michalis had been a little elusive about his work plans. Maybe it wasn't anything to do with a new job. Maybe he was having doubts about their long-distance relationship…

'I… don't have anything booked yet.' She wished this queue would get a move on. She might have to indulge in a sausage roll as well as the coffee. She had been trying a lot of new things lately, including some supplements Michalis had suggested to help ease her back and shoulder tension. Perhaps she still wasn't quite ready for max strength ibuprofen yet, but it was a start.

'Aww look!' Gavin said, thrusting his phone in front of Lucie's face. 'It's Maria, Damocles and the twins! Look how much they've grown already!'

Lucie gazed at the photo of the happy family, all healthy and well, probably forever the only household formed in a swinging egg chair.

'No names yet,' he ploughed on. 'I did suggest Gavin, but apparently they have to be named after their grandparents.' He rolled his eyes. 'Probably another Spiros... oh, no, don't look at that.'

A text had flashed up on screen and although Lucie didn't catch any of the contents she *had* seen who it was from. Nyx.

'Why can't I look at it?' Lucie asked Gavin, now a little suspicious about exactly what was going on with the Andino family.

'Well, you might know this already, but she's started painting. Some woman that gave her dad lessons is teaching her now and she keeps sending me pictures of the pictures.' He shifted along the queue as slowly, but surely, they edged nearer to getting served.

'And why can't I see them?'

'Believe me, I'm saving you from trauma here,' Gavin said. 'Every canvas looks like she's spattered it with pig's blood. It's murderous but, you know, I figure she might be working through some anger issues and that can only be a good thing.'

Lucie looked ahead of them, the need for coffee deepening further still. She definitely wanted to be full of caffeine when this Mr Fox arrived and now she was worried that Michalis was hiding something else from her. Then she scrunched her face up. 'No wonder there's a queue. There's someone new behind the counter.'

'Christ, is there?' Gavin asked, stretching his neck to look along the line and behind the terminal. 'That means Simon will be in a grump later. I've found that the one thing he hates more than re-runs of *Queer Eye* is training people. That girl who started last month didn't even make it to the second day.'

Lucie stepped past Gavin, taking his place in the line and bunching up as much as she could. There was something a little off, she just couldn't put her finger on it.

'It takes skill to be a barista, you know,' Gavin told her. 'Simon has a special coffee maker at his flat and honestly, I know I've done all the nursing training, but it has more buttons than a life support machine. I cannot work it out.'

Lucie felt the hairs on the back of her neck rise as she got a better look at the person making drinks next to Simon. The red baseball hat was pulled low over his head but there was something about the curve of his shoulders and the shape of his hands...

'Gavin,' Lucie said, her voice cracking a little. 'The new barista.'

'Yes? Useless is he? Putting the milk in first on teas and last in macchiatos?'

'No,' Lucie said. 'I think... I think it's Michalis.'

Her heart was hammering in her chest now. This was crazy! It couldn't be, could it? And had he really had a change of career?

'You're mad,' Gavin stated with a laugh. 'You're so obsessed with the guy that you're seeing him everywhere. Which is kind of good I guess. It means this is the real deal!'

She closed her eyes. Was she dreaming him up? Or could it be possible that he was here? She opened her eyes again and, this time, it wasn't just her vision jumping to conclusions, it was her heart too.

'It's him, Gavin,' she breathed, feeling a little unsteady. 'I know it's him.'

It was time to stop being British and forget the queuing. She needed to know for absolute certain. She grabbed her tray and rushed down the line towards the front.

'Lucie!' Simon greeted all smiles. 'Sorry, there's a bit of a wait. I'll just serve Graham then I'll do you something quickly if you've got to head back.'

Lucie frowned. 'There was someone else here just a second ago. Someone helping you with the coffees.'

'There was,' Simon said with a sigh. 'He's not very good. To be honest I think he would be much better off taking another career path.'

'Well, that sucks for both of you, I guess,' Lucie answered. God, she really was seeing things. 'I'll have a hot chocolate. And a sausage roll.'

'Shall I bring this to a table?'

Now a divine shiver ran the length of her back as that beautiful voice spiralled around her eardrums. Turning a one-eighty, Lucie's jaw dropped open as there was Michalis standing right in front of her in baseball cap and matching red apron, the uniform of Café Connexions employees.

'Oh my God! I can't believe it! What are you doing here? When did you get here? When?'

Lucie got caught between jumping at him and remembering she was in the middle of the canteen so the move looked like something out of a Morris dance but with a plastic tray instead of handkerchiefs. She dropped the tray and tried again, launching herself into his arms and squeezing him to check he was truly flesh-and-blood reality. She inhaled, breathing in that musky scent and manliness that had always ravaged her senses.

'Yesterday,' he admitted. 'Last night.'

'What?!' Lucie exclaimed, holding him away now and thinking about all the sexy things they could have been getting up to the night before. She felt bereft.

'I wanted to give you a surprise,' Michalis told her. 'Did it work?'

She nodded, reaching for his hand. 'Yes it worked. I can't believe it.' She frowned then. 'But... what are you doing here? And why are you dressed in barista clothes? Did you forget to pack?' And how long was he planning on staying?

Michalis shook his head then. 'I have a suitcase.' He gave her hand a squeeze. 'And... a new job!' He let her go then, spreading his arms out wide.

Wow. She knew not all his interviews had gone well but she hadn't really expected him to be frothing frappuccinos.

'You're going to be working here?' Lucie asked, still a little confused. Living here? He was going to be *living* here? She was going to get to see him all the time!

'I am,' he confirmed. 'And I know that this is a change. A big change, for us. And I very much hope you will think it is a good change.' He smiled. 'Do not worry. I have my own place to stay for now so we can find out all the annoying things about each other before we commit to anything else but... oh, God, Lucie, tell me, please, that you are happy.'

He looked so incredibly nervous, but her heart really was bursting with nothing but the most concentrated feeling of pure joy. He was here. He was moving here for her. So they could become a couple without the distance between them.

'Oh, Michalis, it's the best thing! The most wonderful, lovely, fantastic thing in the whole world!' She squealed then, uncaring for their audience and wrapped herself around him again to rapturous applause.

'I know you,' he said, the words tickling into her ear as he held her.

'I love you,' she said, the tears beginning to gather. 'So much.'

And then all at once he let her go, dropping her back down and looking at his wrist.

'Is that the time?' he asked.

'Is what the time?'

'I have to be somewhere else. I am sorry,' he apologised, taking off the red cap and throwing it across the counter where Simon deftly caught it. 'We will have more time later, I promise.'

'What's going on?' Lucie asked as Gavin arrived on the scene, a white bundle in his hands.

'I have to be in another department,' Michalis said, stripping himself of the red apron and giving her a flicker of that glorious ab show before he could tuck his shirt back in. 'Somewhere called... the ward... Adrington? No, that's not quite it... um—'

'Abbington,' Lucie stated, the word falling from her lips as her mouth dried up completely.

'Dr Andino,' Gavin greeted, holding out the bundle. 'Your white coat.'

Lucie couldn't believe this. She *had* been right all along! But all she could do was spill out more tears of delight as her Greek boyfriend slipped that too-small white coat over his shoulders and turned into the village doctor she first fell in love with.

'These are happy tears?' Michalis asked, putting a finger to one of the teardrops and swiping it away down her cheek. 'For the new geriatric consultant here at the hospital?'

She both shook her head and then nodded, unable to say anything.

He smiled. 'What can I say? With all my experience with one of the oldest populations in Europe, I was top of the shortlist I think.' He whispered. 'They have even promised me my own skeleton for my office.'

Lucie held Michalis close and let the moment sink right down into her bones as the applause around them continued. Here was her fresh beginning, right here in the canteen of her hospital. It was time to jump heart first into a brave new world and now her gorgeous, kind, loving Greek was going to be right by her side, every step of the way.

'Can I ask you one thing?' Lucie asked, lifting her head away from him.

'Anything.'

'Are you Greek Orthodox?'

He smiled. 'Not practising. Is there—'

She muffled his words with another fierce kiss and secretly wondered if one day she might be back in that big, fat, Greek wedding dress…

Acknowledgements

As always, I have plenty of people to thank for keeping me sane and motivated during the writing of this book. People that deserve all the gratitude are:-

Tanera Simons and all the Darley Anderson team

Hannah Smith and all the Aria Fiction team

My lovely Bagg Ladies

The members of The Mandy Baggot Book Club on Facebook

Sue Fortin

Rachel Lyndhurst

Angela White and Michelle Terrell – forever bonded by Greek travel tweets!

I went to some fantastic places in Corfu last summer and have included many of them as locations in this book. Special mentions to some of my Corfu friends I got to spend so much time with given all the restrictions:-

Harry from Harry's Taverna, Perithia – for keeping me in swordfish

Mairi and Polymeros from the cafeneon, Perithia

Agelos and all the Dimitras family at Jelatis Taverna, Perithia

Sofia and Manthos, Villa Corfu Panorama, Perithia

Theotoky Estate, Ropa Valley – for the amazing wine tasting experience

Dear Reader,

I love a big, fat, happy ending, don't you? Well, there was never any doubt, was there? I loved writing Lucie and Michalis's story and I really hope you enjoyed every single word of *Staying Out for the Summer*. I hope it's made you long for your own Greek getaway!

Now, Sortilas is a fictional Greek village but Villa Psomi (Villa Bread) – where Lucie and Gavin stayed (with the tortoises!) is heavily inspired by my new Greek home! Yes, during a global pandemic, Mr Big and I thought it would be the ideal time to purchase a new house on Corfu! Given the situation with worldwide restrictions, it finally became ours just before Christmas 2020 and we are itching to move in as soon as we can! It's not the first time the house has featured in a book either! It was formerly owned by James Chatto and is written about in his memoir – *The Greek for Love: Life, Love and Loss in Corfu*. After I fell in love with the house, I fell in love with the book too and would highly recommend it for a real taste of Greek life.

If you enjoyed *Staying Out for the Summer* I would love

it if you would leave a review on Amazon. I read every single review and reviews – even a few words – inspire new readers to buy and try a Mandy Baggot novel. Your review could help someone discover my stories for the very first time!

Don't forget you can visit my website to sign up to my monthly newsletter (always with a chance to win) and follow me on social media and keep up to date with all my news!

Website: www.mandybaggot.com

Twitter: @mandybaggot

Instagram: @mandybaggot

Facebook: @mandybaggotauthor

Join The Mandy Baggot Book Club group on Facebook!

Happy reading and get ready for Christmas...

Mandy xx

About the Author

MANDY BAGGOT is an international
bestselling and award-winning romance writer.
The winner of the Innovation in Romantic Fiction award
at the UK's Festival of Romance, her romantic comedy
novel, *One Wish in Manhattan*, was also shortlisted for
the Romantic Novelists' Association Romantic Comedy
Novel of the Year award in 2016. Mandy's books have
so far been translated into German, Italian, Czech and
Hungarian. Mandy loves the Greek island of Corfu,
white wine, country music and handbags. Also a singer,
she has taken part in ITV1's *Who Dares Sings* and
The X-Factor. Mandy is a member of the Society
of Authors and lives near Salisbury, Wiltshire, UK
with her husband and two daughters.

Hello from Aria

We hope you enjoyed this book! If you did let us know, we'd love to hear from you.

We are Aria, a dynamic digital-first fiction imprint from award-winning independent publishers Head of Zeus. At heart, we're committed to publishing fantastic commercial fiction – from romance and sagas to crime, thrillers and historical fiction. Visit us online and discover a community of like-minded fiction fans!

We're also on the look out for tomorrow's superstar authors. So, if you're a budding writer looking for a publisher, we'd love to hear from you. You can submit your book online at ariafiction.com/ we-want-read-your-book

You can find us at:
Email: aria@headofzeus.com
Website: www.ariafiction.com
Submissions: www.ariafiction.com/
we-want-read-your-book

f @ariafiction
🐦 @Aria_Fiction
📷 @ariafiction